Down with a world in which the guarantee that we will not die of starvation has been purchased with the guarantee that we will die of boredom.

> Raoul Vaneigm
> *The Revolution of Everyday Life*

Copyright © 2005, 2009 by D. R. Haney
ISBN: 978-1-4276-2499-4

All rights reserved, including the right of reproduction in whole or in part without the written permission of the publisher, except in the case of brief quotations embodied in critical articles and reviews.

This book is a work of fiction. Names, characters, places, situations and incidents are the product of the author's imagination or are used fictiously. Any resemblance to actual events, locals or persons, living or dead, is purely coincidental.

Printed in the United States of America

D. R. Haney
Banned for Life

And/Or Press
VANCOUVER

This book is for my beloved grandmother Cornelia
who would not have approved
and for all the Peewees there ever were
or ever will be

One...

State your age
Set the stage
Start a fire for something new
Where's your energy?
There's no energy

Unwound

IT ALL BEGAN WITH A FUCK. What doesn't? I fucked the wrong person; I fucked up the right one; somebody played me a song. It changed my whole life, that song. That's why I later went to so much trouble to find the guy who wrote and sang it. His name was Jim Cassady, or at least that's what he called himself. His real name was Eddie Brown, but he'd changed it in tribute to Jim Morrison and Neal Cassady. I'd never heard of either one before I discovered punk rock. I grew up in a small city in North Carolina where I'd never known a soul who listened to the Doors or read Jack Kerouac. I was a jock—a varsity pitcher and All-District linebacker who dressed like a preppie and hung out at frat parties. Even in high school I was hanging out at frat parties. My girlfriend was a cheerleader. My parents were diehard Republicans. Life was good. I hated my life. Nothing ever happened in North Carolina in those days, the early eighties. I used to *pray* for something to happen, and I'd stopped believing in God at fourteen.

Then one night I heard a song by Jim's band, Rule of Thumb, and thought, "My God, somebody out there gets it. Somebody out there feels just like I do." I started listening to other songs by Rule of Thumb, as well as songs by other punk bands, and shaved off my hair and dyed the stubble blue. I slashed up my clothes and put them back together with safety pins. I bought a used Fender Mustang and taught myself to play it. I was the second punk rocker that town had ever seen, so it goes without saying I got a lot of shit, but I used to fantasize that Jim Cassady could somehow see me and was looking on with approval. I knew he'd been through similar things. I'd read a zine interview he gave in 1979 in which he talked about his love of the Stooges and the Velvet Underground back when most of the world was ignoring them. He was a strange kid who was constantly getting slapped around at school, and one of his worst tormenters was his classmate Buddy Lavrakis, with whom he later founded Rule of Thumb. They bumped into each other on the Sunset Strip in the summer of '75, when Jim was home from college, and, realizing they liked some of the same

3

music, started jamming with Buddy's younger brother Gary on drums. They were almost certainly the first punk band on the West Coast, and, as such, no one knew what to make of them. It wasn't till punk took off two years later that they started playing regularly around Los Angeles, and even then they were never that popular. Jim's literacy may have been part of the problem. He also wrote poetry (he'd majored in English at UC Berkeley), and his lyrics were filled with grim forebodings of a mechanized world gone mad.

But I liked that about him. He made me want to learn things. He opened my mind. In that zine interview, for instance, he talked about the Romantic poets and their relevance to rock & roll; popular music as protest art; the Beat and hippie influence on punk. The last he cited as the inspiration behind his adopted name: he was demonstrating the line of continuity. Then, toward the end of the interview, he was asked where he saw himself in the years ahead, and here I'll quote directly, since it's interesting in light of what became of him. "Oh," he said,

> I don't know. I always thought when the band broke up I'd get more into writing, but now I'm not so sure. Nobody reads anymore. You'd have to go back twenty years to find the last truly relevant writer. And right now there's no danger of the band breaking up, even though I'm starting to wonder if we're ever going to get played on the radio. But that's OK. I figure all we have to do is reach a few kids that aren't robots and, if they keep spreading the message and multiplying, my work is done.

In fact, by the time I read those words, his work pretty much *was* done. But he did manage to reach a few kids who weren't robots, and one of them was a fifteen-year-old squirt named Bernard Mash, or, as I called him, Peewee.

PEEWEE WAS ORIGINALLY FROM BROOKLYN, but he'd been sent to live with his sister in North Carolina after accidentally-on-purpose burning down part of his last school. That was only the latest incident in a tragicomic history of academic disaster, yet he was easily the most brilliant person I ever knew. It was unbelievable, the shit that kid could say. At fifteen he'd soaked up more knowledge than most people twice and three times his age, and he'd ramble through it in breathless monologues, veering from subject to subject like a house-trapped sparrow trying to find an open window: it's here, it's there, it's in the kitchen, it's in the attic now. I met him shortly before I disgraced myself by beating up a former friend who'd spread gossip about me fucking around on my girlfriend. She was a sensitive girl who was so upset she tried to kill herself, and I almost killed the guy I held responsible, and, two months shy of graduation, I was kicked out of school as well as my house. It's a long, painful story, and I'll tell it eventually, but for now this is all that matters: in the aftermath I started hanging around with Peewee, who was the *first* punk rocker that town had ever seen. He was the one who turned me on to Rule of Thumb. He made me tapes and showed me zines; he loaned me half of what I needed to buy my first guitar. He'd recently bought a guitar of his own, and he was always saying we should start a band, but to me that was almost beside the point. I was trying to emulate Johnny Ramone and Steve Jones and ROT's Buddy Lavrakis, and didn't care if it was in public or private. I just wanted my hands to produce those same brazen sounds.

One Thursday night in November '81, I was about to hit the sack when Peewee came pounding on my door. It seemed he'd just gotten off the phone with his friend Terrence in New York, and guess who was playing at CBGB's the following night? Go on and guess. I said, "No!"

"Yes!"

"No!"

"Yes! This time tomorrow night Rule of Thumb is going to be onstage at CBGB's, and we're going to be there!"

But I couldn't go. I had to wake up in a few hours to work my house-painting job, and my boss was always reluctant to let me have a day off. I said as much to Peewee, who said, "Jason, are you out of your fucking mind? This is Rule of *Thumb* we're talking about! You can always find another job, but this may be the only chance you ever get to see this band! Now go call your boss and tell him you *have* to have the day off, and if he still says you've got to come in, then tell him you fucking *quit!*"

So I did. I called my boss and said I was sick—I was practically dying, I was so sick—and he said, "Well, Jason, you know I can't spare you." I said, "Okay, I quit, bye," and hung up, and Peewee said, "Yes! Jason, I am *so* fucking proud of you! Now let's smoke some hash and get some sleep. We've got a long drive ahead of us." We left in the morning while it was still dark, and I tore up that highway; I drove like a felon trying to beat a roadblock at the Virginia border. That was as far north as I'd ever been. I'd been as far south as Myrtle Beach. And we raced through Washington, and we mowed through Maryland, and we passed through Delaware in all the time it would take a parched drunk to polish off a six-pack; and for much of the way we blasted tapes of ROT while Peewee bounced in his seat going, "They'd better play some old stuff! If they don't play 'Banished,' I'm going to tear that place to pieces!" The sun was almost gone by the time we reached the city. We parked in the Village, where Peewee's friend Terrence Haggerty was waiting to meet us. He'd come equipped. He led us straight to a Greek coffee shop and back to the bathroom to snort some coke—the first time I'd ever done that. He'd also brought a bottle of Jameson's, and we walked around the Village, getting good and fucked up, till we came to the Bleecker Street Cinema and Peewee looked up to see that his all-time favorite movie, *Taxi Driver*, was playing on a double bill with his second all-time favorite, *Mean Streets*. He went berserk when he saw that marquee. We *had* to go in; we just *had* to.

But Terrence wasn't interested. He'd seen both movies many times. Peewee said, "Well, Jason never has! I've been telling him about these movies since the day we met, and the one time we come to the city they're playing together! It's synchro-fucking-nicity!"

"Yeah, but I haven't seen you in months. Let's hang out, man! I don't want to see some goddamn movie!"

Terrence had grown up with Peewee, so he should have known that resistance was futile. They bickered till Peewee eventually exploded and said, "Just leave, you shanty Irish bitch! We'll see you later at the show!"

So Terrence took off, never to be seen again that night, and Peewee and I watched half of each movie and grabbed a cab to CBGB's, where the doorman took one look at Peewee's fake ID and refused to admit him. That was strange, as I later learned. There wasn't much carding in New York in those days. Still, for whatever reason, the guy wouldn't bend, refusing even to accept a bribe. As for me, I was eighteen—the legal drinking age till the Reagan Administration bumped it up a few years later—so I could easily have gone in by myself. Yet I couldn't. How could I see Rule of Thumb without Peewee? He'd never let me hear the end of it. Besides, I couldn't enjoy the show—not like this.

And so we both remained outside, trying to catch the music over midnight traffic cannonballing down the Bowery. We couldn't hear much, yet, somehow, I wasn't that disappointed. I was in New York City and standing by the door of CBGB's! Who knew how many famous people had stood in this very spot? And all the people who passed us seemed like such characters—bikers and bums and bag ladies and hipsters (who were clearly identifiable as such, with their Beatle boots and bandanna headbands and black leather jackets)—and, for this moment, I was here among them. Even the pavement beneath my feet struck me as special. It was New York pavement, and I'd taken to the city the second I'd seen its horizon rising through my bug-splattered windshield. And now at night, a part of the city, I loved it that much more.

The show ended, or so we gathered from the little we could overhear. We'd been looking around for ROT's van, thinking it must be parked nearby, but we saw no vans, or at least no vans with California license plates. Still, Peewee said we'd probably get a chance to meet Jim if we kept hanging around, and sure enough, covered in sweat, he walked outside and lit a cigarette. He looked nothing like I thought he would. In all the photos I'd seen he came across like James Dean's slightly older brother; but in person he had a moon-shaped face, longish hair streaked with premature gray, and teeth that looked like they hadn't been on friendly terms with a toothbrush in a good two years. Peewee, bold as ever, ran right up to him and said, "Hey, Jim! We drove all the way from North Carolina to see your ass, and that pig-fucking doorman wouldn't let us in!" And Jim said, "Wow, I'm…really…flattered…" That was how he spoke. He had a whispery, spaced-out, spooky voice, and all his sentences were…broken up…like…this… I'd certainly imagined him sounding very different. Nor, as I'd expected, was he especially eloquent.

On the other hand, Peewee did most of the talking. He wanted to discuss the implications of some of Jim's lyrics. Was sex really going to be supplanted by technology, like he'd sung in "Artificial Pussy"? And did he really think, as the lyrics of "Lockstep" suggested, that the human race was headed for a time when cultural differences would no longer exist, replaced with a bland monolith along the lines of the American middle class? You have to understand that nobody was talking that way in 1981, or at least nobody I'd ever met, and this kid was barely sixteen and drunk and drugged to boot. Even Jim looked like a lightweight next to Peewee. He could hardly find answers to half his questions, and when he did it came out like: "Well, that song…it's sort of a…warning…like you find in…science fiction…" To which I remember Peewee responding: "Jesus Christ, Jim, what the fuck are you talking about? Science *fiction*? That shit's for geeks!" He kept referring to him as "Jim," like he'd known him his whole life, and me—I barely said a single word, I was so beside myself. I was standing three feet away from Jim Cassady! And, no, he wasn't exactly impressive with his spaced-out voice and fucked-up teeth—in fact, the whole time we spoke, he kept playing with one, like he was either trying to work it out or work it back into place—but he was *still* Jim Cassady, and to me that was better than being God. At one point he asked if we had our own band, and Peewee said, "No, but I *want* to start one. Would you please tell my friend Jason we should start a band? He'll listen to *you*, Jim."

And by God, that motherfucker—my hero, God Himself—he stopped fucking with his tooth long enough to look directly at me and say, "I really…think you should…start a…band…Jason…" He said my name and everything. That was right around the time Buddy Lavrakis walked out. He was big and blond and dressed like Jim in a plaid flannel shirt, and to meet him was almost as mind-blowing as to meet Jim, though he barely said two words to us. He just took Jim aside with an air of emergency, and, after they'd whispered for a couple of minutes, they walked inside and didn't come back.

Still, not for the first time and not for the last, Jim Cassady had changed my life: for the next few hours I walked the streets with Peewee, all the way from CBGB's to 59th Street and back down Broadway, plotting out the future. We decided we'd pack up our stuff as soon as we returned to North Carolina and move to New York, where we'd live with Peewee's parents—or at least he would—till we got a place of our own. (Of course we had yet to ask, and when I met his parents the next day, I could tell they were both afraid of him.) We bandied about band names and settled on the Widowmakers, which is what we called ourselves for the next year and a half; and we also talked about how big we wanted to be, as if we had full say in the matter, and decided rock stardom wasn't for us. No, that was for dumbfucks. We just wanted to be an East Coast version of Rule of Thumb, a cult band with fans as cool as we were. And I guess, in the smallest of ways, we finally got our wish.

OF COURSE, BEING CHILDREN AT THE TIME WE STARTED, we didn't realize how tedious it could be. We may have worshiped at the altar of rock & roll, but to say we never got our share of miracles—a few small graces to justify the grind and hard knocks—would be the understatement of all time. The Widowmakers fell apart after playing six shows. The survivors formed Scratch. Then, after many jealous scenes, I broke off to front the short-lived Dockside Hookers, and Peewee started the Egonauts. That name was partly a dig at me—Jason and the Argonauts, get it?—but eventually we made up and regrouped as Superego, the band we were sure was headed for greatness when everything literally came crashing to an end. As for Rule of Thumb, things didn't work out well for them either. Within months of that conversation outside CBGB's the band dissolved, and Jim Cassady seemed to vanish right off the face of the earth. Every time we met anyone with ties to the L.A. music scene, we'd ask what Jim was up to, and even when they recognized the name, which wasn't often, they'd say, "Gee, I don't know. Hasn't he got a new band or something?" If so, we never heard about it. There was nothing in the zines; there was never a new record. We spoke constantly of what might have happened, and once, I remember, Peewee read a poem that sounded a bit like Jim and decided that must be it: he must have retired to write poetry using a different name. Later we decided he'd probably OD'd or possibly died of AIDS, since in retrospect we realized he'd been smacked up the night we met him. By then we'd had some dealings with smack ourselves.

In fact, in the movie I later made about our lives in New York, I depicted Peewee as a hopeless junkie. It wasn't true. I was just combining that phase, his "junkie" phase, with a few of his many others. Plus having his character fatally overdose was a less expensive way of killing him off than the way Peewee actually died: in a car wreck while touring in the spring of '88. The movie was called *Sick to Death*, which speaks volumes about the way I was feeling. I never wanted to be in another band as long as I lived. I barely listened to rock & roll. But then I came by some money to make my own film, and the subject seemed to choose itself. I wrote the script in a manic burst and cast four actors with a music background, rehearsing them for a month like a regular band. Then, when the guy playing "me" dropped out, I personally filled his shoes. I wasn't interested in acting, but I hated all my backups, and I figured I at least could help sell the movie band as the real thing. A sense of authenticity was key. We booked and shot actual shows at clubs in New Jersey. We shot in real-life shooting galleries, in hipster dives like Max Fish, on Avenue C in the middle of the night—a dangerous move at the time. I wanted something that felt like a documentary, and no question, I got it, though technically the movie was a mess. There were scenes so dark you could barely see, and others where you wished you *couldn't* see, the acting was so shitty. I always regarded myself as one of the worst offenders, though many assured me that wasn't the case. As the critic from *Variety* kindly wrote: "Helmsman Maddox is a natural as Brian, but pointless squabbling by petulant rockers ultimately makes for a tiresome experience, thus justifying pic's title." Thanks, guy!

Still, even those who'd disliked the movie, including that critic, often praised the soundtrack. Most of the songs I chose came from my own bands, but I stole some from others, thinking I'd pay for the rights if and when I sold the film. One especially I wanted to buy: "Raft at Sea" by Rule of Thumb—probably the most beautiful song Jim Cassady ever wrote. I used it for the final scene, as the main character walks down rainy 42nd Street, reflecting on his shaky future, and everything about it fit the scene like a dream: the chiming guitars and ghostly vocals and lyrics that, over time, had taken on telling significance.

> *But all I want to do is disappear*
> *Beyond the hold and expectations*
> *Of those held dear*
> *And broken records of record dreams*
> *Pizza for breakfast and scenes within scenes*
> *It was never meant for me*
> *The second act begins in exile*
> *As I drift unseen at sea*

Once the film was finished and playing on the festival circuit, where it bounced around for over a year, I was asked about that song many times. There were people who'd come up and say, "You know, I was on the fence about your movie till that final shot. But that really did it. That song—I had tears in my eyes." Cy Parker, who would soon become my agent, was one of them. He approached me at Sundance and said that even though he didn't think the movie would ever get distributed (and he was right: it never did, not even on video), he saw in me a "great raw talent" and would be interested in signing me on the condition that I move to Los Angeles. And he specifically mentioned "Raft at Sea." He knew I'd written most of the songs from the post-screening Q&A, and he repeatedly praised the closing song, assuming I'd written that one as well. I did set him straight, but, all the same, I now give Jim Cassady partial credit for setting me on the road to Hollywood.

JIM WAS BORN IN HOLLYWOOD and grew up over the hill in Burbank. As far as I knew, he'd always lived in Southern California, except for his time at UC Berkeley, and he dropped out of Berkeley after his junior year to start Rule of Thumb. He once referred to L.A. as "a gulag with palm trees," but he also said that made it perfect for punk rock, since "this music thrives on boredom and, trust me, there's always going to be plenty of that in Southern California." He said that in 1979, when the punks in New York were looking down on the punks in L.A., but that was never true of me and Peewee. By the time we were living in New York, a lot of great bands had come out of L.A., though we still dismissed it as a city. We played there once on tour with Superego, and to me it looked like a landfill, particularly after playing in San Francisco the night before. Then again, we only stayed for half a day. Maybe it was time to reassess.

So, in the spring of '91, I flew out for a month, camping on the sofa of a *Sick to Death* actor, and quickly saw I'd gotten it right the first time. It was always sunny, every single day, yet the sky seemed covered with dirty glass, and the light was crude and merciless. Strange that a town famed for illusion could have such brutal light. It spared nothing, exposing every flaw, making the many strip malls look worse than their builders intended. Some of the residential zones were nice enough, but they seemed so perfect, with their roll-up lawns, it was hard to believe people actually lived there. The houses appeared as empty as the sidewalks. It was as if somebody had phoned in a citywide bomb threat and the whole population was out driving in circles till the danger had passed. And they drove fucking *fast*, and that was something else that bothered me, having barely survived the crash that killed Peewee and two others besides, lucky to have kept my right leg. In New York I never *had* to drive, but suddenly I was on the L.A. freeway, lost and trying to make sense of directions while other drivers cut me off and tailgated me. The aggression was all in their driving. They frowned upon it, face to face. I'd never met so many people who came across so blank: no wit, no charm, no spark or bite.

So that's what I didn't like about L.A. What I did like was the way Cy Parker gushed over me. And not just him. The first time I dropped by his agency, the prestigious ETA, he called a meeting with his fellow agents, and they likewise blew a lot of smoke up my ass. Did I realize they handled Joe Strummer? Well, Joe was looking for a new film project, and if they showed him *Sick to Death*, he'd sign up for my next movie immediately! In fact, I'd brought a new project with me—a script I'd banged out on speed, much like *Sick to Death*—and Cy promptly read it and set up meetings with production companies. So there I was, a punk-rock guy from the wilds of arty Williamsburg, driving up to the gates of Warner and saying, "Yes, Jason Maddox to see Phyllis Stein," and lo and behold, the gates parted as they never had for my band. That's what a Cy Parker can do for you, not to mention Sundance. These days a movie like *Sick to Death* would never find its way into Sundance, lacking name actors and/or not directed by an Eskimo lesbian; but I'd applied at the perfect moment, before money and politics were determining the schedule, and thanks to hits like *sex, lies and videotape*, independent film was the happening thing. I wasn't too concerned with selling out, whatever that meant. I wanted to make movies, and art and commerce had always intersected, so why fight it? Sure, I might lose something by way of experimentation, but I'd never been much on offbeat flourishes where they clouded more than they clarified. Even Nietzsche—one of Peewee's big influences and, through him, one of mine as well—chose not to express himself in the convoluted esoterica that would have come naturally to him, but in to-the-point aphorisms, reaching out for the man in the street. And so it was with rock & roll. And so it was with Hollywood. There was no contradiction, as I saw it at the time, and I could always find ways to subvert from within. My new script, for instance, was a kind of postapocalyptic *Bonnie and Clyde*, with all the action sequences Hollywood could wish for, but, at the same time, a satire of contemporary consumerism: even in the middle of a nuclear winter the characters couldn't stop *acquiring* things.

But the subtext I never mentioned around the suits. I could tell some of them weren't sure what to make of me, but I tried to seduce them the same way I'd seduce a woman in a bar, repeating back whatever they said but using different words. Meantime, as much as possible, I let my appearance speak for me. There's no other way to say it: I was a big, tall, handsome guy—"a better-looking Roger Clemens," as my ex Suzanne used to say—and while that had never been particularly useful in the underground-music scene, in Hollywood I was hoping it would be.

Looking back, that may have helped me most of all. Almost every day I went on meetings, and whenever I called Cy for feedback, he'd say, "They loved you! You're going to make a sale, I can feel it in my bones!" Cy's bones were psychic: by the end of that month I'd gotten an offer, and I flew to New York to pack my things and find somebody to sublet.

JIM ONCE REFERRED TO BEING IN A BAND as "dating three guys"—the best description I ever heard. You're constantly having to put up with shit, but you do it for the sex, which in band terms translates as music. With movies you're dating many people, and those who work in development are often among the ugliest. The notes! For a year and a half they would not stop with the notes! First the protagonists weren't "sympathetic" enough—how about a cute child mutant who tags along with them? Then the "stakes" weren't high enough—how about a bad guy who's out to kill the mutant? They neutered the sex, they toned down the violence, and as for my so-called satiric elements, those bit the dust right away—we're not making a comedy, you know! Fighting did no good. I tried a couple of times, but everybody just sat there looking embarrassed, and besides, I wanted to get this project greenlit by any means possible. I was even compliant when they shopped the script to name directors. Fine by me. I'd still be the screenwriter, and once this movie got made, I'd be sitting pretty so that next time around *I*'d be the one directing. That's all a screenwriter really is—someone who wants to be anything but—and for some reason the work came naturally to me. On the other hand, it's not what you'd call creative—not by my standards.

But it did pay well. That was one reason I had few regrets about going Hollywood: for the first time ever I was earning good money. I treated myself to a classic ride: a 1966 Ford Mustang, bright red with a white interior and a rebuilt 289 V8 engine. My dad used to have a '66 Mustang, so maybe for that reason I felt safe behind the wheel. I also got an apartment in Echo Park: a picturesque one-bedroom built on the edge of a steep bank with train tracks at the bottom and the house-lined hills of Cypress Park on the other side. It was mostly a Mexican neighborhood, but the higher you got, the whiter it got, which is how it always seems to go: almost every place I've ever been, the rich live in the peaks, while the poor make do in the flatlands. There were three other units in my building, which had a kind of Cape Cod look: red shingles with white trim and a white rickety staircase leading to my front door and, from there to the street, a serpentine flagstone path. The yard was filled with trees, so that even on the sunniest day it was always shady, and especially at night it was always quiet, the only noise coming from the trains below. Which also put me in mind of my childhood. I grew up not far from a trucking depot, and back then I used to fall asleep to the sound of forklifts and braking semis.

Another L.A. perk: for about three months I was fucking a bona fide *Playboy* centerfold. She was a local girl I met at the laundromat, and when she first told me she'd done *Playboy* I thought she was joking, but then she showed me her layout, and it was her all right—only the name had been changed. She was nothing like you'd think a centerfold would be: an English major at Occidental College who wrote short stories and liked French films. Not quite as interesting as that may sound, but not a bimbo either. I got her on the rebound, and eventually she reconciled with her ex, but for a while it gave me bragging rights when I called my friends in New York. I told them L.A. was an interesting place if you didn't judge it as you'd judge a conventional city. At times it reminded me of a Doors song: laid-back on the one hand, ghostly on the other—a hammock stretched between tombstones. It always struck me as haunted, somehow; but like a lot of people with a background in punk, I was fascinated with crime, and L.A.'s got quite a history that way. One Sunday the Playmate and I visited crime scenes all over town, from the lawn in South Central where the Black Dahlia was discovered to Sharon Tate's house in Benedict Canyon. We couldn't see much from the driveway, so I drove to the top of the opposite hill, where we could just make out the roof, and even though it's hard to explain, being at the exact spot where the sixties had reached their bloody climax was weirdly kind of romantic. It's a shame that house was later destroyed. In my view, considering the turning point it symbolized, it should've been preserved as a cultural landmark.

ONE NIGHT, AROUND THAT SAME TIME, I went to a barbecue in Silver Lake. Barbecues were big in L.A. in the early nineties. I remember many stops at the store to pick up meat and beer. This particular barbecue was hosted by a German director I'd met through the Playmate, and the house was packed with actors and writers and directors and composers and their various hangers-on. That was another reason I rarely missed New York: I used to meet the same types there as well. But the ones in New York could at least show a little passion. Here, once a conversation struck a nerve, it was usually over.

For some reason the Playmate wasn't there that night—she was probably off banging her ex—and I was bored and ready to leave when I started talking to a guy who claimed to have been a major player in the Hollywood punk scene. I never caught his name and wish I had, since it might have proved helpful a few years later. But he was pretty stupid and drunk to boot, dropping names of supposed friends like Lee Ving and Jeffrey Lee Pierce; and when I asked if he'd ever seen Rule of Thumb, his eyes practically bugged out of his head.

"Dude!" he said. "Nobody *ever* mentions them anymore. They were so good, man. They were the fucking best!"

"They were something, yeah."

"Yeah, nobody put on a show like—what was that guy's name?"

"Jim Cassady."

"Yeah, nobody put on a show like *that* guy. And you know what's weird? He had, like, unbelievable stage fright."

"Really."

"Yeah, I got drunk with their drummer one time—what was his name?"

"Gary Lavrakis."

"Yeah. Jerry. And he told me Jim would, like, freak out every time he got up there. You would never have known it, man, 'cause when that guy was on, he was fucking *on*. And the music was so fucking awesome. What was that one song he used to sing? The one about"—and here he paused and looked around to make sure nobody else was listening—"niggers?"

"Oh. Right. 'Nigger Pearl Harbor.'"

"Yeah, I don't know why he'd want to sing a song like *that* one. But I got to say it rocked. I mean, fucking whoa!"

He played a few bars on air guitar. I felt like I was back in the sixth grade.

"Well, you know," I said, "it wasn't meant to be racist."

"It wadn't?"

"Not really. It's such a forbidden word, you know, so Jim was kind of going, 'All right, I'm going to take this word you're all so afraid of and rub it right in your faces.' Especially white liberals. You know how self-righteous they can be. Jim was taking on political correctness before anyone knew what it was."

"Yeah, he was a real deep guy, I guess. I remember one time I saw him at the Starwood, and he was throwing all these big words around, and I was like, 'Whoa, dude, I think I need a dictionary!'"

"Well, the one time I met him, he could barely talk."

"Drugs, probably."

"That's what I always figured."

"Yeah, he was big on that shit. Must have been. 'Cause he ended up homeless, you know. I knew this—"

"Wait a minute, hold on. He ended up *homeless*?"

"Yeah."

"Are you sure?"

"Yeah, this friend of mine—he ran into him on Hollywood Boulevard, and Jim was, like, wearing rags and shit and begging for change with a coffee cup."

It was so shocking, I had him repeat it several times. I kept asking for details: when it happened, who his friend was, how well he knew Jim. He knew him well, I was told, and it wasn't that long ago—maybe two or three years at most.

"And he was absolutely certain it was Jim Cassady," I said.

"Yeah, dude. Like I said, he was friends with the guy. He offered to, like, take him to a homeless shelter, but Jim was like, 'No, dude, just buy me a cheeseburger.'"

"So he was coherent."

"Well, I guess so. I mean, he asked him for a cheeseburger."

I still wasn't sure if I believed it. Not that it was *that* far out, but I knew from firsthand experience how a rumor can take on a life of its own. Still, that was the first time I thought of trying to track Jim down. I remember I stopped at Pioneer Market on the way home and saw a bum begging for change in the parking lot, and I thought, "You know, if this story is really true, it'd make a great idea for a movie. A famous musician ends up begging for change near the site of his former glory." Of course, Jim was only a cult figure at best, but I was trying to see it as a producer might. And then, very quickly, I forgot all about it. There was so much else to think about: the Playmate, my screenplay, all that money I was socking away. Plus Jim was from another part of my life completely—a part that, on some level, I *wanted* to forget. I wasn't ready at the time to fully face my ghosts. In the meantime they came to me in dreams, and sometimes I'd wake not knowing where I was: in New York or L.A. or some city I'd played on tour, expecting to find my smelly bandmates snoring all around me.

AFTER I GOT REPLACED BY ANOTHER WRITER on my lovers-of-the-apocalypse project, Cy assured me this kind of thing happened all the time, and what I should do is write something new and let's get it out there right away. So I did, and he sold that script as well, and I spent months in development with the same result as before: the meat removed, the shell stuffed with cotton candy, a second writer brought in for a "fresh take on the material." It happened a third time too, and that script, like the others, never came close to being made.

During this period, which lasted over three years, I directed a few videos for mediocre bands. One video was shown twice, I think, on MTV: skinny kids banging around in cages, with cuts to a dog catcher making his rounds. I'd pitched the band a lot of interesting ideas, but they opted for the weakest in the bunch. The song was called "Stray Heart," so they thought a dog catcher was a great way of punning on the title and publicizing animal rights in one fell blow. But this all came at the close of the great video boom, when MTV and the major labels were backing off on promoting artists other than top-selling acts, so that took care of that.

Frustrating? You could say so. I was in my early thirties in a town obsessed with youth and barely out of the gate. Fortunately I looked years younger than I was, though I'd lost some hair and gained some weight. Still, I knew the clock was ticking. I figured my best shot at breaking through was to produce my own movie, so I wrote a script for a contemporary film noir—my favorite genre—and spent the next two and a half years meeting with potential investors. The story was inspired by *Hamlet*, of all things. I'd caught the Olivier version on cable one night and thought, "You know, if Ophelia was secretly bad, and *she* was the one who'd killed the old man and married his brother, it might just work as a thriller." It was a great script, the kind everybody likes but nobody wants to make—or not with me attached as director. Finally I met with a company called Avatar, who said they'd let me direct if I altered the script to their specifications. They wanted more sex, more blood, way more tits and gunplay. B-movies were a thing of the past now that A-movies *were* B-movies, except with bigger budgets; but Avatar was still cranking out the real deal, and they were willing to give me a chance. I decided to go forward. I was broke by then and dying to make a movie.

For seven months I slaved on that thing—three in rewrites, one in preproduction, one on the shoot, and two in post—and for all that I was paid just fifteen grand: after taxes, barely enough to keep me in bread and water. Needless to say, the result was shit—so bad I took my name off it—yet ironically, unlike the far-superior *Sick to Death*, this movie got distributed: for a while I couldn't watch TV late at night without seeming to pass it on Cinemax. I cringed every time, particularly at the sight of the half-rubber lead actress. But all the girls I'd liked refused to take their clothes off, and the girl I was forced to hire could barely keep her clothes *on*. Even in dialogue scenes it was always: "Don't you want to see my tits?"

Still, Avatar liked her, and they liked me too. They were proud of that movie. They thought it was good. They offered me another one, which I turned down. I'd rather temp! And did, actually—pretty embarrassing for a failed director of thirty-five. In my spare time I hacked out a new script—my best, I was sure—but after years of developing screenplays that never got made, Hollywood had turned frugal. Now most big movies didn't start as scripts, they started as concepts put together by executives, and screenwriters were the puppets who fleshed them out. Of course, they'd *always* been puppets, but not like this. So my script didn't sell, and, fed up with temping, I got in touch with Avatar, who gave me a job knocking off teleplays for a softcore cable series with the working title of *Secrets and Lays*.

Meantime my use-by date was fast approaching with Cy Parker. By then he'd moved to another agency and taken me with him, but I could tell he'd lost interest, and I'm sure my erotic *Hamlet* was a contributing factor. He'd seen it, of course, and said it was "a lot of fun," meaning it was too trivial to dignify with further discussion. I agreed, so why not say so? But that would have been a breach of Hollywood decorum, just as when I was bound for the chopping block, he danced around that too, sometimes taking as long as a week to return my calls. I was dealing with his various assistants, who were constantly being replaced, far more than I was with Cy. Then one day I called and got the usual thing: "He'll have to get back to you." No, I said, I have to talk to him right this minute.

I was put on hold. Through the receiver *Sgt. Pepper* was playing, and I remember thinking how sad that was, how this once-groundbreaking music was now Muzak. Then the assistant popped back on and said, "Still there?" and I said, "Yep," and she placed me on hold again. Then Cy picked up, and as soon as I started talking, he said, "Wrong line," and popped back off. I was pacing around my apartment thinking, *I am going to kill somebody!* when the assistant came back and said, "Go ahead, Jason," and a second later there was Cy, already sounding impatient.

I asked about my check. (Avatar, like all my Hollywood employers, paid me through Cy so he could take his ten percent.) He knew nothing about my check, he said, and why was I bothering *him* with something like that when I could easily ask his assistant?

"But I've asked her about it, and she says she doesn't know anything either. Besides, she's not my agent, man. And lately I can't seem to get you on the phone; and I realize you're busy, Cy, I realize you've got other clients, but if you can't take two minutes to help me find my check, then what's the point of going on?"

I hadn't planned on giving him an ultimatum. It just came out that way. And I'd long known he was fucked up, with his barely-concealed coke habit and his abuse of past assistants. Still, nothing quite prepared me for the pissant contempt of his next remark. It's one of those slaps in the face that still grate after all this time.

"Well," he said, "it's not like *my* phone is ringing off the hook with people begging to hire you!"

"You're dead."

No, I didn't say that. He would have called 911 immediately. It was pretty clear, though, that we'd come to the end of the road, so I told him thanks and goodbye. I got drunk that night, or maybe it was the night after, and found myself watching *Sick to Death,* and Jim Cassady's lyrics to the other song I'd stolen from Rule of Thumb, "Sonny in the Morgue," hit me like they never had before.

> *Son of the east*
> *Lured to the west*
> *Glory-seeking like all the rest*
> *This town is filled with guys like you*
> *Yeah, and the cemetery too*
> *Tell me something, Sonny*
> *Did you see it coming?*
> *They almost never do*

A COUPLE OF WEEKS BEFORE THAT CHRISTMAS, which was the Christmas of '98, my old bandmate Terrence Haggerty flew to L.A. for a job interview. He was one of very few people from the old days I hadn't lost touch with—not because I'd chosen to cut myself off, but once your friends marry and mature, you can pretty much leave them for dead. Terrence, though, was still single and working the same job he'd worked since the mid-eighties, as tech support for a major Manhattan securities firm. When I first knew him, he wanted to be a film director, but then he realized he lacked the requisite drive. In fact, he'd never had much drive, period, which is why I was so surprised to learn that he was now in his third round of interviews with Apple. I knew he wasn't happy living in New York—there'd been quite a few hints to that effect—but I never dreamed he'd get off his ass and *do* something about it.

Ironically, he arrived as I was thinking of moving back to New York. I knew it would be difficult, not to mention expensive, since, due to some misbehavior on the part of my sublessee, I'd long since lost my apartment. But the half-life I was leading in Los Angeles was sapping me. Terrence noticed it right away: I didn't even look the same. It wasn't just age. The person I saw in the mirror put me in mind of a shellshocked soldier after marching for weeks through sludge and snow. Terrence's looks had also changed. He'd put on weight, especially in the face, reminding me of a young Jackie Gleason. Still, beneath the extra weight, he was the same old affable Terrence. You would never have guessed he was as miserable in New York as he claimed he was.

"Believe me," he said, as we had a drink in Santa Monica, "you're better off here. That place has changed like you can't believe. Do you realize there's a fucking Kmart in the East Village now? Everywhere you look it's just chain stores and trust-fund kids. And they're so rude! New York used to be a friendly town, but those trust-fund kids are the fucking worst!"

"Well, do you think it's any better here? I've been living in the same place for seven years, and my next-door neighbor still doesn't speak to me. I'll pass her at the mailbox, and she pretends like I'm not even there."

"Can you blame her? Hey, speaking of pretending you're not there, guess who I saw a few days ago?"

It was my ex, of course. Terrence said he'd been in Soho when he bumped into Suzanne with what he assumed was her new boyfriend: some bald guy decked out in Armani. He said she'd asked about me and he told her I was doing well, that I'd recently finished my second feature, and, contrary to expectations, she said she was really happy for me.

"If she only knew," I laughed.

"Well, you did make another movie. I don't think you realize how well you're doing. Most people never make *one* movie."

"Yeah, I'm doing great, man. Softcore porn—it doesn't get much better than that."

"As a matter of fact, it doesn't. And so what if this last thing didn't turn out great? You'll get other chances. You're the Killer!"

"Killer" was a nickname Peewee had bestowed on me. Meantime Terrence hadn't flown 3000 miles to listen to me moan. It was his first time in L.A., and like so many lifelong New Yorkers, he'd never learned to drive, so I chauffeured him down the Sunset Strip and up along Mulholland. He loved that, especially when we saw a coyote staring us down by the side of the road—a rare sight in Manhattan! Then, because he wanted to sample the nightlife and possibly meet some girls, I took him first to the Dresden Room and then to the Derby, where we tried talking to a pair of would-be actresses over 200-decibel swing music. They were not only retarded but extremely sarcastic, and after they skulked off, I told Terrence he'd meet plenty more like them if he moved to L.A.

"The most superficial girls on the face of the earth," I said. "And they're not even all that good-looking, compared to their reputation."

"Well, *they* weren't bad. You just scared them away, that's all. Boy, you're really out of practice, huh?"

"What can I say? I'm past my prime and broke. I don't have the bank these bitches are looking for!"

"Man," he cracked up, "this is more serious than I thought. Well, I'll tell you what: I brought you a birthday present I think is going to do you right. It's at the hotel, and I've got to get up early, so maybe we should pack it in."

I knew what that meant: Terrence had always had a huge appetite for drugs. I drove him back to Santa Monica, where Apple had booked him a room, and, sure enough, he opened his shaving kit and took out a tiny packet filled with smack. At first he said it was all for me, but he changed his tune as soon as I diced some lines. We both sat there sniffing away, and, man, was it good—the first smack I'd done in years. It's not what I'd call a social drug. The more you ingest, the more your tongue feels weighted down; but somehow we managed to speak anyway, reminiscing about the old days and working our way forward, so that finally Terrence was wondering out loud why he was trying to land a job with a multinational corporation that, in principle, stood for everything he didn't.

"God," he said, "good thing Peewee's dead. Otherwise I'd never hear the end of it."

"Oh, come on, man, he wrote you off years ago. The whole last year of his life, that's all he talked about: how disappointed he was in you."

"Wow. Thanks. That's good to know."

"Well, you think he'd be any happier about *me*? I can hear it now. 'You're a sellout! And not even a very *good* sellout! You're not making any money!'"

"Well, at least you stand for something. You might not be doing as well as you think you should, but at least your balls are on the line. Me—I think about ending up with nothing, and it scares the fuck out of me."

"It scares me too. Why do you think I'm hanging on? I'm no hero. I just fucked up so bad, this is the only shot I've got."

"So you're scared too. You know, sometimes I think that's what our generation is all about: fear. That's what fucked up New York. Everybody got so scared, they went to the other extreme. And I don't know about you, but I *liked* the danger. I mean, I'd rather walk around thinking I'm going to get robbed any second than walk down some boring street where nothing ever happens. I mean, at least the first way you're feeling something."

"Well, hello, Peewee. Where've you been all these years?"

"Well, come on, he was right! And, you know, I can understand cleaning up crime, but *everything's* cleaned up these days. Like, on the plane they were showing *Saving Private Ryan*, and I'm sitting there thinking, 'What the fuck? Tom fucking Hanks?' That guy's about as interesting as a lawnmower salesman at Sears!"

"Yeah, but people love him."

"Exactly. And you know why? He's safe. That's how scared people are these days: they're afraid to see a fucking *movie* that's going to make them feel a little uncomfortable!"

We continued in this vein till six in the morning, so, knowing how tired Terrence was going to be, I figured his interview wouldn't go well. It didn't, to say the least. We'd already arranged for him to spend a few days at my place, so, after his disastrous interview, I drove out to Santa Monica to collect him, and halfway to Echo Park we stopped at a liquor store to pick up fortifications. We also picked up the *LA Weekly*, and later, flipping through it, Terrence stopped short.

"Well, what do you know," he said. "Combover's playing tonight."

"Who?"

"It's a New York band. They're great, man. I see them every chance I get. But where exactly is the Silverlake Lounge?"

"Nor too far from me. But I think it's a Mexican drag-queen bar."

"Oh, it can't be. They'd never play at a place like that."

He was partly right: on certain nights the Silverlake Lounge was an independent music venue—something I didn't realize, since I so rarely ventured out. We got there at eleven o'clock, and outside on the sidewalk a lot of kids were smoking, many wearing thrift-store clothes and, with their pasty faces and dyed-black hair, looking much like we used to look in the New York eighties. It was exactly the balm I needed. I thought, "I'm home again." Even the place itself reminded me of New York: a shadowy dive with a blue-lit bar and, beside the jukebox, tacked-up photos of trannies dressed like Madonna. The stage was tiny and set near the back and, above it, a four-foot sign with a downturned curve spelled out the word SALVATION in beaming white bulbs.

Terrence and I had often locked horns when it came to music, so naturally I wasn't that taken with Combover. To me they were just another Pixies rehash: a few good riffs here and there, and a so-so chick singer who talked too much between songs. In my day we only did that when something was malfunctioning, which was pretty much always. I tuned out the band and checked out the crowd, and there, standing a few feet behind me, was the most beautiful girl I'd ever seen. She had straight dark hair parted neatly in the middle and a softly-sculpted face with pouty lips and pearly skin. You know the kind of skin small children have, so pure it seems to glow? Hers was no less radiant. There was something angelic about her, but something vampiric too—mainly because of her coloring—and she wore a tan suede jacket with fringe on the sleeves and a kind of Navajo handbag hanging off one shoulder. A number of kids in the club that night were dressed similarly—neo-hippies of the nineties—but, somehow, she didn't seem like any of them. You definitely don't tend to see girls as stunning as her in dives like that one, but it wasn't just that, it was something else—something I couldn't quite lay my finger on.

Naturally Terrence noticed her too. He gave me a nudge and nodded her way (like he actually thought I hadn't seen her!), and for the rest of the show we both kept turning to stare. But I did especially, so that, for just a second, her eyes met mine, and I would love to say something magical happened, but nothing did. She just glanced over as if wondering who it was, this guy who kept gawking, and, seeing it was no one she recognized, quickly looked away. There was a guy with her, a skinny guy with long sideburns who was spooning her from behind, and at one point he pulled her closer and shot me a look as if to say, *She's mine, all right? Now back the fuck off!* Pretty brave for a runt like him. But I did look away, and the next time I looked, they were walking out the front door. And that was it. I never thought I'd see her again, but oh how wrong I was. That girl was going to lead me to some places I never thought I'd go, and somewhere along the way, she would literally reintroduce me to Jim Cassady.

I MET HER IN THE MOST ROUNDABOUT WAY, after months of temping and the ongoing search for a new agent, which led straight to nowhere. I had nothing to show for myself but a handful of videos, some unproduced screenplays, and two features that, in one case, I never mentioned; even so I couldn't get over the arrogance of these glorified secretaries. In the animal world they'd be the weak links, the also-rans forever getting humped by the alpha beasts. In the human world they ran the whole show. How, I wondered, could we develop a system so perverse, so contrary to the laws of nature, and still expect to flourish? On the other hand, the day's still young.

That May Avatar called with a directing gig: a kiddie movie, incredibly. The story concerned a mad scientist of a ten-year-old who invents an invisibility formula and uses it to expose his corrupt principal and reconcile his estranged parents. Very low-budget, of course, and completely the opposite of my other movie; but the people at Avatar didn't type you the way most people in the film business do, thinking, "He's a thriller guy" or "He's only good at comedy"; they just assumed if you'd done a good job one time around (and I really hadn't), there was no reason you couldn't do an equally good job on something very different. I polished the script, which was pretty much set, and a few weeks later we started production at a small Venice studio a couple of blocks from the ocean.

Even though I used my usual pseudonym on that movie (Simon Ritchie, Sid Vicious' real name), I have to admit to a certain affection for it, partly since I wasn't compromising my own material as I had with my film noir, and partly since it put me in mind of those Disney things I saw as a child: *The Love Bug, The World's Greatest Athlete, The Computer*

Wore Tennis Shoes. I also got a kick out of the kids, though I constantly had to mind my language around them, and, what with the child-labor laws, they could only work so many hours a day. It took a lot of planning and a lot of speed. (I took a little speed myself!) Fortunately all our kids were pros, and their parents were standing by to beat them silly if they fucked up. I'm kidding, of course, but I definitely didn't think much of the parents. There was one father who, spotting a piano on the set, banged out the score of *Annie*, forcing his daughter to sing along. Another kid, eight years old, was supporting her entire family, including her mother's gigolo boyfriend. I could see a lot of drugs in that girl's future.

But the mother of the lead was great: laid-back about her son's career, and a big flirt too. I was sure we were going to hook up, but then the wardrobe girl got a better-paying job on another movie, and that changed everything. I didn't even know she was leaving. The production manager never bothered to tell me, and one especially hectic morning I looked up and saw another woman adjusting something on a kid's costume.

"Excuse me," I said, "but what do you think you're doing?"

"Sewing his button back on."

She had an English accent, really smug, and I've always had a problem with Brits. I don't mind the working class, but the rest drive me right up the wall.

"Well, why are *you* sewing his button?" I said. "Isn't that Julie's job?"

"Julie got another film."

"Oh, that's great; it's always good to be informed of these things. Now, get out of my frame, please. We've got to shoot." Then she protested about the button, and I said, "We don't have time to sew any fucking buttons! Now, get out of my frame *now*!" And the boy she'd been fooling with burst into giggles, and, rolling her eyes like I was leagues beneath her, barely human, she stalked off.

Her name, I learned, was Astrid. She had dark blonde bangs, a strong jaw and hooded eyes that reminded me at times of a cobra's; yet, taken on her own terms, she was weirdly attractive. There was a certain irony I came to appreciate, a certain smirky sarcasm. Once I heard her mumble something about one of the kids being "the most awful little brat," and there was something about the way she said it, like a wicked Mary Poppins, that really made me laugh. She was also bright and well-informed, as I learned one day when I found myself sitting beside her at lunch. Usually I sat with the kids and their parents, including the one I liked; but on this particular day their table was full, so I moved to the one next to it, where Astrid was having a heated debate with the props guy and a few other members of the crew. The subject was the president's affair, and so far as I could make out, the props guy was saying Clinton ought to be removed from office, and everybody else was ganging up on him, Astrid leading the pack in her patronizing way. I had no interest in getting involved, but then Astrid turned to me and said, "So what's *your* opinion, Mister Director? You're being awfully quiet. Do you like a nice witch trial or don't you?"

"Well, I definitely don't believe in persecuting somebody over a couple of blowjobs, if that's what you mean. But I still think Clinton is a loathsome man."

"Thank you!" said the props guy.

"But *why*?" said the makeup girl. "I think he's the best president we ever had!"

"Based on what?" I said.

"Like, the economy. He really turned the economy around!"

"Well, maybe you've benefited from it, but I sure haven't. I'm still struggling, thanks. And even if Clinton is responsible for this so-called boom—and I'm not sure he is—it's because of globalization. He's after the complete annihilation of human difference."

"You can't be serious," Astrid snickered.

"Well, isn't that what globalization amounts to? Homogenization? I mean, look at what's going on in Yugoslavia right now—"

"Yeah," exclaimed the props guy, "and you know why we bombed *them*, don't you? To make people stop thinking about Monica Lewinsky!"

"For God's sake," Astrid said, "we *had* to intervene with those people. Are you *aware* of the crimes going on there?"

"There's crimes going on everywhere," I said. "Why don't we bomb Turkey? They've been taking out the Kurds for years already. But, no, they're part of NATO, so it's hands off. And I don't think Clinton was bombing Yugoslavia to hide his affair, but I think his true motives are just as reprehensible."

"And what *are* his true motives?" Astrid smirked.

"I think it's vanity. He's looking at his place in history, and I think after this scandal and all the others, he's trying to beef up his legacy. And

Milošević—he's a very convenient target. We don't have the Cold War anymore, so we need somebody like him. He's the new bogeyman."

"Well," Astrid said, "my brother happens to be married to a Serb, and even she says Milošević is pure evil. He's just the most awful kind of thug. It's as if Al Capone were running that country, having people whacked and so on."

"Clinton does that all the time!" said the props guy. "Just look at Vince Foster! He was going to blow the whistle on Whitewater, and they took him out and shot him!"

But nobody was paying him any mind. Astrid and I were the only ones halfway qualified to hold that discussion, and even I was talking through my hat. I didn't like Clinton because of his association with Hollywood elites and his shameless-yuppie stamp on the cultural climate of the nineties. That was a bad, bad time, as far as I was concerned. I was just giving a running tour of my standard bias.

"Well," I told Astrid, "I'm sure you're right about Milošević. But I really don't think Clinton cares about that. I think the mistake Milošević made is resisting Western imperialism. He's the only thing standing in the way of a completely unified Europe."

"And that's bad?"

"If you want diversity, yeah. And right now it hasn't affected things much, but, ultimately, you're going to get a situation where you can't tell Sweden from Italy. Or Beverly Hills, for that matter."

"My God, that's *so* Luddite! Tell me, should Texas belong to the same country as New York? Because, by your reasoning, they should be exactly the same by now. But I don't believe that's quite happened yet, has it?"

"You said it yourself: not yet." And she looked right at me with her trademark smirk. "*Touché,*" it seemed to say; and for the rest of that day and the next several she was constantly finding reasons to approach me. She told me her life story in bits and pieces. It turned out she came from a well-to-do family with a country estate so grand it was something of a tourist destination. Her mother was related to Princess Diana. Her father was in the House of Lords. Not that her life had been a bed of roses, mind you. She'd basically been raised by nannies—"really cruel, some of them"—and, at least till she was shipped off to school, her only companion was her brother David. Now he was a movie director, while she, of course, was a costume designer, who back in the U.K. had worked on a wildly popular TV show, as well as with the Royal Shakespeare

Company. She loved to work, she wanted me to know, but her posh accent had cost her points with the middle-class types who ran things, so she and her brother both preferred living in Los Angeles. I was flabbergasted. What was somebody like her doing on a set like that one? Oh, she said, she was only helping out a friend, and she might easily ask the same of me: What was *I* was doing on a set like that one? It didn't seem my "sort of fare."

"Oh? So what's my sort of fare?"

"Well, I certainly don't see you working with children. Not unless they're in bustiers and stiletto heels."

Translation: You're a filthy pig who interests me greatly. I invited her out for a drink one night. She suggested the Good Luck Bar in Los Feliz, not too far from her place. She couldn't have made it more convenient: by the second round she was eating my face, and two rounds later I was pounding her sweet spot in her beaded-curtain bedroom. She was one of those women who don't look particularly busty in clothes, but once those come off, you do a Tex Avery: projectile tongue, eyes springing out on coils. As for Astrid, she seemed fascinated by my scarred-up body and asked how it had gotten that way, and I gave the barest-bone answer I possibly could, since that was something I rarely discussed, and besides, I knew already I could never fall in love with her. The next day was a Sunday, our one day off, and after sleeping late, we decided to have breakfast a few blocks away at a French café called Belle Époque. It was late June, and the weather was so nice we sat outside on the sidewalk, and almost the second we did the door opened, and out came that stunning girl I'd seen six months before. She was wearing sunglasses and a babydoll dress—a very different look, yet I recognized her right away, such was the impression she'd made on me. She wasn't alone. There was a kid with her, a different kid dressed like the other one in hipster hand-me-downs, and they were just about to walk up the street when Astrid turned to see what had me so captivated, and, to my surprise, she called to the girl by name.

"Irina!" she said; and the girl stopped and came back, her faux-seventies friend lagging behind her like a self-loathing puppy.

She struck me as a little nervous, somehow. She stood by our table and rattled off a story about rehearsing a scene for an acting class, and as soon as I heard those words, I thought, "Figures. A girl this beautiful would *have* to be an actress." Meantime she had an accent I couldn't quite place. It was slight—her grammar was perfect—but it definitely registered. Then she asked how the movie was going, and Astrid cupped her hand over mine and said, "How would *you* say?" I wished she hadn't made it so fucking obvious I was fucking her! I was the director, she told Irina; and Irina said it was nice to meet me; and I said, "You know, I think I've met you before."

"Really?"

"Well, we didn't talk very much. It was last December at the Silverlake Lounge, and I was there to see a band called..." What *were* they called? Several awkward seconds passed, Astrid giving me the strangest look, when it finally came to me: Combover.

"Oh," Irina said. "Yes, I was there. I didn't like them very much."

Good God, neither one of us liked Combover! Would wonders never cease? And maybe there were *lots* of things we had in common, and I wanted to learn every last one of them—in fact, I was just about to ask if she wanted to join us when Astrid headed me off.

"Where's David?" she asked.

"At home," Irina sighed. "He's meeting with some writer and didn't want me there, so I thought I'd go rehearse."

"Well," Astrid said, really trying to shoo her away, "maybe we'll drop by later and say hello."

"Oh, I don't think that's a good idea. He's in one of his moods, you know. But maybe we'll see you when the movie's over?"

"If not sooner. Give him my love, will you?"

Then, after saying it was nice to meet me—"again!"—Irina walked off with her retro friend, Astrid keenly watching them go.

"My sister-in-law," she explained with a roll of her eyes. "God, poor David!"

ACCORDING TO ASTRID, IRINA WAS A SLUT. She didn't come right out and say it, but that was clearly what she meant to imply. She said Irina had a habit of getting "very friendly" with "a lot of guys," and while David was sure she'd never been unfaithful, Astrid had her doubts.

"She's the flower, and they're the bees, all buzzing around. It's just amazing, how many men are always phoning the house. David finds it all very funny. He says it isn't her fault if men find her attractive. But

I've seen guys touch her in *very* inappropriate ways, and she does nothing to stop them. So I'm afraid David's deceiving himself. He's such a sweetheart, you know. Hates to think a bad thought about anyone."

"And she's an actress?"

"Well, that's *one* way of putting it. She has no talent whatsoever. Even David admits that. He's tried to dissuade her from acting, but she insists on doing it. And the irony is, she's a brilliant painter. Well, that's going a bit far. But she has enormous talent, and she does nothing with it. She just goes on auditions and does her little plays and that sort of thing."

I asked how David had met Irina, and she said, "Well, it was—five years ago? Yes, that's right, I'd just broken up with Nicky. David was making a film in New York, and Irina came in to read for him. She was modeling at the time, but she quit that as soon as they got married. She just sits back and lets him support her, except every so often she'll get some little acting job. As a matter of fact, David's planning a new film, and she's been hounding him for a part. And I expect he'll give in to her. He always does."

"You really hate her, huh?"

"No," she said, taken aback, "I like her. I don't like some of the things she does, but she's no fool, I can tell you that. For a girl from a place like Yugo*slav*ia, she's done very well for herself. I have to give her that."

Then she gave me a funny look, sheepish and sharp at the same time, and said, "Now, please don't tell me you're infatuated too."

"I just met her."

"I thought you met her before."

"Oh, that. I bumped into her, and she spilled her drink, and I offered to buy her another one. We barely said two words."

I was lying because I'd lied to Irina, trying to mine a connection we didn't have, and now I had to lie again to cover my tracks. But Astrid wouldn't let it go. She asked if Irina was alone that night, and I lied still again, saying I couldn't remember. The whole thing was really touchy, since, no matter what Astrid said, it was obvious she couldn't stand Irina. And if her suspicions were correct, I could definitely understand. She had every right to watch her brother's back. I just wished she'd stop watching mine. She'd been clinging to me all morning while gawking at me with moonstruck eyes that seemed to ask, "Are you okay? Am *I* okay? Am I still to your liking, dearheart?" Where was the saucy woman I'd taken to bed? She'd turned to jelly overnight. Still, I hoped to keep seeing her, at least till the end of the movie. It had been so very *long*.

I needed to go home. She wanted to come with me. Fine. I took her over. She liked how it looked from the outside, but inside she mentioned right away how "dusty" it was. Then, glancing at the sink: "I see you're not much on washing dishes." However, she was very impressed by all the books I owned, and she lingered for quite some time by a framed photo taken on the set of *Sick to Death*.

"Weren't you something," she said. "How old are you here?"

"Twenty-seven. It's from my first movie. Want to see it?"

"Now? Well, all right. Maybe a little."

I popped it in the VCR, and we sat on the sofa, watching. At first she laughed at some of the funny bits, but that soon stopped as she stifled back yawns, looking like she needed a pair of toothpicks to keep her eyes pried open. I'd only seen that thing 10,000 times, but somehow I could always get into it, regretting mistakes and praising myself for the good parts; recalling what had taken place on a given day. But because Astrid was making it so painfully clear how bored she was, I clicked it off.

"It's very good," she said.

"You can be honest."

"No," she roused herself, "it reminds me a little of Ken Loach—do you know his work at all? And it's certainly very exciting to see you play guitar. You still play?"

"A little. More lately. Want to hear something?"

She didn't. She gaped at me with goo-goo eyes and said, "Do you know who'd really like your film? David. He likes anything with a lot of grit."

"Is that the kind of thing he does?"

"Well, he'd like to, but his agent—you know how those people are. They keep thrusting these silly little scripts at him. It drives him mad!"

"At least he's got an agent."

"And you don't?"

"Not right now I don't. They only want names or kids."

Then, as if struck by a thought, she said the words that would shortly alter the course of my life: "Could you give me a copy of your movie?"

Of course, I told her.

"And do you have a script you've written? Something you're especially proud of?"

"I'm sure I can dig something up."

"Well, let me pass those along to David. Of course I can't make promises, but if he likes them enough, he might be willing to pass them along to his—"

"Sure. Thanks. That's very nice of you."

Then she started kissing me, and even though a few minutes before she'd been close to passing out, suddenly she was raring to go.

I TOLD ASTRID FROM THE BEGINNING that I wasn't looking for anything serious, and she claimed she wasn't either, but that wasn't the way she acted. Sexually she treated me like rough trade, like the servant servicing the lady of the manor in some torn-stocking fantasy of hers; but outside the bedroom she'd fix me again with goo-goo eyes, and if I didn't behave exactly like she wanted, she'd force me into one of those relationship powwows of the American kind, demanding to know what I felt and weighing my feelings against hers. Yet because she made herself so readily available, I continued to see her even after the shoot had wrapped and I'd moved on to the editing room. As for the script and video she'd given her brother, he never responded. I wasn't expecting a response, since even your best friends won't watch something unless you prod them, and even then. Six months later you'll say, "Hey, did you ever check out that thing I gave you?" "Sorry, man, haven't had time. But I will, as soon as I get home, I promise." Six months later, same dialogue. Repeat.

One Saturday morning, maybe a month after that day at Belle Époque, I was sleeping at Astrid's place when the doorbell rang. Astrid wasn't there. She'd gone off to fit an actor for a job she'd just gotten, and I was exhausted after a long day in the cutting room and a romp with Astrid afterward, so at first I tried to fall back asleep. Then I remembered Astrid saying something on her way out the door, that David was going to Vegas for a couple of days and he might stop by to leave his keys so she could feed his cat. I still hadn't met David but felt like I had, Astrid talked about him so much. And once again he rang the bell, so that, cursing to myself, I got up and threw on my pants and went staggering into the living room.

Well, it wasn't David. It was Irina. She was walking away when I opened the door, but she turned and came back and said she hoped she hadn't woken me; she'd left the keys in the mailbox. She also said she'd liked my movie. At first, being so muddy-headed, I thought she meant the kiddie flick, but as she kept talking, I realized, no, she'd watched *Sick to Death*. She said it was the funniest thing, that the tape had been sitting on top of the TV "forever," and she thought it was one of David's audition tapes—"because he's casting this new movie, you know"—and eventually, curious, she slipped it in the VCR. Only one thing kept bothering her: she'd seen the lead actor somewhere and she couldn't place where. Later, she said, she mentioned the movie to David, asking where he got it, and he told her it was something Astrid gave him, and that was when she finally realized who the actor was: Astrid's boyfriend.

So, great, I was Astrid's *boyfriend* now. Not only that, I was an *actor* to boot. Irina started talking shop, asking what kind of "technique" I'd studied, and I said, "Well, I don't really have a technique. That's the only time I ever acted."

"You're kidding!"

"No, that's it. And I wasn't supposed to do it that time, but the guy who was supposed to do it dropped out at the last minute."

"That's so funny," she said. "You know, I had a teacher who used to say the best actors are the ones who never do it professionally. She said it comes so naturally it's not enough of a challenge, or something like that."

"Well, I don't know, I never thought I was that great. I mean, I wrote the movie, so I had an advantage there. And I fronted a band for a long time, so to get up and play a guy in a band—it wasn't that hard, you know? The hard part was trying to direct and act at the same time. And I was a lot more focused on directing, so I always kind of felt like the acting suffered."

"But it didn't. And I could tell you were probably in a band. The parts where you're playing—those are the best."

"Yeah, well. Those were the parts I felt the most comfortable."

"And did you write the songs?"

"Well, most of it them, yeah. But there's a few by other people. Like that one at the end—"

"Yes, that's the one I'm thinking of. Who *did* that?"

Now, over the years I'd been asked that question many times, and whenever I said Rule of Thumb, people always said, "Who?" So that's what I expected her to say. But instead, when I mentioned ROT, she said, "Oh, I've heard of them."

"You're probably thinking of someone else."

"Well, aren't they from L.A.? In the seventies, I think it was?"

"Jesus Christ, that's right! How'd you ever hear of Rule of Thumb?"

Through her friend Jeffrey, she said. Jeffrey knew *everything* about music, and once he'd shown her a video compilation of punk bands from the late seventies. She couldn't remember that much about it—"They all sounded the same to me"—except for one band she really liked: the Avengers. Had I ever heard of the Avengers?

"Of course! I must have played that one EP till my ears bled! And that girl—Penelope Houston?—she was like the perfect punk chick!"

"She's a folk singer now."

"She is? How do you know?"

Jeffrey again. She said Jeffrey had seen Penelope play at some club in San Francisco, and apparently he bugged her so much afterward, asking about the Avengers, she told him to fuck off. Irina found that very funny.

"If you knew Jeffrey, you'd understand," she said.

"Is he that guy you were with at the Combover show?"

"Yes, that's him. Did you speak to him that night?"

"I didn't, no. But I wonder if he knows what happened to Jim."

"Jim?"

And I told her about him. I described him as a kind of shaman, as a poet and prophet who vanished after his band broke up, only to end up panhandling on Hollywood Boulevard. At least that's what I heard, I said. I told her the story that guy had told me all those years before and how for five seconds I'd thought of basing a film around it, and she said, "Well, why didn't you?"

"I don't know. Punk rock—it's not the most commercial subject."

"God," she sighed, "you sound just like David. Every time he has a good idea, he never does anything with it. It's never 'commercial' enough. And I say, 'Is that the only thing that matters? People never think anything is commercial unless you force them to.' And then he'll complain about how bad movies are! Well, yes, they *are* bad, but they're never going to get better if we're all too weak to take a stand."

Man, how beautiful is youthful idealism? As beautiful as Irina, standing there on Astrid's porch, her dark hair blowing around that creamy skin. And this was the closest I'd ever been to her, except for that time at Belle Époque, and that time she'd been wearing sunglasses that hid what I now decided was, physically, her most remarkable trait: her eyes. Not only were they beautifully shaped, with lashes out to here, but they were a color I'd never quite seen before, like brand-new pennies rolled in gold flakes. And she wasn't wearing a speck of makeup, and she was tall and thin, but not *too* tall and thin, and she had those pouty lips—what a sight to wake up to! I asked if she wanted to come in for coffee, but she said she couldn't, she had to go, yet she just kept standing there, talking about New York now. She said she used to live near St. Mark's Place—a prominent location in *Sick to Death*—and that was something else she liked about my movie: it made her miss New York. Of course, she only lived there for about a year, but she considered it the best year of her whole life, even if she *had* been modeling—"the dumbest job in the world," she called it.

"Yeah, it was kind of like that for me. I used to work these shitty jobs, but I always knew it was worth it. But now everybody says it's changed so much."

"Yes, but people always say that. They were saying it when I lived there, but I didn't know any better, so for me it was perfect. I wish L.A. was that perfect."

Then we started talking about L.A., and somewhere in the middle of that, she finally agreed to come in for coffee.

"But I can't stay long," she stressed. "After a few minutes, you have to kick me out."

I led the way to the kitchen. Astrid owned one of the most complicated cappuccino machines I'd ever come across, and I tried to figure it out till Irina laughed at my helplessness and made the coffee herself. Meantime she ran down Los Angeles, expressing herself in a forthright way I'd almost forgotten existed. She complained about the air, the isolation, the architecture and, most of all, the people—especially the white ones living on the west side. Sometimes, she said, it felt like the only people she met in L.A. with a trace of passion were black or Latin, and she wondered if the reason was poverty.

"I mean," she elaborated, "once you have money, I think you just stop caring, you know? But when you struggle, you know exactly how much life is worth."

"Yeah, but don't you think it's a cultural difference? They've got more of a pleasure ethic, whereas white people are all about work. But that's not true. In Europe it's the Protestant countries where people work the hardest. Catholics—they're not really famous for their work ethic."

"Well," she laughed, "I'm from Yugoslavia, and we're Orthodox—or we are in Serbia, where I grew up—and we definitely have no work ethic there. We're extremely lazy!"

"Including you?"

"Well, David thinks yes, but I don't think so. I've always worked *very* hard when something interests me. At acting, for example, I've never stopped taking classes. And I've worked constantly at perfecting my English. Not that I've succeeded!"

"But you have. You speak better English than most natives."

"Thank you," she said, "but that's not what casting people say. Every time I go for an audition, they say, 'Well, we really like you, but unfortunately the character doesn't have an accent.' When, many times, there's no reason she couldn't. Why *couldn't* this girl be European? It's not like it matters either way."

"Well, why don't you try to work in Yugoslavia? That would seem to be the ideal situation."

"There's no work in Yugoslavia," she said, as if I should know better, "and it's very regimented. You go to the academy, and from there you do theater, and maybe then you do films. It's not like that in America. And there's no future there. Not just for me, for everybody. It's very depressing."

"Well, it must be pretty weird to live in a country that's bombing yours."

"Well, yes, I was very upset when the bombing started, but then I realized this may be the only way things will ever change. None of my Serbian friends agree with me. We've had many bad fights about it. I don't know. Maybe I'll change my mind the next time I go home, but I don't think so. I think, in the end, it really is for the best."

By this time we'd moved to the dining room, both of us drinking coffee, when Irina fell quiet and gave me a blank look. I had no idea what was going through her mind. She just stared at me, and I stared back. Finally she asked the strangest question: "Do you believe in God?" I asked why she wanted to know, and she reached toward me and picked up a small silver cross dangling from my neck and held it for a second.

"Oh," I said, "that. I just wear that because—well, I was in this really bad car wreck, you know. I'm still not sure how I survived, but I just happened to be wearing this thing, and when I was in the emergency room, this guy cut it off and put it in my hand and said, 'He was really looking out for you tonight, wasn't He?' So, after that, I kept on wearing it."

"Then you must believe."

"Not really. It's just a kind of superstition."

"Isn't religion always superstition?"

"Not if you believe. And if you make a comment like that, I assume you don't."

"Well, I believe in *something*. I don't know if you'd call it God, though. It's closer to astrology, but it's—it's very hard to express! But you know how in astrology, if you're born under a certain sign, you have this kind of personality, and this kind of talent, and no talent for something else?"

"Of course."

"Well, I think the same. But it's not because of this sign. And it's not the personality you get from your parents, and it's not the way they raise you, it's… Okay, my mother has a friend in Belgrade who loves dogs. And he *looks* like a dog. Even people who don't know he likes dogs call him a dog behind his back. Now, why would people who don't know the first thing about him say something like that?"

"Maybe he spends so much time with dogs he's started to look like one."

"No, it's something else. It's what in art you'd call a motif. And with me—well, there are many things but, for instance, the month of June—all the big things happen to me in that month. That's when I was born, that's when my father died, that's when I left Yugoslavia. I met David in June, and we got married in June a year later. And it wasn't that I was planning it. He just said to me one day, 'Let's get married,' and we flew to London and got married."

"Yeah, but I bet a lot of big things happen in other months too."

"Oh, so you're going to fight me. No, I'm sure I'm right. It took me a long time to realize. And if you really looked at your life, you'd see the same thing. You'd see all these patterns that don't make sense, and they *don't* make sense, because where's the sense in them? But that doesn't mean they don't exist."

So then it was my turn to sit there staring. She actually *thought* about things—abstract things she could barely find the words to express, but she still made the effort. I wanted to leap across the table and kiss her, and she stared back, and once again I had no clue what was going through her mind, when she suddenly looked at her watch and said, "Oh my God!" and jumped up and ran into the living room. I followed, and at that second the door opened, and there was Astrid. The look on her face was priceless. I wish I'd had a camera, as they say. I knew what she must be thinking, with me half-naked and Irina so flustered, and I was about to explain when Irina spoke first. She said she'd stopped by to leave the keys and woken me, and David was going to kill her; she really had to go. She thanked Astrid for looking after the cat, kissing her on the cheek, and then, to my surprise, she ran back to me and kissed me on the cheek as well.

"It was great," she said, and she gave me a last flash of her copper-gold eyes and raced out the door, leaving me alone with an English statue. I could sense the storm about to come, but Astrid stood as if frozen. Then she moved. She moved to the dining room, where, spotting the empty espresso cups, she said, "Well, that's odd. If Irina was in such a hurry, then why did she come in for coffee?"

"Because I asked her to."

"Oh," she said. "I see." Then she moved to the kitchen, where, like Mama Bear detecting the presence of Goldilocks, she said, "Oh my God, look at this mess! Who *made* this mess?" There wasn't much mess—just a few grains of coffee spilled on the counter—and I told her I'd clean it up, but she refused to let me. She grabbed a sponge and started swabbing the whole place down, and when I walked up and put my arms around her, she jerked herself free.

"What the fuck is wrong with you?" I said. "We just had fucking coffee!"

"Oh, really? Is that why you're being so loving all of a sudden?"

She had me there. Come to think of it, that *was* the reason I was being so loving all a sudden: she was a substitute for what had run out the door. Of course I couldn't tell her that, so I had to go on convincing her she was out of her mind.

"Why don't you give the girl a break?" I said. "You walk in here and treat her like crap. She's perfectly nice to you."

"Well, if you prefer her way, then go right ahead. Let's see how far you get."

"Oh, really. I thought you said she sleeps around."

"And I think she does. But I wouldn't get any ideas if I were you. She likes them young or rich."

Ouch! Astrid had fangs when she wanted to use them, as I would eventually discover in a major way. She was jealous of everybody, not just Irina, and I was getting sick of it, so I told her I was leaving, and went to the bedroom to get my shirt and shoes. I'd almost finished putting them on when she appeared in the doorway and stood watching me with bovine eyes.

"I'm sorry," she said. "I know I'm being difficult. I just wasn't expecting to arrive home and find you alone with *her*."

"Well, come on, she's your brother's wife. What do you think? I'd fuck her right here? Give me a *little* credit."

But if I could've, I no doubt would've. Plus, if there was any truth to Irina's "motif" theory, I had a long history of semi-incestuous romances, and that was running through my mind even as I told Astrid she had nothing to worry about. Once again she apologized, blaming her mood on a frustrating fitting with a hard-to-please actor, and soon I was doing to her everything I would've loved to have done to Irina, only minus the tenderness I would've put into it.

BACK WHEN I FIRST HOOKED UP TO THE INTERNET, I'd done a search on virtually every person I ever met just to see what came back. I don't think I ever turned up anything especially startling, except when I searched my own name. In *Sick to Death* I'd appeared nude for all of two seconds, changing clothes before a show, and incredibly, even though the movie had never received any form of distribution, somebody had gotten hold of a copy and posted stills of my butt crack on gay porn sites. Also, with Superego, I'd made a record and now discovered it was being sold at fairly steep prices by specialty stores and collectors. I wrote to one collector, curious; were there actually people willing to pay fifty bucks for that thing? There were for a fact, he responded; he'd recently sold his only copy at that price exactly, and he asked if I could send him a few more copies, offering to pay as much as thirty for each one. I replied that I had just two left and intended to hang on to both, having long since lost track of the masters. "LOL," he wrote back.

Naturally I'd done a search on Jim Cassady and gotten somewhere, I think, around 200 hits. Most concerned other Jim Cassadys: brokers from Wisconsin, lawyers from Massachusetts. Maybe twenty pertained to *my* Jim Cassady, but they were nothing remarkable: sketchy reviews of ROT records, and still more collectors looking to sell them. A search under Rule of Thumb led to so many sites that I soon stopped sifting through them, the band's name being a household expression. I did find an ROT shrine put up by a moron named Josh, but it was so badly put together, I barely looked past the opening page.

A few days after that talk with Irina, however, I was stoked enough to give it another try, and this time I had the inspired idea of searching under idiosyncratic ROT song titles such as "Sonny in the Morgue" and immediately pulled up a substantial number of band-related hits. "Josh's Rule of Thumb Page" headed the list, and two years later it looked and read exactly as I recalled:

> Rule of Thumb was a great band that desserved a lot more credit than they have ever receved. I was disterbed when I found there was no pages for them anywhere on the web so I have put this up so youll see for yourself how great they where. They were true punks not posars they wrote great songs that told the truth they refused to play the game thats why they never got big as they shoud. There sound was uneeke they didnt sound like every other punk band they deserve to be remmembered as the pioneres they were.

Who the fuck was this guy? He read like a brain-damaged twelve-year-old, but I was constantly coming across similar writing on the Internet, and it couldn't *all* be the work of brain-damaged twelve-year-olds. Plus how could somebody who couldn't spell the simplest words favor a band with a frontman as brainy as Jim Cassady? Still, whomever this Josh was, he had a few links on his site, one of which led to the zine interview I quoted a few times at the start of this book. Now, reading it again for the first time in over a decade, I couldn't get over Jim's prescience. For instance, his remark about Southern California—how, being so boring, it was the perfect environment for punk—was borne out by later developments: no other region was nearly as influential in the years following punk's first wave. And then there was this forecast from the same interview, equally astute:

> I mean right from the beginning, rock 'n' roll has either been banned or sanitized. It's really kind of a running battle. They cleaned up Elvis and gave us Frankie Avalon. Then the British came along to bail us out and, after five or six years of really good music, it's right back to crap. And I bet the same thing will happen with punk. One day a few bands will go Top 40 and they'll phase them out and gives us, you know, the Osmonds doing "God Save the Queen".

Well, close enough. Led by Nirvana, punk went mainstream in the early nineties, and a few years later the only "punks" at the top of the charts were virtual boy bands like Blink 182. Elsewhere, Jim explained the effect of punk as a religious experience akin to Bible-thumping tent revivals, and he even claimed to see a precedent for punk's do-it-yourself ethos in the "Let's put on a show!" of Mickey Rooney musicals. And there were links to still other sites on Josh's page, including this ROT bio at musicgeek.com:

> Assembled in 1976 by singer Jim Cassidy [sic] and guitarist Buddy Lavrakis (b. 1955), Rule of Thumb was the wild card of the early Los Angeles punk scene. Their eponymous 1978 EP had them as forerunners of thrash, but their sound later softened, with catchier hooks and nuanced songwriting. In 1980, they released *Pathology of Least Resistance*, their finest hour, but clashing temperaments and audience indifference took their toll and, shortly after releasing the melancholy *Tinderloin*, the band broke up. Lavrakis and his brother Gary later went on to form blues-punks Tornado Bait.

In fact, the band got together in '75, not '76, and I personally preferred *Tinderloin* to *Pathology*; but the yield here was learning that Buddy and Gary had been in Tornado Bait. I'd very nearly seen that band! Back during my ten-minute career as a video director, I was supposed to go to the Troubadour one night to catch some kids who'd expressed interest in working with me, but my car wouldn't start. It was too late to find a ride, so the next day I phoned the band to apologize, and they said it was no big deal; I'd only missed their best show ever. Why, they'd blown the headliners, Tornado Bait, right off the stage. I had a very distinct memory of this, since "tornado bait" was one of Peewee's favorite expressions for poor white trash. If I'd only known!

Aside from Josh's page (which was pretty threadbare; no mention of Jim's present-day whereabouts), I still couldn't find anything about Rule of Thumb beyond the usual record reviews and collectors. Then I did a search on Tornado Bait, and that eventually led to this 1996 profile from *The* (Portland) *Oregonian*. It was entitled "'Tornado' Sweeps Into Portland" and included a small photo of the band—Buddy's hair dyed black and his face a bit bonier, but otherwise looking exactly as he had in ROT.

> Buddy Lavrakis feels no shame about touring with his band in a broken-down van at age 41.
>
> "Blues artists only get better with age," he says, "so I never understood why people don't cut rockers the same slack. That's something I'm hoping to change. A big part of this band is introducing kids to a little thing called experience."
>
> Lavrakis, whose band, Tornado Bait, performs tonight at St. John's Pub, certainly has a lot of experience. A California native, he takes pride in being one of "America's first punk rockers. I don't think kids these days realize how hard it used to be. Everybody wanted to beat up punks [in the 70's]."
>
> For a while, Lavrakis set music aside. He married and fathered a child, working for his in-laws as an auto detailer. But drugs and alcohol abuse caused the marriage to end and Lavrakis decided he missed music, after all.
>
> "I wasn't looking to start a new band," he remembers. "My brother Gary was in bad shape, too, and I thought if we got together and played every once in a while it would be like therapy. But it turned out I was the one who got the most out of it. In all my earlier bands, I was never able to do what I wanted. There was always some lunatic insisting we do things his way. So, now I finally had a chance to get it right. We started booking shows and it all just snowballed from there."
>
> Lavrakis admits he can be a stern taskmaster. In 1991, he fired Gary, who died a year later from a heroin/cocaine overdose.

"It probably would have happened no matter what," Buddy reflects, "but I still feel bad about it because I'm the one that got him into music in the first place. And there are certain friends of mine who got him into drugs and I feel responsible for that, too. But some of them are dead themselves now, so I guess they got what was coming to them."

He calls the ferocious witches' brew that is Tornado Bait—equal parts metal, punk and swampwater blues—"everything I've been through in one neat package. I was never that into roots music when I was growing up, but maybe that's something you come to appreciate over time. You look up and see you've survived and start relating to music that's survived, too. The only thing is you can't make much of a living at it. But that's OK. I feel privileged to do what I do. Most people my age hung it up a long time ago."

Anything else?

"Yeah," he says, "make sure you bring your earplugs. I may be getting up there, but I play real loud!"

So Buddy had become a kind of roots-rock missionary, and Gary was dead. Plus it sounded like Jim was dead as well. I mean, what other "lunatic" who'd refused to let Buddy play his own way could he possibly have had in mind? Then, with equal bitterness, he'd mentioned "certain friends" who'd gotten "what was coming to them."

I sent this article to Terrence in New York. He'd never idolized ROT to the extent that Peewee and I had, but I wanted a second opinion: did this sound to him like it did to me? "Definitely," he wrote back. Intrigued, he did a search of his own, and a few days later he sent me a link to another website: a kind of punk archive containing an interview with an aging scenester named Billy Bash. At first I didn't see any connection, but finally, close to the end, there was this bit, way too little information for all the questions it raised:

BB: [...] but out of all those girls, the one I liked best was Cybil Disobedience. She was from Vancouver, or maybe I just think that 'cause she used to go out with Joey Shithead. Anyway, she came down to LA to try and start a band, but she wasn't much of a singer, she wasn't much nothing as far as music goes, but one thing she did have, she could make a scene like nobody else. She'd do wild shit like, one time, I was at a show and this guy was fist-fucking her right there in front of everybody. And she dressed real crazy. I mean she was way past wearing garbage bags and shit like that. One time she took a bunch of latex gloves and made a dress out of 'em.

Q: Vivienne Westwood lives!

BB: Yeah well, Cybil didn't make it too far. She hooked up with that jerk Jim Cassidy [*sic*], the only person around as fucked-up as she was. That's where she died, his apartment. They ruled it a suicide, but the kind of relationship they had, I was never sure.

I WRAPPED POST ON THE KIDDIE FLICK at the end of September. Any time you work on a movie as hard as I did on that one, there's a sense of achievement but, at the same time, a terrible sense of emptiness. You cast and shoot and cut and mix—hundreds, even thousands, of tiny decisions—and you want to feel good about it, but you know the movie's a piece of shit destined for an audience of twenty. You start to wonder why you made it in the first place, except you also know why: if you hadn't, you'd be sitting in the dark eating ramen noodles!

Meantime Astrid's brother had gotten his mega-movie greenlit. She'd been talking about it, practically, since the day we met, and it was finally going to happen, thanks to some TV pretty boy who'd accepted the lead role. Now David was headed to Europe to scout locations, but first he was throwing a party to celebrate the movie and his thirty-ninth birthday. I was curious to meet him after weeks of hearing so much about him. I wanted to see who was married to Irina. I picked up Astrid the night of the party, and she'd really decked herself out for the occasion, wearing a kind of flapper dress and a matching sequined turban—her own designs. From there she directed me to David's house, high in the Los Feliz hills. The house was a Spanish-style mini-castle painted rustic red, with a tiled roof and turret and spade-shaped windows and a big Moroccan door. There was no place to park nearby, so I dropped off the flapper and kept searching till I found a spot a five-minute walk away.

Now, I knew already this wasn't going to be my kind of party, but as soon as I stepped inside, I almost felt like throwing up. The living room was filled with high-end furniture and industry types from every white nook of the globe. The men were mostly eunuchs, and the women mostly she-males, which was par for the course for the movie business: if a man had balls, he had to hide them, and if a woman *didn't* have balls, she had to pretend like she did. But both sexes were equally full of shit; neither knew the first thing about life aside from shopping and work. Even parties were work. They weren't about having a good time; they were about networking, about showing the host what a pal you were for turning up in the first place and fleeing at the first opportunity. A handful might stick around to dance, but, trust me, that's a sight you'd never want to see. I noticed a few chicks-with-dicks bobbing their heads to Massive Attack. Goddamn, I wanted to remove that record! I wanted to put on Cockney Rejects and clear the room. Then again, I could also clear the room simply by being a man with balls.

I saw a dark corridor off to one side and bumped shoulders down the length of it. The talk around me was typically bloodless: "I picked up the best pair of shoes…" "We worked together on…" "The food is great but the location…" Photos lined the walls: some of David, some of Irina, some of David *and* Irina. Most were small and simply framed, but one was biggish and framed expensively: a black-and-white nude of Irina. She was lying in a tub half filled with water, her arms folded across her chest like a pharaoh. You could almost make out a nipple. She smiled a knowing smile.

I found Astrid in the kitchen with David. I would've known it was him even if I hadn't just seen his photos, they looked so much alike. Unfortunately for Astrid, he'd gotten the better end of the bargain: her strong jaw and hooded eyes looked fine on him. I had to admit he was a handsome guy, but that was all I could say for him. He struck me as a typical Englishman of his class, mincing around, superficially charming and playful, but cold and hard at heart. When Astrid introduced us, he limply shook my hand and said, "Well, we've certainly been hearing a lot about you."

"Yeah, I've heard a lot about you too."

"Oh," he said, "I'm afraid to hear what this one's been saying," meaning Astrid, who pitched her turbaned head back, laughing insanely.

"HA, HA, HA, HA, HA, HA, HA!" she shrieked. She wasn't being sarcastic either. She responded that way to half of what he said, no matter how unfunny, and he clearly relished the attention. You would almost have thought they were sleeping together, despite their creepy resemblance. I can only speculate that with their cruel nannies and remote parents and isolated country estate, they'd formed the kind of bond that went far beyond the sibling norm, except, here again, Astrid came out on bottom: David had married, and she never had. No wonder she hated Irina! Not that she was about to step aside. I'd barely met David, in fact, when he ran off to welcome a new set of guests, and Astrid—his de facto wife—trotted off behind him. And so it went for the rest of the night: where he led, she followed, and you always knew right where they were from the HA, HA, HAs.

Not that I cared. I was free to search the house alone for the one I'd come to see, dodging interactions till I opened a door that led to the backyard. That was where I found her. She was standing on the pampered lawn in a black minidress so skimpy it looked like a slip, her legs long and luscious, her dark hair pull back in a tight little knot. There were two guys with her, both tall and swarthy, and, walking toward them, I realized they were speaking Serbian. At least I *assumed* they were speaking Serbian; I'd never heard it before. Then Irina saw me coming and met me halfway with the oddest smile, fixed and phony, and said, "You made it," kissing me lightly on both cheeks.

The older of the two guys was named Milan. He was balding with a kind of samurai ponytail and watchful, serious eyes—a very talented film director, Irina told me. The younger was her cousin Bora, who'd recently moved from Belgrade to study engineering. He had the family good looks but the kind of dumb grin you see on panting dogs. We all spoke in English before Irina lapsed back into Serbian, which was weird to hear. It's a harsh language, full of guttural sounds, and whereas in English she came off as soft and sweet, in Serbian she seemed earthy and a bit raucous. Then Milan turned to me and said in English, "You're musician too?" So, obviously, she must have mentioned something about *Sick to Death*.

"Well," I said, "I wouldn't call myself a musician. I played in a few bands, but it's not the same thing."

"How is different?"

"Jimi Hendrix—*that's* a musician. I'm okay, but compared to somebody like that, I don't think I qualify."

So that kicked off a music talk. Milan said he'd been in a band himself back in his student days, and he recited a list of their influences, eager to demonstrate his knowledge of American music. Bora seemed bored, though every once in a while he'd chime in with, "What you think of NBA?" or "What sports you are playing?" Irina barely said a word. She just smiled her frozen smile and stared off into space, her shoulders hunched and arms clenched as if fending off the cold. I offered to let her wear my jacket, but she said no, she was going to get a sweater, and off she went.

She never came back. I was stuck talking to Milan and Bora while, from inside the house, I heard the insincere strains of "Happy Birthday." Finally I made an excuse and returned to the kitchen, where Astrid came up and said, "Where have you *been?*" and dragged me away, stuck to my side like flypaper. Then David appeared and she attached herself to him instead. We danced that dance a number of times, and at one point I tried talking shop with David, but he looked past my shoulder the entire time, which wasn't very long. The first guests were slipping away, and younger guests were arriving—friends of Irina's, I figured, but she wasn't there to greet them. I hadn't seen her since she'd supposedly gone to fetch a sweater.

I made another search of the house, cracking doors till I caught a glimpse of luscious legs stretched across a bed covered by a white comforter. I cracked the door some more. She was smoking a cigarette with her back against the wall while talking to a kid who was perched on the edge of the bed. He was dressed like a hipster, like the other kids I'd seen hanging around her, and whatever it was they were talking about, it seemed pretty serious. Then they realized they were being watched, and I entered the room and said, "So this is where the action is," and the kid laughed slightly as if to say, "Yeah, right." Irina, meantime, seemed downright hostile. Even her weird, frozen smile had disappeared. There was a painting on the wall above the bed—a portrait of a dark young man done in swift strokes, with gloomy gray washes sloshed over the lines—and when I asked who'd done it, she almost seemed to roll her eyes and said, "*I* did."

"Wow, that's pretty good."

"Thanks," she said, as if forced to.

"No, it reminds me of—what's that Austrian guy's name? The one who painted all those skinny people with contorted faces? Egan...?"

She refused to be baited. However, when the kid asked about it, she talked away, saying the painting dated from her last visit home and the subject was a family friend: a pimp and a pusher, but a good person in spite of it. She discussed him at some length, but, again, this was all directed at the kid, not me, and when I asked if her friend was still pimping and pushing, she shrugged a cool shrug as if she didn't have a clue.

"So you don't keep in touch with him?"

She shook her head. I could tell they both wanted me gone, and I was sure they must be lovers, or had been, or would be; and now that I'd met David I could certainly understand why she'd want to fuck around, but why did it have to be with this twerp? Why couldn't it be with me?

Because she likes them young or rich, stupid. Just leave. But, no, I hung around for more, asking when her friend Jeffrey was going to show up, and she acted as if she had no idea what or whom I was talking about.

"You know. The guy who knows everything about music?"

"Oh," she said. "I don't think *he'll* be here."

"Well, I'd love to talk to him at some point. Because—remember how we were talking about that band, Rule of Thumb? Well, I did some research and found out some pretty fascinating stuff."

Of course, I was hoping to discuss it with her, not Jeffrey. I was hoping she'd say, "Wow, really? Tell me all about it." But all she did was lazily stub out her cigarette.

"Jeffrey," she said, "doesn't speak to me anymore. So…" And her voice trailed off in a way that announced she had nothing more to add. I took the hint that time. I walked out, and that was the last time I saw her that night. I didn't care if I *ever* saw her again. I returned to the kitchen, where I drank every last beer I could find and chased it down with vodka. A *lot* of vodka.

LATER THAT NIGHT, LYING IN BED AT ASTRID'S PLACE, I got a bad case of the spins. I tossed and turned, trying to find a position that would make the spinning stop, but I knew it wasn't going to work. Soon I felt the inevitable coming and charged for the bathroom, puking on the way, and fell to my knees in front of a white blob vaguely shaped like a toilet. It felt as if my guts were tied to a hook and being yanked out through my jaws. I retched and heaved and retched some more. Then the light flipped on, and there was Astrid.

"Oh my God!" she screeched. "Oh my fucking God!" I raised my head. Every surface in sight was splattered with chewed-up party snacks. I'd even managed to hit the tub on the far side of the room. Astrid stormed out, skating in my puke, and came back a minute later with a sponge in one hand and a skillet in the other. At first I thought she'd brought the skillet to dash out my brains, but, no, apparently I was supposed to take it back to bed for use as a makeshift chamber pot. She refused to let me help with the mess, so I took the skillet, and after she slammed the door behind me, I sat in bed for at least ten minutes and listened as she cleaned the bathroom. She cleaned about as loudly as it's possible to clean, obviously wanting to make sure I heard, and every so often, like she'd found my leavings in some strange spot where she never expected to find them, she'd scream "Oh *no!*" or "Oh my fucking God!" and mumble through a list of my many faults. She was already mad at me for having supposedly flirted with another woman right in front of her at the party. Had I? Yes, I probably had, drunkenly thinking it would somehow even the score with Irina. *She* was the reason I'd stayed with Astrid, the chances it gave me to see her, and if she'd turned out to be something more than a bitchy slut with no interest in me, I might have tried to mend things with Astrid. But since she *was* a bitchy slut with no interest in me, I might as well make the break. I should've done it weeks before.

So I got up and dressed (a painful operation, that!) and knocked on the bathroom door and told Astrid I was leaving, never to return.

"Good!"

"Don't worry, I can drive."

"I'm not worried!"

In other words, I hope you crash into a tree and die!

Amazingly, I wasn't pulled over by the cops. I got home and passed out and woke the next day to find the whole top half of my mattress drenched in watery puke. It felt like somebody had wrapped my head in a burlap bag and struck it with a hammer while simultaneously spraying my eyes with battery acid. It was all I could do to stagger to the bathroom, where I soaked in the tub with a washcloth covering my face till, some time later, I peeled back the washcloth and saw it was dark.

Still later, after I'd scoured the mattress and hacked up some bile, I checked my e-mail. Terrence had hooked me into a thread of New York office workers, most of whom I'd never met, who seemed to do nothing all day long but send each other goofy one-liners. And then there was something from somebody calling himself Frick Frack. Who the fuck was that?

> i dont know where you could find jc these days or anything about cybil disobediance [*sic*]. i didnt do the interview with bb thats something I got off rippedtoshreds.com. i do know that patrick fitzpatrick is back in boston and has his own label called bolloxchops. good luck.

I was still so massively fucked up, my brain operating at a fraction of its normal speed, it took me a few reads to decode this thing. Eventually I realized it came from the guy at the online punk archive, the one with the Billy Bash interview. I'd written to both him and Josh of "Josh's Rule of Thumb Page," asking after Jim, but only "Frick Frack" had bothered to reply. As for Patrick Fitzpatrick, he'd played bass in ROT's final lineup.

I found the Bolloxchops website. They were hawking a catalog of twenty or so records, each with a thumbnail cover scan and a brief description of the music. It was mostly hardcore. I never much cared for hardcore. I turned off the computer and turned on the TV, channel-surfing in a sensory freeze till the sun came up.

TWO DAYS LATER, MUCH IMPROVED, I'd just gotten home from Pioneer Market when my phone rang. My caller ID said: PRIVATE. I picked up and heard a sweet, familiar female voice with a trace of a European accent. My heart slammed against my rib cage.

"I hope I didn't catch you at a bad time," she said.

"Not at all," I stammered. I asked how she'd gotten my number, and she said it was on the cover of a screenplay I'd left at her house.

"*Landmine,*" she said. "That's yours, yes?"

"Oh. Yeah. Astrid took it over a few months ago."

"Well, that's strange. I just found it yesterday. Do you need it back?"

No, I told her, just throw it away; but she said, "Oh, I'd never do that. I'll take it with me and read it on the plane." It seemed she was accompanying David on his European location scout, and at some point she was going to break off and spend a few weeks with her family in Belgrade.

"Lucky you," I said.

"Not really," she sighed. "I mean, yes, it's always good to see my family. My mother—she's a brilliant woman, I miss her very much. And my brother and cousins and friends—for the first few days it's great. But then you walk around, and it's so depressing. Everyone complains, nobody's working, they're all cut off from the rest of the world. And I'm sure, after the bombing, it's going to be worse."

"Well, at least you're getting out of L.A. That's got to be good for something."

"That's true. L.A. always looks good after being in Belgrade. The only times, actually."

There was an English twist on "actually." There were many such touches in the way she spoke. I heard a cat meowing in the background and what sounded like an electric can opener, so she was obviously feeding her cat. To the cat she spoke in Serbian babytalk, and to me in English she said, "So I understand you got very drunk the other night."

"I did, yeah. There was kind of a bad scene over at Astrid's."

"Yes," she laughed wickedly, "this is what I hear. Not from her, from David. She would never tell me that kind of thing."

"I know."

Tick-tock, tick-tock.

"So," she said, "she's spoken about me." Then she tried to shake me down for details, and I bobbed and weaved till she finally said, "Never mind, I'm sure I can guess. She hates me, and she always has."

"No, she told me she really likes you." Which she had, even though I knew she was lying.

"She's lying!" Irina said. "She doesn't know the truth herself, she lies so much! She's—no, I'm not going to say anything. There's always a chance you'll get back together."

"No chance."

"Well, good. You're much too good for her. I thought that from the first time I met you."

What was it with this girl? Why did she freeze me out one minute and praise me the next? Yet, right as I was thinking this, she apologized for the party, saying she hoped she hadn't been too rude but she'd been having a lot of "problems," that it was "that time of the month" and she hated playing hostess to David's friends and "all these people I don't even know. And I hated them. I don't understand it. I don't understand how you can get all dressed up and go to someone's house and then, when you get there, talk about *nothing*."

"I couldn't agree more."

"I'm sure. But you seemed okay. My friend Milan liked you, and, believe me, he doesn't like anyone."

Then she went into an unbelievably long thing about Milan, how he made a much-loved movie in Yugoslavia and it looked like he was going to be a big success when the war broke out and he moved to America to start a new life. But he would have come anyway, she said, because he loved American movies—but *old* American movies by John Ford and people like that; he didn't seem to realize those days were over. She rambled on and on till she cut herself off and said, "Wait a minute, there was something I was going to tell you. Oh, I remember now! I'm so confused these days! Yes, I heard from my friend Jeffrey. I thought he was mad at me, but he called yesterday and wants me to see a band with him Wednesday night. Distortion Felix—you know who they are?"

"I've heard of them. They're always on those e-mail fliers I get from the Silverlake Lounge."

"Yes, exactly, that's where they're playing. I shouldn't go out, I've got so much to do, but I love these guys; I see them all the time with Jeffrey. So, if you want to talk to him, that's where he's going to be."

"Well, okay. Maybe I'll drop by, then."

"Great," she said. "It'd be so nice to see you before I go." And, in the background, I heard the cat say, "*Mierrrrr.*"

THE *LA WEEKLY* HAD DISTORTION FELIX playing on Tuesday night, not Wednesday, but Irina had never given me her number, so I couldn't call to say as much. I drove down anyway, but she wasn't there, and neither, as far as I could recall him, was her friend Jeffrey. Earlimart, a local band, had just gone on—really catchy pop-punk, though the kids playing it seemed kind of bored, making wise-assed comments to the kids in the audience. There weren't that many, maybe twenty or twenty-five, and most were clearly friends with the band, making wise-assed comments right back. The others stood around with hipster pouts and that "impress me" stance I knew so well. It was the same in my day.

This wasn't the first time I'd returned to the Silverlake Lounge (or the Fold, as it was called on non-drag nights). Ever since that Combover show, I'd gone as often as possible. At first I thought it was because of the milieu, the way it evoked my youth. I wondered if I was having a midlife crisis. The seven years I'd spent in L.A. felt like seven decades, for all the damage they'd done to me. But rock & roll had inflicted far worse damage, and for that reason it took me a while to realize it wasn't simply nostalgia that made me want to return to the Fold, it was first and finally the music. Every so often I'd hear a song or part of a song or maybe just a single chord, and something stirred, something I never thought I would feel again, and I gradually came to know that, deep down, in spite of myself, in spite of everything, I still loved this shit, it moved me still like nothing else, it made me feel alive. So why did so many kids I saw at the shows look so dead? But I knew that too. They were *kewl,* man, and some were trying to find themselves, as kids have always tried to find themselves in the underground-music scene, while others were kingpins who weren't going to give up for just any band. No, the *kewl* factor trumped all for those kids.

Earlimart finished up. Distortion Felix took the stage, and they were every bit as good as Irina had said they were, like the *Nevermind* Nirvana with a touch of Latin Playboys but bathed in feedback. Most of the audience had left, and those that stayed barely seemed to listen. I listened. I bobbed my head like a six-foot jack-in-the-box. The show was nearly over when I felt a hand press softly against my back and turned to find Irina standing behind me. She was by herself and seemed out of sorts, making a face as if to say, "You don't know what I went through to get here!" She glanced around and sighed. She bit her nails, distracted. Then she walked to the back where the bathroom was, behind the stage, and returned a minute later and, pulling out a pack of cigarettes, nodded toward the door that she was going outside to smoke. Fine, go. I didn't have the patience to deal with this moody shit. Talk about motifs!

But where Irina was concerned, my own motif was helplessness; I went looking for her a few minutes later, and there she was, standing in front of Café Tropical at the corner of Sunset and Silver Lake.

A still-open liquor store was across the street, neon beer ads burning brightly in the windows, and she was staring vaguely in that direction but staring obviously at nothing at all. It put me in mind of an Edward Hopper, this pensive girl smoking alone on a late-night street. Then, as I got closer, she turned and, not moody in the slightest, asked what I thought of the band.

"Great," I said. "Best I've seen in a long time."

"Yes," she said—and here she hit the mood pedal—"too bad I can't enjoy them. God, I just don't understand people!"

I bummed a cigarette and asked what was going on.

"Oh," she sighed, "I just had dinner with Jeffrey. It was exactly what I was afraid of. But never mind. I don't want to bore you."

"No, I want to hear it. Go on. I'm curious."

"Well"—she took a deep breath—"he's in love with me. At least he thinks he is, and I knew that's how he felt, so when he stopped calling me, I thought I understood. But the other day he calls and says everything is under control now. He says he understands we're just friends, and he likes this other girl anyway, so we can start seeing each other again. So okay. Tonight we decide we're going to have dinner before seeing the band, and everything is fine at first, but then he starts crying. I said, 'What is it? What's wrong?' And he said, 'I thought I was ready for this, but I'm not. I'm still in love with you.' I said, 'But I thought you liked some other girl.' And he said, 'Oh, I just said that because I wanted to see you.'

"So we sat there, and he cried, and I tried to explain things. I said I like him as a friend, but he knows I'm married, and I never tried to give him the wrong idea—but he says I've done nothing *but* give him the wrong idea. He was really mean. I've seen him this way with other people, but never with me. He started calling me names like 'emotional pervert.' He said, 'I know a lot of girls like you. I knew you were an emotional pervert the minute I met you!' I said, 'Well, why did you keep seeing me, then?' And he said, 'Because I have a thing for emotional perverts!'"

I cracked up. She asked why I was laughing with an air of gloom, and I said he sounded like someone I used to know.

"Well, believe me," she said, "when you're in a situation like this, it's not so funny. He was threatening to kill himself! Then he tried to get me to get in his car with him, and I wouldn't do it. I thought he was going to attack me! I said, 'Jeffrey, I can't be around you when you're acting like this. Maybe we can try again in a few months.' Then he told me to fuck myself and drove off like a maniac."

"Well, good riddance, right?"

But she stared across the street and sighed.

"Everybody's always mad at me," she shook her head hopelessly. "Every time I look, there's some new thing I've done to make somebody upset. And I don't think I'm a bad person. People just expect too much from me!"

"Well, there could be a reason for that. I mean, Jeffrey was holding you the first time I saw you—as a matter of fact, it was right here—and I thought for sure you guys were together."

"So—what? He's right? I gave him the wrong idea?"

"Well, come on, you're not twelve years old. If you don't like a guy, you shouldn't be letting him hold you. I mean, guys—we assume every time a girl *looks* at us, there's some kind of sex going on. We can't help it. That's just the way we're put together. So it's sort of your job to lay down the boundaries. Otherwise you're going to find yourself in some fucked-up situations. We'll try to fuck you every chance we get if we think you're open to it. And even if you're not."

"You sound like a Serbian man."

"Somehow, I don't think you mean that as a compliment."

"It's not."

"Then I guess I won't be holding *you* any time in the near future."

She laughed, the gold in her eyes sparkling.

"Well," she said, "you never know. I mean, you talk about your nature, but what about mine? I'm very affectionate. Am I not supposed to touch my friends?"

"Oh, come on. What if David told you that? What if you went out one night and saw him holding another woman?"

"He'd never do it," she said glumly.

"But what if he did?"

"I wouldn't have a problem with it. He needs to start showing his feelings more. In fact, I've *told* him he should have an affair. Maybe then he won't complain about me so much."

"Really. What does he complain about?"

"Oh, I don't know. I can never do anything the right way. Today I go all the way to Santa Monica to pick up the plane tickets, and when I get back, he's mad I haven't taken his clothes to the cleaner. He's always got me running around doing things for him. Sometimes I feel like his assistant."

"Isn't that what married life is all about?"

"Are you sure you're not Serbian?"

"You know what I mean—it's a partnership."

"But we aren't really *partners*," she sighed. "He wants me there when he wants me there, and when he doesn't, I can do what I want. Not because he's so generous. He just doesn't care about the same things I do. He doesn't read, he doesn't like music, he hates going to the theater. I don't even think he likes people all that much. The other night at the party—did you ever get a chance to talk to him?"

"Not really. Just small talk. It was almost like he was avoiding me."

"I knew it," she snorted. "And do you know why? He could tell you're nothing like him. He's never honest. He's got this sort of menu for the way he deals with people. It's like, if you say A, he looks in column A. If you say B, he looks in column B. It's always what he thinks is—*appropriate*—to the situation. But then later, when he's alone with me, he'll say, 'Oh, that Richard is such a moron, and his movie is just awful.' 'Well, why did you tell him it was good?' 'Because that's what he wants to hear. He doesn't want to hear the truth.' But, you see, David is really speaking of himself—because *he* would never want to hear the truth. And that's why he would never want to be around someone like you. You're too—*real*—for him."

"Well, I was also with Astrid. And she's been through a lot of guys, so why make the effort when he knows it's not going to work out anyway? And it didn't! We didn't even make it through the *night!*"

"No," she said emphatically. "Even if you'd come alone, it would have been just the same. It's something I can always count on: if I like somebody, I know he won't."

"Then do you mind if I ask you a personal question?"

"I know. Why are we married, yes? Believe me, it's something I ask myself all the time. And I'm not sure how to answer, except I know him very well and he knows me. And he's really not as bad as I'm making him sound. He's very sweet and very funny, and he's got a good mind, even though he doesn't like to use it. And sometimes I ask myself if I could live without him, and I think…"

And then she broke off and stared away for quite some time before she turned to me and asked if I had ever been in love.

"I mean *really* in love," she emphasized. "The way it is in movies."

"Well, there was a woman I almost married once, and it wasn't quite like the movies, but, yeah, I was in love with her. Or I thought I was. It seemed like a delusion by the end. So I guess the answer is yes and no."

She really seemed to take this in.

"Well," she said, "I can say this about David: I love him very much, but I'm not sure if I was ever *in* love with him—not the way some people talk about it. I never felt like I couldn't eat or couldn't sleep or any of those things. Maybe this is all a big myth, I don't know. But sometimes I feel like I'm missing out on something."

SHE WANTED TO HAVE A DRINK, but not at the Silverlake Lounge. "It's so depressing," she said. I suggested another bar right up the street. It was a dive, I warned her, and probably worse than the Silverlake Lounge, but I often went there to shoot pool.

"Oh," she said, "I love pool, even though I'm awful."

I walked her to her car: a sleek silver BMW 350i. I was embarrassed to be seen getting inside my Mustang. Somebody had done a hit-and-run on the front fender a few years before, twisting it up in the shape of a crowbar. I couldn't afford to have it fixed. I couldn't afford a paint job either. The sun had baked the original red a rusty orange and cracked the leather seats, drying and crumbling the foam inside. I badly wanted to buy a new car, but I could never save the necessary money, and that was mostly due to the car I had. The starter would go out. Then the transmission. Then the generator. It was all I could do to keep that thing on the road, and, looking like it did, it was hardly worth a dime in trade. Nor could I arrange for financing—not after the last few years and the toll they'd taken on my credit rating. I personally didn't care what people drove, but I knew others did, and Irina might be one of them.

Still, she followed me down Sunset to the Short Stop, the place I had in mind. It's since turned trendy, but back then it was sort of a cop bar—"sort of" because the LAPD had recently cracked down on off-hours fraternizing in the wake of the infamous Rampart scandal. That suited me fine, always wary of cops, but it wasn't so great for my friend Thom, the nighttime bartender who would sometimes serve me and select others to the brink of dawn and beyond. Irina parked behind me across the street, and, laughing as she joined me on the sidewalk, said, "Oh my God, *this* place! You really go to *this* place? My friends are all afraid of it!" Inside, a couple of diehards were ass-glued to barstools while Thom read the sports page and watched sports on TV simultaneously—the same old same-old. Country music blasted from the jukebox: not good country, the old-fashioned kind a hop and a skip from rock & roll, but that horrible shit sung by guys who look like soap stars dressed like cowboys. I bought us a round, and we walked back to one of the game rooms, where Irina proceeded to show just how bad her pool-playing was. She'd miss a shot and curse in English and Serbian alike. She'd mock-slap me when I ran the table. I beat her soundly the first few games, so, after we got a second round, I gave her a tutorial—a way of getting fresh that dated from my days as a New York cad. My hands held hers as I guided her cue. Our cheeks touched. My crotch was pressed against her ass. She never pulled away even slightly. I was expecting at least a little resistance—especially since we'd just talked about this kind of thing not an hour before! Then I decided she was playing along to fuck with my head, and, if that was the case, it worked: I scratched on the eight ball, and she danced like a receiver in the end zone—not what you'd call a gracious winner.

"Enjoy it," I said. "It's not going to happen next game."

"Oh no. I won. That's how I want to leave it."

"So how about a victory drink?"

"It's almost two."

"It doesn't matter. I can drink here as long as I want."

"Well," she said after taking a long moment to think it over, "okay. But I'll have to drink it fast."

Thom was blown away by Irina. He wished me luck and set me up, and I took the drinks to the game room, where she was now checking out the cop paraphernalia from all over the U.S. that hung in frames on the walls. There was an arm-patch display, including a patch from my hometown force, as I pointed out, and Irina said, "Yes, that's a nice one. Very colorful."

"Yeah, they're a colorful bunch. They colored me right out of high school."

"I'm sorry?"

"Oh, I broke some asshole's nose, and they came to my school and arrested me. It was a huge scandal—you don't *know* how huge it was! That was right around the time I got into punk rock, and those fuckers—they'd never seen anybody who looked like me, so they'd pull me over every chance they got. And what's funny is, I did some pretty bad shit, but they never stopped me for any of that. It was always over nothing."

"And you're still mad about it?"

"Do I sound mad?"

"You sound a little…bitter."

"Oh, I'm definitely bitter. Not about that, though. I'm just bitter because things aren't going so great. But I figure I've got lots of company in that department."

"Really."

"Well, yeah. The movie business is filled with bitter people. The music business too. I mean, they're dream professions, you know. You go in with a lot of expectations, and ninety-nine percent of the time they don't work out. One plus one equals two."

"Yes, but you have to make adjustments. I have trouble too, but I try not to be bitter. It's not such an attractive quality."

"Really? I don't mind bitter people. I find them a lot more interesting than happy people."

"Well, if that's so, they were probably interesting to begin with, and the bitterness is something on top. It's like a painting, you know. I don't think it's the grime on a painting that makes it beautiful; it already *was* beautiful, and the grime gets in the way."

"Sometimes it contributes."

"Not usually. But I was just making an example. I think bitterness is the worst thing there is. That's why I could never live in Yugoslavia: it's poisoned with bitter people."

"So? L.A.'s poisoned with stupidity. How's that any better?"

"Well, at least everybody's not complaining all the time. And I think you *like* being bitter. It's the—*reward*—you give yourself for not being successful. Do you think that's possible?"

"Probable, even."

"So? Whose fault is that? I think you blame other people. And I know this is a difficult business—believe me, I know this very well!—but I think it's really your own problem. Because I wasn't going to tell you this, but I read your script, and I hope you don't mind if I say it's very terrible."

She was so blunt that, even though it stung, I burst out laughing.

"I'm glad you take it so well," she said, laughing along with me.

"No, there's just something about the way you said it. But go on. Tell me why it's so terrible."

"Because it's not *you*. I thought it was going to be just like your movie, and I *loved* your movie. I've watched it several times—have I told you that?"

"No, but I'm flattered."

"I'm not saying it to flatter you. There's something honest about it, something true. But this script—it's just some stupid action thing. I would never think it's the same person who did both."

"Yeah, but it's much better written than *Sick to Death*. I was so clueless when I did that thing. I was like a blind person trying to feel my way through something. And I'm really proud of it in certain ways, but, you know, you can't make money doing movies like that. In fact, you'll lose money. And I did. That was my own money that paid for that thing, and, believe me, it didn't come easily. And the thing is, nobody got to see it, except for a few people at festivals. So the best I can say for it is, it got me through the door."

"And what have you done since?"

"Not much."

"And do you know why? Because you're not doing what you *want* to be doing, you're doing what you *think* you should. Like this action script—it could have been written by anyone."

"Yeah, but that's true for almost every movie out there."

"So is that what you want to do? Make the same movie *everybody* is making?"

She was so earnest, so reminiscent of a different period in my life, I found it really endearing. And that was more or less what I told her. I said, "I appreciate what you're trying to say. And I think it's sweet."

"Thanks," she said acidly.

"Well, I do. But, come on, you're—what?—twenty-six? Twenty-seven?"

"Twenty-four."

"Twenty-*four*?! And you've been married five years?! Jesus, *David* wasn't robbing any cradles!"

"We've been together five years, but we've only been married for four. But please don't change the subject."

"I'm not! You're twenty-four years old! And do you know how old I am? Thirty-six. I'm thirty-six years old, and in two months I'm going to be thirty-seven, and when you get to be that age, boy, you *cling* to those last two months—especially in *this* business! I might as well be ninety as far as these people are concerned! And when you're up against it like that, you aren't thinking a whole lot about 'artistic integrity,' or whatever you want to call it. And I'll tell you something else: every time I did anything with 'artistic integrity,' people took it right away from me. I spent years trying to get movies made the right way, and all people did was strip away the good parts. So at a certain point you think, 'Why fight it? Let's just give them what they want right up front.' Because I don't want to be driving a fucked-up car when I'm fifty years old. I don't want to be temping. And, you know, the one thing I can get hired to do right now is to knock off shit. So, if it's got to be shit, at least let's make some fucking money."

"Yes, but how can you be happy that way?"

"Well, 'happiness' is sort of like 'artistic integrity.' It's great if you can afford it, but right now I can't. And I really hate to say this, but it's pretty easy for you to be saying these things. I mean, you're—what?—twelve years younger than I am, and who's driving which car out there on the street?"

"So," she said, offended right away, "in other words, I'm a *sponzoruša*."

"?"

"It's a Serbian word. A *sponzoruša*—she's a girl who's sponsored, you understand? She's like a kept woman, but not so nice. Well, that's not what I am at all. I'm not with David for his money or what he can do for me; I'm with him because I care about him, and I would feel that way if he had money or not, just like I'm with him even though he's not very talented. There, I said it. It's something I don't like to admit, not even to myself, but I know it's the truth. But you—I think you're different. You could do *much* better than you're letting yourself do, but it's like you're giving up before you have to. Thirty-seven—it's not so old, not for a man. You have much more time than *I* do. How do you think it will be for me when I'm thirty-seven and still trying to get parts with an accent? The only reason people want me now—and they usually don't!—is they like the way I look. Would you even be talking to me right now if I was old and ugly? I doubt it very much."

She said this all so quickly and so forcefully that, once again, I started laughing. She asked me why with a look of annoyance, and I tried to explain but couldn't.

"Tell me something," I said. "Are there any more like you in Belgrade?"

"What do you mean, like me? Like me, how?"

"You know. Smart. Beautiful. Passionate. Your basic all-round perfect."

"Oh," she relaxed. "Well, I can tell you Belgrade is very famous for pretty girls. Every time we go, David says he can't get over it."

"Well, why don't you pick one up for me the next time you're there?"

"I'll see what I can do."

"Yeah, but she's got to be *exactly* like you. Do you think that's going to be too hard to find?"

"Oh, I don't know. I understand I'm a lot of trouble. Maybe I can find something a bit better."

"No, I think I'll stick with the original, thanks. See if you can find someone exactly like you, and if you can't, don't worry, just come back and I'll clone you. I promise there won't be any pain involved. I'll just set up a lab and read up on the latest—"

And suddenly she planted one on me. We weren't that far apart, and she leaned up and kissed me hard on the lips, and my dick turned to quartz. Then she pushed me away, and there was a look on her face I don't think I could fully describe if I spent a year trying. There was lust and fear and guilt and shock, like she couldn't believe herself what she'd just done, and there was also something coy, like a little girl who knows she's been very, very naughty.

"I shouldn't have done that," she said.

Well, too late now! I was back on her in seconds flat! I pulled her close and kissed her again, and at first she seemed to melt. Her breathing changed; she tilted back her head; she raked her hands over my back. Then she tightened and squirmed and shoved me away, and now there was nothing coy in the look on her face. Now she just looked scared.

"I can't," she said.

But I just had to try one last time. I wanted to fuck her so bad! And she wanted me too—I could feel it, I could *smell* it—but she kept fighting me, saying no no no, so that finally I had no choice but to let her go. She wouldn't even look at me. She immediately collected her coat and bag, and we walked out to the bar, where Thom was now doing the inventory, and I told him thanks and good night. Then we walked across the street, and Irina kept in front of me the whole time, never looking back, not once till she got to her car. Only after she'd taken out her keys and unlocked the door did she finally turn around.

"I want you to know something," she said. "I've never done that before. That's the first time I…"

"Cheated on David?"

"We just kissed, that's all."

And then suddenly she went limp and covered her face with her hands and said, "My God, what's wrong with me? I just go through this thing with Jeffrey, and then I…" She shook her head for quite some time till she unmasked her face and said, "Well, *I* certainly have a lot to think about."

"You know, I only live a few blocks away."

"*No,*" she said.

"Well, it's a great place to think. I do all my best thinking there."

"I'm sure," she laughed in spite of herself; and then for a long time we just kind of stared at each other, just staring for the longest time. Finally she said she'd write to me as soon as she got to Belgrade, asking for my e-mail address and promising to send me "a very long letter" that was going to explain "a lot of things.

"But," she added, "don't be mad if it takes a few weeks. First I'm going to travel with…" And as if the act of saying his name would cause him to appear, she cut herself off. She looked so frazzled, almost dazed, and she apologized for that, saying she was so confused she didn't know if she was coming or going.

"Well, you're going, right?"

"Yes. Yes, I am."

"Then maybe you should go."

"All right. I will."

Then she went to hug me good night, and next thing you know, we're making out again. I dry-humped her against her car; I pinned her knees open and slammed my crotch against hers, and she half resisted and half went along, and I wasn't that far from creaming in my boxers when she shoved me away, and, bam, she got in her car, and, zoom, she was out of there, man—that road was practically paved with butter, she moved so fast. And I watched her go, I watched her taillights turn to tiny red specks on a big black flag before they disappeared altogether.

Life, huh? One minute you're making out with a stunning starlet from Eastern Europe, the next you're all by yourself on some bleak street like the cover of a Frank Sinatra record circa 1955. I was hoping Thom would set me up one last time, but he didn't answer when I knocked at the door, so I drove home and jerked off and tried to fall asleep. But I couldn't sleep. I got up and poured myself a drink and kept drinking till a band of birds sang the sunrise song. And I thought about Irina, I thought about everything I knew about her—Astrid's assessment, my own instincts, all those boys I'd seen hanging around her—and I thought, "Do you *really* believe she's never fooled around?" Yet she'd seemed so credible when she claimed she never had, and what difference did it make either way? We might get together, we might not, but even if this was all that ever happened, I'd still reaped the benefits, and I don't mean sexually. Because she was absolutely right with all that talk about the "reward" of bitterness and blaming other people for my fuckups. I was obese with bitterness. I was bloated with blame. How had I strayed so far from the idealistic kid who made *Sick to Death* and, long before that, slept on floors and lived on potato chips for the sheer love of playing music? Like most people past a certain age, I thought I was being realistic, but also like them, I'd dropped something along the way without realizing I'd lost it, the same way you don't realize you've packed on the pounds even though you see yourself in the mirror all the time. Then you catch some telltale snapshot and that's when it finally sinks in. And I wanted to get back to my fighting weight—I wanted to get back to the person I'd been—but where and how to begin? And it took me half the night and half a bottle of whiskey to realize I'd begun weeks before.

SO THIS IS WHEN THE SEARCH FOR JIM REALLY GOT GOING. I had just enough money from the kiddie flick to last a couple of months, and I was hoping that within that time I could speak to Jim, or at least find someone who could flesh out his missing years should he prove to be dead. It wasn't like I needed strict fact before sitting down to write, but on *Sick to Death* I'd stuck to the facts as much as possible, and that was the kind of movie I wanted to make this time as well. I was just hoping it wouldn't prove your run-of-the-mill drug drama, but maybe Jim had actually killed Cybil Disobedience or done something just as nefarious—what a story that would make! Still, I had no idea how to conduct research except through the Internet, and as I've said before, I had never found the Internet particularly useful. There was a brief moment of promise when I first made contact with Patrick Fitzpatrick, but since I saved our correspondence, you can see for yourself why it didn't pan out. I won't bother with my query letter, which basically said I was a director with an interest in doing a movie about Rule of Thumb, and was wondering how and where I could locate Jim. Patrick replied on October 14, 1999:

> Thanks for the kind words re: ROT. You are not the first person to contact me about Jim. There have been others but I haven't spoken to Jim in almost ten years. The last I heard he was still living in the LA area. Buddy would know more and it should be easy for you to speak to him as I understand he plays around LA all the time. But if you do speak to him please leave my name out of it as that guy is very bad news! Good luck with your project. Who else have you spoken to?

I wrote back immediately:

> Good to hear from you! Actually, I haven't contacted anyone besides you, but I'll be sure to keep an eye out for Buddy's band, and don't worry, if we meet, I'll never mention your name. But what exactly do you mean when you say he's bad news? It might be good to know beforehand. Also I was wondering if you could tell me something about a girl named Cybil Disobedience. A friend sent me an article in which it was speculated that Jim was somehow responsible for her death – do you know anything about that? In fact, I'd be interested in *anything*

you have to tell me about Jim and ROT. If it's too much of a pain to write, feel free to call me collect at 323 *** ****.

Thanks a million –
Jason

I thought he sounded like a friendly guy, what with his warning about Buddy, and I was thrilled to get a message from a member of ROT, even if Patrick *had* joined them late in the game and was never any match for Clint Cancer, the guy he replaced. But he turned out to have an agenda, as his next e-mail made abundantly clear:

Dear Jason,

Yes I knew Cybil very well and would be willing to discuss her and any other questions you might have re: Jim, Buddy etc. However since this is my own life we're speaking of I don't think I should do that until we've worked out some kind of fee. The fact is I've often thought of writing my own script based on those years and if I gave you what you're looking for I'd be losing something without getting something in return. So make me a proposal and if it's fair we can talk at that time. You can reach me at my home number which is (617) *** ****.

Look forward to hearing from you.
PF

Man, everybody wants to get into the movies! Plus the second money comes up, I suddenly get a salutation with the word "dear" in front of my name. I thought about calling to see if I couldn't coerce him into seeing things my way, but then I decided it was less risky to plead in writing. So here's my reply, which I slaved over like you cannot believe, rewriting a single paragraph again and again over the course of a couple of hours:

Dear Patrick:

Obviously, I am very curious as to anything you might be able to share, but first let me explain something about my circumstances. By no means am I Steven Spielberg. I'm a punk rocker, much like yourself, who got into filmmaking after hanging up my guitar, and I've struggled mightily ever since. No one is paying me for this script, should it become one, and I would be very lucky to raise the funds to shoot it. In other words, I'm in no position to offer you any money, unless I could provide you with something as technical advisor *after* the film is financed. But first I need a screenplay, and then I have to find a producer who'd see this project as viable, and as I'm sure you know, ROT, great though it was, is bound to be obscure as far as most producers are concerned. Nor are there likely to be many directors with a background similar to mine. I understand that you might wish to do something yourself, and if that's the case, I wish you all the best; but perhaps before making that decision you could take a look at my first feature, "Sick to Death," which debuted at Sundance and is based on my own life in punk bands in New York City during the eighties. I would use a similar approach here, and, as I'm sure you'll agree, it would serve the ROT story well. So, unless you instruct me otherwise, I'll prepare a video and drop it in the mail to the Bolloxchops address provided on your website.

I will never march in chains –
Jason

That "chain" line comes from a Rule of Thumb song called "Lockstep." I knew it was corny, and it really didn't make a lot of sense in the context, but I wanted this guy to see me as a fellow traveler, not a potential source of income. In any case, he tersely wrote back a few days later:

Send the video and I'll let you know after I've had a look

So I sent him the video, and he never responded. I couldn't believe some guy from a little-known band, now running a two-bit label in Boston, would hold his palm out that way. On the other hand, I'm sure that *was* the reason. Still, what a jerk. What a disgrace to the punk race. And yet I might well have written again to grovel if I hadn't gotten lucky elsewhere. In fact, even as I was corresponding with Patrick, I was putting up "Does anyone know what happened to Jim Cassady of Rule of Thumb?" posts on every message board on the Internet where I could think to place them. There weren't many replies, and the ones

I received were mostly pretty out there. From "ponyboy" on a Hüsker Dü board, there was:

> didn't jim cassady become a moonie? that's what my sister told me and she was into rot big time

From "Macon Bacon" on the Ripped to Shreds board, I got:

> Jim Cassidy [sic] is a Meth Freak living in Atlanta!! I met him at Six Flags five years ago and We talked about ROT for an Hour!! He was really Cool too!! ROT ROCKS!!

On a site called Thrash and Burn, "tony68" posted this story, which I now think is more than likely true:

> i dont know if it was really him but one night i was in a 711 in ontario this real fat old guy came in and talked to my friend a clerk at the store. he stank real bad he acted like he had a lobbotomie and when he left my friend said do you know who that was? that was jim casidy [sic]. maybe my friend was pulling my chain i don't know. but if its him you would never know its him.

The "real old fat guy" could only have been Jim if the 7-Eleven was located in Ontario, California, not Canada; but since "tony68" never responded to my follow-up post, I'm assuming it was the former. Then, the strangest post of all, possibly a prank, came from "iggypox" on a Stooges board:

> jim cassady had a sex change operation and now races cars under the name gloria west

And just for the hell of it, I did a Google search on Gloria West, and there *was* such a person, a stock-car racer, and in the one grainy picture I found, she actually looked a bit like Jim. So it's possible "iggypox" saw the same picture and decided it *was* Jim, or maybe he (or she) just thought it was funny to say it was. But since that was iggypox's only post, I'll never know for sure.

Those four responses are the only ones I got out of maybe fifty queries. Or that's not quite true. There was one more from "panthergirl" at Groupie Central, though it wasn't pertinent to my search:

> i always wondered what happened to him too. i slept with him one time. he was really weird, didn't want to fuck, wanted me to play with my pussy while he beat off. not much in the meat section either. that must of been twenty years ago. hate to date myself that way! i was jailbait!

"panthergirl" at least wrote back when I asked if she knew anything about Cybil Disobedience.

> never heard of her. was she a groupie? i didn't hang around the punk scene too long. moved on to the big leagues. in all senses!

I also wrote to a handful of musicians who'd been active in the West Coast punk scene, and all I got there was a note from Joey Shithead of DOA politely saying he'd never in his life met a girl named Cybil Disobedience. Meantime I dropped a note to Buddy care of Tornado Bait's label, but nothing ever came of that, just as Tornado Bait never showed up in the *LA Weekly* club listings. For good reason: they'd broken up, as I learned from Scott Sterling, the guy who booked the Fold. He was practically a music encyclopedia, and said as far as he knew, Jim had OD'd. Meantime, even though Buddy had never played the Fold, he'd been known to see bands there, and Scott told me he'd pass along my number if and when Buddy turned up. Still, he added, "I'm pretty sure Jim Cassady is dead. I'm not sure where I heard that, but I'm almost positive I did." And I believed him. And I knew all those Internet rumors were probably false, but at the same time they intrigued me. Why couldn't Jim have joined a cult or moved to Atlanta? Was that really less credible than begging for change on Hollywood Boulevard? And the more tidbits I collected, the more intrigued I became. This was no longer about writing a screenplay (as if it ever had been), it was about getting to the bottom of a mystery. I at least had one advantage: I was living in the heart of ROT country, and so, undoubtedly, were a number of people who knew the truth—but how to get in touch with them?

I wrote to Terrence for suggestions. I wrote to him many times during this search, and he told me I should run an ad in the *LA Weekly*. I ended up running three, in fact, for over a month—one in the *Weekly*, one in the *Times*, and one in the *Recycler*—and out of that came two callers: a woman who wanted to know why I was looking for Jim but wouldn't say why she was asking, and a guy who, somewhat like Patrick, tried to shake me down—not for money but for lunch! He called himself Frenchy and said he and Jim were "great friends" who went "way back," and he'd give me all the information I needed if I took him out for lunch. I was naturally suspicious and, as a test question, asked if he could tell me Jim's real name, and he mumbled something and abruptly hung up. He later called a few other times, and one of those calls came late at night, and that was especially eerie. He never spoke when I answered, but I knew it was him, since his number appeared on my caller ID. Who was that guy, and why was he calling? At the time I thought he might be Jim, but now I'm sure he wasn't. And who was the woman who called and wouldn't say why? They're micro-mysteries unto themselves.

I killed the ads. I'd always known there was one sure way of finding Jim, and now I decided to explore it: I looked up a private detective in the Yellow Pages and asked for an estimate. Even the best-case scenario was more than I could afford. The detective said that with Jim being a "former public figure," she might be able to turn up something relatively quickly, but I didn't have a previous address, and his real name (Eddie Brown) was so common, it wasn't like she could phone up a friend at the DMV and that would be that. So there were no guarantees, and being broke, I'd exhausted my investigation budget running the ads. I just kept calling every person I could think to call: friends and kind-of friends and friends of their friends—anybody who might know somebody who dated from Jim's day in the L.A. punk scene. And, finally, I got a little luck.

ONE OF MY NEIGHBORS WAS A CANADIAN EXPAT named Paul Bertolette, a film editor who, before he got married, used to throw a lot of parties. That's how I met him: I crashed one. Like me and Irina's friend Milan, he'd been in bands before getting into film, but he was never into punk. Hanging out at Paul's house, you'd hear anything from Nat King Cole to Buddy Holly to the score of *Twin Peaks*. But again, as a former party guy, Paul was acquainted with many people from all walks of life; and when I asked if he knew anyone who might have known Jim, he mentioned a friend named Michelle, an L.A. native and a former punk. He promised to give her a call, but—story of my life—every time I checked back, he'd say, "Sorry, I forgot." It went on for weeks that way. Finally I stopped bugging him. Then one night he called out of the blue to say he'd just spoken to Michelle, who'd be more than happy to speak to me—in fact, he said, this might be the perfect moment to call.

She picked up right away. She didn't sound friendly, or she didn't at first, but the second I mentioned Jim, she laughed and said, "Yeah, I knew him. What do you want to know?" It caught me up short for a second there. I hadn't expected success! I asked when she'd last seen him, and she said, "God, it's been years. Isn't he dead?"

"Well, that's part of what I'm trying to find out."

"Oh, he's got to be. He really had a problem with the bottle. One of the worst drunks I ever met, as a matter of fact."

"And a junkie too, right?"

But she wasn't sure about that. She knew Gary had been a junkie, and Clint too, but as far as she remembered, Jim had always just been a big drunk. She said she first met him when they were both living at the Canterbury, which she described as a kind of Hollywood flophouse where a lot of punks used to hang their shingles.

"It was a really crazy place," she said, "and Jim and his girlfriend lived right down the hall, and I don't think I ever saw him when he wasn't blasted or well on his way to getting there."

"Was his girlfriend Cybil Disobedience?"

"No, but I knew her too."

There was no curiosity as to how I might know about Cybil, just as she was in no way nostalgic. It was as if those days were a bygone lark, something she'd long since disavowed, and as for Jim, he was just "some pretentious guy who was dying to be Jim Morrison. Yeah, right! If he'd *really* been Jim Morrison, I would've married him!"

"So you weren't that impressed with him."

"Well, maybe at first. He was really arty, really creative and all that, but after a while that stuff stops working. You're never friends with the artist, you're friends with the person, and as a person he was really self-absorbed." She also described him as "really dark, like he walked around in his own private rain cloud," and as "the worst mama's boy I ever met. Every time he had a problem, he'd go running to Mama and she'd fix it all up for him."

Nevertheless she'd gotten "sort of" close to him, since "for about ten minutes" she and Gary had been joined at the hip. This was after she moved out of the Canterbury and Jim had taken up with Cybil at a place on Argyle near the Cahuenga ramp off the 101 freeway. She and Gary used to drop by "all the time," she said, "and it was so creepy, you know. I mean, I was used to people staying up late, but they took it to extremes. They always slept all day, so the windows were all blacked out. And the house was so filthy. There were cigarette butts on the floor and bottles everywhere. And Cybil had these cats she never cleaned up after, so the whole place smelled like cat piss. Plus she had her gear sitting out, her whips and chains and shit like that."

So it turned out "Cybil Disobedience" wasn't just your standard prankish punk name; the girl behind it had supported herself, and Jim as well, as a dominatrix. She'd come to L.A. to be an actress or singer, but too lazy or crazy to make it happen, she eventually settled for being a singer's girlfriend.

"Really hung up on fame in the worst way," said Michelle, "and Jim couldn't have cared less about that stuff, not really. But she had this ridiculous idea he was going to be the next big thing, so she sunk her claws in and never let go." She also thought Cybil might have done some streetwalking, but mostly she was into whipping ass and just loved to brag about her celebrity clients.

"But," Michelle emphasized, "you couldn't trust one thing she said. She lied about everything. Like, one time she told me her grandfather was the guy who invented Spam. What a thing to make up! You're the goddamn Spam heiress! And she'd slept with every rock star in the world, don't you know, people you knew she could never get near if she lived to be a hundred. She told me some pretty vile stories about some of them."

"Like...?"

"Oh, I really don't want to get into that. Just imagine the sickest shit you can possibly think of, and that's the kind of shit she did." I asked if Jim had likewise been into S&M, and she said, "I have no idea. But I can tell you this: one time Cybil had a black eye, a real shiner, and I asked her how she got it, and she said, 'Jim hit me.' And Jim—he was sitting right there—said, 'No, I didn't.' And she said, 'Yes, you did; you just don't remember. You were blacked out.' See, that's the kind of drunk he was: he'd black out and do all these things, and the next day he'd have no idea what he'd done. I remember a few times he disappeared and everybody would be calling around looking for him, and just when you thought he was dead for sure, he'd turn up in San Diego or someplace with no idea how he'd gotten there. I mean, how do you not remember something like that? And his wallet and all his money would be gone, so his mom or Cybil or somebody would have to wire him something to get back home. He was such a sponge, that guy. In fact, the last time I saw him, he asked to borrow money."

I asked her what year that was, and she said, "Oh, '90, '91. I was sitting outside the Onyx Café with my friend Trixie, and this guy walked by and said, 'Michelle?' I didn't even recognize him. He'd gained a lot of weight and gotten kind of old-looking, and I found that really sad, you know. I mean, when I first knew him, he was a really good-looking guy. And we talked for a few minutes, and he said something about moving to Seattle or someplace to work for a relative. And he'd lost his wallet, same old story, and asked if he could borrow some money, and I felt so sorry for him I gave him twenty bucks."

"Did you have the impression he might be homeless?"

"Well, he *always* seemed homeless. He was never a neat freak. He always looked like he needed a good shower." Then I told her that story about him begging for change, and though she didn't have much to say about it, I think her Onyx story may be the one that later found its way to me; it just got scrambled as it made the rounds. I also asked her what, if anything, she could tell me about Cybil's death, and she said, "Well, all I know is what Gary told me. He said Jim and Cybil had gone to bed late, same as always, and at some point the cats jumped on the bed and started going crazy. Then I guess they woke Jim up and he found this suicide note Cybil had put by the bed, and Gary said it was pretty upbeat for one of those. She even drew a little happy face on it! Then Jim went in the bathroom and found her hanging from the curtain rod with one of his belts, and he cut her down and tried to revive her, but it was too late."

"So do you think he had anything to do with it?"

"You mean, do I think he killed her? No, I don't believe that for one minute. I remember a few people wondering the same thing, but I don't think so, because Jim had had a lot of trouble with the cops already. We all had. We were like Public Enemy Number One or something. So I think if the cops had had any reason to blame him, they would have locked him up for life. Also, just knowing Cybil, it was totally within her to do something like that. She was completely obsessed with Jim, and I think she knew it wasn't going to last, and this was the one way she could *make* it last, if you know what I mean. She knew he'd be the one to find her. She used his belt to do it with. And I think she had it figured just right, because he was such a downer, that guy, so something like that just finished the job. I know the band never did much after that. I mean, yeah, they put out one more record, but that was nothing but a self-pity thing all about Jim and Cybil. So you could really say she killed them both, even though they took one body away."

Altogether I must have spoken to Michelle for ninety minutes, and past the first hour I could tell she wanted to go, but I kept her on the phone to ask, for instance, if Jim had started Gary on drugs.

"Absolutely not," she said. "Gary never needed any help in that department." I also asked what she could tell me about Buddy, and she said, "Kind of a redneck. Kind of belligerent, kind of a bully." She hadn't seen him in a long time, though. As for ROT's live performances, she thought they were pretty good, but the band itself was never a big favorite.

"I was more into X and the Germs," she said with just a hint of wistfulness. "If you ask me, *they're* the ones who'd make a good movie. I always thought Darby was the most interesting guy around. Once he died, it was no fun anymore."

ALL DURING THOSE WEEKS WHEN I WAS RUNNING ADS and posting on message boards and trying to solve the Jim mystery, another mystery had opened beside it: Irina. She'd never written as promised. She'd never called either, and since I had no way of calling her, there was nothing to do but wait. I tried to forget her. I told myself she was nothing but trouble and married to boot, but it got to the point where every time I went to my favorite video store—Jerry's Reruns in Los Feliz—I'd drive past Irina's house to check for clues of return. There were a number of clues. At night the lights were often burning, and not always in the same windows. Sometimes her car was there, and sometimes it wasn't.

Astrid might be stopping by to feed the cat, or maybe she or somebody else was house sitting, but would that person also be driving Irina's car? Why *her* car and not David's SUV, which was parked in the driveway in a spot it never left? No, I decided, she was obviously back and choosing for whatever reason to tune me out.

One night in late November I was making my usual detour when I saw Irina's friend Milan crossing the street in front of her house. I recognized his samurai hairstyle right away. I stopped and honked and waved to him, and he walked up to my window and, squinting in the darkness, said, "Oh. The musician. How are you?"

"I'm adequate. What's going on?"

"Not much. I write the script, you know. I try writing at home, but my roommate—I do nothing with him there, so Irina lets me do it here."

"Oh," I said, "she's back." And he looked baffled and said, "Back?"

"Yeah, wasn't she in Europe for a while?"

"Oh no. No, she does the play, you know. Some stupid thing. And she is forcing me to go, and now I guess I will have to. She is terrible actress! The worst!"

And so the mystery was solved. She'd never left in the first place; she'd been in town rehearsing some play the whole time. Milan said he was going on Friday and asked if I wanted to go with him, and at first I said no, but then I thought, "Fuck it, I'm going. Play *me* for a fucking chump." I wanted to see the look on her face when I showed up—assuming there *was* a look. Sociopaths aren't much known for their expressiveness.

I told Milan I'd see him on Friday. I told him not to mention he'd seen me, that I wanted to surprise Irina, and after I got home, I checked the theater listings in the *LA Weekly*. The play was called *Forever and a Day*—a "fairy-tale pastiche," the critic summed it up, and without panning the actors by name, he cited the "subpar" performances as one of several reasons not to attend. It was running at a theater on Melrose Avenue, which was maybe my least favorite street in all of Los Angeles, full of pseudo-bohemian shopaholics with smack-like cappuccino dependencies. Good God, was it really worth it? No, I decided. Forget the whole thing.

Well, that Friday around 7:45 I just happened to find myself on Melrose, even though I hated it, and somehow I walked by the theater and some money flew out of my pocket, right in front of the box office, and the person sitting there picked up my money and sold me a ticket. Strange! Then, next thing I knew, I was inside the theater, which was small, with maybe three-quarters of the seventy or so seats filled with mostly middle-aged people dressed as if for the mall. Two stools shaped like mushrooms were sitting in the center of the stage, and a painted backdrop of a cottage in the woods was draped behind it. I had to walk across the stage to reach the seats, and there in the back row was Milan, laughing like a cutup at a high-school assembly, and the girl and guy beside him, both dark and attractive, were also laughing. The girl's name was Maja—I would later get to know her well. I've forgotten the guy's name, but he, like her, was a Serb. I waved to Milan, who waved me up, and we all small-talked in English for a couple of minutes, but for the most part the Serbs spoke to each other in Serbian while I read the actors' bios in the program. Well, *one* I read, and it listed a handful of prior credits, including a part on *Friends*. ("She is basically extra," Milan said when I asked him about it.) Then the house lights dimmed and the stage lights rose on a young couple perched on the mushrooms, the guy dressed a little like Peter Pan, the girl in white like Ophelia. They talked broadly about being in love, mugging and flailing and camping it up, and there was nothing funny about it, but for some reason the audience laughed at everything they said, including the Serbs, though you could tell they were doing it sarcastically. Then a woman dressed like a witch came running out with a broom and told the lovers they could never marry, being under a spell, and she likewise gorged herself on the scenery, but after she ran off, everyone in the audience but me and the Serbs applauded. Then an old guy playing an apothecary hobbled out, and Peter Pan asked his advice for lifting the spell, and the apothecary said he would have to travel to a distant kingdom and pluck a magic flower guarded by Valentina, the most beautiful woman in all the world, and it was a treacherous journey from which Peter Pan might never return, since as soon as he saw the ruthless Valentina, he would surely fall in love. I knew from the program that Valentina was being played by Irina, and I thought, "Huh, typecasting." Meantime I sure hoped he'd meet her soon. My ass was starting to understand what the playwright had in mind when he'd named this thing *Forever and a Day*.

But, no, I was in for a long, long wait. First Peter Pan had many adventures with thieves and knights and elves and ogres, all played by shitty actors. And then, at last, he found her. She was standing in a red light in a red dress with a red bouquet of flowers, and it was impressive, that first sight; but then she spoke, and it was all downhill from there. She couldn't project; her line readings were off; it took her forever to say the slightest thing. It was so strange, since in real life she spoke near-perfect English, but onstage it was like she was trying to speak it better than she already did. All her offstage presence was lost. She was slow, dull and stilted. But Peter Pan fell in love with her anyway, and when he didn't come back, Ophelia went in search of him, and eventually, after many adventures all her own, she found him with Valentina and plucked the magic flower, causing Valentina to clutch her heart and die. Then, after the wedding finale, the cast took its bows and the house lights rose, and I sat there with the Serbs, stunned. None of us could believe it. Why would anyone bother to write and stage such an utter piece of shit? We all got up to leave, crossing the stage when Irina walked out, still in makeup and costume. She was smiling at first, but her smile vanished the second she noticed me. I could see it in her eyes: *What are* you *doing here?* That, of course, was the reason I'd come, to see that look, but once I did, there was no sense of comeuppance or any of that. I just felt like crap.

But then something interesting happened. She pulled herself together, and if I hadn't seen that look of distress a second before, I would've sworn she was happy to see me. What a great actress! She asked how I was doing, and I said, "Fine." Then I asked how she was doing, and she said, "Oh, you know." I didn't, of course, but that was as far as it went; she turned to the Serbs, and they spoke for a long time in Serbian, and never once did she look at me. Then she did. She said, "We're going to have a drink up the street. Would you like to come?" It was hard to tell if she was still acting, but, after all, she didn't *have* to invite me; she could've blown me off, as she'd done already for the last two months. I told her sure, I'd love to have a drink. Then she ran backstage, and the Serbs started to walk outside. I said, "Hey, aren't we going to wait for Irina?" And they said, "No, she will meet us there."

We were headed to a place about five blocks away called Café Luna, where the cast and some of their friends were getting together on the back patio. A waiter was pushing tables together, and as more and more cast members and their friends showed up, more and more tables were added. I sat with the Serbs and saved the seat next to mine, fighting off a number of people who tried to take it, including Peter Pan. Finally Irina showed up, and I called to her, but, as if she couldn't hear me, she sat at the far end of the table, ten or more feet from me. There was a guy with her—a young, square guy I'd seen in the audience—and he sat beside her and she talked to him, ignoring me and the Serbs, who were talking to each other in Serbian. Then somebody ordered a bunch of food, which meant I was going to have to contribute to the bill, even though I wasn't hungry. Then a husky girl who'd played an elf started bugging me, or she and her mother both did. They asked who I was and what I did, and when I mentioned something about making movies, the mother said, "Oh, how *exciting*! Have you done anything *we'd* know?"

"Well, possibly. But I work in adult films."

"*Oh,*" she said, laughing nervously. So that took care of her and the elf! I stole looks at Irina, who was lit by candlelight and talking to the square, and at one point she gave me a smile as if to say, "Having a good time?" Yeah, slut, I'm having a great fucking time! I gave her every opportunity to walk down and say something, but she never did, so that I finally got up and threw some money on the table and said good night to the Serbs. I promised myself I wouldn't so much as glance at Irina on my way out the door, but I broke that promise, and she glanced back with an expression of pity, and pity was the last thing I wanted. Besides, she must have really perfected that look, having practiced it on so many others. I drove home and did the same thing I'd done the last time I'd seen her, the same thing I did every time I saw her: I hit the sauce. I was well on my way to getting drunk when, at one in the morning, the phone rang, and I fucking knew it was her. She'd done her cold-hot-cold routine; now it was time for the heat again. I checked my caller ID. UNAVAILABLE, it said. Yeah, you got *that* right! And I was *not* going to answer.

"Hello?" I said, after I did.

"Hey, why'd you leave so soon? I was going to talk to you, but then you just left."

"I had some stuff I had to do."

"Well, I wish you'd said something. I got caught up with Bruce, you know. He's the director."

It sounded like she was in a wind tunnel, so she must be on her cell phone or, possibly, on her broomstick. She asked if I could meet her someplace. I couldn't, I said, I'd been drinking.

"Oh. Well, I can come to you, then."

"I don't think so."

"How about tomorrow?"

"No," I said. "Irina, I'm too old for this shit. If you want to play games, go do it with somebody your age. I'm sure you've got all the volunteers you can handle."

But she ignored that.

"Can't I just stop by for a few minutes?" she begged. "Please? I really want to talk to you. I promise I won't stay long."

Why couldn't I ever tell this girl no? It was like I was Peter Pan and she was Valentina. I gave her directions. She wasn't that far away, she said, and I hung up and thought, "What the fuck have you done?! You know she's only coming over to fuck with your mind!" I steeled myself with still more beer, and maybe fifteen minutes later I heard her footsteps coming up my stairs, and there she was.

SHE LOVED THE LOOK OF THE PLACE, even though it was messy.

"It's exactly how I pictured it," she said. "Very *you*." She asked if I had something to drink. Only beer, I said, and she made a face and said a beer would be fine. Then we sat in the living room, where she got around to the point of the visit, lamely explaining her two-month silence and phantom trip to Europe.

"This is what happened," she told me. "I was ready to go—I had my bags packed and everything—and Bruce called and offered me this play. And I was fighting with David about something else, and I decided I'd rather stay and do this play than travel with someone who's mad at me. And I'm going home for Christmas anyway. It all happened at the last minute. I know it looks like I lied to you, but I didn't. I really thought I was leaving."

"Yeah, but that's not the issue here. I mean, it's not like I expected much. When you said you were going to write me, it's not like I sat here counting the seconds till your letter came through." (Hours, perhaps, but not seconds.) "But the thing is, you were here the whole time and you never let me know."

"Yes, but I've been so *busy*. The play—it may not look like much, but it's a lot of hard work. And David was calling from Europe and making me do errands, and then he came home for a couple of weeks, and I couldn't call you *then*. I've really *wanted* to speak to you, but I haven't had a minute."

"Well, you had plenty tonight. You could've walked down and said something, but you spent the whole night sitting with some guy at the end of the table. And, okay, he's the director, but this isn't the first time you pulled something like this. You did the same thing at David's party. And when I saw you tonight, I could tell you were freaked out I was even there."

"Because I knew you wouldn't understand!" she fairly shouted. "I could tell you were mad at me the minute I saw you, and I didn't want to deal with it. And I couldn't. Because to speak to you—I'd have to say things I can't say in front of other people. And I don't think it's fair for you to show up without telling me you're coming and expect me to have some big talk right away."

"Hey, I'm not asking for a 'big talk.' If you don't want to fool around, just tell me. It's no big deal. Just say, 'That's something I don't want to do,' and we're all set. But don't tease me, and don't play hide-and-seek. Those are the only rules."

Then she asked if I'd be upset if she only wanted to be friends. That was all she could offer, she said; and I said, "Well, there you go. See how painless that was? That's what you want, and that's the way it's going to be. Case closed."

"No," she sighed, "you're upset, I can tell. I *knew* this was going to happen."

"Then why did you *make* it happen? I didn't make the first move, *you* did. You called me up and asked me out and then you started kissing me. I mean, that's what happened, right?"

"Yes," she sighed again.

"Well, good, we've got *that* straight. And now you're here, and I didn't even want you to come over, but you insisted—and you know what? I'm always going to have a problem that way. I'm not going to lie to you. I want something more, and now you're saying it's not going to happen. I mean, Jesus Christ, you're married! So, no, I don't think I can be your friend. Remember when you said I wouldn't even speak to you if you were old and ugly? Well, I almost wish you were—because *then* I think we could just be friends."

Then, for a long moment, she fixed me with a completely unreadable expression of the kind she'd given me before at Astrid's. Then, very quietly, with an air almost of resignation, she said, "Okay, I think we should do it."

"I'm sorry?"

"You know. I think we should sleep together. I've been thinking about it for weeks, and I told myself no, but now that I'm here—yes, I think it has to be."

We hadn't so much as touched. She was on the sofa, and I was in a chair four feet away, and after two months of nothing, I was sure she was playing another head game. Yet she seemed serious—a little *too* serious, almost.

"Don't you want to?" she said. "There's something I need to find out, and it's never going to happen if we don't sleep together."

"So what is it?"

"I don't know. I mean, yes, I know *something,* but I really don't want to talk about it right now."

"Well, is it something you can only find out with me, or could it be with anybody?" And she looked at me if the answer must be obvious: of *course* it had to be with me. But did that mean "I think I might be in love with you," or "Let's see how you stack up against my other lovers," or "I've never had an orgasm and maybe you can give me one"? She *was* married to an upper-class Brit after all. I didn't want to press her for explanations and have her change her mind. On the other hand, she seemed to have passed the buck to me.

So I sat there, weighing desire against the trouble I knew it would bring, till finally I said, "Well, I guess if we're going to do it, we should go ahead and do it."

"I guess we should," she said, and as if relieved that a decision had been made, she stood and asked where my bathroom was. She leaned down and kissed me briefly before she went in, and I drank the rest of my beer and wondered what exactly I was supposed to do next. Was she inserting her diaphragm or taking a squirt or what? And where should I be when she came back: here in the living room or waiting in bed? I'd almost never been in a romantic situation quite this weird!

So I put on a record and went to the bedroom, which I tried to tidy up a little. Then I heard the toilet flush and, through the doorway, I saw her walking toward the living room, naked except for a tiny T-shirt and panties. I said, "No, I'm here," and she circled back to the bedroom, where the bed stood between us, and said, "Do you have any protection?" I did,

I told her, and I walked around the bed on my way to the bathroom and took her in my arms, and for the first time that night we really made out. I wasn't nearly as excited as I thought I would be, but I was sure it was all going to kick in later. I found a condom in the bathroom and came back and got into bed, and once again we fooled around. Off came her T-shirt, and out of respect for Irina, I'm not going to get too graphic, but I'll say this much: she had one of the most beautiful bodies I've ever seen—guitar-shaped, a fuller bottom than top, but don't take that to mean she was flat-chested. No, she was perfect in every way. And off came her panties, and we kissed and fondled and kissed some more, and again, I don't want to get too specific, but let's just say she did everything she could to make things happen and my dick wasn't having it. I got a little cooperation before I put on the condom, but once I did that, everything went south again. I was pissed at myself, pissed at *it*, but Irina didn't seem bothered at all. She just laid her head on my chest and chalked it up to drinking.

"Well, I'm not *that* drunk. I've been a lot drunker than I am right now, and this almost *never* happens. Jesus Christ, look at you! I bet this has never happened to *you* before."

"It's happened. But this is fine, like this. I really like being around you."

"Yeah, because I'm such a great lover."

"I'm sure you are, actually."

"What makes you say that?"

"Something about you. Something in your eyes. You have the most beautiful eyes."

"Yeah, but *your* eyes—*those* are the ones. Jesus Christ, what the fuck is wrong with me?!"

But, deep down, I knew. I was afraid of her, or, rather, I was afraid of my feelings for her. I'd be crushed if we fucked and she brushed me off afterward, so my dick was trying to protect my head. Still, Irina said she'd known for a long time that we were going to make love, and if it didn't happen tonight, she was sure it would happen eventually.

"I think we have to," she said. "There's something between us. Don't you feel that way?" And I told her I did, even though I knew I shouldn't: the more she thought she had me, the less she'd no doubt want me. Then she started talking about David, saying she was going to have to leave him, that things had gotten pretty bad of late, and it scared her; she'd been with him so long, she wasn't sure how she'd get along without him.

"You mean financially?"

"Oh no," she laughed. "No, I can take care of myself. In fact, I'd *like* to get a job. I think I need some time to myself, you know? I haven't had that since I left home, and then it just lasted a couple of years. I met David, and he wanted to get married, and I married him. I knew I was too young. But I did it anyway."

"Why?"

"Because I didn't want to lose him. He was at an age where he felt he should be married, and I knew if I said no, he'd find somebody else who'd say yes. There were a lot of women after him. And I don't regret it, because we had a lot of good times; we traveled a lot, and that's something I always wanted to do. But now he wants to have a child, and I'm not ready for that. I'm not sure if I'll *ever* be ready! But he's almost forty, and he's got this schedule, you know. He wants to be able to see his grandchildren, and he's afraid if he waits too long, he'll never have the chance."

"See what happens when you go for older guys? Not only can't they get it up, they start talking about their *grand*children."

"Well, this is something that can't be helped. I've always liked older men. It's because my father died, I think."

Which completely contradicted what Astrid had said, what I'd seen with my own two eyes; but Irina claimed she'd never had a lover who was younger than twenty-five. I asked about Jeffrey and the other boys I'd seen hanging around her, and she said they were just friends, that she had a lot of trouble making friends with girls, they were all so competitive.

"It's not such a problem in Belgrade," she said, "but here—I don't think I have one good American girlfriend. Even when I was modeling, I never got along with the American girls. All my friends were Spanish and Italian."

Then, apropos of nothing, she raised herself and asked what I thought of her performance.

"You never told me," she said. "Am I as bad as Milan said I was?" I danced as fast as I could. I asked if Milan had *really* told her that, and she said, "Yes, but he was funny about it. And I know him—he never likes anything—but what did *you* think?"

"Well," I went on dancing, "I really don't think I'm qualified to say. I'm not a theater guy. And don't you think this play is kind of goofy?"

"Yes, but I think it's always good to do these things. It's like going to the gym, you know? And this part is hard, because Bruce—he wanted a very artificial style, and I think I do better when it's closer to me."

Of course, in spirit, it was *very* close to her. Still, once she started talking about acting, I was off the hook. She'd dreamed of being an actress ever since she was a little girl, she said, and she didn't care about being famous or any of that; she just wanted to be really good, like her idol Ingrid Bergman. She wanted to play Lady Macbeth one day. She wanted to make great films with great directors like Roman Polanski. On and on she went, with a passion I couldn't help but find endearing. She said she was going to have a small part but a good one in David's movie, and she was very excited about that, and I said, "Yeah, but is he still going to let you do it if you leave him?"

"Oh," she said, as if I'd missed a crucial loophole, "I won't leave him until *after* the movie is done. Not because I'll lose the part! Yes, I'm thinking about that too, but that's not the real reason."

"So what *is* the real reason?"

And as if she couldn't or wouldn't explain further, she turned away and said, "It's just not the right time."

LATER THAT NIGHT I DREAMED WE WERE FUCKING. We were in my apartment, in my bed, and I was pounding away on top of Irina, who was staring up with a look of astonishment. It was so lifelike, I started wondering if I was dreaming after all. I wasn't. I was sleepfucking—an old habit of mine. Then I woke up (even though my eyes had never been shut in the first place), and right in the nick of time, since I was just about to come. We were still going at it at when her cell phone rang at six in the morning, and she freaked out, going, "Oh my God, it's David!" and slid out from under me and went tripping toward the bathroom, where she'd left her phone, and shut the door and stayed in there talking for close to an hour. I could hear her voice but not her words, and every so often she'd laugh. I had to take a leak and got up and cracked the bathroom door, but she slammed it shut immediately.

I was close enough then to make out her words. She said, "I'm sorry, the cat's bothering me. What did you say?"

Well, thanks a fucking lot! I went to the kitchen and pissed in the sink. She joined me in bed a few minutes later. She apologized for slamming the door, and I told her I understood, and she said, "Well, I'm glad *one* of us does."

"Is something wrong?"

"Oh, David's all alone in Prague, and I'm…"

"Feeling guilty?"

"Even though I shouldn't," she sighed. "Do you know that's the first time I've made love in months? He barely touches me anymore. And then he wants to have a child! How's he going to have a child when he doesn't want to have *sex*?"

"Well, there's always artificial insemination."

"Or," she laughed, "there's always *you*. Wouldn't it be funny if I had your child and passed it off as David's?"

"Oh, yeah. And then he can kill us when he finds out."

"But he'd never know. You'd be the only one."

"Sorry. No child of mine is going to have an English accent."

"But it's very refined, don't you think? And you wouldn't have to worry about him growing up poor. He'd have a great life. Well, except David would send him off to boarding school. But that wouldn't be so bad. He'd get a great education. And he'd be half-Serbian, so you'd never have to worry about the other children picking on him. We're quite the warriors, you know."

And it *was* sort of funny, us teasing each other, but that mention of poverty—it hammered home my deepest suspicion, that she loved David for his money, and because of it, she'd probably never leave him, no matter what she said. In fact, even though she claimed to feel guilty, she was ready for more, and afterward I slept till I heard her call my name, and there she was with breakfast. She said she'd woken and, finding the refrigerator empty, driven to the store and bought a few things, and now she wanted to feed me. She *literally* wanted to feed me. She cut up my food and held the fork to my mouth, sometimes playing "airplane" and frequently stopping to kiss me. I'd been dying to tell her for weeks about the research I'd done on Jim Cassady, and now I finally found the chance. She seemed fascinated, especially by those bizarre calls from "Frenchy," and said I couldn't stop, I had to keep learning more; this whole thing had the makings of a great movie. I said, "Yeah, but I'm not sure what to do at this point. I mean, I guess I could hire a detective, but a lot of people seem to think he's dead. You know, I don't want to spend all that money just to find out where he's buried."

"Maybe you can speak to Jeffrey. I bet *he* knows what happened to him."

"Yeah, but you're not talking to him anymore."

"Yes, but *you* could call. Or—you know what? I just saw Distortion Felix is playing in a few days. You might be able to speak to him then."

She wanted to hear Jim's music. So, after she fed me, I played her my favorite ROT record, *Tinderloin*, and she said it was so beautiful, she just loved it, and could I please make her a tape? I was about to play her my own record, the Superego record, when she said, "Oh my God, look at the time!" She had a performance in a few hours, but first she had to feed her cat and do a few chores for David. I walked her to the door and asked when I was going to see her again.

"Any time you want," she purred.

"After the show?"

"That's going to be difficult. Some friends are coming, and they'll probably want to go someplace afterwards."

"Well, why don't you call and tell me where you are? I don't mind hanging out with your friends."

"No, you'd just be bored. And I think we're going to have to be very careful with other people. Especially people we know. I don't want them getting suspicious."

She proposed that we get together the following day, after she'd done her matinee; and that just happened to be my birthday, as I told her now, and she got excited and said we'd have to do something special. Then she freaked about the time again and raced out the door, and I thought, "Every time I see that girl, she's in a hurry to be gone." Plus, even after sleeping with her, I still didn't have her phone number.

She never left my thoughts that night. Who were these friends coming to see her play? Were they guys? Did she miss me? What was she wearing right now? I could only fall asleep by jerking off, though I tried not to jerk off, wanting to save it all for her. The next day I got birthday calls from my family in North Carolina, and she called while I was talking to my dad—a weird juxtaposition, that. She wanted to take me out for dinner, but I told her no, I just wanted to shoot some pool; so we set a time to meet, and a few hours later I drove to the Short Stop and found it desolate, same as always. Christmas was less than a month away, and the daytime bartender, a woman named Mickey, had done the place up with decorations: garlands on the gun locker, frosting on the badge displays. Thom and I talked till Irina walked in a half-hour late carrying what looked like a bottle of booze. My present, she said. That's why she was late: she wanted to wrap it. I said, "Oh, you didn't have to do that. I'm just going to rip it off anyway."

"But I wanted to," she said sweetly.

I tore off the paper, and rolled inside a Glenfiddich gift box was a painting she'd done of herself, similar in style to the portrait I'd seen before in her bedroom: quick black strokes and washes of gloomy gray. She wondered if it wasn't vain, giving me a picture of herself, and I said, "No, it's great, I'm honored. But you didn't do it just for me, did you?"

"No, it's from a couple of years ago."

"You look sad. A little like a goth."

"Sometimes I *feel* like a goth."

"Well, great. I have a genuine goth painting now."

Thom bought us a round. He knew it was my birthday. He'd watched me unwrap the painting, and he was obviously impressed. He asked Irina if she painted professionally, and she laughed, flattered, and said no, she just fooled around a little. This was something Astrid had mentioned, Irina's nonchalance toward her painting; and I asked why she didn't take it more seriously, and she said, "Oh, that's what everybody says. It's just something I've always done, you know. It's really not much of a challenge."

"Well, there's always room for improvement, right?"

"Of course. But I feel I can always paint—it will always be there—but I only have so much time to act."

Man, that girl had it going on in so many ways! My heart was hanging by a few frayed strings: a couple of whacks and I was a goner. And that was what I didn't want at all. Well, I did and I didn't. But I didn't think a future was possible, since she was married and used to luxuries I couldn't afford, so I was just trying to content myself with the here and now. And I'm capable of that—I would never have been able to survive otherwise—but this girl was such a rare find, it was hard not to wish for something more.

Still, as great as she was, and apart from the wedding band she rarely wore, there was a huge price to pay, being with Irina. That night, shooting pool, two cops wanted to play us, even with an empty table in the next room. I knew why, of course, and could hardly blame them. How many ex-models showed up in that dive? But one of them chatted her up right in front of me, and she could easily have shot him down, but, no, she played along, laughing at his corny jokes and coyly responding to his stupid questions. Finally, to spell a few things out, I put my arms around her and gave that guy the same look her friend Jeffrey had once given me: *She's mine, all right? Now back the fuck off!* And it worked: he and his friend left after playing one game. Except now I couldn't enjoy myself. I kept thinking about that grand talk of hers—"There's something between us"—when, clearly, there was something between her and a lot of guys. She noticed the change in my mood and asked if something was bothering me, and part of me wanted to talk about it, and part of me felt I had no right. We'd only been together, if you could call it that, a couple of days; who knew how many more there'd be? I just told her I didn't feel like playing anymore, so we went to my place and made love; and there I was with so much doubt, yet I felt something different that time, something I'd never quite felt before, as if I wasn't just fucking with my body, I was fucking with my soul, and my soul was dissolving into hers. It wasn't as if I tried to feel that way—I tried to shake it off in fact—but I did want to give her pleasure, that I wanted, and the more she responded to the pleasure I gave her, the more I felt my boundaries give way. *Tinderloin* was playing in the background, soundtrack to some of the most profound changes I'd ever been through, and as spooked as I felt, that record didn't help. Nor did the look in Irina's eyes. She clearly felt as spooked as I did, and afterward she was especially affectionate, especially talkative, and told me about her father's death when she was eight and he was thirty-six—"that age you were until today." He died of a stroke, she said, and life was so hard afterward; she had to help raise her younger brother and was never allowed to be, simply, a child. She also told me about her first love at sixteen, with a man of thirty—another director, it turned out. She'd met him on the set of a commercial (she started modeling when she was fourteen), and eventually he became so insanely jealous, she thought he was going to kill her if she didn't get out of Yugoslavia. What a surprise, huh? She also asked questions about my past, and I answered sparingly, since I'd coughed up a chunk of my soul already, making love. Some questions—the lighter ones—I didn't dodge. She wanted to know how many women I'd slept with, and I said, "I don't know. Ninety. A hundred."

"That many!"

"It's not that many. I've known guys who slept with way more. And most of that's from my twenties. I was a pretty wild guy in those days."

"So what's the wildest thing you ever did?"

"It all depends on what you mean by wild."

"You know what I mean. The most—decadent."

There was a fair amount to choose from, but the *most* decadent, as moral types would probably see it, was too personal to share. I said, "Well, I was at an orgy one time."

"Really!"

"No, not really. What happened was, I was touring with my band, and we spent the night at this girl's house, and she had a few friends over, and everybody was really drunk, so we all started fucking around. But there were certain guys the girls wouldn't touch, and it was a really small place, so the ones that weren't getting any—they had to just sit there and watch."

"But I bet you weren't one of them."

"No, I did all three, as a matter of fact."

"How nice for you."

"Yeah, but they all were pretty ugly. And it's so weird to be in a room with a bunch of guys with hard-ons. Especially when you know them well. It's like, 'Oh my God, how am I ever going to get that picture out of my head?' And like I say, certain guys were being excluded, so it created some pretty bad feelings in the van for a few days. But, you know, that's always going to happen anyway. Touring is—it's really a nightmare in a lot of ways."

Then, a little afraid of what I might hear, I asked about her own wildest experience. She refused to say at first, but I said, "No, I told *you*. It's fifty-fifty around this house."

"Well, okay. This happened when I was living in Paris. I was eighteen and going out with this photographer, this Italian guy, and he had a friend who was so beautiful I thought I was going to die! And one night he was staying at my boyfriend's place, and my boyfriend went to bed, and I made love with his friend on the sofa. I don't know how we managed not to wake up my boyfriend! I think we made a lot of noise. And the next day it was so strange, acting like nothing had happened. Very uncomfortable. Like you were saying about your...orgy."

"Did your boyfriend ever find out?"

"Well, I never told him, but he probably knows by now. I broke up with him a few days later and started seeing his friend. It was all a big secret, you know. Then my agent sent me to New York. And a few weeks later I met David."

I didn't consider that terribly wild as far as sexual exploits went, but it was troubling nonetheless. She'd cheated with her boyfriend's *friend* while her boyfriend was sleeping in the *next room*—*that* was the girl I was giving myself to. I barely slept that night. I remember staring at the ceiling as Irina slept beside me and that record played in the living room: the songs of a ghost recounting his love for another ghost. Yet one of those ghosts wasn't truly a ghost at all, as I was less than twenty-four hours from learning.

THE NEXT DAY WAS A MONDAY, and I had to get up early to work a temping job out in the Valley. Irina reminded me that Distortion Felix was supposed to play that night and Jeffrey might be there, so maybe we should think about going. Regardless of Jeffrey, I was badly in need of a live-music fix; so we made a plan to meet, and that night I drove to the Silverlake Lounge, where there was quite a scene outside by the door: lots of kids lined up, many more than usual. I asked the one in front of me what the big deal was, why the crowd, and he said it was because of ...And You Will Know Us by the Trail of Dead.

"Who? What?"

"They're from Austin. Fucking rad, dude."

Inside, the place was also packed, and I looked around for Irina, who naturally wasn't there. I got all the way to the front of the stage, and by then Distortion Felix was about to play, so I stopped to watch, and they were just as good as last time. It's a shame they aren't better known. Then they finished, and these kids from Austin started setting up, and all four had black bowl haircuts, and they all seemed pretty fucked up—not the most auspicious first impression, the mod look in particular. Then Scott Sterling, the Fold promoter, sort of pushed his way past me and said, "Did you see him?"

"See who?" I said.

"Buddy Lavrakis."

"Where?!"

And he pointed to the back, where the bathroom was. It was hard to move with so many people crushed around the stage, but I kept trying to force my way through when I heard Irina shout my name and turned to see Milan's ponytailed head moving like a periscope above the crowd and, looking small behind him, Irina. I had no idea why she'd invited Milan, since days before she'd expressed concern about socializing with people we knew. But I stopped till they got to me, trying hard to act cool with Irina, who asked if I'd seen Jeffrey. I said, "No, but I think Buddy Lavrakis is here."

"Who?"

"He played guitar in Rule of Thumb."

Then the Trail of Dead show started. They've since blown up and tweaked their sound, but in 1999 they were still unknown, except to hipsters, and they obviously had a lot of cache in those circles. I thought they were incredible! Their drummer was a phenom in the Keith Moon style who'd sometimes switch to guitar and sing, and that was something we used to do in Superego, changing roles that way. And he and all the others were jumping off the stage, breaking down the fourth wall in every way they could think to do it, and that was likewise a Superego specialty. I thought for sure the band was on ecstasy, but then one of them shouted, "I am *so* fucking drunk!" On what? Cough syrup? But it was such a powerful experience, I could barely tear my eyes away, Buddy Lavrakis or not. For their last number they went hog-wild insane—drums crashing, debris flying, frenzy, chaos, freakout—and that was how it was in Superego too. And it really did me a world of good to see all this. Rock & roll was alive and well. Superego had an heir. I was sure they'd never heard of us, but I felt like I was watching the baton being passed to a new generation that was going to take it places we never did or could.

Yet once they started playing, the crowd thinned out, as if instantly bored with the band they'd driven out in the cold to see. And that made it easier to scan the place for Buddy, and there he was, standing ten or so feet behind me. Man, was he intimidating! His face had hardened, he was dressed all in black, and he was heavily muscled like he'd just escaped from Rockabilly State Prison. Plus he had a friend beside him who looked like a psycho in his own right. They were still hanging around when the show ended, and I suddenly felt shy about approaching Buddy, but Irina said, "Oh, go on. He's nobody special. I'm sure he'll be very flattered." I thought, "Yeah, stop being such a pussy," and walked up and said, "Buddy? I just wanted to tell you what a huge fan of Rule of Thumb I was. Still am, actually. I was just listening to you guys last night."

"Oh," he said. "Thanks. Thanks a lot." He was obviously disarmed. He shook my hand and asked my name, and I poured it on even thicker. I said, "You're the reason I started playing guitar in the first place"—which was true, though I was equally inspired by others. He asked if I was still playing, and I told him no, I'd gotten into making movies; and I thought about mentioning the ROT project, but, after my experience with Patrick Fitzpatrick, I decided that might not be a good idea. Instead I asked, like a casual fan, if he was still in touch with Jim, and his face, which had softened, hardened again on the spot.

"Well," he said, "not really."

"Is he alive?"

"He's alive."

"Well, that's good to know. Does he live in L.A. or—?"

"Kind of. But, you know, I barely talk to him. He's a really fucked-up guy. Dangerous, you could even say. So, you know, I keep my distance, and he keeps his."

"Do you know what he's up to?"

"Not much," the psycho-looking friend laughed. Then I asked if there was some way I could speak to Jim; and I had a feeling that was probably one question too many, but even so Buddy flipped out in a way that took me aback.

"Didn't you hear what I just *said*?" he growled. "The guy is fucked up and dangerous. I barely talk to him. He barely talks to me. And I don't think he wants to talk to you either."

Fine, man, subject dropped. Then I asked a little about Buddy's life since ROT, and though he'd clearly lost interest in talking to me, he did mention something about starting another band. I thought he might be more approachable at some later date, so I told him I'd love to try out if he got something going, just managing to slip him my phone number before he and his friend took off. Then I went back to Irina and told her what had happened, and she said, "Well, at least you spoke to him. Maybe he'll call you."

"I doubt it."

Meantime the Trail of Dead drummer had set up a merch table by the side of the stage. I told Irina I'd be right back, and it took a while before the drummer got to me, and when he eventually did, I told him how blown away I'd been, but he seemed too drunk to care. He was selling two records for ten bucks each, and I had about fifty to see me through the rest of the week, but I thought, "Fuck it, it's worth starving for something this good," and bought them both. By then at least ten minutes had gone by and Irina was no longer at the bar, where I'd left her with Milan. I looked all around and walked outside to the sidewalk, where I spotted her smoking with Buddy and his buddy. (Milan had apparently gone home.) I thought, "My God, don't tell me she's cockteasing Buddy Lavrakis!" Sure enough, I got closer, and Buddy was practically foaming at the mouth, bragging about the many times he'd toured Europe—"Yeah, and then we got shut down in Paris" and blah-blah-blah—and Irina was playing right along. He talked and talked till he glanced at me like I was there for him, not Irina, like I was going to bug him with still more questions about Jim when he'd made it perfectly clear he had nothing more to say. He broke off his lame story and said, "What's up, dude?"

"Oh," Irina said, "this is my friend Jason. You already met, didn't you? He's a really great director, and he wants to make a movie about your friend." I thought, *Goddamnit, don't fucking tell him that!* and Buddy, as feared, looked at me like I was a complete moron and said, "A *movie*? Don't even waste your time. There ain't no movie with that guy. He's just a fucked-up loser, that's all he is." Then he turned back to Irina and started chatting her up again, and, thoroughly disgusted, I headed back inside the bar, where I bought myself a beer. I sat there for at least ten minutes, getting more and more furious with Irina, who finally strolled inside with a big smile and said, "Well, *there* you are. Why'd you walk off like that? You should've stayed."

"What for? He's a fucking asshole, that guy."

"Oh, he's not so bad. He talked a little about Rule of Thumb. He said he's got some old outtakes, and he's going make a tape for me."

"Isn't that sweet."

"Yes, he's going to bring it when he sees my play."

"*What*? *Excuse* me? You made a *date* with that guy?"

"Only to see my play. He probably won't come anyway, but I thought if he did, you could come too and maybe you could talk to him again."

But I had a hard time believing she could be that thoughtful, and besides, I'd seen too much of this kind of thing already. I sat there staring her down, and she stared back and said, "Well, you don't really think… Oh my God, that *is* what you think."

"Well, what am I *supposed* to think? Every time I turn around, you're gone. And two days ago you run off to meet your 'friends' and tell me I can't go. Then David calls, and you stop in the middle of sex and slam the goddamn door in my face."

"Well, I had to! He wouldn't call my mobile if he hadn't tried the house. I don't want him to get suspicious!"

"Okay, he's your husband, we'll give you that one. But last night—why did you talk to that cop?"

"I don't know what you mean."

"I'm sure you don't."

"Well, why don't you explain? He talked to me, so I talked back. What am I supposed to do when somebody talks to me? *Ignore* them?"

"Yeah, you know what? You are. If we're together, you don't even *talk* to other men. Not some guy who comes up to you in a bar."

But, of course, we *weren't* together—not really. I was calling her on shit I had no right to call her on. And she looked at me as if seeing who I really was for the first time and said, "You're just like a Serb. The way you're speaking—it makes me sick."

"And how do you think I feel watching you shake your ass for other guys? You think I *enjoy* that?"

"I do not," she said, "'shake my ass' for anybody."

"So what do you call it, then? Being friendly? There's no such thing as being friendly when a guy comes up to you in a bar. He's after one thing, and you know it too, and it's disrespectful to flirt with guys when you're with somebody else."

"I don't want to have this talk right now," she said, turning to go. "If you want to talk about it later, give me a call."

But how was I supposed to do that? I *still* didn't have her phone number. And she walked out of the bar, and that pissed me off even more, the way she'd effectively hung up on me. I wasn't going to follow, but then I did, catching up to her as she rounded the corner at Café Tropical.

"You know," I said, "you could make a living at this."

"Make a living at *what*?" she snapped.

"Disappearing. Is that what you do with David? Does he have to spend half his life trying to figure out where you've wandered off to?"

"No, he doesn't," she said, still walking. "He trusts me."

"Well, you've sure done wonders with that!"

Then she turned to me for a second with a pierced look and said, "You wouldn't understand."

"Why, because I'm not some cosmopolitan European? What, do you guys have an 'arrangement' or something? Is that what you were doing in the bathroom the other day? Jerking him off with your latest misadventure?"

"You're *so* disgusting. I had you mixed up with somebody else. My mistake. Sorry."

"Yeah, I thought *you* were somebody else too! I never know *who* I'm going to get the next time I see you! One minute you're one way, the next you're another!"

"Because you expect things from me. I can only be what I am. And David understands that. He doesn't try to make me feel guilty about it."

"Well, maybe he should. You're fucking other guys behind his back! I mean, tell me the truth here. I'm not the only one, am I?"

"Of course not."

"So how many others are there?"

"So many you wouldn't believe it."

"I bet I would."

Then she stopped and turned to face me and said, "I bet you would too. There's no point, is there? If that's what you think of me, there's no point in going on."

"Well, where were we supposed to be 'going' in the first place?"

"Well, I didn't have a *plan*. I just—" Then she broke off, and I said, "Yes?" and she said, "I just wanted to figure some things out. And I was hoping I could help *you* figure some things out. But I guess that's not possible. I guess I've made another mess. But that's not what I wanted. I just wanted us to *help* each other."

She seemed perfectly sincere when she said all this. On the other hand, she always seemed sincere, even when she was flirting with other guys. Where was the truth with this girl? Did she even know herself? But she obviously didn't, which she was pretty much admitting. And she looked so sad and lost, I wanted to take her right back home and into my bed. But I couldn't. Because then the whole thing would start up all over again.

"I'm sorry," I said.

"For what?"

"Everything. I wanted something to happen in the worst way, and I still do, but I don't think I can handle it. These last few days—they've been great, but if it keeps up, one of us is going to get hurt, and I think I know which one it's going to be. So you're right: I think we should call it a day."

"And we can't speak anymore?"

"Not a good idea."

"Not even on the phone?"

"It's just going to make me want to see you."

Then she stared into my eyes, her pupils going back and forth, and it seemed like she was going to say something—several things—but all she finally did was ask for a hug. Of course, I said; but the hug was too much, and I was about to cave and kiss her when I gently pushed her away. She was crying when we broke apart, and she wiped away her tears and laughed slightly, as if at her own sappiness, and said, "Well, I wish you all the best things."

"I wish you the same."

Then she walked off, and I stood there watching her go, and isn't it breaking your heart? Can't you just hear the string section? But I hadn't heard the last of her—nosirree, not by a long shot. It was only a matter of days before we spoke again, and, boy, did she have a few surprises that time!

BUT JUST THEN I THOUGHT IT WAS OVER. So I went home to yodel in the old thundermug, and at three in the morning called Terrence in New York—woke his ass up—and gave him a rambling account of my three-day affair with that amazing girl we'd seen at the Silverlake Lounge; how I'd just come from there and seen Buddy, and Jim Cassady was alive, he was alive, and I loved Irina—why did she have to be married? But it wouldn't have mattered anyway, she shook her ass for everything in pants, and there was a band playing, they were so great, so great, Peewee would have flipped, and I loved Irina still. And Terrence listened with great patience till he finally said, "Jason, what are you doing for Christmas?"

"No plans."

"You want to fly back here?"

"Can't afford it."

"I'll pay. I think you need a break from that place. You're cracking up."

"Just drunk."

"No, I think it's worse than that. You ought to move back here."

"What are you talking about? A year ago you told me to forget it!"

"Yeah, and a year ago you were sane. And I guess I've made my peace with it. It's fucked up everywhere. It's only a matter of degree."

He said he'd find a bargain ticket on the Internet, and I could crash on his sofa, and he knew of some great parties we could hit for New Year's. And this, of course, was a really important New Year's, concluding the century and the nineties too. That decade couldn't end fast enough as far as I was concerned. I never thought anything could be as dull as the seventies, but I now stood corrected. I kept telling Terrence I couldn't let him do it, but he said, "Shut up. You're coming to New York, and that's it." Great friend, yes? And he really has been, even though that trip was a minor catastrophe. But just in case I didn't seem grateful at the time: Thanks, man, for that and everything else.

At any rate, that gave me something to look forward to: Christmas in New York with Terrence. But I was at least two weeks from leaving, so to keep myself busy I started a script: an old idea I'd never thought commercial enough to sit down and write, much like the one about Rule of Thumb. It started off as a traditional Western, with a group of outlaws riding into town and stumbling on a lynch mob about to string up a piano player. His crime? Playing bad music. What kind of bad music? He's allowed to demonstrate. He bangs out a few chords of "Copacabana," and one of the outlaws shoots him dead and asks the mob if they want to hear some *good* music. Then we cut to the outlaws rocking out with electric guitars and everything, and the whole saloon—lynch mob and cowboys and barkeeps and whores—is moshing away at the foot of the stage. But corporate types from back east want to kill the outlaw-rockers and replace them with bland knockoffs they can easily control. Eventually, after a blazing gun battle, they succeed. The last of the great outlaw-rockers has bitten the dust. The Wild West has been tamed. But those are just the broad strokes. I had a lot of funny ideas, and I was making rapid progress when that Thursday, about midnight, the phone rang, and I saw a strange number on my caller ID. Curious, I picked up, and there was Irina, sounding so terrified from her first words there was no time for any I-thought-we-weren't-going-to-speak stuff.

"Thank God I got you!" she said. "Can you give me a ride?"

"Why? Where are you?"

"Eddie's house. I mean Jim. I'm here with Jim Cassady."

"*What?*"

"Please, I can't explain. The police are going to be here any minute."

"Is this some kind of joke?"

"No," she said urgently, "it's not. Can you please come get me? I don't have my car, and it's too far to take a cab, and I don't even know where I *am* right now."

There was a lot of commotion behind her: a barking dog, a running TV, lots of yelling and talking. I heard her ask somebody to tell me how to get there, and a second later an old lady with a voice like a parrot's came on the line and said, "Hello? Are you there?"

"I'm here. Who is this?"

"Never *mind* who this is. Are you going to come pick up this girl or aren't you?"

"Sure, I'll come get her. Where are you?"

Then she started spitting out very confusing directions, all leading to Rancho Cucamonga, wherever that was—a left here and a right there and two blocks later I'd see a tan house with a plastic Santa by the door. She was very impatient, and some guy was ranting in the background, and she broke off to say, "Shut up! Would you please shut up? I can't hear myself think!" I never had a chance to read back the directions. I tried, but she said, "The police are here," and, just like that, she hung up. My writing looked like hieroglyphics, I'd been rushed so badly, so I tried to call back and got a busy signal. What the hell was going on?

It sounded almost like a party. That was my first thought: that maybe Irina had gone to a party where, by a fluke, she'd met Jim Cassady, or maybe she just *thought* she had. But she'd specifically said she was at his house, so how had she managed to get there? And I was fairly sure I knew how, so why couldn't *he* drive her home? Especially when I'd have to spend my last few bucks for the gas to do it myself.

Still, I left immediately. I drove for maybe a half-hour down the 10 East, passing through at least a dozen suburbs—lots of fast-food signs lit up by the side of the road; not much traffic aside from big rigs. It was very cold and so windy that, at one point, I drove over a palm frond blown loose from a tree and dragged it for a stretch before pulling over to remove it. Finally I got to Rancho Cucamonga, and, Jesus, what a wasteland: just blocks and rows of stucco ranchhouses, one the same as the next. I kept trying to read the directions, but they made no sense, and passing a minimart with a pay phone outside, I stopped and called the crone, who picked up with: *"Yes?"*

"Yeah, I'm supposed to pick up my friend?"

"Well, it's about time! Where are you? Do you realize it's after one in the morning?!" There was no noise behind her now; it was all very quiet. I told her I must have the directions wrong, and she said, "Well, aren't *you* a prize?" and started spitting them out again.

"You can't miss it," she squawked. "It's the tan house with a plastic Santa on the porch."

"Can I speak to my friend?"

"You can speak to her when you get here. I'm not getting up one more time tonight. My feet hurt!"

Her revised directions weren't much better than the first, but I followed them till, maybe ten minutes later, I found myself on one of the streets she'd mentioned. It was higher in the hills, and some of the houses had boats in the driveway, but the houses themselves all looked the same. Finally I noticed a plastic Santa on the porch of a house with a blue television light flickering in the window. The Santa wasn't lit, so it didn't exactly leap right out at you, but this had to be the place; I parked across the street and walked to the edge of the property and read the name stenciled on the mailbox: McDANIEL—the same name I'd seen on my caller ID. Then I continued toward the front door, and the closer I got, the more I could make out the sound of the television—an episode of *M*A*S*H*, it sounded like. I rang the bell, and right away a dog started barking, and a second later the door swung open, and there was Irina. She looked terrible! Her skin was sallow, circles ringed her eyes, and her hair was lank and dirty and pulled back in a haphazard ponytail. Of course, compared to most people, she was still the most beautiful thing you ever saw, but for her, she looked like shit.

"Thank God you finally got here!" she said.

"Do you want to tell me what's going on?"

"I'll tell you in the car."

Then she went to join me on the porch, about to close the door when I stopped her. I said, "Is that really Jim in there?"

"Jason, please."

"Well, is it him or not?"

"It's him," she sighed.

"Can I see him?"

"You don't want to do that."

"Why not?"

"You just don't."

"Well, is he sleeping? I mean, come on, I've driven all this way. At least let me say *something*."

Then she sighed again and cracked the door, and to someone I couldn't see, she said, "My friend would like to come in for a minute. Do you mind?" The dog was barking; the TV was going; she stood there with her back turned to me. Then she turned around and gave me a look as if to say, "Well, okay. But don't say you weren't warned!" The way she was acting, you would almost have thought there were body parts lying around that place. There weren't, but, in its own way, it was still pretty grim.

I THINK THE FIRST THING THAT HIT ME, walking inside, was how hot it was, and then the odor. That house was like a giant ashtray. You could smell the smoke of countless cigarettes baked into the walls, and there was also a kind of burning-lint smell, like the heating vents were filled with dust accumulated in the warm months, and now, in winter, it was being fried. The carpet was grayish-green, matching most of the furniture, and there was a big cheap print of an autumn landscape hanging on one wall and, beside the front door, a wooden chair that leaned to one side as if broken. There were no books or plants; the only light came from the television; and sitting in profile watching *M*A*S*H* was an old man of sixty pressing what looked like a folded-up washcloth over one eye. It was a washcloth; I got a little closer. He didn't turn around, but at one point, almost as soon as I walked in, he leaned down to stub out his cigarette, and when he did that, I saw the flesh on the bottom of his arm do a kind of wiggle. He was as fat as a nursing sow, with a medicine ball for a stomach and a ball of white wax for a head; and it was soft wax, not hard; what with the heat it seemed to be melting. He was wearing a white T-shirt lightly stained with what looked like coffee, and his hair was white as well, or what was left of it—he was almost completely bald. He was also obviously drunk. A number of beer cans were on the coffee table in front of him, and after stubbing out his cigarette, he reached for a beer and sank back in his armchair, sipping it. The dog went on barking from someplace inside the house, but he didn't seem to hear it, just as he didn't acknowledge us. He just sat and drank beer while watching TV as if hypnotized.

Now, I honestly had no idea who this guy was till Irina came up beside me and gave me a glance as if to say, "Well, that's him. Pretty sad, huh?" He looked exactly as "tony68" had described him, assuming that story is true. I could've passed him on the street every day for a year and never recognized him. Then Irina called his name—"Eddie," not Jim—and he finally turned around, but even seeing him full-face instead of in profile, I could not identify this bloated, decrepit, one-eyed man as Jim Cassady.

"Eddie," Irina said, "this is Jason. Remember when I said I have a friend who's a fan of your band? Well, this is him." She spoke as if to a brain-damaged child, and he said, "Oh, that's nice," or something like that, and his voice was as wispy as the way I recalled it from our first encounter at CBGB's, with just a trace of the grain I knew from the records. Or at least it *seemed* that way—it was hard to hear between the sound of the TV and that fucking dog. Then he lowered the washcloth, revealing his hidden eye, and held out a couple of fingers for me to shake. His fingers were soft and damp like sponges, and his eye was red and swollen. It looked to me in the dim light like he might have conjunctivitis, and I was just about to ask when he suddenly shouted, "Shut the fuck up!" I freaked. I thought he was talking to me. But then he did it again—"SHUT! THE FUCK! UP!"—and I realized, no, he was shouting to the dog.

"He wouldn't be barking if you didn't have people here!" the crone yelled from another room.

"Go to hell!" Jim yelled back.

"I'm not kidding, Eddie! I want them gone!"

"Yeah, yeah, yeah!"

Then, like an afterthought, he mumbled, "You old battle-axe," and started cackling and looked up at me said, "Don't you love that?"

"Love what?" I said.

"When people say 'battle-axe.' They always say it on *The Flintstones*."

"Yeah, but you know what I like? Those dinosaurs that help around the house. They'll be washing the dishes, you know, or they'll be part of the stereo, and they'll stop working for a second and look up and say, 'It's a living!'"

But he'd turned back to the TV, and once he did that, he was hypnotized all over again. Then Irina started whispering something I couldn't make out. I kept saying, "What, what?" and she'd roll her eyes and repeat it in a voice still too low to be heard. Then Jim looked up and said, "Did you say something?" and I told him no, I was talking to Irina.

"Oh. Well, here, have a seat. You want a beer? There's plenty in the kitchen. Go help yourself."

"Thanks," Irina jumped in, "but we can't. Poor Jason has to drive all the way back to L.A."

"L.A.," he repeated, as if he'd never heard of it.

"That's where I live," I said.

"Oh? Which part?"

"Echo Park."

"Echo Park?"

"Yeah, it's near Dodger Stadium."

"I know. I used to live around there."

"Really. Which street?"

He just sat there staring at me.

"I'm sorry," he said finally. "Did you just say something?"

"Yeah. Which street in Echo Park did you used to live on?"

"Avon Street," he said, after taking a long moment to percolate.

"Oh? The hilly part or down around the park?"

But then he turned and shouted again for the dog to shut up—it was still barking after all that time—and the crone shouted back, "Eddie, are those people still here?"

"Go to sleep!"

"I *can't* sleep! Do you have any idea what time it is? *Some* people have to get up in the morning!"

"And some people kill their mothers!"

She fell silent, and Jim cackled and asked if we'd ever seen *Psycho*.

"Many times," I said.

"It's pretty great till the ending, don't you think? Don't you think the ending is kind of lame?"

"*Really* lame, yeah. The whole movie goes downhill after the shower scene."

"Yeah, the shower scene is great."

"But, you know, the best thing in the whole movie is when Janet Leigh is driving down the highway and hearing all those voices. I mean, all she's doing is driving, you know, but it's the scariest thing in the whole movie."

"What is?"

"When Janet Leigh is driving down the highway."

"Yeah," he said. "That's right." Yet I could tell he had no idea what I was talking about. What the fuck had happened? How could anybody disintegrate this thoroughly? It went way beyond Buddy's talk of fucked-up losers. And Irina was clutching me, tugging me toward the door, and I really couldn't blame her. Besides, I was going to take her home and fuck her three ways from Sunday. I mean, give me *something* for driving all that way.

So I told Jim we had to go, and he looked kind of sad and said, "No, have a seat. Get yourself a beer. There's plenty in the kitchen."

"Thanks," I said, "but we can't. We've got to head back."

"Oh? Where do you live?"

"Echo Park."

"Echo Park?"

Then we went through the whole thing all over again! But at least this time, when we got to the part about Avon Street, he said he used to live near the park. I said, "Yeah, I love the park. I like to go hiking in there."

"I used to do that. I wrote a poem about it."

"Oh? You still write poetry?"

"Write what?"

"Poetry."

"Yeah," he said, as if he wasn't so sure, "I write poetry."

"And music? You still play music?"

"I play music."

"So do you have a band or—?"

"Oh no," he said right away. "Just me."

I found it interesting, how fast he answered the band question. It was like a hint that he might have a bit of a brain left after all. But Irina looked like she was going to have a nervous breakdown if we didn't leave right that second, so once again I told Jim good night.

"It was a pleasure," I said, going to shake his hand again. "I can't even tell you what Rule of Thumb meant to me. You changed my whole life."

"Ha!"

"No, you really did. When I was eighteen, I quit my job and drove to New York from North Carolina to see you guys play."

"Really! How were we?"

"Well, I never got to see the show. My friend—the guy I was with—was underage, so they wouldn't let us in. But later on you walked outside and we talked to you for a long time."

"You did?"

"Well, it was mostly my friend. I was feeling kind of starstruck, you know. But you guys were really getting into it. You must have talked for a half-hour."

And then something truly remarkable happened. We were shaking hands, and he tightened his grip and looked at me—really *looked* for the first time—and at that moment I could see some resemblance to the person I'd met almost twenty years before. It was all in the eyes. One was red and watery, and the melting-wax lids partly concealed both, but something in the expression brought Jim Cassady before me.

"Was this at CBGB?" he said. "Did I meet you at CBGB?"

"Yeah, it was outside after the show."

Then he further tightened his grip, using his other hand to enclose mine, and he said, "Oh my God, you're that kid! You're that little kid that wouldn't shut up!"

"No, that was my friend."

"A real little kid, right? About this tall?" He said this with a hand held four feet from the floor, and Peewee wasn't *that* small, but I told him yes, I was so happy this was happening.

"And he had red hair, right? And he was smoking a cigar?"

Well, I'll be damned! When Terrence met us that night, he'd brought with him not just booze and coke but a couple of cigars, and later, outside CBGB's, Peewee and I smoked them. For some reason I'd blanked that part out, but now I caught just a flash of Peewee trying to light his cigar against the wind (*"Goddamnit! Motherfucker!"*) and got so excited I practically jumped up and down.

"That's right!" I said. "I'd forgotten all about that!"

It was a miracle! He couldn't remember what he'd said five seconds before, yet he still remembered Peewee and a detail I didn't. Even Irina seemed to share my excitement, as much as she wanted to go. I asked Jim if he remembered anything else, hoping he'd place me too, and he said, "Well, that night—I think Gary got in a fight or—I know something happened—and I walked outside to clear my head and that kid came up, and, man, that kid blew my fucking mind! I mean, ten years old and—*wasn't* he ten?"

"No, but he *looked* about ten."

"Yeah, but he was *so* smart. That kid was a fucking genius!"

I had goosebumps; I was close to tearing up. I wanted to grab a beer and keep talking, except Jim shouted again for the dog to shut up, and the old lady shouted back—still another reenactment of the call that had brought me there. Then I heard a door open and a wretched-looking mongrel came running into the room. I mean, this thing was misshapen to the point of freakishness, with a face like a sheep skull attached to a dog's body, and so fat it looked like a giant meatball with four straws sticking out of the bottom. It charged right up like it was going to bite us, and Irina cowered behind me, but the dog stopped short at the last second and retreated to a corner, still barking. Then the old lady walked in, and this, of course, was Jim's mother, yet the dog looked more like him than she did. She was really thin, for one thing, and she had a mess of curls dyed muddy brown and a face so wrinkled it looked like a piece of paper that's been crumpled and spread flat again. She marched right past us in a robe and slippers and opened the front door and said, "I'm sorry, but you've got to go. *Some* people have to get up in the morning!"

"Don't pay any attention to her," Jim said. "You can stay as long as you like."

"No, they cannot! You made me get up four times in one night, and you *know* I hate getting up! My feet hurt!"

"Would you shut up about your goddamn feet? I almost got my eye taken out, and you don't hear *me* complaining!"

"Serves you right! Inviting all these people into my house!"

Then Irina grabbed me and yanked me out the door, and I tried to say good night to Jim, but it wasn't like he or his mother noticed, they were so busy fighting. The dog noticed. It walked up to the door and barked as if to say it would bite us for sure if we ever returned. Then the old lady pulled the dog back and shut the door, yet halfway across the street, you could still hear them inside the house, going at it.

"Now, Eddie, I want you to go to bed! I will not have you waking me four times in one night!"

"Yeah, yeah, yeah!"

That was the last exchange I could really make out. My mind was reeling—I was still trying to process this whole bizarre scene—when suddenly, as if things weren't bizarre enough already, as if she had to raise the level that much higher, Irina came flying at me and said, "I love you!" and showered my face with kisses.

THIS IS WHY IT TOOK A WHILE before I could find out exactly how she'd come to be at Jim's place: first, before we'd even gotten in my car, she had to tell me what a terrible week she'd had; that ever since our fight she couldn't eat and couldn't sleep, and she'd never felt this way before, she was in love and there was no use fighting it, that was just the way it was. She didn't even want to go back to L.A., not yet; she wanted to find the nearest hotel and spend the night there. I was broke and said as much, but she said not to worry, she'd pay.

Then we got in my car, and I drove off trying to remember how I'd gotten there in the first place. I asked how *she'd* gotten there in the first place, and practically the first word out of her mouth was "Buddy."

"I knew it!" I said.

"Jason, you have to understand, I was so upset. For three days all I did was sit around and cry. And I wanted to call you, but you told me not to, and I was hoping you'd call me, but you never did."

"I couldn't have called even if I'd wanted. You never gave me your number."

"Of course I did."

"No, you definitely didn't."

"I'm sorry, I thought I had. I'll give it to you now."

"No, just tell me what happened."

"I've forgotten where I was."

"You were sitting around for the last three days."

"Yes, doing nothing. I couldn't sleep, I couldn't eat. All I did was cry and sit by the phone. And then tonight Buddy calls."

"So you gave Buddy your number."

"Yes."

"You gave your number to Buddy but you never gave it to me."

"Jason, please, I thought I *had* given it to you. It's been so crazy these last few months! My marriage is falling apart, my family is getting bombed, I'm doing this play, and all my friends keep turning against me. I feel like I'm losing my mind!"

"Okay, all right, go on."

"So," she collected herself, "Buddy called. And the only reason I gave him my number was so he could see my play and maybe you could speak to him again. And he asked me out for a drink, and I said I couldn't, I'm married, and it's one thing if he wants to see my play, but my husband wouldn't like it if I met him for a drink. And he said, 'That guy you were with the other night—that's not your husband, is it?' And I said no, and we started talking, and somehow I told him everything."

"What do you mean, everything?"

"I mean about us. I had to talk to somebody, and I can't tell my friends because most of them know David, and Buddy doesn't know one person I know, so it was like that made it all okay. And he was really understanding. He said he's been married three times and he cheated every time, and it's always a bad idea to cheat, it always comes back to hurt you—just giving me all this advice, you know. And he said, 'Are you sure you don't want to have a drink?' And I thought, 'You know what? I'm going. I've got to get out of this house or I'm going to go crazy!' And I was really enjoying our talk, and I thought, 'What harm can it do?'

"So we met at this place Cobalt—it's right down the street—and Buddy kept telling me all these things about himself. Like he has a daughter in—oh, I forget where—but he has a daughter he never sees, and he feels bad about that, and he used to have a brother, and his brother was a junkie who died from an overdose. He was in Rule of Thumb too, but I guess you know that."

"Of course."

"Yes, I knew you would. And he told me he used to fool around with drugs himself, but he was never a junkie, but Jim used to be a *terrible* junkie. Then he started talking about Jim, and I mean he *really* talked about him. He said he has all these phobias and he's afraid to leave the house, and Buddy's tried so many times to help him, but every time he does, he gets kicked in the teeth. That's what he said: 'I just get kicked in the teeth!' But you could also tell he admires him in a way. He said he was so smart and talented, and it was such a shame this smart, amazing, talented person was so fucked up. I said, 'Well, I'd love to meet him one day.' And he said, 'Why?' And I said, 'Well, Jason's told me so much about him, and he played me one of your records, and I thought it was really beautiful.' And he said, 'Would you really like to meet him? I could take you over. He's not doing anything. He *never* does anything.' And I can't believe he's saying this! I thought, 'Poor Jason! He tries so hard to find him, and now Buddy is talking about taking me right over!'"

"And he offered just like that."

"Just like that, yes."

"And you weren't flirting with him."

"I don't think so."

"Well, either you were or you weren't."

"Yes, but, Jason, people *always* think I'm flirting when I'm not trying to flirt at all! I just try to be nice, you know, and they think things and get mad at me when I'm not the way they think I am. And if I'm *not* nice, they say I'm a bitch. They get mad no matter what."

"Yeah, but how many times do I have to tell you this? You bring it on yourself. I mean—remember that time we played pool? I was practically feeling you up, and you just stood there letting me!"

"But I wanted you to. I was in love with you."

"Even then?"

"Well, I didn't want to admit it, but I think I was. It started when I saw your film. I was *so* impressed. I thought, 'I've really got to meet this guy!' Then I realized I'd met you already, and then I met you again that day at Astrid's, and that's when it really hit me. I was afraid you might be disappointing, but, no, I loved everything about you. You looked so sleepy and you had your little beer belly, and I thought that was so cute; I hate it when guys look so perfect. And we talked about all these big subjects, and you said such smart things, and I *loved* the way you smelled. It was—I don't know—everything together. And I could see you had problems, I could see you weren't happy, but this was something I liked too; I'm not so happy myself. I was dying to kiss you."

"I felt the same way."

"I know you did, I could tell. That's why I wasn't so nice that night at the party: I didn't want to encourage you. Or myself either! I was having all these problems with David, and you were going out with Astrid—someone who hates me already—and I thought, 'You must really want trouble, to fall in love with this guy. You can't fall in love with *anybody*, but especially not *him*.' And that's why I didn't call you all that time: I was afraid if I did, I'd sleep with you. I was dying to sleep with you! You don't know how close I came the first time we kissed. After I drove away, I almost turned around and came back."

I got violently turned on when she told me all that. I wanted to pull over and take her right there—not a great idea on a cold night in a small car by the side of the road. Meantime I'd gotten lost. I had no idea where I was; I might be headed in the wrong direction altogether—only a local would know the difference, and possibly not even a local. And Irina kept pouring her heart out, and I was getting more and more turned on, when she somehow resumed her story about Buddy. They were leaving Cobalt, she said, and she was going to follow him to Jim's place, but Buddy had insisted she ride along with him, since it was so far she'd probably get lost.

"Also," she said, "I was a little drunk, and Buddy didn't seem drunk at all. I thought it was probably in Santa Monica or, you know, someplace like that, so I got in his car, and he never tried anything in the restaurant, but as soon as he started driving, he kept touching me."

"What do you mean, he touched you?"

"I mean he touched me! He'd put his hand on my knee or he'd put it around my neck, and I acted like it was all a big joke, you know; I'd push his hand away and ask him how much further it was. I was so scared! I thought he was going to take me out to the desert and kill me! I mean, how stupid could I have *been*, to get in a car with somebody I barely know! Then we get to this place, and I can't believe this is where he would live. I said, 'Are you sure this is right?' And he said, 'Yes, I'm sure it's right.' Then this fat old man came to the door, and I thought, 'Oh, this must be his father.' Because you showed me that record, and I thought he looked sort of beautiful, and I know that was a long time ago, but Buddy—he's Jim's age, and he doesn't look so bad. But I guess he's had plastic surgery."

"Has he?"

"Well, he never said so, but I think he has. Then we went inside, and the house smelled awful, and Jim was really drunk, even though you could still sort of talk to him. He wasn't as bad as he was when you got there. I just wanted to go, you know, but we'd come so far, so I was hoping we'd just stay for a couple of minutes and leave. And that dog—it was acting like it wanted to kill me. It must have smelled the cat on my clothes—don't you think that's it?"

"Maybe."

"Yes, I think that's what it was. And Jim's mother—she was so rude. She told us to leave as soon as we got there, and Buddy and Jim were yelling at her and she was yelling at them—it was completely insane. Then she took the dog and left us alone and Buddy started drinking, and he tried to get me to drink with him, but I wouldn't do it. I didn't even want to sit down! He and Jim were talking about all these people—'Have you seen Trudie?'; that kind of thing—and I was so bored. I kept saying, 'You know, I really have to go,' and Buddy said, 'We'll leave in a minute,' but he just kept sitting there, and he kept trying to touch me, and finally I said, '*Please* don't do that,' and that's when he got mean. He was mean to both of us, but he was *really* mean to Jim. He said, 'Where's that five hundred dollars you owe me?' And Jim said, 'What five hundred dollars?'

And Buddy said, 'You know perfectly well what five hundred dollars. I want my money, and I'm not leaving till you give it to me.' And I knew something bad was going to happen, and I kept trying to get Buddy to leave, but he wouldn't. Then Jim's mother came back and said, 'If you don't leave right this minute, I'm calling the police!' and I thought the dog was going to attack me and I asked her to please hold it, and she yelled at me for yelling at her about the dog! Then—the next thing I saw—Jim had his hand over his face, and Buddy was standing there hitting him. It was terrible! You could see Buddy is so much stronger than he is, and Jim was going, *'Mom, help, he's hitting me! Help, help!'* I kept shouting at Buddy to stop it, but the more I did, the more that stupid dog acted like it was going to bite *me*, not Buddy, even though he was hitting his own master! Then I looked up, and Jim's mother was running in with a chair, and she hit Buddy over the head with it."

"No!"

"Yes! Then Buddy ran out the door, and I went over to see if Jim was okay and I heard Buddy's car starting, and I tried to get outside, but that dog—it had me cornered! Then, somehow, I got outside, and Buddy was gone, and I stood there waiting for him to come back, but he never did. I was going to call him, but—can you believe this?—my phone was dead. And I hated to go back inside that house, but I really had no choice.

"So I knocked on the door, and Jim's mother—I didn't think she was *ever* going to let me in. I said, 'Please, Buddy left me here, just let me call someone to get a ride home.' Then she finally opened the door, and she called me all these names—I was a whore and a drug addict; I must be if I was hanging around with Buddy—and you were the first person I tried, and thank God I got you! Then the police got there, and they were mean to me too, like 'Where do you come from? Are you in this country legally?' and thank God I just happened to have my passport or they might have arrested me. Jim's mother told them Buddy had come over to try and sell drugs to her son, and they asked me if it was true, and I said, 'No, it's not.' And she said, 'Don't listen to her, she's on drugs too,' and I was so scared they were going to arrest me, I almost wet in my pants."

"So who do you think they believed?"

"Well, they didn't arrest me, so I guess they believed *me*. But I think Buddy could be in a lot of trouble. And I hope he is, leaving me like that!

Then the police left, and I sat there with Jim and his mother, and that dog—it just sat there growling at me. I hate that dog! I was *so* afraid you weren't going to come. I swear, every second felt like hours."

"Yeah, but the directions were all fucked up. I tried to call back and couldn't get through."

"Yes, she didn't put the phone back the right way. I tried to call you again, and the phone was off the hook. So we all sat there waiting, and Jim and his mother—it was so strange—they'd be really nice to each other, and then they'd be really mean. Then she went to bed again, and—was that you that called?"

"Yeah, to get directions."

"Yes, I thought it was probably you. The phone rang, and I was going to get it, but I heard her get it in the next room. I just sat there watching TV with Jim, and he barely said a word the whole time. God, he's strange. They're *all* strange. I thought it might be a *little* strange, but not like that. What's *wrong* with them?"

SOMEWHERE BETWEEN RANCHO CUCAMONGA and Who The Fuck Knows, we passed a motel by the side of the road. By then Irina was saying we should head back to my place, but I was in the kind of state where I couldn't hold off; so she paid for a room with a credit card, and all I can say is, if beds could talk, we sure gave that one a filthy mouth. Again, I'd prefer not to elaborate, but at one point I told her I wanted to carve my name inside her, I didn't want her to ever make a single move where she couldn't feel it; and when I said that, she came in a big way, and I did too, pulling out in the nick of time—or just about. And that room was so antiseptic it smelled like the passenger cabin on a jumbo jet, but just then it felt like the most romantic place I'd ever been—the sound of lonely cars driving down the road; headlights forming patterns on the wall. We made love till the brink of dawn, and afterward Irina said she'd leave David as soon as his movie was over, that she couldn't do it before because she knew if she did, he'd never get over it, and that was something she simply couldn't live with.

"I still care about him," she said. "Not the way I care about you, but I care. He's been trying to make this movie for ten years, and all his others weren't so good, you know? So there's really a lot at stake."

"And for you too, right?"

"Oh, Jason, please. *Please* don't say things like that; it makes me sound so *awful*. Yes, I'd like to do that part, but that's not the real reason. It's just not the right time. And it's not so long to wait. The movie will be over in a few months. I can tell him then."

"Yeah, but if you do this movie, who are you going to stay with? David, right? And, look, I know you're married—I knew that from the get-go—but things are different now. If we're going to be together, we're going to be together. You can't go off and live with somebody else for the sake of a movie, even if it's somebody you're married to."

Finally she said I was right. She'd tell him at Christmas, she said. He was in Prague in preproduction, and she was going to spend Christmas in Belgrade, where at some point he was supposed to join her. Then she asked about my Christmas plans, and I told her my friend Terrence was going to fly me to New York.

"Is he the one Jim was talking about?"

"No," I said, "that's Peewee."

"And who's that?"

"You know who he is. He's the guy that overdosed in my movie."

"You mean that actor?"

"Oh, no. Fuck, no. He would have killed me if he'd seen the guy I had playing him. No, I mean the guy he was based on."

"So all that really happened?"

"Well, most of it, yeah. I mean, it didn't happen exactly that way, because—you know, it was so complex, what went on, there was no way I could've told the whole thing in ninety minutes."

"But he overdosed. That happened, yes?"

No, I said. I told her how he really died, and then I took her back to the early days. I talked about things I hadn't talked about in years, since there was no way she could know me without knowing all that. We spooned in bed in a room that smelled like an airplane, and I talked and talked while the sun came up, and the world looked brighter all the time. And, more or less, this is what I said.

Two...

You made me what I am
And hated what you made
When I dared to contradict you
But I was so confused in those days
And you were just as crazed in your way
The doctor and his monster
Both so full of contradiction

                                          Superego

T HE FIRST TIME I SAW PEEWEE was shortly after the start of my senior year of high school. Every day I used to get to school early and sit around the cafeteria with a group of my friends, most of them athletes, just sort of shooting the shit and waiting for the day to begin, when one morning a second-string football player named Mark Powell froze in mid-sentence and started gawking across the room. Everybody else was gawking too, and we'd just gotten a fresh batch of freshman girls, so I turned in my seat, expecting to see the pick of the litter, and instead noticed a strange little kid turning the lock on his locker. He was tiny, maybe four foot ten, but he wasn't just tiny in the short sense; everything about him was undersized, from his bird-boned build to his scaled-down head. Yet everything he wore was a size or three too big: a motorcycle jacket covered with brightly colored pins and baggy pants tucked into work boots with no laces. His nose was pug, his jaw was soft, his eyes were black and beady. And then—the final touch—he'd shaved off most of his hair. Nobody did that in those days, not in that town, aside from state troopers and Moose Lodge types.

Well, we all just sat there staring at him—in fact, the whole cafeteria seemed to come to a halt. And he kept trying to open his locker, and for some reason the door was stuck, so he started slamming it with his tiny fist. He slammed it several times before he walked away, but after a few steps he ran back to kick it, limping slightly when he walked away again. Then he passed by our table, and, taking us in, he nodded with an impudent, closed-lip smile and said very casually, very simply, "Hey." And nobody said a word back. We just watched him limp off in his floppy boots, and after he'd gone, Mark Powell shook his head and said, "What the hell was *that*?" Which, since every one of us had been wondering the same thing, had us in stitches.

Now, at most high schools there are certain clothes you *have* to wear, and ours was no exception. It was khakis and Izod shirts and Oxford button-downs—if you deviated in any way, you were dead and buried socially. And this had everything to do with the local university: a prestigious school mostly attended by affluent northerners who often liked the town to the point where they stayed on after graduating. These were leaders in their fields in some cases—doctors, lawyers, professors, architects—and my friends were their children, and they set the standard for every white kid at my school. They were smart and glib and going places. Yet they were also incredibly narrow-minded. Their instinct for class was infallible, so that if you weren't one of theirs—and they always *knew*—you were mercilessly excluded. I was only allowed in because I played sports and took the same collegebound classes. And even then I knew my standing was shaky.

So that's how it was for a lemming like me. I'm sure you can guess how it was for Peewee. He got to that school and people couldn't stop talking about him. Even people at other schools were talking about him. I remember once I was at a party and some kid from way out in the sticks asked if I knew Bernard Mash. (His nickname wasn't coined till some time later, and nobody in North Carolina referred to him by it, apart from me.) I said, "Well, I know who he *is*. We don't hang out or anything." And he said, "Yeah, I met him over at Planet Records. Man, is he *gay* or what?"

That's what a lot of people decided, though he wasn't effeminate in the slightest. He was a brainy Jew from New York City who dressed like TV's Fonzie, but he rarely got shit for any of that; it was mostly for being "gay." He was weird, right? Wasn't that the same as gay? Redneck kids would taunt him with the usual slurs—"fag" or "faggot" or "homo" or "queer"—and usually he'd shrug it off, but sometimes he'd take on guys more than twice his size. I never saw it myself, but I heard stories; and once, walking down the hall, I passed our principal, Mr. Wright, frog-marching Peewee toward his office after breaking up a fight. Peewee's face was a bloody mess, and he cursed like a cathouse parakeet, going, "I'll *kill* his ass! I'll motherfucking *kill* him!" And Mr. Wright said, "All right, that's another day. You want to try for the whole week?" Suspension talk. I was soon to hear something similar from Mr. Wright, but worse. Much worse.

But the elite kids were too sophisticated for outright taunts. They treated misfits like unwitting jesters, and Peewee treated them much the same way. He hated conformity above all things and considered my friends the worst offenders, so in the morning, while we sat in the cafeteria, he'd amuse himself by playing the role of freak to the hilt. He'd scratch his ass and sniff his fingers with gusto. He'd talk out loud to invisible people. Then he'd shut his locker with a judo kick or a butt of the head soccer-style and, passing by our table, spout off a twisted catchphrase like "I love the smell of Nikes in the morning!" or "Things go better with codeine!" And sometimes we'd laugh, and sometimes we'd glare till he walked out of sight and ask each other what *that* was supposed to mean. Things went better with what? Was that some kind of drug? Well, that explained everything! Yet, secretly, I think we all looked forward to those early-morning shows. He was really kind of riveting in a way. What strange thing would he say or do next?

Well, one morning, maybe a month after he first appeared at school, he passed by our table with his hair dyed red. *Blood* red. And guys didn't dye their hair back then, and certainly not a color like that. We were more than shocked; we were morally affronted. Mark started calling him to the table, and Megan, my girlfriend, said, "Mark, *please* leave him alone." She was afraid he'd do him physical harm. Mark said, "I'm just going to talk to him"; and he kept calling Peewee to the table, and Peewee kept ignoring him till, finally, he closed his locker and walked up with a kind of *"Yes?"* look on his face. And Mark said, "What's going on with your hair?"

"My harem? They're fine, thanks for asking."

It took a few seconds for that to sink in. Then Mark said, "No, you dyed your hair."

"You mean my hair is *dead*?" He reached up to feel it. "Are you sure? Feels alive to me."

His dumb act disconcerted Mark, who, now pissed, said, "You know what I mean, fag. It's red."

"Really? Oh my God, I must have a massive head injury! I *knew* I shouldn't have hit myself with that hammer!"

Then he turned and, clutching his scalp while babbling to himself like a disoriented trauma victim, walked away. At the time I thought that was the strangest, sorriest, most pathetic thing I'd ever had the misfortune to witness, but when I think about it now, when I think about Mark Powell watching him go in a state of exasperation, I want to dig up that kid and hug him.

I NEVER SAID A WORD THAT DAY. I barely spoke to him for most of that year. Later, after my whole life had been shattered, I would finally get to know him; but before then we had just one semi-lengthy exchange, and that took place on a late-fall day in the library. He was always in the library. I knew because there was a long balcony that ran above it, and since he didn't look like anyone else I'd ever seen, he was very easy to spot. He was usually reading at a table by himself or sitting by a window that faced the parking lot and, just beyond it, a road that led to Interstate 40. I saw him there many times, slouched and staring out that window, looking like the loneliest kid in the world. Which, in those days, he may well have been.

But on this particular day *I* was the one sitting by the window. A few weeks before I'd fractured my ankle in a key game with our crosstown rival, and I'd been doing so well before then; I'd been Player of the Week and knew for certain I was being scouted by at least one college, and coming from a family that struggled to get by, I was badly in need of an athletic scholarship. So now I knew I'd blown my chances, and I was feeling kind of sorry for myself, though, looking back, it was all a pipe dream anyway. I was good at football, but not what I'd call a blue-chip talent. I played with a lot of heart, as they say. I played to get my aggressions out. And I had a lot of them: the town, the school, that constant status anxiety. Plus I was horny to the point of priapism, but I'll get to that later. And then there were the times themselves. Because I wanted something to happen, I didn't know what, and I was stuck in a place still mired in the seventies, and, next to the nineties, those were the dullest damned years I ever lived through. I mean, I was pretty dim in those days, and even *I* knew something was missing. Yet for all that, my dream was to head off to college and get a good job and live in a big house with a preppie wife and all the Oxford button-downs money could buy. I just didn't want to do it in North Carolina. I didn't care where it was, so long as it wasn't there.

So that's what I thought as I sat by the window. Not that I remember *that* exactly, but since that's all I ever thought about (when I wasn't thinking about sex), it's a safe bet I was thinking it then. It was sixth-period study hall, the one class I shared with Megan, and she had to write a paper on Freud, so she'd gone to find a book about him, and she stayed so long I started asking everyone who passed me if they knew where she was. Finally somebody said, "Yeah, she's back there talking to Bernard Mash." (That's the way he was always referred to in high school: always by the first and last name, as if to keep him separate from the other Bernards, though he was the only one.) And the second I heard that, I knew exactly what had happened. She'd bumped into him and said hello, the same way she said hello to everybody, and he'd taken it for a sign of genuine friendliness, which in a sense it was, and now she was stuck talking to him. It happened all the time. She didn't know how to say "Got to run now." Her first priority was being liked, so she was nice to everybody, including misfits; and since most cheerleaders kept to their own, she was easily the best-liked girl at our school. It didn't exactly hurt that, except for a too-high forehead and a hefty rack and shoulders, she looked like a real-life Barbie.

I thought about leaving her back there. I was always telling her she needed to assert herself (a big word back then: everyone was always *asserting* themselves), but she'd still strand herself with people she didn't like and bitch about it later. So maybe this time she'd learn her lesson. But then she didn't come back, and she didn't come back, and I thought, "All right, let's go bail her out. I'm sure she'll appreciate it. Maybe she'll give me a blowjob later." (Dream on!)

So I reached for my crutches and pulled myself up and gimped my way to the stacks, where this kid had said he'd seen her, and sure enough, there she was, and there was the freak, who was running his rodent mouth a mile a minute. Megan's back was turned, and the closer I got, the more I could make out what the freak was saying, and, holy shit, it was a language I'd never quite heard before. Yes, it was English, but he was talking about Freud, about whom I knew nothing, and sounding almost like a book himself. It was: "This whole idea Freud had, that people have to repress parts of themselves in order to function in society, is complete *bullshit* in my opinion, because *animals* have societies, and *they're* not doing much repressing. I mean, apes, yes, that might be possible. And dogs—dogs are very similar to people; their brains are virtually the same, apparently. But a lot of *lower* animals have societies. Fish, for instance. And birds. And ants. Now, how much repressing do you think *ants* do?"

Now, maybe this doesn't sound particularly impressive, but you have to understand it was coming from a sophomore in high school who looked more like a fourth-grader, and yet he spoke with such authority and near-fanatical fervor. He looked like a fucking maniac while he stood there, his black eyes like BBs lit from within, his hair like a blood-soaked beanie. There was a sense of stumbling on a secret somehow, as if I'd tripped on a rug and discovered a cellar that wasn't in the floor plan. And that window in the library was really big, so if it happened to be cloudy outside, it got dark in the library too, particularly back in the stacks. And it *was* cloudy that day, and the darkness was part of the spook factor. Then he saw me and broke off, and Megan turned and saw me as well, and her eyes met mine as if to say: *Did you hear all that? Can you fucking believe it?* She moved to me and said to Peewee, "Well! Thank you for that! That was very...helpful!" Then he gave a kind of "Aw, shucks" shrug with his face averted, and Megan held up the book she'd gone to find as if to say, "Got it! We can go now!" Yet I couldn't move. Because now that I'd heard this creature speaking in tongues, I had to know more about his—its—background.

So I said, "Hey, Bernard. That's your name, right? Bernard?" And he looked like he couldn't believe I was speaking to him in a somewhat friendly voice, like it was all a trick to set him up for the inevitable insult.

"Uh-huh," he said.

"Somebody told me you burned down your last school. Is it true?" And with that he lowered his guard a shade.

"Well," he said, "kind of. See, what happened was, I was smoking in the boys' room, and instead of throwing my cigarette in the toilet, I threw it in the trash and the bathroom caught on fire. Well, the bathroom and part of the hallway. They caught it before it spread too far, but it was bad enough they had to shut down the school for a couple of days."

"And this was in New York?"

"Brooklyn," he nodded. Which meant practically nothing to me. I knew vaguely that Brooklyn was close to Manhattan, but just how close I couldn't say. I asked how he'd managed to end up here, and he said it was where his parents had sent him after he set fire to that bathroom. His sister was a graduate student at the university, he said, and his parents were essentially paying him a salary to live with her and away from them.

"I'm quite a handful," he told us proudly.

"So what do you think of this place?" And he laughed a do-you-really-want-to-know-what-I-think laugh and said, "Does the word '*hell*' mean anything to you?"

And it's funny; I thought it was hell myself, but when he said that, I almost felt like sticking up for it. Why didn't he run away if he hated it so much? Nobody liked him anyway. And there were a few other things I wouldn't have minded asking, such as why he never seemed to change his clothes, and why they didn't fit, and what was the meaning of all those buttons he wore, and why, of course, the red dye-job? I knew the last must be connected with rock music in some way, since I'd seen pictures of David Bowie, for instance, with his hair dyed even stranger colors; but why would anybody want to look like David Bowie? And why did he act so weird in the morning? *Why?*

But I'd had all I could take for the time being. Somebody might see us together! I hobbled off with Megan, and as soon as she thought he couldn't hear, she said, "God, he's strange. But he is awfully bright, don't you think?"

"He's a Jew," I shrugged. Which was all I'd ever been told about Jews: they were very smart. Not to mention evil.

THAT CHRISTMAS MEGAN WENT TO KENTUCKY to visit her father. Her parents had recently divorced after her father had run off with a woman half his age, and Megan was pissed about it, while her mom sought comfort with old John Barleycorn. Not that she barhopped. She only drank at home, and even then she wouldn't touch the stuff till six or seven at night, but once that rolled around, she couldn't mix the drinks fast enough. Sometimes I'd drink with her. I'd drop by, and she'd say, "Well, Jason, can I get you a beer?" And Megan would say, "No, Mom, you cannot." And Gail, her mom, would laugh and say, "Oh, Megan, stop. We both know Jason drinks." I drank quite a bit, as a matter of fact. I'd only been going to frat parties since I was fourteen. And Mark

Powell was a pothead, and so were others in that crowd, so I'd certainly done my share of weed; and I liked how Gail took that kind of thing for granted, whereas my own parents didn't. Both were teetotalers. And both had strong Southern accents, and I was really embarrassed by that; I used to cringe when they got around my friends. But Gail came from the Midwest, so she spoke like a normal person, and she'd traveled and lived around the country before settling in North Carolina, while my own parents had barely left the state. So I would have much preferred to have a mom like Gail, even if she was a drunk, and I knew she liked me too. She always talked a lot to me when she answered the phone or I came by the house, so much so that Megan would get jealous. She'd say, "For God's sake, Mom, he's *my* boyfriend." Other times, if she didn't like the way Gail was acting, she'd tell her to go to bed—and I don't mean she'd *ask* her, I mean she'd say, "Go to bed, Mom! *Now*!" And Gail would do as told. It was a very strange relationship. They were more like sisters than mother and daughter, and so far as that went, Gail was more the daughter and Megan more the mom. They even looked like sisters. Gail would have been around forty at that time, but in the right light she could easily have passed for ten years younger—blonde, like Megan, with Megan's big tits and too-high forehead, but without the boxy shoulders Megan had gotten from her father, who'd once been the lacrosse coach at the university. Then he met this girl at a game in Kentucky and took a job there, and since he now planned to marry her, he wanted Megan to come up for Christmas so the two could meet.

At first she refused. She was intensely preoccupied with what people thought of her, and her father's affair had been reported in the paper—the worst thing that could possibly happen to a girl who once stayed home from school for nearly a week on account of a cold sore. But she was also an only child who knew she'd have to bury the hatchet sooner or later, so it might as well be now. That was Gail's advice, and mine too; so the night before Christmas Eve I drove her to the train station, and right before she left, she said, "Jason, would you do me a favor? If you aren't doing anything tomorrow night, could you stop by and see my mom? Because she's going to be all alone, and we've never spent a Christmas apart, and I'm a little worried about her." I would, I said, and then the train started moving, and I ran down the platform waving goodbye while she waved back from her window. And that's my fondest memory of Megan. She really was a sweet girl, even though it was partly camouflage. The real

Megan was much more complicated than she liked to let on—in fact, I didn't know myself how complicated she was till a few months later, and I definitely found out then!

At any rate, the next night I dropped by Gail's, as promised, and I could tell she'd been drinking the second she came to the door. Not that I cared. I was used to it. I'd brought her a gift—a box of chocolates—and she seemed pleased about that and invited me in for a beer. As I say, that was par for the course, so I went inside, and she got us some drinks, and we sat in the living room talking. I remember a lot of it was about my future plans: the schools I'd applied to, and what I should study if and when I went to one. I'd never been sure about that. When I was really young, I wanted to be an Apache Indian, then a cement-truck driver, then a professional football player; and none of those paths were looking too promising, except for driving a cement truck, and that was exactly the kind of life I was hoping to escape. So we talked about that, and Gail said, "Well, you're young. You've got plenty of time to figure it out." She got me another beer, and that was *not* par for the course—usually I'd have just one—but it was Christmas Eve, and there was a really nice feeling in the room. It was like, without Megan there, we were a little more natural, a little more the way we really were. I had another beer and another one, and Gail kept drinking herself, and I knew I should be going, I knew my parents would start to worry, and a few times I said as much, but somehow I just kept sitting there. And everything was fine, Gail didn't seem to have a care in the world, when she started crying. It came completely out of the blue. One minute she was chatting away, the next it was, *"Waaaaaa."* I said, "What is it? What's wrong?" and she went, *"Waaaaaa."* I said, "I'm sorry?" and it seemed like she was trying to explain, but it all sounded like *"Waaaaaa"* to me. I was half wasted and out of my depth, so I put my arm around her and tried to comfort her as best I knew how; and she sobbed on my shoulder for quite some time till, finally, she stopped moving altogether. I thought, since she'd had so much to drink, she must have passed out.

So I was stuck. I sat with this drunken woman sleeping on my shoulder, afraid to move, otherwise she might wake and start crying again. The TV was going next to the Christmas tree, and *The Homecoming*, that freaking CBS Christmas movie that used to come on every December, was playing at low volume. Then *The Homecoming* ended with—what else?—a homecoming, and the local news followed with its annual disadvantaged-children-celebrate-the-holiday story. Or maybe somebody's house had burned down due to faulty electric decorations—that was the other annual Christmas story. And Gail continued to sleep on my shoulder. And I realized I had a hard-on.

Now, in those days I had a hard-on around the clock. I could hardly look at a half-attractive woman without wanting to fuck her, and for that matter I could sexualize almost anything. I'd see a chair and think, "I wonder how many pussies have sat in that thing?" Instant hard-on. I'd pass a motel and think, "I wonder how many people have fucked in there?" Instant hard-on. I used to jerk off two and three and four times a day, and, boing, the goddamned thing would spring back up all over again. It was like a movie monster that will not die, and Megan was no help at all. She would not let me fuck her. I could dry-hump her, I could play with her tits; once she started giving me a handjob, but after a few strokes she stopped and made me take her home. More reputation paranoia. And no way could I break up with her, and no way was I going to fool around, because she was *Megan*: cheerleader, homecoming queen, queen of the junior prom. Which made me king. That's right, I ruled the fucking prom, and half the school got laid afterward, and guess what the king got? Blue balls, same as always. Yet I knew I was unbelievably lucky that Megan had ever agreed to date me in the first place. Even my own parents used to tell me that. They adored Megan. They loved her, I think, more than they even loved me. And I loved her too in my teenaged way, but to be with her was also torture.

So there I was with Gail, who, as I've said, was a dead ringer for Megan, and I'd be lying if I said I'd never thought about fucking her, but, again, I thought that about most women. And, obviously, I knew the difference between thinking and acting. But then she rearranged herself, inching a little closer. Then she did it again, stroking my chest as if acting out a romantic dream on a pillow. She was breathing kind of hard—it was hot on my neck—and I was getting more and more excited but also more and more nervous. I couldn't see her face—I couldn't see anything but the top of her head—but more all the time I had the impression that she was feigning sleep and hoping I'd make a move. And I did *not* make one. I was too scared to move at all.

Then she did the unthinkable. Her hand was on my chest, right? And she was stroking it? Well, gradually she moved her hand to my crotch and started rubbing my dick through my pants. I was sweating; my heart was pounding; I could not believe this was happening. Then she opened her eyes and smiled drunkenly and moved to kiss me, and at first I didn't kiss her back, but she kept stroking my dick while pressing her mouth against mine. Then I *did* kiss her back; our tongues rolled around, and I groped her tits while she pulled down my zipper, pulled out my dick, and that was the deal closer, right there. I was no longer scared in the slightest. I loosened my pants and climbed on top of her, but the sofa was so cramped, and the Christmas tree seemed like a note of reproach. So I started to get up, and she tried to restrain me, and I said, "I'm not going anywhere," and picked her up and carried her down the hall to her bedroom with my pants falling off and threw her down on her bed. We dry-humped, and I said, "I want to fuck you so bad!" and she said, "I *want* you to fuck me! I want your big, hard dick inside me!" That's pretty much an exact quote, and hearing it, I almost shot my wad on the spot. We tore out of our clothes—and they came off fast!—and, naked, she spread so far apart it looked like she'd snap in two and I popped my dick inside her, and, man, she felt like she was coated with hot syrup, and every time I thrust, she'd whimper and moan while staring up with wide, astonished eyes. And that look and her smell and the way she looked like Megan—all of it sent me right over the edge, so that I probably wasn't inside her a good twenty seconds before I started convulsing. I said, "I'm going to come!" and she said, "Don't come inside me!" and I pulled out just in time, and, man, the hole in my dick opened to the size of a dime; cum was just flying out, and every time some of it splashed on Gail, she'd jerk in a really violent way and say, "*Oh! Oh! Oh! Oh!*" I felt that blastoff in every nerve in my body, as if every last inch of my skin was charged, and finally I stopped convulsing and collapsed on top of Gail. I wasn't a virgin; I'd fucked a few girls before I started dating Megan, but I hadn't lasted long with them either, so now that I had Gail I was going to ride her as long as she'd let me. I fucked her a second time, harder. A third time, ditto. Every time we did it, I could last a little longer, so that somewhere in the middle of the fourth round she said she couldn't take it anymore.

"I can't," she panted. "You've worn me out."

But she wouldn't leave me hanging. No, she flipped around and sucked my dick while I ate her raw pussy, and when I came, she licked up every last drop, going *"Mmmmmmm"* the whole time. And I write all these details so there's not a single doubt she was an eager, willing participant every step of the way, and also because, frankly, it still turns me on after all this time. It was the purest fuck I ever had—the most animal, the most apocalyptic—and when it was over, when she finished drinking my load, she moved back to the pillow and stroked my face and cried again. She didn't explain, and I didn't ask, afraid she'd mention Megan. She cried till once again she appeared to pass out, and I got up and dressed and drove home to face my parents, who were both awake and beside themselves with worry. "We thought you were dead! We called the rescue squad three times!" I told them I'd gotten a flat and the spare was flat too, or some bullshit, but they weren't buying it. They grounded me for the rest of Christmas break, sure I'd been up to no good, and I lay awake for a long time that night, plotting ways to sneak out of the house and have another go at Gail.

⌒

WELL, OF COURSE I WAS DREAMING. She called a few days later and said, "We need to talk," sounding so serious I almost felt like throwing up. She claimed she couldn't remember exactly what we'd done, so I led her through it as tactfully as possible, and she said, "Oh my God, we did *that*?" and started crying yet again and said she was so sorry, she was such a bad mother; poor Megan, and poor Jason too. She begged me not to tell Megan—"It would kill her," she said—and I thought, "Yeah, like I'm going to go tell Megan!" I wasn't so confident about Gail. Still, we both promised we'd never say a word. "It never happened," she said. So, fine, got *that* settled.

But then Megan got back from Kentucky, and talk about wanting to throw up! She was so glad she'd gone now. Her father was so happy with his fiancée, and Megan really liked her; they'd gone shopping together and blah-blah-blah. Why'd she have to be so goddamned sunny? It made me fucking hate her. Plus if she'd fucked me or blown me or something, this might never have happened. I could barely meet her eye, and she asked me several times if something was wrong, and I kept telling her nothing.

"Are you sure?"

"I'm sure."

"Then why are you acting like this?"

"Like what? I'm just not in a great mood, okay? I mean, just because I don't walk around smiling every second of the day means something's wrong. Not everybody's you."

So then it was *her* turn to cry. I should've broken up with her, except lashing out made her so upset I couldn't see myself doing it. Besides, what reason could I give? We'd been getting along so well before then. Plus, by losing her, I would've been losing the status that came with her. Selfish, I know, but that's how it was in that town: you were gold or shit, take your pick. Which is how it remains. And that's one reason, you may have noticed, I never mention the name: even to write or say that word can make me nauseous. There are also legal reasons why, but I'll come to that later.

I tried to do right by Megan. I became the nicest boyfriend you ever saw: tender, generous, so perfectly attentive she should have been suspicious, but somehow she never was. I guess I was *so* perfect she didn't want to rock the boat. I bought her things, expensive things, and got a part-time job bussing tables at a steakhouse to pay for them. As spring got closer, I made a big point of not playing baseball so we could spend more time together. (I'd lettered as a pitcher my junior year.) Plus I stopped bugging her for sex, but that was because I'd lost interest in sex, or at least sex with her. Not that I wasn't horny! I still wanted to fuck almost every woman who crossed my path, but with Megan I felt so guilty I could barely raise a hard-on. Yet the more I backed off, the more she started bugging me for sex. Un-fucking-believable! For almost a year she'd freak out if I tried the slightest thing, and suddenly she was mine for the taking. I kept saying, "Are you sure about this? It's an awfully big step, you know." And with no pause at all she'd say, "I'm sure."

So, finally, I was forced to do it. I fucked the pussy that came out of the best pussy I'd ever fucked. This occurred at the Ramada Inn, a local Mecca for devirginizing, and let's just say it was pretty weird, especially the blowjob. Gail was a champ at sucking dick. With Megan all I felt was teeth. At one point I tried to coach her, but then I realized it was all coming straight from her mom's playbook, so I shut my mouth and let her munch away. Fortunately the next day she was full of paranoia, afraid I'd lost respect for her, and I implied I had to get her off my back. But there were other little problems I was always having to face, such as how to behave around Gail. We barely spoke when I called the house. I'd make up excuses not to come over, and when I did come over, I'd beep in the horn in the driveway instead of going inside. And then there were times when I had to go inside, and Gail would shoot me fleeting looks, some guilty, some with a hint of lust, and God only knows how I looked at her. I was constantly afraid that Megan would piece it together. Maybe Gail would get drunk one night and spill her guts. Maybe she'd tell a friend of hers, who in turn would tip off Megan. For myself, I kept it quiet for the longest time. Which was killing me. I wanted to say something to *somebody* and get it off my chest.

Well, one night that March I was smoking pot with Mark Powell in the woods behind his house, and he told me that a few nights before he'd fucked the school slut, the shameless Tammy Ducey, in the high-jump pit. *Everybody* fucked Tammy Ducey. I'd fucked her a few times myself before I started seeing Megan. But the thing was, Mark was seeing somebody himself: a good friend of Megan's named Paula Welk who was also something of a queen bee, though nowhere near as nice. In fact, she was a stuck-up bitch—just perfect for Mark Powell! So when he told me about Tammy, I figured here was my chance to talk about Gail. I saw it as a kind of nuclear pact: two nations who'd never strike first, since each had the power to annihilate. Plus I considered Mark one of my best friends, even though I knew he somewhat looked down on me.

So I told him. And, stoned and stunned, he said he didn't believe me. Then I swore on my father's life it was all true, and he said, "Man, three times in one night!"

"Four, including the blowjob."

"And she really knew how to do it, huh? She really knew how to clean your pipes!"

"Buddy," I said (since in that circle everyone was referred to as "buddy"), "you have no idea."

He didn't blame me at all, he said. Megan's mom was hot. If he'd been me, he'd have done the same thing. Which was pretty reassuring. For some reason we never talked much about sex in that circle, and when we did, nobody ever came across as chronically aroused as I was. It made me feel like a freak, like some kind of hillbilly breeding animal. But here was Mark Powell with the big thumbs-up. I was all right. I was a regular guy. And right before I left that night, I said, "Hey, buddy, let's keep this between ourselves," and I have to give him this: he never specifically promised me anything. But he did give me a look that said, "What, are you crazy?" And that was good enough for me.

Well, a week went by, maybe two. And then one day at school I was walking down the hall, and whom should I pass but Paula Welk? I said hi, same as always, and she shot me a look like I was the lowest life form ever to crawl out of a compost heap and kept going. Like I say, she was never that nice, so at first I wasn't concerned. But then she did it again. Then it happened with another girl who was close to Megan and Paula: I said hi, and she said nothing back but just kept going like I wasn't there. So at that point I *was* concerned, and I sought out Mark and said, "Hey, buddy, you know that thing I told you about?"

"What thing?"

"About Megan…?"

"Oh. What about it?"

"You didn't say anything to Paula, did you?"

"Why?"

"She's acting kind of weird."

"What do you mean, weird?"

"I mean weird. Like she's mad at me or something."

"It's your imagination."

But he wouldn't meet my eye when he said all this. And, come to think of it, he'd been acting strangely himself—a little more distant, a little less friendly—and suddenly I looked at him and knew he'd done it. I knew he'd told Paula. I said as much, and he swore he hadn't, and I said, "Look, buddy, just tell me the truth. Because I don't want Megan hearing it from anybody but me."

"But I didn't *tell* Paula."

"Mark, man, I know you did."

"And I'm telling you I didn't. But you know what? Maybe I should. I think it's really shitty, what you did. It's low, man. Megan's a great person. She doesn't deserve that kind of shit."

I wanted to kill that motherfucker! But that would've caused still more talk. By keeping my cool, I was thinking magically, as if the way I presented myself could somehow make the talk stop. It didn't. More girls glared as I passed them in the halls. Guys smirked—that is, if they weren't themselves glaring. I told myself I was being paranoid, but pretty soon a sort-of friend named Steve Horn came up and told me the story that was making the rounds: I'd forced myself on Megan's mother. I forget his exact phrasing, but that was the idea, and he obviously didn't believe it, otherwise he would never have approached me as if to share a joke. Even so, I snapped and pushed him against the wall, demanding to know his source, and he named some kid I barely knew, and then I pushed *him* against the wall, and he swore he had no idea what I was talking about, and so convincingly I decided Steve must have fed him to me to keep me from confronting the real deal. You didn't want to cross those elite kids. For myself, I'd all but stopped hanging out with them. What was the point? I knew they all knew. Besides, they were a lot closer to Mark than they'd ever been to me.

The weird thing is that, for the longest time, Megan had no idea what was going on. To this day I'm not sure how she stayed in the dark for as long as she did. I guess people liked her *so* much they formed a wall of silence around her to prevent her from being hurt. Also, being a girl, it wasn't like Steve Horn or somebody like him was going to walk up and say, "Hey, what's all this about Jason fucking your mom?" However, she did notice that I'd stopped speaking to Mark, and when she asked me why, I said he was, simply, an asshole.

"What makes you say that?"

"Because he is."

"Well, did something happen or—?"

"Nothing happened. I just don't like the way he treats people, that's all."

Nor did she. Megan had her own misgivings about the school and town both, which was probably the one thing we most had in common. We were equally hypocritical insofar as we sought approval from the very people we partly disliked, but we had an unspoken pact about that: you don't call me on my bullshit, I don't call you on yours. I later learned that's how a lot of relationships work. But now my own bullshit was spinning out of control. The girl had to know. But how was I supposed to tell her? There were so many times when I almost said something, but the circumstances were never quite right. And then one night I was driving home from the steakhouse and decided I'd write her a letter. More than one English teacher had told me I showed a flair for writing, and I thought I might be able to explain myself better without the pressure of doing it in person. I started the letter that night, after my family had gone to bed, and the next day at school I was still working on it till, finally, I felt fairly satisfied. I'd love to see it now. I remember trying to adopt a worldly tone—"There's no one to blame, it just happened"—with many assurances that I'd never sought to hurt her, which I hadn't. And this was on a Thursday, and my plan was to give her the letter the next day so she'd have the weekend to collect herself.

But that wasn't the way it worked out. That Thursday Paula took it upon herself to tell Megan what was being whispered all over school. Megan went home and confronted Gail, and after what had to be a gruesome exchange, she locked herself in the bathroom and swallowed half a bottle of over-the-counter sleeping pills. Then she panicked and alerted Gail, who rushed her to the hospital, where she had her stomach pumped and passed the whole thing off as an accident. So she wasn't detained, as often happens with attempted suicides, and when I called the next day to see why she hadn't been at school, she let me have it. Only, of course, she'd been misinformed. Gail had told her I'd "taken advantage" of her when she was too drunk to know what she was doing. But she knew. Besides, I'd been drinking myself, and she was the one who served me the beer—who'd taken advantage of whom? But Megan was too upset to give me a fair hearing. She cursed me out and told me never to speak to her again and hung up; and that night, overwrought, I confessed to my parents, hoping they could tell me how to make amends. And that's when things got *really* ugly.

ONE THING ABOUT MY PARENTS: they were Jesus freaks. Not as bad as some of our relatives, but my mom did pray on her knees every night, and my dad—he usually kept his views to himself, except when a crisis hit, at which point he'd start quoting scripture left and right. "It says it right there in James three, verse two!" But a situation like this—there was nothing in the good book about fucking your girlfriend's mother. Not even God was ready for that! Still, my parents kept bringing His name up anyway, and after so much of it, I said, "Would you guys stop with all this God stuff? I don't believe in God!"

"What? What did you say?"

That's right, Jason, let's get it going in *all* directions! But at least that admission led away from Megan and onto the larger matter of my immortal soul. By the end of that night we were having a relatively peaceful conversation about why they believed and how I'd come to decide I didn't. It wasn't very complicated. I just didn't see the proof that God existed. There *was* no proof, my parents said; that was what faith meant, and maybe if I spent a little more time in church, I'd know that. Finally we all went to bed, and even though I never thought I'd manage to sleep after a day as hellish as that one, in fact I slipped into, virtually, a coma. I woke briefly in the morning to hear my family—mom, dad, two kid brothers—leave the house for a Little League game. Then I dozed back off, and when I woke again at noon or so, the house was still empty.

By now, twenty-some years later, I've lived through situations far worse, but this one still hurts, since I was so young, and the pain you suffer at that age has a way of sticking with you, or at least it has with me. I felt as maimed as an amputee, ambling around the house that day, and Mark's betrayal was the salt in my wounds. He seemed to forget the means I had of retaliating. If he was so big on talking to Paula, then maybe I should talk to Paula myself. It seemed kind of pussy, but fuck it; pussy measures for pussy people. I picked up the phone. I put it down. Something in me was balking. I was supposed to work a shift at the steakhouse, and at first I was going to blow it off, but then I decided the distraction might do me good. Sure enough, I was so busy bussing half-eaten sirloins for the next few hours, I could barely think about anything else. Then the restaurant closed and I saw my boss, Nick Campanis, doing the books, and I had a lot of respect for Nick, he'd fought in Vietnam and traveled the world, so I figured here was somebody with advice worth taking. I walked up and asked if I could have a word with him, and for the second time in twenty-four hours I told the whole story, and he was a little shocked and a little amused, but he assured me that I was a good kid who'd made a big mistake, and the important thing was I'd graduate in a couple of months and after so much time it would be like this whole mess had never happened. As for Mark Powell, I should leave it alone. "He'll get his," he said. Yes, and who'd give it to him? Not me. I'd never have the satisfaction. Besides, Nick was originally from a podunk town in Pennsylvania and probably didn't realize how rich preppies like Mark Powell always got away with murder.

So I shrugged off Nick's advice. I called Paula the following night, and as soon as she heard my voice, she said, "What do *you* want?" in her frostiest tone. I said, "Oh, not much. Megan tried to kill herself, but I guess you know that. You should. You're the one that caused it."

"And you're the one that—never mind. You know what you did."

"Yeah, you know what? I do. And you *don't*. There's a lot of things you don't know. Like Mark and Tammy Ducey—I bet you don't know about that."

"What are you talking about?"

"Oh, you don't know? Yeah, he fucked her in the high-jump pit."

She freaked the fuck out. I savored every second of it. At the same time I had a sick feeling in the pit of my stomach. I knew I'd just opened a huge can of worms. I knew I might come to regret it. But if I was going down, I was taking Mark with me, and maybe my strike hadn't damaged as much as his, but a little damage was better than no damage at all.

That was Sunday night. The next day I thought about blowing off school, but I didn't want to be like Mark, spreading stories and pretending I hadn't spread them. I'd done what I'd done. I wasn't going to run away. I drove to school, where people shot me hostile looks the second I pulled up in the parking lot. By then it seemed like the whole student body knew about Megan's suicide bid, and even though nobody had the balls to confront me, I was obviously being blamed. Even black kids, who seemed to exist in a parallel dimension with their own styles and hierarchy, were staring me down, which says a lot about Megan's popularity. They all loved her and they hated me, and if that was how they felt, then fuck them. Fuck every last goddamned one of them.

Then it happened: I ran into Mark. Right after lunch I was walking down the hall and, through the crowd, I saw him coming toward me. His eyes met mine, and I was all pumped up, heart beating fast, still feeling sick, but sometimes, like any performer can tell you, a rush of nerves can serve you well. He got closer and closer, and right as we were about to pass, he looked away, like I wasn't worthy of his full attention, and said something out of the side of his mouth. It sounded like "You're dead." It was: a number of witnesses later confirmed it. I stopped and turned around and said, "Did you say something?"

"You heard me."

That he said loud enough for me to hear. But he'd never broken stride, so I went after him and said, "No, I don't think I *did* hear you. Why don't you say it to my face?" Then he stopped, and I could sense other people stopping around us, but I barely noticed, I was so microfocused on Mark. I could tell he was a little high—he often had a puff in the parking lot during lunch—and he looked right at me and said, "I'll deal with you later."

"Yeah? Like when?"

"You'll find out."

"So, what, you're going to sneak up on me? Yeah, that sounds about like you. Well, I'm waiting, buddy. Whatever you want to do, whenever you want to do it, I'm right here."

Then there was a kind of flash in his eyes, and he shoved me, and that was it: I barely know what I did after that. I literally saw red, as if a strip of red nylon had been tied around my eyes and the whole world had taken on a pinkish-orange glow. I remember hitting him in the face and crushing his nose as I did it, the way it imploded with a silent pop. And I remember him falling to the floor and raising my foot to kick him after he went down. It all seemed to happen in a second or less. It didn't, from what I was told later, but my sense of time was askew, along with everything else. Then somebody grabbed me from behind, their hands digging in like hooks, and I kept trying to break free and get back to Mark. Then there were more hands, and next thing I knew I'd been slammed against the wall and a teacher named Mr. Gillespie was looking straight at me. I'd never liked him. He was a preppie motherfucker, always trying to act like one of the students. He pushed his face inches from mine and said, *"Stop it! Do you hear me? Stop it right this minute!"* Then I realized somebody was standing beside him, a black basketball star named Boyd Mosby, who was staring at me like I'd gone insane, which at that moment I probably had. Boyd was the one pinning me—Mr. Gillespie couldn't have done it—and he said, "Chill out, man, calm down, cool out," in a soothing voice, and the world began to lose its reddish glow. I kept looking past him and Mr. Gillespie for a sign of Mark, but all I saw was a circle of students staring down at the floor. Then Mr. Gillespie told me to follow him and Boyd let me go, but after a few steps Mr. Gillespie stopped and said, "Get your books," and I saw that my books and Mark's were scattered all over the floor. It was hard to tell which were which, but I leaned down to collect the ones I thought were mine, and while I was there I noticed a gap in the crowd surrounding Mark and caught just a sliver of his light-blue Oxford button-down speckled with what looked like cranberry juice. Then a female teacher came running down the hall and toward Mark, and when she got there, the gap in the circle closed.

All the way to the administration office, two wings away, Mr. Gillespie walked in front of me, opening doors and holding them till

I'd passed through. We didn't speak for the most part, but at one point he gave me a grave look and said, "You'd better hope he's okay." I didn't say anything. Then he asked if I'd "mind" telling him what the fight was about, and I said, "None of your fucking business." I remember it felt so good to say that. I was already in trouble. I could say whatever I felt like saying. We got to the office, where I sat in reception and Mr. Gillespie walked up to the secretary and said, "Is Mr. Wright around? Jason here just beat up Mark Powell pretty bad." The secretary's eyes met mine for a second—a maternal look of disappointment, or so it vaguely seemed—and Mr. Gillespie walked down the hall and came back a minute later with Mr. Wright. He was somebody else I'd never liked. He looked like a mortician. He acted like one as well. He gave me a nod as if to acknowledge he knew I was there and walked out the door with Mr. Gillespie, and he was gone for—five minutes? ten?—while I sat and listened to typewriters and ringing phones and footsteps thumping up and down the carpet, feeling disengaged from everything and everyone, including myself. Nothing felt quite real. Finally Mr. Wright came back alone and said, "Jason, you can wait in my office," and I started down the hall as, behind me, I heard him say to the secretary, "We're going to have to call for an ambulance. This boy is messed up real bad." That's when I knew I was in deep, deep shit. I knew it already, but if they were sending for an ambulance, it must be worse than I thought. Yet none of it still felt real. I sat across from Mr. Wright's desk and realized for the first time that my jaw felt funny, like it might be popped out of place, yet I had no memory of Mark laying a hand on me. Plus my knuckles hurt. Plus my shirt too was splattered with blood. Was it my blood or Mark's? I had no idea. Then Mr. Wright walked in and shut the door behind him and sat in his rolling chair, and I saw that he was holding a rolodex card, and I knew what that card contained: contact numbers for my parents. And he didn't say a word to me—not then. He just picked up his phone and called my dad to say that I was being expelled from school and the police were on their way to arrest me.

SO I SAT AND LISTENED, a nightmare beyond my wildest imagination, and thank God I couldn't make out my dad's voice. Not that I had to. I could easily fill in the blanks. Mr. Wright was saying things like, "Well,

Mr. Maddox, I'm sorry you feel that way, but if you could see what Jason did to this boy, I'm sure you would understand. He's got cuts all over his face, his eyes are swollen shut, he was out cold for a couple of minutes. And I realize Jason's only got two months to go before he graduates, and I realize he's been a model student up till now, but we simply can't allow this kind of thing, and if I made an exception for Jason, I'd have to make one for everybody else." This went on for quite some time, and I kept hoping my dad would turn him around, but finally Mr. Wright hung up and said he had a message for me: I was "on my own." Which meant—what? I could rot in jail? I could feel myself close to tears, and I tried to fight them back but couldn't; I broke down sobbing and said, "What am I supposed to do now? I can't even *graduate*?"

"Well, you can still make it up. If it's not too bad with Mark—and that's a big if—you can go to the community college and pick up the credits you need and take it from there. But I cannot allow you remain at this school, that's something I cannot do." Like any mortician, he had a box of Kleenex on hand, but I couldn't bring myself to reach for it. I asked if I could finish my classes at home, and he told me no. Then I asked if I could re-enroll if Mark was okay, and he told me no again. I kept looking for the magic words before the police got there, or hopefully the police wouldn't show; but then the secretary knocked on the door and said, "The police are here," and Mr. Wright stood and said, "Let's go." I just sat there, and he said, "Come on, Jason, let's not keep these men waiting. They've got a job to do."

So I dried my eyes as best I could and followed Mr. Wright down the hall, where, at the far end of it, I saw two cops giving me the once-over. Administrators stood in open doorways watching as I passed, almost as if I were being drummed out of the army. I was frisked and cuffed and read my rights. The cuffs were too tight, but the cops ignored me when I said as much. Then they led me outside to their waiting cruiser, and just before I was caged in the back of it, I glanced up and saw a long line of students staring down from that big window in the library. It was a partly cloudy day (I've never forgotten the date: April 6, 1981), and for much of the drive to the police station, ten minutes away downtown, one cop talked about buying a house while the other one gave him real-estate tips. Pedestrians and people in the cars around us peered at me as if wondering what I'd done. What *had* I done? At the station, the cops who'd arrested me weren't even sure what to charge me with. Eventually, after a long discussion with the desk sergeant, they decided on a misdemeanor assault charge, only if Mark's injuries turned out to be worse than believed, I might later be looking at felony assault or even attempted murder. They removed the cuffs and told me I could make a phone call, and I was positive my parents had conferred by then, and I wasn't sure how seriously I should take this business of being "on my own," but when it came to trouble, I much preferred dealing with my mom. I tried at her work, but she wasn't there. A female colleague said she was on her way to me. I said, "Does she know where I am?"

"Well, you're at the police station, aren't you?"

She was very tactful about the whole thing, and I'm not being sarcastic in any way; she really was. It meant something at the time. I hung up and sat for a while with the house-hunting cop, giving a statement for the arrest report, and afterward he or somebody else led me away to be fingerprinted, and the guy doing it looked at me funny and said, "Hey, don't you play football over at the high school? Yeah, I thought so. My boy was on your team." He never asked why I was there; he just talked cheerfully about our season the whole time I was being fingerprinted. Then I was taken to a different room to be photographed, and somebody told me my bail had been set at $200, and I said, "Well, I guess my mom will pay it. Or I *hope* she will." Because I could picture her arriving at the station and somebody saying, "Two hundred dollars, ma'am," and her saying, "Two hundred dollars? Forget it!" But then somebody told me the bail had been paid, and, free to leave, I walked back to the front desk, where I found my mom waiting. Her eyes were covered with sunglasses, but even so I could tell she was livid. She stood with barely a glance my way and said, "You got everything?" And I said, "There's nothing to get."

Her car was parked in a five-story garage a few blocks away. Neither of us spoke on the walk there. Then we got in the car and rolled out to the street, and I was just about to thank her for bailing me out when she started talking. She sounded calm at first, but her voice was trembling, and the more she talked, the more she lost control.

"Jason," she said, "I think you're going to have to get your own place. Your father feels the same way. Sleeping with Megan's mother, and sending people to the hospital, and getting kicked out of school! You have two younger brothers—did you ever think about *them*? What kind of example are you setting?! Where did we go wrong, would you at least tell me that?! What did we ever do to make you act like this?!"

"You live here, don't you?"

"What the hell is that supposed to mean?" And my mom never cursed, never, so I figured if she could, I could too. I said, "What the hell do you *think* it means? Look around you! We're nothing as far as these people are concerned! We're *shit*!"

Then she hit the brakes in the middle of moving traffic and slapped me. She got me in the face, the chest, the legs, the shoulders—anyplace she could land a swat—saying, "How *dare* you speak to your mother that way! Do you know what your grandparents would have done if I'd spoken that way to them? *Do* you?" Cars were backed up behind us, pedestrians stopped to watch, and somehow I managed to get out and stormed off down the sidewalk. I stared straight ahead as I walked, but I could sense my mom pull up and drive alongside me.

"Jason," she said, "you get back in this car!" I kept walking, and she said, "Jason, you get back in this car or your *father* is going to have something to say about this!" Then I stopped and faced her and said, "He already did! I'm 'on my own'! And you're saying the same thing, so, fine, that's what I am! You think I'm *happy* about this? You think I *enjoy* being arrested? But you don't give a shit! All you care about is what other people think about you! Which makes you just about perfect for this place!" I was saying shit I hadn't even known I thought, and people stared, and I couldn't have given a fuck less. Stare, bitches! *Stare* at the freak having a fit on Main Street! And don't forget to tell the whole world what you saw!

So, after that, my mom drove off and left me there. I was glad to see her go. Well, I was and I wasn't. But if I'd gone home, there would've been weeks of cold shoulders and quoted scripture and constant reminders of what a fuckup I was—no thanks. I just kept walking with no idea where I was headed, depressed one second, pissed the next. At one point I came to a bridge and, stopping in the middle, seriously thought about jumping. Megan had chickened out at the crucial moment. I wouldn't. But then I pictured Megan and all my former friends crying at my funeral, and thought, "What, are you fucking nuts? They'll be so happy they'll practically throw a dance to celebrate! No, you've got to live and make them feel worse! And I hope Mark is laid up for a long time! I hope he's got fucking brain damage! It'd be worth it to spend a couple of years in the state pen, knowing I cracked that fucker's skull!"

So I kept walking and, feeling hungry, found I had just five dollars. There was one cheap meal. What about the others? And how was I going to pay for my own place? There was a lot to think about, but first things first: I walked back to school, where my car was still in the parking lot. By then it was getting dark and there were chains drawn across the parking-lot exits, so I drove my car over the curb and a bed of flowers planted to spell out the school initials. Ha! How do you like your flowers now, motherfuckers?!

I'd hazily planned on heading to the steakhouse, but if I did that, I'd have to tell Nick how utterly I'd failed to take his advice. I decided I'd go to my grandmother's instead. This was my father's mother, and she was no stranger to scandal herself, having dumped my grandfather for another man when I was five years old. What a war that started! Half my family supported her, and the other half, including my dad, refused to have anything to do with her till she broke her hip two years later. But I'd always been her favorite grandchild, so that even during the time when she was kept from seeing me, she always found a way to slip me presents. My car was one of her later presents. After I got my license, she bought herself a new car and gave me the one she already had: a 1970 aqua-blue Chevy Impala—not much to look at (or so I thought at the time), but at least I had wheels.

She was startled by the blood on my clothes when she answered her door. I told her I needed a place to stay and explained why. I told her everything, omitting only the part about Gail, though I was frank about having cheated on Megan. She said, "Well, you're a young boy. You've got a lot of wild oats to sow. And that friend of yours—he had no right to go running his mouth that a-way. He's just lucky *I* wasn't around. I'd've smacked his face good!" God, I loved that woman! She cooked me dinner and went upstairs to prepare a room and came back down and said, "Now, honey, you know you're welcome to stay as long as you want. It's been pretty lonesome around here since Luther died." (Luther was the feud-causing second husband.) "But don't you think your momma and daddy are going to be worried about you? Here, let me just give them a call and let them know you're safe with me."

So she picked up the phone, and, just as I feared, a fight ensued. My parents demanded to speak to me. My grandmother told them no—I'd been through enough for one day. Soon the old matter of Luther was exhumed, and I listened and realized I'd fucked up yet again. I couldn't live with my grandmother and potentially spark another two-year rift. I told her I was leaving and staying with friends, assuring her I'd be just fine. She was still on the phone when I walked to the door, still getting shit from my parents, and though she tried to stop me, I drove to the steakhouse, where I told Nick the whole story and asked if he could put me up till I found a place of my own. At first he told me to go home, but I said no way, I was *never* going home, and he said, "Well, I think Rico's looking for a roommate. Why don't you speak to Rico?"

Rico was the dishwasher, a Latin-American guy from, I think, Colombia. There weren't a lot like him around town, but you could never really ask him about it, since he spoke practically no English—in fact, I wasn't sure how Nick had managed to learn he was looking for a roommate in the first place! But I walked back to kitchen, where Rico was scrubbing the floor, and said, "Hey, Nick says you're looking for someone to live with you."

"?"

"Me. Live. With you?"

"Oh, yes yes yes! *Si*, yes!"

"My own room?"

"?"

"Place. Sleep. Me. My own?"

"Sleep. For you. Yes yes yes, *si*, yes!"

I returned to Nick in the dining room and said, "You know, I think he thinks I just need a place to crash."

"Good. I mean, nothing personal, Jason, but you're a big guy and we haven't got much room as it is. So see what's up with Rico, and if it doesn't look good, give me a call and we'll work something out."

So I went back to the kitchen and told Rico in sign language I wanted to see his place, and after he'd finished his final chores, I followed him to an apartment complex just inside the city limits. It was relatively new and cheap—a kind of mini-city unto itself, not unlike those gated communities in retirement states, but without the gate. I parked next to Rico in the parking lot and trailed him down the courtyard toward his apartment. By then it must have been midnight, and most of the windows were dark, but somebody was playing music. Loud. It was a pissed-off, ragged sound I knew I'd heard a few times before, yet it was all I could do to give it a name: punk rock. And guess who was playing it? Guess who was about to be my neighbor?

Welcome to the new world.

MARK'S INJURIES FELL OUTSIDE THE FELONY RANGE. He had a broken nose and a mild concussion, and the cuts on his face, caused by my class ring, were scratches more than gouges. He was back in school a week or so later, and the judge, by way of teaching me a lesson, sentenced me to six months on probation and ordered me to perform fifty hours of community service at a state-run home for handicapped kids. But that wasn't the end of it. Mark's parents filed a lawsuit against me, claiming he was damaged for life, so I was forced to hire an attorney and submit to a long, embarrassing deposition in which I was asked about everything from the time I slept with Gail to the time I told Mark to Mark's encounter in the high-jump pit with Tammy Ducey. She was deposed too. So were Mark, Megan, Gail and Paula. So were people I barely knew, people who'd witnessed the fight. One said Mark had bitten me—had he? Others mentioned his overheard threats and his shove that got the fight going. He clearly wasn't going to make a sympathetic plaintiff, as his lawyer started to see; so, after weeks of uncertainty, I was asked to pay a nominal fee for his pain and suffering and the suit was dropped. I was lucky. Even though my classmates held me in contempt, those who'd seen the fight told the truth anyway, and for that I'm still grateful. Meantime my parents kicked in for my legal bills, and I'm grateful for that too. Of course, it's been thrown in my face in the years since, and to this day my relationship with both my parents has never fully recovered. I'm sure they'd say otherwise, but, in their heart of hearts, I don't think they ever quite forgave me for spoiling their good opinion of me. Still, seven years later, after a trauma so bad it made this one look like a stroll at the beach, they never hesitated to help me out.

As for Megan, this is one of those things that boggle the mind, but shortly after I moved in with Rico, she somehow learned my new address and, turning up unexpected one night, proceeded to fuck me blind. I kid you not. She claimed she was there to return my many presents, and I choked up and told her to keep them, and suddenly she was all over me. But this had nothing to do with forgiveness. No, she wanted to get even with me and Gail, and I was going to let her. No more hesitations on Jason Street. Now that everything was out in the open, I was *more than willing!* I whisked her off to my mattress on the floor, and the whole time she bit me and scratched me and called me names like *you pig* and *you filthy piece of shit*. She covered my neck with black and blue hickeys!—and that was just the first of many occasions. For months she'd drop by every weekend and do it again. It wasn't always so rough, but it was usually fast, since she was seeing me on the sly. She was terrified that word would get out. In fact, that's what led to my talking to Peewee. The second time she came over, she darted inside and said with a look of terror, "You never told me Bernard Mash lives here!"

"He does?"

"He must! I just saw him outside! And he saw me on your porch! Oh my God, he *saw* me here!"

Then, right on cue, we got a blast of souped-up music, and I said, "Oh, *he's* the one." I'd been wondering. By then I'd left the steakhouse for a full-time job painting houses, and it was tedious, tiring, soul-sucking work, and almost every night I'd drag myself home to some jerk putting on a punk show for the entire complex. Not that I ever had a problem falling asleep—not after the days I put in. It was the lack of consideration that drove me up the wall, and I'd often thought of saying something but never had for fear of starting another fight. Weren't punk-rock fans known for being violent? I dimly thought they were. So I pictured myself being arrested again, and I wasn't looking for any more trouble of that kind or any other. I wanted to keep the lowest possible profile—to eventually get my diploma and head off to college and put this mess behind me.

But now—*now* I knew who was blasting that crap. And Megan was afraid he'd tell people he'd seen her at my place, so she asked if I'd go over and "have a word with him. You know, just kind of tell him to keep it to himself." In other words, she wanted me to threaten him, which before then had been very unlike her. It wasn't as if anybody was going to listen to a goddamned word he had to say anyway, but I did want to speak to him about the music; I told Megan I'd be right back and followed the sound across the courtyard and up the steps to his landing. It was warm that night, so the main door was open, and through the screen I could make out the living room, which was almost as threadbare as mine: a nondescript sofa and shelves filled with books and a turntable sitting on cinder blocks with at least 150 records lined up beside it. (Some belonged to his sister, but this was only half his collection. The other half was in his bedroom, including most of his singles.) And I think, but I'm not positive, the record playing was *Sandinista!* by the Clash, since I have a distinct memory of seeing that cover on top of the stereo; yet nobody was in the room to listen. I knocked and nobody came. Then I knocked again, and Peewee walked out from what I knew was the kitchen, since all the apartments in that complex were laid out exactly the same, and the second he saw me standing on his porch, he just fucking froze, man. He looked like he'd seen a ghost. He turned down the stereo and walked up to the screen door and said, "What are *you* doing here?"

"I live here."

"*Where?*" And I motioned down the courtyard, and he suddenly got very excited and said, "Oh my God, that's like living next door to Muhammad Ali! Do you know I even told people in New *York* about that fight? You ought to think about turning pro! *I'll* manage you! I won't charge you a dime as long as you beat up people like *that* guy!"

So, at that point, I forgot why I'd come over in the first place. I asked if he'd seen the fight or just heard about it, and he said, "Oh no, I saw it. I saw the whole thing. Didn't you see me? I was standing right there."

"Well, to tell you the truth, I'm not sure *who* was there. I was pretty out of it. I almost felt like I wasn't there myself."

"Wow," he said, almost with the air of a scientist, "that's the way *killers* talk. 'I was in a dream, I didn't know what I was doing, it felt like somebody else.' But, see, I always thought that was bullshit, because—did you ever read *The Executioner's Song* by Norman Mailer?"

"Who?"

"Yeah, I didn't think so. But Mailer's a writer, right? He's maybe the best American writer going, and as a matter of fact, I went to school with some of his kids. He's got more kids than a Catholic cop! Anyway, he wrote this book about Gary Gilmore. Now, *him* you've probably heard of."

"He's that guy that got shot a few years ago."

"Right, by a firing squad, exactly. And when he confessed to killing those people—those Mormons he robbed—he threw in all that dream stuff because he knew that's what killers are *supposed* to say. Because it made him sound insane, right? As part of his defense? So when I read that, I figured that's why other killers say the same thing."

"Yeah, but I didn't kill anybody."

"Well, it definitely *looked* like you were going to. And I almost wish you *had*. I think everybody there felt that way, only they'd never admit it. You know, people get really aroused by the sight of blood. It's this animal thing we've got. Even a hundred years ago—which you realize is just a drop in the bucket, time-wise—everybody just took it for granted; it wasn't all mixed up with 'morality' the way it is now. They'd make an announcement they were going to hang somebody, and it was like, 'Oh, great, they're going to *hang* somebody! Let's pack a picnic basket and round up the kids!' Executions—*that* was entertainment! But these days people don't think like that, and do you know why?"

I never got to say a word, since he charged in right away.

"Because we can see the same thing in movies! We don't *literally* have to see people getting killed now that violence in movies has gotten so realistic. Now, if we didn't have that, I think we'd go right back to the way things used to be, where somebody's head would get chopped off in the middle of town and everybody would go running up to collect a souvenir. Which they'd do, you know. Everybody would bring a handkerchief to the executions, and after the head came off, they'd go running up to collect some blood with their souvenir handkerchiefs. And this was just Mom and Pop who ran the liquor store down the street, not a bunch of psychos. But now you've got movies like *Taxi Driver* where people's hands are shot off and their brains are splashed all over the walls, and it looks so real you don't *have* to see it in real life. And that's exactly what's getting attacked right now. Because people think *that's* why Reagan got shot. Jesus Christ, how can people be so *stupid*? Reagan got shot because that Hinkley guy's a nut, and guess what, people, that's what happens to leaders, they get assassinated. I mean, Julius Caesar got stabbed to death on the floor of the Roman Senate. Now, what are you going to blame *that* on? Did Brutus go out and watch *Friday the 13th* and think, 'Hey, you know what? That movie gave me a good idea! I think I'm going to get a knife and stab Caesar to death on the floor of the Senate!' I mean, Jesus fucking *Christ*!"

And he was off and running. From there he jumped to pornography, how it wasn't the *cause* of rape, it was actually a substitute, but "dumbfuck" feminists and born-again Christians were joining forces to try and ban it. But they were just a bunch of hypocrites, since there'd never been a human being yet who didn't like porn. Even the Pope liked porn. The Vatican was filled with porn passing as "art." Besides, there were so many different *kinds* of porn. For instance, McDonald's ads—hadn't I ever noticed those hamburgers buns were lit to look like a woman's ass? So there was food porn, and car porn like *Smokey and the Bandit*, and gore porn like *Taxi Driver*; and then he got back on that again, and since I'd never seen it, he told me the plot, as well as the plot of *Mean Streets*, meantime citing still more of his favorite movies, such as *Straw Dogs* and *The Battle of Algiers* and *Bring Me the Head of Alfredo Garcia*—wasn't that the greatest movie title *ever*? And he was going to be a director one day. He was going to help lead the revolution. No, not the Castro kind, the cultural kind, the kind that should've happened back in the sixties, only those fucking hippies had dropped the ball. But that was okay. There was a whole new generation on the rise, *our* generation; all over America there were kids who thought like he did, and once we came of age, look out, boy, we'd take the world by storm. It was a speech I was soon to hear many times: how, once our generation took control of The System, we'd change everything from the kind of movies that got made to the kind of music played on the radio to the way people actually thought; and I've got to say that, even then, his speech rang false. Because where were all these kids who were going to set the world on fire? I'd never met one of them. Or, yes, I'd met Bernard Mash, but he was just a little freak who couldn't seize control of a locker, let alone the world.

And yet I had to admit he was weirdly magnetic. He was like a cross between a junior dictator and a sweet little kid—sweet in the sense that he seemed so innocent when he spoke about grisly shit like people getting their heads chopped off in the middle of town. Plus he was *very* funny, almost like a stand-up comic. (In fact, Lenny Bruce was one of his heroes, as I would shortly learn.) We probably talked for close to an hour, or mostly he talked, while I just listened. I forgot all about Megan. Then I remembered and said I had to go, and even then he kept talking, so that, trying to shut him up, I said, "Hey, you know where I live. Drop by some time."

"Oh, you *know* I will."

Then I ran back to my place, where I told Megan I was so sorry, I couldn't get away; and she said, "Well, at least you spoke to him." But

I'd never managed to work in a word about Megan or the music either. Already, down the courtyard, he'd cranked his stereo back up to full volume.

⌢

SO THAT WAS IT. After that I saw him every day. I'd get home from work and change my clothes, and right about then he'd knock on my door, or sometimes he'd charge inside without bothering to knock and start yakking away. It was almost like turning on the radio, except he at least was interactive—or just barely. Other times I'd walk past my place and head straight to his, and from there we might sit up all night long, talking and drinking beer or, occasionally, smoking pot with his sister Suzanne. She was almost as bright as he was. Even a simple comment like "Bernard, are you ever going to clean the tub?" could turn into some long confabulation about the history of cleanliness and whether deodorant was fundamentally bourgeois, and after all the French didn't wash, and the French were the most cultivated people on earth. Or was that the British? No, the British couldn't paint or cook or make movies. Now, Hitchcock—*he* could make movies, but you know what they say: the exception proves the rule! And so on. It was very intimidating. Even their less pointy-headed talk could be intimidating. One night, for instance, very early on, they amused each other with anecdotes about a New York friend named Al. It was: "Yeah, and remember the time Al came over at one in the morning? And I think he had Jill with him."

"It wasn't Jill. It was Tuesday Weld."

"Are you sure?"

"I'm positive. It was right after *The Godfather* came out."

And suddenly I knew which "Al" they were talking about. My God, they knew Al fucking Pacino! Well, mostly their father did. He was a well-known playwright who wrote screenplays on the side, and very successfully, to the point where he once moved his family to a beachfront house near Malibu. Peewee was a tot at the time. But his mother and sister hated California, so before long the family moved back to New York, though Peewee's dad continued to spend weeks every year in L.A., as well as flying around the country to repertory theaters staging his plays. Peewee's mother was a big-time editor at Simon & Schuster, so between her and her husband, the Mash kids had grown up surrounded by books and ideas and, yes, by a number of celebrities like Al Pacino. Not that, in the last case, Peewee was inclined to brag. He was never impressed by mainstream fame, and definitely not by wealth—he'd grown up surrounded by that as well. His parents weren't millionaires by any means, but they weren't exactly hurting; and so he'd been sent to exclusive schools with classmates who really *were* the kids of millionaires and never let him forget it. And then one day in the sixth grade he clubbed one of them on the head with a microscope, and that kicked off his career as a problem child. He told me the guy had been "fucking" with him. He never mentioned why, though I'm sure I can guess: he couldn't bear being teased about his size. He'd take a lot of things in stride, but if you did that—look out, boy, there's a twister coming through! And I think his size lay behind most of his problems. He had the mind of a giant but the body of a pygmy, and he bitterly resented the disparity, and I think (since it's something I don't remember him ever discussing) he deep down blamed his parents. Neither was especially small, as I later found out, just as Suzanne wasn't either, but Peewee had been stuck with an aberrant shortness gene that made him a target for bullies and persona non grata as far as girls were concerned, and he was going to make his parents *pay*. He brought home Cs and Ds instead of the straight As they knew he could easily make. He threw tantrums and got kicked out of school—repeatedly. It happened the first time when he attacked that kid with a microscope. At the school after that he was caught with a switchblade. At his next school he formed a covert group with a handful of fellow students called the Substitute Teachers, in which points were allotted for various feats of terrorism, anything from posting porn shots on the bulletin board (20 points) to stinking up the building with dead fish hidden in the heaters (500). His best friend Terrence Haggerty was a member of the Substitute Teachers, but it was mostly Peewee's personal operation, and once he was found out, he was kicked out of that school as well. Then came his *pièce de résistance*: The Great Bathroom Fire. He was very lucky not have to ended up in juvenile hall, but in fact his parents were considering something just as bad: on the advice of his latest shrink (there'd been a number of shrinks before), they were planning to ship him to the nuthouse. He told me it wasn't a *real* nuthouse; it was a place in Connecticut where rich people sent their incorrigible kids, and there were classes during the day, and at night you did therapy, and if you fucked up in any way, they'd take away your privileges and lock you in a special ward. Well, no way was he going there! He threw tantrum after tantrum, which only made things worse. Then Suzanne stepped in. Despite their eight-year age difference, she and Peewee had always been close, and she proposed that he live with her for a year in North Carolina, where he could enroll at the local high school and, through his grades and good behavior, re-win their parents' trust. He wasn't exactly thrilled with Suzanne's plan either, but it sure beat the nuthouse; and finally, after much discussion, his parents agreed, and now every month they sent him a nice, fat check for food and supplies (which he mostly spent on books and records), and so far it was working out better than expected. Of course, he'd been suspended a couple of times for fighting, but he was making great grades, since "you guys are just learning shit I studied in the fifth grade! I don't even *try*, and I *still* get straight As. My parents are so fucking happy! And I'm going back to New York in a few weeks, and I am never coming back to this goddamn shithole as long as I fucking live!"

At the same time he knew he'd miss his freedom. Suzanne spent half her life at her boyfriend's place, so he was often left alone for days on end. He bought his own groceries and cooked his own meals—in many ways he was living like an adult. He'd blow off school to check out movies at the local art house (I barely realized we had one till I got to know Peewee) or attend lectures at the university with Suzanne's friends. None of them could get over how bright he was. Like her, they were going for advanced degrees in English, and he understood most of their references to books and writers, at times raising points they'd never considered. He especially liked debating Suzanne's boyfriend, who was an older guy, a professor and a bit of a hippie. I remember once, with his usual air of laid-back condescension, the boyfriend said something like, "Bernard, you're really going to have to start reading some new philosophers. I'm afraid all that Nietzsche is warping your mind." And Peewee said, "Yeah, maybe you ought to loan me your copy of *Jonathan Livingston Seagull*. And make me a tape of the Grateful Dead while you're at it. My trash can could use some friends!"

Yet for all his intellectual precocity, he was emotionally stunted. The slightest thing could trigger an outburst. One night, stoned and starving, we started making pancakes, and he somehow managed to burn his hand and picked up the bowl with the batter in it and smashed it against the wall, making the biggest goddamned mess you ever saw. He'd do similar things with records. He'd buy a new one and, after playing it just one time, he'd say, "This fucking sucks," and break it over his knee or hurl it across the room like a Frisbee. He once took a huge stack of records out to the woods behind our complex and shot them up with a BB gun. I participated. I wasn't so mature myself, looking back. But we were the only ones there, and that was an important consideration in the early days, when I'd go to almost any lengths to avoid being seen with him. He attracted too much attention, looking like he did, and as soon as he realized people were gaping, he'd turn it up all the way, talking as loud as he could about subjects intended to keep the gapes coming: "Yeah, and after they stabbed Sharon Tate sixteen times, they were going to cut her baby out of her stomach and take it back to the ranch as a present for Charlie. But it was getting kind of late, you know, so all they did was stick a towel in her blood and write the word 'pig' on her door." (He was fascinated by the Manson case, having lived in L.A. at the time of the murders, and his worn copy of *Helter Skelter* was one of the first books he loaned me.) He was also a huge cop magnet. It seemed as though the cops stopped us every time we went anywhere, and after fucking with us for a few minutes, after frisking us and giving us sobriety tests, they'd finally get around to the point: "Why's your friend dressed that way? What's going on with his hair?" Grown-up civilians would walk up and ask similar questions while eyeing me as if to say, "What's a nice, *normal* boy like you doing with a freak like him?" Other people would shout "faggot!" from passing cars. It was almost as bad as being in school! And that was another reason I rarely went out in public with him: I was afraid one of my former classmates would spot us together and start a rumor that I was now Bernard Mash's gay lover. (And, eventually, one of them did.) I told him not to talk about me. I told him I wanted those people to forget I even existed, and he said, "Well, you *know* that's never going to happen. They're going to be talking about that fight for the rest of their lives. And I think you should be *proud* of that."

"Well, I'm not, okay? It fucked up my whole life."

"No, it didn't. You didn't want that life in the first place, you just *thought* you did. That's the whole reason you pulled that shit."

"What shit?"

"What do you *mean*, what shit? You fucked your girlfriend's mom—which is a pretty transgressive thing to do!—and then you tell the one person where it's practically *guaranteed* to get back to her, and then you call his girlfriend and try to get a fight going. Don't you see what you were doing?"

"No. What was I doing?"

"You were *protesting*! Jesus Christ, do I have to spell it out? You *hate* those people, and you hate this town, and you *should* hate this town, it's the worst fucking place in the *world*! It's kind of like me and that fire, you know? When I got to that school, I was so fucking scared. My parents were all *over* my ass, and I was like, 'Gotta do good, can't fuck up, this is my last chance.' But, deep down, I hated that place, and that fire—I mean, I never *told* myself I was going to start it, but come *on*, if you throw a burning cigarette in the trash, what do you expect? And that's the way it was with you. You *knew* what you were doing. Deep down, you were looking for any excuse you could find to beat that guy's ass. And you didn't just beat his ass, you almost *killed* the guy!"

That was the kind of comment that made me discourage him from testifying in the suit brought against me. Even so, I decided he was right. He always saw me as one of his kind, as a rebel, and I've got to say it was flattering to be seen that way. Rebels are brave. They think for themselves. Even unconscious thinking is thinking, he told me, and I clearly had the right idea. And yet if he'd just *said* all that, I'm not sure it would've made much of an impact. But all during that spring there was one thing he did every day without fail: he played music. His stereo never stopped turning. And one night, very early on, he played me the song that changed everything, though it took a few months to fully sink in. It was two minutes of the most vicious, feral, ferocious guitar and drums I'd ever heard, half sung and half shrieked by a guy named Jim Cassady, frontman for the Los Angeles punk band Rule of Thumb.

> *I've stood in many poses*
> *I've stood on my head*
> *And begged you to like me*
> *And what I do I get?*
> *Slings and arrows*
> *A knife in my back*
> *A smile that hides*
> *A plan of attack*
> *And what's my crime?*

Just being alive
Just lifting back the veil
Where the good folks hide!

I'm BANISHED!
I'm BANISHED!
I'm BANISHED!
I'm BANISHED!

I'm a prodigal son
But a stand-up guy
Let me buy you a drink
Here's mud in your eye!
Hey where are you off to?
What did I do?
I guess I must have gotten
Too close to the truth
I'm guilty of something
Guilty of nothing
Guilty of looking
Where no one looks!

I'm BANISHED!
I'm BANISHED!
I'm BANISHED!
I'm BANISHED!

EVEN THOUGH PEEWEE DRESSED like your basic punk rocker, in certain ways he was more of a punk wannabe. That was partly because, in those days, punk was thought to be dead. It was a weird sort of transitional period in which the founding scenes, such as the one at CBGB's with Television and Patti Smith, had been over for a couple of years, and something new starting up, but almost nobody knew about it, and the New York scene especially was dominated by working-class kids who were naturally suspicious of kids from money like Peewee. He had a few friends among them, like this guy Matt he used to call and their mutual friend Terrence; but Terrence likewise came from money and was never as diehard a fan as Peewee. He certainly never dressed the part—and speaking of that, it's true that Peewee wore the official punk uniform while at the same time loathing conformity, but that was one of his many contradictions, and at the time he was trying to nail down his punk identity, which, though I didn't know it, the kids in New York found questionable. Plus in North Carolina there was the irresistible bonus of shock appeal. And yet I can't recall a single person at school linking his appearance to punk rock. I know *I* never made the leap. As I've said, I thought that with his hair dyed red he was trying to look like David Bowie, and I mentioned that one of the first times we hung out, and he said, "Oh *God*, no. That guy's a hack. He stole everything from Lou Reed and Iggy Pop."

"Who?"

"Jason, don't *tell* me you don't know who they are. I mean, come on, you must know Lou *Reed*. You never heard 'Walk on the Wild Side'? *Everybody* knows that."

He hummed a few bars to refresh my memory. He didn't own the record. He hated it and everything else Lou Reed had ever done, except for his stuff with the Velvet Underground—*that* he owned and played for me. He also played me the Stooges, including *Raw Power*, and asked what I thought, and I said, "I don't know. I guess it's pretty good."

"Pretty *good*? That's one of the greatest records ever made! What kind of music do *you* like? And don't you dare fucking say Led Zeppelin! I *know* you're going to. What's the *appeal*, would you mind explaining that to me? Is it the *mystical* thing? Do you want to *transcend*, is that it? Do you want to climb a stairway to heaven? Or do you get off on long-winded guitar solos? I can't stand that shit! It sounds like fucking *math*!" And so on. And, yes, he'd nailed me: I liked Led Zeppelin. I liked Cheap Trick and Aerosmith and the seventies-era Rolling Stones. I liked what it was safe to like, what my former friends had liked as well, and that definitely wasn't punk, which to me was "My Sharona" or "God Save the Queen." Yes, I'm sure I must have heard "God Save the Queen" before I met Peewee, though I couldn't have described the Sex Pistols for the promise of a date with Miss December. I was also familiar with Devo and the Cars and, of course, Blondie, who in those days were the hottest band in the world—in fact, their song "Rapture" was a big hit around the time I got kicked out of school. But that was all considered "new wave," which Peewee said was a bullshit term invented by record companies who didn't want to sully their reputations by distributing punk. That was how scary punk was. And that was how scary it had *always* been. It wasn't just music, the way most people seemed to think it was; it was a whole approach to life that went way, way back: even during the Roman Empire there were poets who wrote poems with the words "shit" and "fuck" in them, and some were jailed for openly taunting Caesar—*that* was punk. And there were French poets in the nineteenth century who'd dyed their hair green and stabbed people with sword-canes, and eminent painters from the same period who'd graphically painted pussies; and Brando was a punk, and so was Bob Dylan, and so was Jesus in a weird way. Punk was *dissent,* as Peewee defined it. It was giving the finger to the status quo. He showed me zines and played me records (which he was constantly having mailed to him from New York specialty stores like Bleecker Bob's), and he'd spout off facts about the bands—"These guys are from Minnesota," or "These guys just moved to New York from D.C."—but none of it really impressed me till, one night, as I was going through his porn stash (and he had quite a big one!), I happened to catch some of the lyrics of the song playing in the background. I asked him to play it again, which he did, and halfway through he started talking, and I said, *"Shhhhhhh!"* Then, once it stopped playing a second time, I shook my head and said, "Man, that's my whole life, right there." And a wistful expression crossed his face, and he said in a soft voice, very unlike himself, "Me too."

I asked him to play it again. I asked him to play it every time we got together for weeks afterward, and at first he was eager to comply. Rule of Thumb was his favorite band, and their singer, Jim Cassady, was only a fucking genius. Here, read this interview. Here, listen to some other songs by Rule of Thumb. But "Banished" was the only song that really grabbed me at that point. Then one night I asked him to play it and he told me no. He said, "I like that song too much to start *hating* it. Let me make you a tape, and you can play it as much as you want when you're by yourself." Yes, and when was that? Almost every minute I wasn't working was spent with him. I still saw Megan, who would stop by once a week or so to bite and scratch and curse and fuck me; and she knew I was hanging around with Peewee, and she warned me that I'd better watch out or I was going to wake up one day with my hair cut funny and dyed bright red. (She was only off on the color, as it turned out.) I said, "Oh, come on, we're not even *friends.* He's only fifteen years old!"

"Well, you sure spend a lot of time with him."

"Yeah, he's got some great pot. And I feel kind of sorry for him, and he's not going to be around for long. He's moving back to New York as soon as school is over."

Meantime the tape he'd made was playing in the background. I've still got that tape. It starts off with "Banished" and all the other songs from ROT's EP on Dangerhouse, as well as most of their first full-length, *Pathology of Least Resistance*. The rest of *Pathology* is on side two, along with songs by other bands: "Nobody's Scared" by Subway Sect, "Public Image" by Public Image Ltd., "Academy Fight Song" by Mission of Burma. He loaned me a boombox, and that was a fairly new invention back then, so the first day I took it to work all the other guys hovered around it like aborigines seeing a cigarette lighter for the very first time. Then I played that tape, and one of them, a tractor-capped redneck in his forties named Raymond, winced and said, "What the hell is that?" Music, I said, and he shook his head and said, "That ain't music. I don't know what the hell it is, but it sure ain't *music*." Peewee loved it when I told him that story. To him it confirmed that punk rock had the power to rattle even those who'd never heard the hype surrounding it. (Rico was also put off by it, but Rico worked nights and I worked days, so for the most part our paths never crossed.) And as I say, at the beginning all I liked was that one song, and what I liked about it was the lyrics, but I quickly came to like the sound as well. It was aneurism music; you could very well suffer a concussion just by listening to it. It reminded me of playing football, all amped up before a big game; and when I said as much to Peewee, he said, "What the fuck are you *talking* about? This music has nothing to do with *football*."

"How do you know? You never played it."

"Hey, I don't have to play the accordion to know it's *boring*. It's just a stupid allegory, that's all it is. *All* sports are allegories. The goal's an *egg*, and the players are *sperm*, and who wants to waste time pretending to be a sperm?"

Not him, that was for sure—and the same goes for almost every underground-music type I later got to know. There were fairly rigid rules about what you could like and what you couldn't like if you were going to be really *kewl* like them, and a love of sports could potentially mark you as a meathead. You likewise weren't supposed to admit you'd ever been a fan of, say, Led Zeppelin; but I think for me bands like Zeppelin were another bridge into punk. I mean, it's all guitars and drums after all, and how's a song like "Custard Pie" less punk than, for instance, "I Want You Around" by the Ramones? I just kept playing that tape every day as I worked, and Peewee made me more tapes with songs by other bands I started to get into—"Fragile" by Wire, "I'm Not a Fool" by Cockney Rejects, "The American in Me" by the Avengers—but for Peewee and me both, the best band of all was Rule of Thumb. They had a song that suited my every mood. If I wanted to rock out, there was "Lockstep," "Artificial Pussy," and "Banished," the last especially good for those times when I was pissed off at the world. If I was sedate and craved something softer, there were medium-tempo songs with a trace of pop like "Big Sur," "Hostage," and "Passion Takes a Dive"; and if I felt dejected, as I often did in those days, there were songs full of what Peewee used to refer to as a "sweet sadness." "Raft at Sea" was one of these songs, but we hadn't heard it yet. That was on their last record, *Tinderloin*, which they were soon to release. But there was another song called "The Coldest Beer in Town," a little in the style of the Doors, in which Jim recited a poem about waiting for a girl across the street from a Mexican market with a sign that read, yes, COLDEST BEER IN TOWN. Rule of Thumb broke new ground in the sense that almost no punk bands in those days were doing songs so slow and pretty. And then they had a song that, musically, could sear the top of your head off but, lyrically, was the vilest thing I'd ever heard: "Nigger Pearl Harbor." I remember being horrified when I realized that Jim was for a fact bellowing the word "nigger" again and again. I had relatives who were racists, such as one of my cousins, who regarded desegregation as an offense to God, whereas I thought of myself as the enlightened type as found in droves at the university. Yes, I'd once made that remark to Megan about Peewee being Jewish, but that was more a case of a hick kid trying to sound worldly. And here I'd gone and gotten into this band, only to realize they were dumbfuck racists, except Peewee said I'd misunderstood the song, or, actually, I'd reacted exactly as Jim intended.

"It's kind of like Lenny Bruce," he told me. "You know, they hounded that guy till he killed himself just because he used 'dirty' words, and now nobody gives a shit; you hear the same words everywhere. One day the President of the United States will get on TV and say, *Fuck* those fucking commies, they can suck my fucking *dick*!' and nobody will even blink. But one thing he *won't* say is, 'Those niggers sure like playing basketball!'

See, that's the *new* taboo. It's like my parents—they hear something that sounds a *little* bit racist, and they're ready to tar and feather somebody! And that's exactly what Jim is going after. He's going, 'Oh, I'm not allowed to say this word? I'm not? Well, guess what? I'm *saying* it!' And I think that's *great*! I think it's *visionary*! All these other people think it's taboo to say 'fuck,' and he's onto the *real thing*!"

He also made another good point: if ROT was truly a racist band, there'd be a lot more songs like that one. So it was okay to like them again, and Peewee promised that, after he got back to New York, he'd buy me a copy of *Pathology* and a few other records besides and mail them to me, his treat. And that day kept getting closer and closer till, next thing I knew, he was packing and preparing to take off with Suzanne and her boyfriend. (They were driving him up, but coming back in a few weeks to spend the rest of the summer in North Carolina.) We stayed up all night before he left, and I helped him load the car in the morning, and right before he hit the road, I said, "Oh, hey, let me run back and get that boombox."

"No, you can keep it. You fucked it up anyway. You've spilled so much paint on it, it's starting to look like a Jackson Pollock." And I laughed. Just from being around him and Suzanne, I knew who Jackson Pollock was.

"Well," I said, shaking his hand, "give me a call sometime."

"Oh, you *know* I will."

Then he got in the car, and I stood watching as it disappeared and thought, "What am I going to do without him?" He was too young, too weird, too smart, too talkative—nothing like the ideal friend I might have chosen, and yet I suddenly knew he was the best friend I'd ever had. And now, with his many distractions in the city, I figured he'd soon disappear from my life altogether.

BUT HE HADN'T BEEN TALKING SMACK about keeping in touch. He called me constantly to brag about all the fun he was having. Yes, he was seeing shows almost every night, and he'd met a girl named Mouse at one of them, and he was *pounding* that Mouse ass, and he and his friend Terrence were getting *so* fucked up. One night he put Terrence on the phone so the two of us could "meet," and Terrence said—his very first words—"Is this the killer?" I hated the thought of Peewee describing me that way, even to people I didn't know; and I was also jealous that he was in New York while I was stuck in North Carolina. So I said, "Yeah, well, I guess everybody seems like a killer when you're a midget like Bernard." Then Terrence burst into stoned laughter and said, "Hey, Bernard, the killer just called you a midget!"

"Well, fuck *him*, that redneck motherfucker! And he's *literally* a motherfucker, did I tell you that? He fucked his girlfriend's mom!" I'd opened Pandora's box. He was railing in the background in a voice so high he sounded like a talking tea kettle, but I barely heard a word he said, I was laughing so hard. I said, "Whoa, tell Peewee back there to take a fucking chill pill!" and at that point Terrence lost it completely and said, "Oh my God, *Peewee*, that's too fucking much!" and called to him like a dog, going, "Hey, *Peewee*! Roll over, *Peewee*! You want a bone, *Peewee*?" Then Peewee (since that's who he'd just become) went five-alarm berserk, and I heard him say, "Yeah, you *wish* I was fucking Peewee, you potato-face bitch! Now give me that fucking phone!" Then Terrence kind of yelped in pain, and a second later Peewee came on the line and said, "Hey, white trash! Yeah, I'm talking to *you*, white trash! I was going to mail you all those records I bought for your white-trash ass, but you know what I'm going to do now? I'm going to break them! Here, cunt, *listen*!" And, sure enough, I heard something break and Terrence yell, "No! Don't do that! Bernard, I said to stop it!" It sounded like a wrestling match had broken out—boom! crash! bang!—and then, with a thud, the line went dead.

Now, I'd seen this kid mad a few times, but never at me, and never as bad as he sounded on the phone. The rage in his voice! But ten minutes later he called again and acted like the whole thing had never happened, so I did too. Even so, he was always "Peewee" to me and Terrence after that; and to get even with Terrence, he'd made cutting remarks about his being Irish, while I became officially known as—what else?—"Killer," though that never quite caught on the way "Peewee" did. It just suited him perfectly, as he eventually admitted, but you had to know him well before he'd let you call him that. (He likewise refused to answer to "Bernie," as people sometimes addressed him. "My name is Bernard," he'd correct them on the spot. "Bernie's the guy that does your taxes.") And at least twice a week he'd ring me up, saying I should drive to the city, and of course I was dying to do exactly that, but I had to work, and, being on probation, I wasn't allowed to leave the state without permission. I asked but was told that, first, I should I finish my community service. So every weekend I worked at the home for handicapped kids, washing dishes and cleaning toilets and, once, driving a van full of head cases on a field trip to the petting zoo. (What an experience that was! "Bucky, put the stick down! Goats don't like it when you hit them with sticks!") And I was almost done with it—in a couple of weeks I could finally hit New York City—when one night toward the end of July, with no advance word whatsoever, I heard a knock on my door, and there he was.

"They threw me out," he said.

"Why? What happened?"

Well, it was a long story, but in a nutshell, his mom had found a vial of cocaine while going through his laundry, and during the shouting match that followed, he'd thrown a butter knife across the room, almost hitting his dad. Afterward there was still more talk of shipping him to the nuthouse, when he'd somehow managed to convince them to send him back to North Carolina instead. I'd never seen him so down. He'd been having the greatest summer of his whole life. Now he was stuck in hell for at least another year. I said, "Well, that's okay. We're going to have a great time, even if it *is* hell." I drove to the store and bought us some beer. He gave me the presents he'd bought me. He'd broken a few, of course, but there was still a big bag filled with T-shirts and buttons and five or six records, including a brand-new release by Rule of Thumb. I didn't know there *was* one! Peewee said, "Yeah, I didn't either. I found it at Bleecker Bob's the day those cunts busted me. I never got a chance to listen to it."

So we had a first listen that night. *Pathology of Least Resistance* had been a step down from the jackhammer-hardness of ROT's debut EP, and this latest record (which, sadly, was to be their last) was softer by far than *Pathology*. Some songs were fast and bluesy, a bit in the style of the Flesh Eaters, but most were pensive and sparely arranged, almost like a punk-rock version of Nick Drake, if that makes any sense. There was one song, "Raft at Sea," I loved right away, but Peewee thought that one sucked as well. He said ROT was finished, or the way he put it, "They could have led the revolution, and now they're fucking *Wings*!"

But that opinion was premature. It wasn't what we'd hoped to hear, but *Tinderloin* is the kind of record that opens up a little more each time it's played, so that finally it's one of your all-time favorites. I know

Peewee came to see it that way, and as for me, it was the one ROT record I continued to play long after I'd lost my taste for punk and rock & roll in general. Then too it was the soundtrack to the rest of that summer, when I cut my last remaining ties to my old identity. It started with the T-shirts Peewee had given me. They were just fucking *T-shirts* for bands like the Clash, but people were so disturbed by those alone, I thought, "Fuck it, might as well go all the way." I buzzed off my hair and dyed the stubble black, but that was *so* normal, I soon bleached it white. Then I switched to blue with the aid of food coloring, and the guys I worked with flipped the fuck out. "Good Gawd, yore hayer is *bloo*! Wachyoo doin' with bloo hayer, boah?" But they were supporting families on the same pay that barely supported me, so they had more important things to worry about than some teenage co-worker dyeing his hair blue. Megan, on the other hand, stopped coming by to fuck me, sure I'd lost my mind; and my mom *cried* the first time she saw me with blue hair, and my dad took one look and banned me from seeing my brothers. I said, "What is *wrong* with you people? It's just hair! And one day *everybody's* going look like this! There's going to be a revolution, and everything's going to be different by the time it's over!" But I could never make that speech work the way Peewee (almost) could, and my parents accused me of trying to (further) embarrass them. But it wasn't that, and it wasn't punk either—or not completely. I'd just been through so much in such a short span of time; I was being *bombarded* with so many new ideas and influences, so that I think my appearance *had* to change in order to signify, at least to myself, I wasn't the same person I had been. Plus I'd been mortified to be seen with my best friend (just as Megan had been mortified to be seen with me), so I was sort of saying, "That's right, I hang out with a freak. And I'm a freak myself. Want to make something out of it?" As a matter of fact, people did! I was refused service in restaurants. I was laughed at, spit at; kids and sometimes fucking grownups would shout "faggot!" from passing cars, the same as they did with Peewee. A rumor started circulating that he and I were lovers, and my brother Keith, who was fourteen that fall, got in a fight because of it, and that in turn brought me still more grief from my parents. It goes without saying they both despised Peewee. They thought he was the devil incarnate, and in a strange way I think they were right. Lucifer, after all, means "the bearer of light," and the crime that got him kicked out of heaven was thinking for himself. And that's why, I've come to decide, original thinkers throughout history have so often been persecuted: they're devils, don't you know! The Athenians poisoned Socrates; the Italians burned Giordano Bruno; and Sequoya, the Cherokee silversmith who came up with an alphabet so his people could communicate with a written language, had his fingers chopped off for his troubles. Not that I'm equating us with the likes of Sequoya. We were just kids going against the grain, and we got so much shit for it, you would almost have thought we raped a baby.

Yet the more that happened, the more defiant I felt. I started taking things in directions even Peewee never had, cutting up my clothes and putting them back together with safety pins. I wore a chain and padlock around my neck and painted my shirts with words—BANISHED and HOSTAGE and REVOLUTION ROCK—so that finally Peewee said, "Um, you know, Jason, nobody's really doing that anymore. That stopped about five years ago." Well, so what? I was *doing* it! I started going out in public with him, everywhere and all the time, and if the cops stopped us, let the cops stop us; they couldn't arrest us for looking weird, and we never left our building stoned or drunk. Luckily, most of our neighbors were university students who, wary of the cops for reasons of their own, weren't inclined to complain about noise. Peewee had bought a G&L Telecaster while he was in New York, and he taught me the few chords Terrence had taught him—A, C, D and E major, and A-shaped barre chords—and we strangled many a cat while playing along to records. "Lockstep" was the first song I learned to play from start to finish. Then, very quickly, I taught myself "Sweet Jane" and "Wild Thing" and half the Ramones' first album. Peewee was impressed. He said, "Jesus Christ, Killer, you're a fucking natural! You should get your own guitar, and all we have to do is find some more people and we can start our own band!"

"Like who? Who's going to want to play with us? And there's no place *to* play."

Oh, he said, we could always find that; I wouldn't believe some of the places people played in New York. He posted a notice looking for musicians at the only halfway-decent record store in a 100-mile radius, and though I don't remember any musicians responding, we did get a call from a guy who wanted to sell a guitar for $200, mini-amp included. The guitar was an off-white 1968 Fender Mustang with a red pearl pickguard, and, man, to see that thing was to fall in love. Peewee loaned me the $100 I was short to buy it, and one night shortly afterward I was noodling by myself when I realized I'd written a song. I ran straight to Peewee's place and said, "Listen to this! I just wrote a *song*!" I never even got to play it all. He stopped me halfway through and said, "Hey, shouldn't that part go more like…?" and took away my guitar and started rewriting the fucking thing! That was my first hint of what it was like to be in a band with Peewee. He later changed the lyrics I wrote from an account of my fight with Mark Powell to a tribute to Nietzsche's superman, or some fucking shit—I forget. But I know the song was called "A Cut Above," and we never played it for a single soul, aside from Suzanne, who listened with a smirk throughout and afterward said, "That was very sweet." Peewee said, "*Sweet?* That bitch *rocks!*" I shared his sentiments completely. Considering that we could barely play, I regarded that song as a masterpiece.

It was a magical time, those heady months beginning in April of '81 and lasting to, roughly, the end of the year. I suppose all moments of transformation seem magical in retrospect, or they do if you change for the better. But youth is wasted on the young, as the old saw goes, and looking back, I think I was far too immersed in my many problems—lawsuit, parents, harassment, and so on—to fully savor the good. Plus where was it all *leading*? I remember talking about that with my grandmother one time. I used to drop by for dinner as often as possible, sometimes taking Peewee, who was always a perfect gentleman around her, though I could tell she wasn't sure what to make of him. It wasn't because of the way we looked. She'd been pretty wild herself back in her day, so she took all that in stride. But once, when she and I were by ourselves, she asked if I was still planning to go to college.

"You used to talk about it all the time," she said, "but it seems like ever since you got friendly with that boy, you just stopped doing it."

"Well, you know, I feel like I *am* going to college. I mean, I'm learning so much from hanging around with him, and what are they going to teach me at college he and his sister can't?"

"Oh, honey, I think they can teach you a lot of things. They can teach you how to get a good job. You don't want to be doing what you're doing right now for the rest of your life. That's going to get pretty old after a while."

Yes, it was *already* getting old! But one night in mid-November Peewee came running over to my place to say he'd just gotten off the phone with Terrence in New York, and guess who was playing at CBGB's tomorrow night? Go on and guess! I called my boss and quit my job, and the next day Peewee and I hit the road, and that night we met Jim Cassady, who told us we should start a band. Before then I'd never really thought it was possible, but once he said it was possible, or he said it was in so many words, I knew *exactly* where everything had been leading: I was going to move to New York and start a band with Peewee, and that was *it*.

SO AFTER JIM HAD VANISHED INSIDE CBGB'S with Buddy Lavrakis, I walked the streets with Peewee for quite some time, tossing band names back and forth till we eventually settled on the Widowmakers. And Terrence could play bass, and I'd play guitar, and Peewee would likewise play guitar as well as sing. I said, "Wait a minute, why are *you* the singer?"

"Well, come on, I'm the one with the most experience. I must have seen fifty bands last summer!" Of course seeing bands wasn't the same as singing for one, but for the time being I backed off on that account. Our immediate tasks were to find a drummer and to somehow convince his parents to sanction his move back to the city. The latter especially he considered pressing, since the rents in New York were outrageously high, and the way he explained it, we could move right away, with the limited funds we had, if his parents agreed to take us in. I said, "Come on, man, we're going to live with your *parents*? We might as well stay in North Carolina!"

"Well, *you* don't have to, but I've got no choice. They're going to insist I stay in school, and what am I supposed to say then? I want to drop out and start a band? Yeah, right! They'll cut me off in a heartbeat, and I'll have to get some fucking *job*."

That was his true motive. Work was one of his bêtes noirs—and that included schoolwork. If he found a subject interesting, he'd read and study and master it in what seemed like no time at all, and often at that point he'd grow bored and move on quickly to something else. But he was otherwise lazy, as his parents knew, though they continued to spoil him with their lavish monthly stipend—an obvious attempt at buying his love. I think they both felt guilty for being too busy to give him their full attention, while he, of course, was greedy for attention, and that was another reason he acted up and they in turn sent him away: out of sight, out of mind. Plus, as I was soon to see with my own two eyes, they were both afraid of him. We kept walking and talking, all the way to Central Park South and down Broadway to Times Square, where black guys came up and said, "Smoke, smoke," openly selling pot; but Peewee said, "Don't look at them. Never make eye contact with people in the street. That's how you attract psychos." He also told me never to look up at skyscrapers, only tourists did that and tourists got mugged, and when I walked on the sidewalk, I should always stick close to the curb, the better to avoid muggers lying in wait. We passed Macy's and the Flatiron building, and I wanted to stop and get a bite to eat, but Peewee said, "No, I really want to get downtown. I want to hook up with Mouse." Mouse, again, was the hardcore girl he'd been seeing during the summer, though at the time I don't think we used the term "hardcore"; it was all punk to us. He'd met Mouse at a club called A7, which was where we were headed. It didn't get going till really late, he said, and once we got there I was going to have to keep my guard up; the neighborhood was just crawling with Puerto Rican gangs who'd stab me to death on the slightest provocation. Finally we arrived, and he definitely wasn't kidding about the neighborhood. It was right across the street from Tompkins Square Park, which in those days was deadly. The park itself was pitch-black, and some of the surrounding buildings were burned-out hulks, and people would pass us with scarred faces or missing eyes or just something about them where you could tell at a glance these were not people to be fucked with. There was no carding at the door as there'd been at CBGB's. I was thrilled. I was just about to hit my first punk club. I was disappointed the second I walked inside. It looked like a minuscule rec room, with beat-up furniture pushed against the walls and a small stage in the corner where a band made up of high-school kids was playing shitty music. It sounded to me like the Germs. I'd never liked the Germs. I may well have been one of the oldest people there, and very few looked as punked out as me and Peewee. They mostly wore flannel shirts or plain white T-shirts with scruffy jeans and work boots. Some had shaved heads. Others wore motorcycle jackets or studded leather bracelets, but that was generally as punk as they got. Peewee tried to act like a big man on the scene, saying hi to people who didn't speak back, and even when they did speak back, they still seemed vaguely hostile. I didn't realize he *wasn't* a big man on the scene—he'd always made it sound to me like he was—so I thought this was the way real punks acted and tried to cop the same attitude. He asked if anybody had seen Mouse. Nobody had. He introduced me, saying, "Yeah, this is my friend Jason. We just drove from North Carolina to see Rule of Thumb." Kids groaned at those words. "Those guys are nothing," one said. "They're sellouts, man." I tried to defend them, and he said, "What do *you* know? You're from South Carolina." I got quite a bit of that that night. Just because I came from the South and spoke with a slight accent, I was treated like a hayseed, when to me these kids seemed just as provincial, if not more so. Then I met Peewee's friend Matt, who seemed just plain stupid, though he at least was a nice guy. Peewee asked if he wanted to be our drummer, and he said, "Man, you know I can't do that! I'm in four bands already!" One of his bands played next, and all their songs were really fast, none lasting longer than a minute and a half, and every time they started a new one, kids would form a circle and move around the room, shoving each other and people on the sidelines, including me. This was something Peewee had never mentioned, so the first time it happened, I thought somebody was looking for a fight. Then I realized, no, these kids were *dancing*; and the next time I was shoved, I shoved the guy right back, and soon I was part of the circle myself, shoving everybody else. The music was still god-awful, but the shoving part was a *lot* of fun. And even aside from slamdancing (which is what that shoving was), there was a sense of rage in that room, a sense of disaffection, and if you could take all that and multiply it and make it move and march beneath the same black flag—there was your revolution. At least two more bands played after Matt's, all sounding very much the same. It was daylight by the time we left, and I think I had an idea that in New York the buildings were so tall and so close together they'd block out the sun, but, no, it was so bright outside, I felt like I needed a welding mask after so much time in darkness. We staggered across the street to a coffee shop to get some breakfast, and Peewee said we could do one of two things: find a cheap hotel or crash at his parents' place. I was newly unemployed after all, so the less money spent, the better. Besides, I was curious about his parents after hearing so much about them.

"Well," he said, "okay. But don't tell them I blew off school to come here. Let's just say you really wanted to see the city, and last night you talked me into driving up and we're leaving first thing tomorrow. And don't say anything about the band. And if they say anything about the way you're dressed, say that's the way you've always dressed; it's got nothing to do with me. And don't mention Terrence—they don't like him. And don't tell them I have a BB gun, and don't say anything about me spending my money on records, and *definitely* don't say anything about Suzanne spending the night at her boyfriend's place. They'll give her shit for leaving me alone."

And I think there were still more things I was told not to say. We walked back to the heart of the Village, where I'd left my car, and Peewee directed me across the East River to his parents' building in Brooklyn Heights: a large brownstone with a postcard view of the Manhattan skyline from all the windows facing it. He used his keys to let us in, and a second later a blonde woman with a face like his came walking down the hall and said, "Bernard, what in the *world*?" We'd come to see the city, we told her. We'd been driving all night! Then his dad walked out. I liked him right away. His mom struck me as a bit on the cold side and, of the two, far more suspicious, so I tried to set her at ease with my down-home manners, lots of "Yes ma'ams" and "No ma'ams" and that sort of thing. Both she and her husband had voices so loud it took some getting used to, especially Peewee's father, who seemed to speak through some kind of internal megaphone: "JASON, YOU LOOK LIKE THE KIND OF BOY WHO'S PLAYED SOME BALL. EVER PLAY ANY BALL, JASON?" Both had strong New York accents oddly unshared by their kids, and neither seemed nearly as brainy as their kids, despite shelves of books in almost every room. There were also framed posters for some of the movies and plays Peewee's dad had written, and I asked him questions about his career, and he'd say things like, "WELL, THE THEATER'S NOT WHAT IT USED TO BE, I CAN TELL YOU THAT. NOBODY WANTS TO SEE PLAYS ANYMORE. ALL THEY WANT TO SEE IS MUSICALS." He was like his son that way, though I don't think they recognized it. Both were critical of the way things were. They were just taking radically different approaches.

Peewee and I hadn't slept in over twenty-four hours, so I crashed in Suzanne's room and he slept in his, and that afternoon he woke me so

I could "see the city." First, though, we had lunch with his parents, and that's when I realized they were afraid of him. It wasn't just because of the stunts he'd pulled, starting fires and throwing knives and so on; it was also because he was so brilliant, as they obviously knew, and so they responded meekly to half of what he said, like people with painful, secret pasts forced to dine with a psychic. What if he exposed them? What if he uttered something so devastating they'd never get over it? And he was conscious they felt that way and tried to use it to bend them to his will, and that's another reason I think they sent him to live with Suzanne, who of course was also very bright, though she was kind of a "safe" thinker compared to him, and nowhere near as devious. And he could definitely be devious. That lunch was a good example. He described his life in North Carolina as an anti-Semitic nightmare, with kids at school calling him a kike and slapping him around. I sat there listening and thought, "What the fuck is he talking about?" Sure, he got harassed, same as me, but I'd never heard anyone call him a kike. But then, as he kept talking, I realized it was all part of Operation Widowmakers; that by skewing the truth to fit his parents' specific paranoia, he was hoping they'd say, "Oh my God, we'd better move you right back to the city!" It didn't seem to be working at first. They said, "Well, Suzanne's never had a problem. She says it's very nice."

"Yeah, but she goes to the university. It's not like that at *my* school." I backed him up immediately, inventing a teacher who once told me the Nazis hadn't gone far enough. They were suitably outraged. Then Peewee and I left for Manhattan, and the second we hit the sidewalk, he said, "Suckers! Oh, Killer, you were fantastic! I was going to pull you out of the room and tell you what to say, but you read my fucking mind! I should've thought of this a long time ago! And they love your ass, I can tell, and tomorrow I'm going to leave you guys alone, and I want you to make it sound like I'm in mortal fucking danger! I want death threats, I want swastikas on my locker, I want everything you can think of to get those bitches to let me come home!" And it just might have succeeded. But that night we got together with Terrence, as we had the night before, and Peewee asked if he wanted to play bass in the Widowmakers. Terrence said, "Well, yeah, but what about my parents?" It seemed both sets of parents wanted to keep their sons apart. Peewee said, "Oh, I'm sure you can figure something out. I think I got *my* parents exactly where I want them!" We bought some more coke in Washington Square Park and took the subway to Times Square to check out some strippers, and not one person carded Peewee or Terrence either. (He was seventeen at the time, and Peewee had turned sixteen on August 18th.) Then we headed back downtown, where we drank beer at a bar called the Park Inn and topped off the night at A7. Mouse showed up, and she looked just like one, and her date looked like a camel. Seeing Mouse make out with the camel caused some sadness for Peewee, yet we had so much to look forward to, he didn't stay sad for long. We slamdanced till five o'clock in the morning and took the train back to Brooklyn, where I once again slept in Suzanne's room, and once again I was woken by Peewee.

"Get up," he said. "Come on, we've got to go." I could tell something was wrong. I threw on my clothes and walked out to the hall, where Peewee's mom said, "Well, Jason, I hope you had a good time. Maybe we'll meet you again under better circumstances." She was acting as strangely as he was. I never saw his dad. We walked outside, and I asked Peewee what was going on.

"Oh, fucking Terrence fucked up everything! He got home all fucked up and told his parents he was out with me, and they called my mom and told her. Those spudfucker cunts! I'm surprised you didn't hear all the yelling and screaming. You really didn't hear it?"

"I never heard a thing."

"Well, it was pretty bad, goddamn their fucking asses. But they're not going to get in the way of this band! *Oh* no! We're going to go back and pack up our shit and move, and if they don't like it, they can eat my fucking *fuck*!"

BUT THOSE WERE BIG WORDS. He'd changed his mind by the time we got to North Carolina. He said we didn't have the money to make the move, and the best idea was to wait till Christmas, when he could once again work on his parents. He spent two weeks in New York that Christmas (I drove up for New Year's), and though his parents were still implacable, he did meet a kid named Anthony who expressed interest in being our drummer. The plan at that point was to hold off till summer, and if his parents were still against taking him back, we'd move in spite of them. He started saving his money, skimping on meals and buying fewer books, and even though he hated working, he took a part-time job at that record store, walking forty-five minutes to get there after school. (He figured, living in New York, he'd never have to drive, so it wasn't till some time later that he finally learned how.) As for me, I found another house-painting job and, to cut down on my rent, moved in with Peewee and Suzanne, sleeping on their sofa and likewise hoarding most of my pay. Every cent we saved was kept in a strongbox stored beneath Peewee's bed. We counted it constantly while keeping a lookout for amp heads, guitar cabinets and effects pedals we could buy at a discount. At one point we talked about stealing equipment from a cover band playing at the Ramada Inn bar, but we could never find a moment when they left their stuff unguarded. We also talked about stealing a PA from my parents' church, but I wasn't willing to go that far, and besides, all that talk of stealing made me nervous. Yet, ironically, we'd started doing things almost as bad. First Peewee decided the Widowmakers had to have a logo he wanted to spray-paint all over New York once we got there, and he came up with a number of designs—a rifle scope, a tombstone, a wedding band with a slash through it—and we'd drive around town to test them out, defacing walls and buildings in the middle of the night. A few times we brought along eggs, pelting cars and pedestrians, and once we blew up a mailbox with a cherry bomb; but that got written up in the paper with a mention of it being a federal offense, so no more blowing up mailboxes. It was a pointless crime anyway. We had no beef with the postal service. We had a big one, though, with a certain redneck who beat up Peewee, and I'm afraid somebody filled the locks on his car with superglue, as well as supplying him with a nifty Chewbecca hood ornament. Later we learned his mother had died, and we paid a visit to the cemetery (which was right across the street from my grandmother's house) and wrote I SUCK COCK IN HELL in Day-Glo paint on her grave marker. We also took vengeance on Mr. Wright, who from my point of view had expelled me unnecessarily and likewise suspended Peewee: we dialed the time and temperature in Sydney, Australia from a phone booth and charged the call to Mr. Wright and walked away leaving the phone off the hook. And then there was another kid who was constantly fucking with Peewee—a nerd, of all things, who must have been trying to elevate his status by picking on somebody smaller—and we decided his car would be vastly improved with a polka-dot paint job. It's hard to believe we did all that. It's hard to believe we never got caught. We were taking a huge risk, since nobody in that town looked remotely like us, and the police still stopped us every chance they got, though never with the grounds to make an arrest. It got especially bad after we gave ourselves Mohawks. Mine didn't last very long. My boss told me to shave it off, otherwise I was fired. We had plans for getting him too, but we skipped town before we could set them in motion.

But Peewee's boss thought he was just terrific. There was practically nothing Peewee didn't know about contemporary music, including music he despised, so he could answer almost any question a customer posed, and even his appearance was something of an asset as far as his boss was concerned: it made the store seem cutting edge, which, by local standards, it was. Still, I hated that guy. He was a hippie freak whose favorite band was Captain Beefheart, and that kicked off Peewee's Beefheart phase, and I could never get into that stuff, no matter how much he played it for me. Worse, he started talking about some "new way" of making music, whereas I just wanted to play your basic punk rock in the vein of early Rule of Thumb. But that was pointless, Peewee now decided. Nobody would ever do it as well as *they* had, and besides, it was just like Captain Beefheart said: Why did everything have to have that same old heartbeat rhythm?

"Because," I said, "it rocks! And that's all I want to do. I just want to rock the fuck out!"

"Well, so do I! But maybe there's a different way of doing it. I mean, I'm not saying I want to be Beefheart. There's only one of those. But almost every goddamn song I hear is verse-chorus-verse, and it's all so fucking predictable, and if somebody doesn't come along and change things, rock & roll is going to die. It's *already* starting to die. Punk started something, but it's already become a formula, and we have a chance to do something different instead of the same old crap everybody else does. It's kind of like the Impressionists, you know? Suppose they'd gone on painting the same old way instead of freeing up the stroke? Or suppose Rimbaud had gone on writing boring little poems instead of *A Season in Hell*? That's the only reason people remember him. And that's what I want for us: I want us to be *remembered*."

He always maintained that rock & roll was an important art form, and that one day scholars would take the Sex Pistols as seriously as they now took Mozart. Well, maybe. But every time I wrote a song, he'd find a way to change it, and every time we practiced, I'd be playing power chords while he'd bang out some weirdly-paced racket and yelp like a lapdog with its tail caught in a door. That was his idea of "singing." We would tape ourselves and mail the cassettes to Terrence and that Anthony kid who'd talked about being our drummer, and Terrence, I knew, had some serious misgivings—we spoke about it once on the phone. But my attitude was, first, let's get to New York; we can adjust the band later. It was a frustrating period for everybody concerned. Suzanne had broken up with her boyfriend during the winter, which meant she spent more time around the apartment, and she and Peewee were constantly squabbling about his slovenly housekeeping, so, to keep the peace, I was forced to become the resident janitor. He clashed with me as well. Once I got caught in the snow on the way to pick him up from work, and he ranted and raved about freezing his balls off like he actually thought I'd kept him waiting on purpose. There were also some jealous scenes over the fact that I was getting laid and he wasn't. It turned out certain girls liked the punk-rock look. Especially around the university, they'd come up and talk to us; and Peewee, of course, was only sixteen while looking more like ten, and often he'd go off on some tirade filled with a great many four-letter words, so that even if there'd been the slightest chance of something happening, he'd blown it right there. I, on the other hand, was nineteen and looked it, and I was a pretty good-looking guy in those days, with or without blue hair, so I was usually the one they'd wanted to meet in the first place. I had a semi-regular thing going with a girl Peewee dubbed "the albino" on account of her white-blonde hair, as well as another ongoing thing with a girl named Natalie who later moved to New York to study acting. So there I was, hooking up constantly, yet almost every time I walked out the door, I'd get called a fag, or else I'd see people whispering and figure that was what they were saying to each other. I was too big for them to say it to my face—or not unless they were safely inside a moving car or carousing with a pack of friends. I had to restrain myself from responding. I didn't want to get in a fight and bring the cops down on my ass. All the crimes I committed were done on the sly, and every time we pulled one off, it was like getting even with all those others I would have loved to have taken on directly but couldn't.

One Saturday night toward the end of April I went to the record store to pick up Peewee. It must have been around seven o'clock, and halfway home we stopped at a Burger King to grab a bite to eat. We should never have gone there. We should've gone to someplace near the university, where people were typically more tolerant; but even then the manager might refuse to serve us, or other customers might complain or try in more obnoxious ways to start trouble. That was especially true of poor white trash, and this particular Burger King was in a shopping center next to a Kmart where the bumpkins from surrounding counties came to shop. Still, we foolishly stopped there, and just as we should've expected, somebody threw something at us—an ice cube or french fry or something—and we looked across the room and saw four teenaged guys smirking our way, at least one of them wearing a letter jacket from a backwater high school. Peewee still had his Mohawk—I'd recently shaved mine off—and one of the kids yelled, "What tribe you from? The Faggot tribe?" And Peewee said, "No, I'm from the Fuck You tribe." And that was it. There was no escalation, no sense that something bad was about to occur. They left a few minutes later, and we finished eating and walked outside ourselves, and suddenly I heard Peewee shout, "Jason, look out!" and the second he said that, somebody jumped on my back, bringing me down on the pavement. I went down hard—or me and the kid on my back both did—and somehow I managed to shed him and saw another kid raising his foot to kick me while smirking down as if to say, "Yeah, who's talking shit now?" I had no idea where Peewee was. I rolled over to avoid getting kicked and grabbed this kid by the leg, tripping him, and he and I grappled for however long and exchanged a few blows. I must have hit him pretty good, or maybe he just got scared, but he got up and ran away, and then I stood myself and saw a number of people in the parking lot frozen in place and staring with blank expressions. Then somebody else jumped me from behind, once again taking me down, and we rolled over and over on the pavement, duking it out. He was really strong—a farm kid, no doubt—and at one point he had me pinned down, slugging away on top of me, when he suddenly jerked his head back and screamed in agony while clutching the back of his neck. The whole scene was really confusing, but that one moment is as vivid now as it was at the time. He stumbled to his feet and staggered away, still clutching the back of his neck, and a second later Peewee came running around the other side of the Burger King and said, "Let's go!" Everything was spinning. I kept looking around for the car and couldn't see it till Peewee said, "Jason, it's right in front of you!" And so it was. We got in the car and peeled out of the parking lot, and I said, "What the fuck happened?!"

"What do you *mean*, what happened? Those fuckers jumped us!"

"Well, I know *that* happened! But what happened to *you*?"

Well, he said, he saw those guys as we were walking out of the restaurant, and he took off running and one of them chased him all the way to Kmart. Then he realized the guy wasn't there anymore, so he ran back and saw this other guy attacking me, and, knowing the guy would tear him to pieces if he joined the brawl himself, he stabbed him with a ballpoint pen and ran away. The pen was still in his hand. He was very proud of himself, and for a moment I was too. There was a brief sense of celebration, a sense of "We showed *them*," but then I realized something: if that kid was badly hurt, we were deep in shit. I asked Peewee how hard he'd stabbed him, and he said, "*Pretty* hard. But, Jason, I had to do *something*. It looked like he was killing you!"

"Yeah, but you may have killed *him*! Jesus Christ, you know what's going to happen? They're going to call the police and say we started it, and you *know* who they're going to believe."

"But we didn't! They jumped *us*! And it was just a fucking *pen*!"

"It doesn't matter! He could *die* if you stabbed him in the right place! No, man, we've got to get out of here! We've got to pack up our shit and get the fuck out of here *now*!"

"And go where?"

"Where do you fucking *think*? New York!"

But for a few minutes he kept saying it was self-defense, and there were plenty of witnesses who'd back us up, and it was only a goddamned pen, that's all it was, nobody could die from a single stab wound inflicted by a goddamned pen. I said, "Bernard, do you really want to go to jail? Because that's where we're going! And, yeah, they might let us out in a couple of days, but that's still long enough for somebody to rape your fucking ass!"

That sold him. We got to our place—Suzanne wasn't there—and started throwing our shit in the back of my car. I was bruised and bleeding from scrapes all over my body, but there was no time to think about that, I was so convinced we were about to be arrested. Then, as we were taking the stereo apart, Peewee suddenly announced he was calling his parents. I said, "Are you out of your fucking *mind*?! That's like leaving the cops a *map*!"

"Well, I can't just *disappear*. Suzanne's going to come home and find me missing, and they're going to blame *her*. I've *got* to call them, Jason.

I'll tell them—I don't know—we're moving to L.A. to start a band, and maybe in a few weeks I can tell them where I really am."

So he called his parents while I died a thousand deaths, thinking he was going to slip up and tell them what was really going on. But he didn't; he stuck to his story. At first he spoke to his mom, but then his dad came on the line, and he, of course, spoke so loud it was like he was standing in the next room.

"BERNARD," I heard him say, "YOU'RE NOT GOING ANYWHERE. YOU ARE GOING TO STAY RIGHT THERE AND STAY IN SCHOOL. WE'VE HAD ENOUGH OF THIS, AND IF YOU DROP OUT AFTER ALL WE'VE DONE FOR YOU, YOU CAN FORGET YOU'RE EVEN MY SON." And Peewee said, "Yeah, you've done so much for me. You guys don't even want me around."

"I'M SERIOUS, BERNARD. IF YOU DROP OUT OF SCHOOL, YOU CAN FORGET I EVEN EXIST, AND THAT GOES FOR YOUR MOTHER TOO."

Then Peewee's face turned so red it was almost purple, and he said, "WELL, FUCK YOU BOTH THEN! I AM GOING TO LIVE MY LIFE THE WAY I WANT TO, AND THERE'S NOT A GODDAMN THING YOU CAN DO TO STOP ME, YOU WORTHLESS, SOULLESS, TALENTLESS SELLOUT!"

Then his father hung up with a click so loud it sounded like an ammo clip being slapped inside a gun, and Peewee stood perfectly still. Then he moved. He threw the phone against the wall, smashing it. Then he picked up the coffee table and threw that against the wall, smashing that as well. Even as small as he was, he was terrifying at that moment. With his inky Mohawk and face rage-red, he looked like a miniature Travis Bickle. Then he lunged for the stereo, and I said, "Bernard, no!" and once again he froze before he sank to the floor like a marionette whose strings have just been cut, and he cried. He fucking howled, man, and I knew exactly how he must be feeling, since I'd practically been disowned myself. I couldn't take it. I went to his room, where most of my things were likewise kept, and packed and fucking prayed the police wouldn't show up before he pulled himself together. I listened to him cry till he was all cried out. Then he walked back with his eyes downcast and still a bit teary and said, "Yeah, I think we should leave Suzanne something for all the stuff I just broke. You think fifty bucks will cover it?"

"Let's make it a hundred."

"Okay, a hundred. Now let's pack up this shit and get the fuck out of here."

We left maybe a half-hour later, and do you know, after all that, the police never did look for us. I know they never went to my parents' place, and I know they never contacted Suzanne, so I have to assume that kid wasn't badly hurt after all, or if he was, he may have thought I was hurt myself and been too afraid to call the cops. But even now when I go home, I still think about that kid and wonder if he could still press charges after all this time, or for that matter, if Mr. Wright could, or one of those people whose property we destroyed. But every last one of you fucking deserved it, and as for all you others who likewise deserved it and nothing ever happened—I just hope fate took care of you.

WE SPENT MAYBE TWO WEEKS at a run-down hotel in Elizabeth, New Jersey. At least I think that's where it was. I know it was just outside the city, and even with a safe, Peewee didn't trust the staff, so I was left to guard our stuff while he took a bus to Manhattan every day to look for an apartment. It was almost as difficult to find a place in those days as it is now, but one night he came back and said he might have something. It wasn't too far from CBGB's, he said, and it was only $400 a month, which he considered a real steal. I didn't. In North Carolina we'd paid something like $250, split three ways. Still, he was the New Yorker. He must know what he was talking about. He thought the landlords might not approve him, looking so young, so the next day I went alone to their office in Chelsea and basically offered to pay them a bribe (in addition to the security deposit and first month's rent) if they rushed my application. The bribe was Peewee's idea. It worked: the landlords approved me almost on the spot. Trusting Peewee, I never even bothered to see the place. I signed the lease and forked over the money (which, of course, I'd brought with me); and back in New Jersey, Peewee and I packed up the car and drove to Manhattan, where he directed me across town to Rivington Street, a block north of Delancey and the mouth of the Williamsburg Bridge. It looked exactly like the neighborhood around A7: charred buildings, sidewalks strewn with broken glass, scary-looking Puerto Rican guys staring us down. I was in shock! I told Peewee I was driving back to those pigs in Chelsea and demanding a refund, but he said, "You can't do that! You just a signed a lease! And it's really not that bad. You haven't even been inside yet!"

So I took the keys for a look inside, leaving Peewee to watch our stuff. There was a front section and a back section, and the courtyard dividing them was covered with sooty slush that later proved to be rotting green felt, probably placed there to simulate grass. Our place was in the back: apartment 1-R on the ground floor, just behind the stairwell. The door was metal and painted blue, with part of a bumper sticker peeling off the front and three locks that took me five minutes to open. I heard doors slamming, kids crying, people talking loud in Spanish. It smelled like somebody a floor above was cooking cabbage in a pot filled with dirty diapers. Finally I got the door open and saw cockroaches the size of Matchbox cars go racing away. I was standing in a large studio, thirty by fifteen feet, not including the bathroom. The only light came from a single window with a lovely view of a brick wall. The toilet looked like a huge rotting tooth. An ancient carton of milk was still inside the refrigerator. Nobody had bothered to remove a single piece of furniture that was sitting in the middle of the main room: a twin-bed mattress streaked with shit. Or maybe it was chocolate. Or maybe it was blood. I went back to the car and told Peewee we couldn't *possibly* live in this place, and once again he said it was too late. He said, "Trust me, man, this is as good as it's going to get. And I think it's great! We've got our own place in Manhattan! And what'd you expect, anyway? Some nice little townhouse like we just moved out of?"

"Well, I didn't expect *this*."

Still, like he'd said, I'd signed a lease. We started moving our stuff inside in shifts. I remember thinking of Rico, the only Hispanic I'd ever met in North Carolina, and now *I* was a minority. It certainly seemed that way. All I'd seen was Puerto Ricans since driving south of Houston Street. But then, as I was passing through the front part of the building with a load of stuff, I noticed two white guys coming down the stairs. Both were young and dressed in suits. Both had strange, glazed expressions. I saw them again a few days later, and others like them. Some were white, and some were black (though most were Puerto Rican), but they all shared the same foggy expression. Peewee noticed the same thing and said there must be a shooting gallery in the front of the building.

I said, "A *what?*" I knew about junkies, of course, but never realized they convened to shoot up. Peewee told me never to speak to any of our neighbors, afraid it might lead to them stealing our stuff; and for that matter, we had a rule at the beginning that, unless we were practicing, one of us always had to be in the apartment to keep vigil. And that worked out well, since, shortly after we moved to the city, I got a security-guard job at Hunter College, working midnight to eight, while Peewee found a daytime job at a copy shop. I never drove to work. My car was stolen days after making its Rivington Street debut, and I never reported it missing for fear of it being linked to the stabbing in North Carolina. It was weeks before I told my parents I was living in New York and not in California, as I'd lied. Peewee maintained the same lie with Suzanne. He didn't speak to his own parents for over three years, even after they learned he was living a few stops away on the F-train.

One night, a month or so after we moved in, I ran to the courtyard to put out the trash. I *literally* ran, as I often did when I left the apartment in the early days, just about to head inside when a goateed Puerto Rican guy cornered me by my door. I thought for sure I was about to get mugged, but instead he said, "Hey, man, I need—I need—I need to borrow a broom."

"A what?"

"A broom. You know. I live—I live—I live upstairs, and I need—I need to borrow a broom."

I could tell he was a junkie—he had that familiar glazed look—but he seemed so friendly, I went inside and got him a broom. Then I went to close the door, but he just kept standing there, saying, "Yeah, I seen—I seen—I seen you guys. Punk rock, right?"

"That's right."

"Yeah, that's some—that's some wicked shit."

Then Peewee came walking up—he was probably getting back from work—and asked what was going on. So I told him, and he turned to the guy and said, "Hey, man, bring the broom back any time you want, but right now we've got to eat." Then he shut the door and locked it and said, "What, are you fucking retarded?! Didn't I tell you not to speak to these people?!"

"I couldn't help it. He spoke to me first."

"Yeah, and you know why? I mean, you do know what he was doing, right?"

"No. What was he doing?"

"He was *casing* us! He wants to know what we've got in here so he can come back later and steal it!" And I thought, "Holy shit, he's right," and swore it would never happen again, and a few days later *I* came home and there was Peewee hanging out with the same guy inside our apartment! He was even playing him one of our songs with his fucking guitar plugged in and everything, alerting every junkie in the building to the fact that our place was filled with equipment, including a Sunn head we'd recently bought. But that was Peewee. He'd say one thing and do another, and if you pointed out the contradiction, you had to know you were in for a long debate in which he'd try to prove there *was* no contradiction, and if you actually managed to make your case, he'd shrug and say, "A foolish consistency is the hobgoblin of small minds," quoting Emerson, or, quoting Walt Whitman, "I contain multitudes." Still, his getting friendly with that guy, whose name was Nelson, proved in some ways to be a benefit, since we'd been too paranoid to play music in our own apartment, and Nelson said we could play there any time we wanted and if anybody fucked with us, they were going to have to deal with him, and he was "a bad—a bad—a bad motherfucker." Eventually we did practice there a couple of times with the other Widowmakers: Terrence and that kid Anthony, who was twenty-two and lived in Queens with his overweight girlfriend. He was an incredibly dim guy with a mullet and a major Ramones fixation, but he drove a van, which was helpful, and his dad had a business packaging and selling nuts, which was helpful too, since we sometimes practiced at his dad's warehouse.

But our very first practices were held at a place called 171A, right up the street from A7. It was a home away from home for hardcore kids and, briefly, us; but one day Peewee blew off work and got in a fight with some bruiser at 171A and refused to go back. I forget what that fight was about. All I remember is that Peewee came home with a black eye and said he was never setting foot at that place again, and that went for A7 too. Fuck those kids and their simple-minded, two-chord music. We were going to show *them* a thing or two. We were going to do something completely different—though he never could articulate how this something different was supposed to go. He'd say things in practice like, "It should sound like a train about to go off its tracks," and Terrence would look at me if to say, "Did I just hear right? A *train* about to go off its *tracks*?" Yet the truth is, that was how we sounded without even trying. None of us were any good, except for Anthony, and Anthony had one basic beat he'd ripped off from Tommy Ramone. Peewee, inspired by Captain Beefheart, had begun his lifelong experiment with altered tunings, and from that I learned how to tune down to C#, which for me was a huge discovery. I still leaned heavily toward power chords while trying to branch out and play some true leads, though most of my contributions weren't to Peewee's liking. They were all too "conventional" for him, just as my songwriting was conventional too, so no song was complete till he'd made it his own. He was likewise bossy with the other guys, Anthony in particular. I remember once he told Anthony to get a haircut, that maybe if he cut off his rattail, he'd think less like a rat and more like a human being. Other times he'd try to show Anthony exactly what he wanted by playing the drums himself. Not that it did any good. Anthony would nod like he understood, only to lapse back into Tommy Ramone a few minutes later. It was really Peewee's fault for sticking him in the band without so much as a tryout; but he was only sixteen when he met Anthony, and must have figured one drummer's pretty much the same as the next, when by now I know percussion's the most important part. I can't count the number of times I've heard a song with a great guitar intro, and I'll think, "This is going to be something," and it all goes to hell the second the drums and bass kick in.

At any rate, once Terrence graduated from high school, we started practicing five and, sometimes, six times a week. That was what Peewee thought it was going to take to make the band work, and I for one was all for it, that band being all I had. We kept a rehearsal space at a studio on Eighth Avenue in the West 40s. I forget the name, but it was managed by an ancient Irish hoofer named Katie who used to dance with Gene Kelly and loved to talk about what a jerk he was. But she was sweet to us, and I met a number of cute girls at that place. I never brought them back to Rivington Street. Peewee and I had put up a bricks-and-boards bookshelf to split the room in half, but it still didn't afford much privacy. Plus the neighborhood was so dangerous—I was mugged twice by the end of that summer—and with practically no ventilation, the apartment felt like a sauna. I hadn't realized New York could be so brutally hot, and even at night the heat made practice hell, to say nothing of Peewee's outbursts and his constant belittling of Anthony. It's a wonder that kid put up with it for as long as he did, except he was doubtlessly cowed by Peewee's intelligence. But we all were. And Peewee was conscious of that, just as throwing fits was another way of trying to control us, and so was his stinginess when it came to praise. Every so often he'd say, "Wow, that wasn't bad at all," and it was such a great feeling to finally hear something good for a change. But as the weeks wore on, it got tougher and tougher to keep going over the same seven or eight songs. Anthony wanted to spend more time with his girlfriend, and Terrence was gearing up for his freshman year at NYU, and I was starting to feel like death on its feet, working graveyard and sleeping days in that stifling apartment. So, across the board, the passion level was sinking fast, and I was sure it would help if we got out there and played for an audience. Terrence and Anthony thought the same thing, but every time we raised the subject with Peewee, he insisted we weren't ready. We'd say, "We're just as ready as any band at A7. Let's just go over and sign up one night." That was all you had to do to play at A7—it was a bit like open mic—but of course that was the *last* place Peewee was willing to play. Then one night Terrence saw a show at Club 57 on St. Mark's Place and came back and told us about it. He said some of the bands had done some pretty weird shit—as weird as the shit *we* were doing—and he'd talked to the guy who ran the place, who said if we wanted to play next week, it was fine with him. (As at A7, auditions weren't required at Club 57.) Peewee naturally said we weren't ready, and we all said, "Yes, we fucking *are*." I mean, it was insurrection time! And he obviously must have sensed it. He said, "Well, if you all want to play that bad, I guess we'll play. Never let it be said this band's not a democracy." Yeah, right. And the same goes for Stalin's Russia!

So the following week we had last one practice on Rivington Street, and afterward we started loading the van, and at some point Peewee disappeared. I thought, "I hope he's not up there doing smack with Nelson." Yes, we'd started fooling around with smack by then, but I'll get to that in a minute. Then he came back and swore he hadn't done smack with Nelson, he'd just bought some, and I said, "Well, do me a favor and don't do it till after the show. You don't want to get up there all smacked up." He wouldn't, he swore, and we drove a few blocks to Club 57, but it turned out we'd gotten there way too early; there was a play about to go on. We watched some of the play, and it was very weird, which I should've expected, since so much of what was happening in the East Village in those days was very weird. I suppose punk was an influence, but in retrospect a much bigger one was Andy Warhol, especially downtown with its local celebrities very much in the Warhol Superstar mold: John Sex and Diane Brill and Ethyl Eichelberger, who I think was in that play that night. We left at intermission, and I noticed that Peewee was acting nervous in a way I'd never seen before. I was a little nervous myself, but it never occurred to me that he might be afraid of going onstage—not him, with his boundless courage and bottomless need for attention. I asked if he was okay, and he said, "I'm fine! But I wish I had something to drink. Come on, let's go get a beer!" I think the drinking age was still eighteen at the time, but as I've said before, there was never much carding in New York anyway; we walked up the street and got a couple of forties and drank those outside the club. Finally that fucking play finished, and we loaded in, and the first band played—a bunch of kids from Queens or New Jersey trying to be Led Zeppelin, and that was weird because it wasn't weird at all. Peewee had loosened up to the point where he heckled them, saying things like, "Hey, if Robert Plant's such a Druid, why's he try so hard to sound black?!" They had a number of friends in the audience, and I was picturing still more stabbings with ballpoint pens, so I told Peewee to shut his fucking mouth. Then the guy in charge came up and told us we were next, and at some point, as we started setting up the stage, Peewee disappeared again. I looked all over the club and tried the bathroom, where he blocked me from entering and shouted through the door, "Somebody's in here!"

"Come on, man, we're going on."

"I'll be there in a fucking minute!"

I later learned he was throwing up. That's how nervous he was. We had to sound-check without him, and I was just about to drag his ass to the stage when he walked out from the shadows with stooped shoulders and his face a fishy green. Still, I have to give him this: he just strapped on his guitar and counted off the first song and started spazzing, which he always did when he really got rocking, jerking and twitching like a monkey on meth. The kids from the first band took their revenge, taunting him with names like "Napoleon," which I thought was kind of clever, considering the lunkheads they were; but, if anything, that fired him up even more, and I can't even tell you how thrilled *I* was. I was playing guitar in front of a live audience in New York City. Me! A guy from Nowhere, North Carolina! And I knew the band was a work in progress and still had far to go, but I thought we sounded better than we ever had, and Peewee said the same thing after the show. He was even nice to Anthony! We stopped at a liquor store on the way to Anthony's place in Queens, where everybody got roaring drunk and I cornered some friends of Anthony's girlfriend and asked what they thought of the band. They pretty much thought we sucked. One said we sounded like Flipper, whose song "Sex Bomb" was a big favorite of Peewee's, and something else I could never get into. Still, they all thought Peewee was an odd choice for frontman, with his Chihuahua singing and spastic moves. Plus it looked weird, with him so small and me so tall beside him. So hearing all that took me down a few notches, though later that night I bumped uglies with one of those girls in the bathroom. Everybody ended up crashing on the floor, and the next day Peewee and I took the train to Manhattan, and I told him what those girls had told me, and he said, "Yeah, like I really care what *they* think. And they compared us to Flipper. I mean, *that's* good."

"Well, maybe for you it is. But I don't care what you say, Flipper's a bad band."

"No, they're just too sophisticated for your country-fried ass. You ought to break off with Anthony, and he can be Tommy and you can be Johnny, and I'll go find some *smart* people to play with."

I was really hurt when he said that. But then we got home, and he broke out that smack he'd bought the night before, and soon I was feeling no pain at all.

I THINK THAT MAY HAVE BEEN the second time we'd done it. I know the first time was on Peewee's seventeenth birthday, and that was maybe a week before we played at Club 57. Nelson passed us by our door that night—we were getting home late from a bar—and Peewee mentioned something about it being his birthday, and Nelson said, "Well, shit, I got—I got—I got to give you something." Then he went upstairs and came back down a few minutes later, handing Peewee a small tinfoil packet, and I thought, "Oh my fucking God!" Peewee started to open it the second he left, and I said, "Wait a minute. You know what that is, right?"

"Of course."

"And you're still going to do it?"

"Why not?"

"Yeah, but aren't you afraid of getting addicted?"

"Oh, you can't get addicted if you do it just once. Come on, aren't you curious?" And I was. But there were two drugs I was really afraid of, and smack was one of them. (The other was PCP, which I later did also, when Terrence and I dropped acid and realized after the fact it was laced with angel dust.) But in some ways Peewee had a sixties attitude when it came to drugs. He'd get high for the sake of getting high, but he was also looking for insight. Plus heroin had a certain romantic allure, what with all those famous junkies, from Lenny Bruce to William Burroughs to Miles Davis to, well, Jim Cassady, who, from living in that building, we now realized had probably been smacked up the night we met him. Nelson hadn't brought along a needle, so I kept wondering how Peewee was going to do this shit. Then he started rolling up a dollar bill, and I said, "What, you're going to sniff it?"

"No, I think I'm going to give some to George Washington first. Of *course* I'm going to sniff it!"

Well, I just didn't know you could do that! He cut a line and scarfed it down, and I watched and waited and said, "So? What's it like?"

"I can't describe it. But if you're really that curious…"

Oh no! Not me! Thanks but no thanks! But then something interesting happened: Peewee didn't die. In fact, he looked so serene that, next time he went to cut himself a line, I said, "Hey, why don't you cut one for me too? But just a *little* one." So he did, handing me the dollar bill, and five minutes later I thought smack was the greatest thing in the whole world! My thoughts weren't blurred the way they were on other drugs. My mind was sharp while my body seemed to nap in a cradle lined with silk and satin. It was *so* nice I never wanted to do it again—I could definitely see myself forming a dependence. But then Peewee bought some more from Nelson and bragged about it to Terrence, who said, "Shit, *I* want to try it! Can you get some for *me*?" I hadn't realized he was a big drug guy! Yes, he was always sniffing coke, but coke was nothing in those days; it was almost like having a beer. So then it was me and Peewee and Terrence, all sniffing smack, and we asked Anthony if he wanted to join us, but he said, "You guys are nuts! That shit's the devil!" Peewee said, "Hey, *Dee Dee* does smack. Don't you want to be like Dee Dee?" He definitely did not. He was a pothead, and that, no doubt, is one of the reasons Peewee turned against pot, which he now dismissed as a "plebeian drug." He also started talking about shooting up, but I told him to knock it off. We were buying smack from Nelson every two weeks or so, and I figured as long as we kept it at that and stayed away from needles, everything was under control.

That Christmas I went to North Carolina for a few days, and my first night back Peewee asked if I wanted to "get a hooker"—his euphemism for buying smack. My grandmother had given me some money, which I now gave to him, and he went upstairs to Nelson's place, and hours passed and he never returned, and I figured, well, it's one of three things: either he's hanging out with Nelson, or he's been mugged and killed, or he's gone up to that shooting gallery and stuck a fucking needle in his arm. I was fairly sure it wasn't the first, since he couldn't stand Nelson's company for more than a few minutes, and I was also fairly sure it wasn't the second, since he had a sixth sense for avoiding muggers, so that left just one possibility. Finally, around two in the morning, I went looking for him. Nobody answered when I knocked on Nelson's door. Then I walked across the courtyard and up the stairs of the front part of the building to the fifth floor, which I knew was where the shooting gallery was, even though I'd never been there before, and neither so far as I knew had Peewee. I had no idea which apartment it was, but then I heard laughter and knocked on the door from which it seemed to come, and the laughter abruptly stopped and a woman with an accent said, "Who is it?"

"Yeah, I'm looking for a friend of mine? A little white kid? With a black leather jacket?"

"He asleep."

"Are you sure he's *sleeping*?"

But she just said the same thing: "He asleep." She never opened the door, and I was glad she didn't. I walked downstairs and across the courtyard and sat up till Peewee stumbled home at the crack of dawn with a drowsy smile and glassy eyes and said, "Guess what *I* did?" I just had to try it, he said—it was the greatest thing he'd ever experienced, a completely different drug—and I made up my mind then and there I was through fooling around with that shit. I was not about to encourage that kid in any way, and it wasn't till fifteen years later, long after he died, that I finally went near smack again, though I had countless opportunities via Terrence, who continued to sniff and smoke it without developing a habit. Peewee *tried* to develop a habit, but, working for slave wages, he couldn't afford a daily dose. Still, he was so taken with the romance of being a junkie, he loved telling people he was one. Plus, as I say, he was looking for insight, and in that way I think smack helped him. I think he felt obliged to shed some light, at least for himself, on the darkest corners of the soul. A lot of kids are that way, posing questions they're not equipped to handle, but most kids don't have the imagination he did while meantime having the good sense to pull themselves back before going too far. Not Peewee. I remember once he sat for the better part of an hour, staring at a photograph of a POW getting his head sawed off by Nazis in one of his favorite books, *Film as a Subversive Art*, going, "My God, what is he thinking right now? And what are those Nazis thinking? I mean, you can tell they're enjoying it, but can't they empathize at all? And what do you think *we'd* do if we were in a group like that and everybody started chopping people up? Do you think we'd take part or refuse to go along? And if we *did* go along, do you think we'd *enjoy* ourselves?"

So I think smack relieved him of those kinds of thoughts or, anyway, it made them more bearable. I wish I could say it made *him* more bearable, but it didn't, not when it came to the band. He was as tyrannical as ever, though we had to cut back considerably on practice once Terrence started going to NYU. (He was taking film classes, with an eye toward becoming a director, and I crewed on a couple of his projects—my first experience with anything film-related.) I kept writing songs that Peewee kept changing, and some were very personal, such as "I'm a Motherfucking Man." (Gail was even mentioned by name.) I taught him that song, and the first time we took it into practice, he started skewing the rhythm and shrieking improvised lyrics, so that I stopped and said, "No, man, that's not the way it goes. And why don't you try *singing* instead of screaming? You sound like a girl who just got her first period." That pissed him off so much he did something he never had before. He said, "All right, Caruso, show us how it's done." And I fucking well did too. I sang that song the way it was *supposed* to be sung, Anthony and Terrence falling in behind me, and afterward they said, "Wow, Jason, that was great. You've got to do that the next time we play."

"Over my dead body!" Peewee shrieked. "This band *has* a singer, and you're looking at him! All the *really* great bands have *one* singer!"

"Oh yeah?" said Anthony. "Ever hear of a little band called the Beatles?"

Oops! Wrong thing to say! He'd obviously never heard Peewee's patented speech on the many artistic crimes of the Beatles, among them allowing the Barry Manilow of the band (McCartney) to displace the Gene Vincent (Lennon). Well, he sure got to hear it now! Still, that was one watershed practice. It led to a long talk between Peewee and me about the direction of the Widowmakers; and, yes, we'd had plenty of those talks already, but this one was crucial, since we were able to clearly identify exactly where we stood: I was a traditionalist who believed a song in the old form—verse-chorus-verse and using a few simple chords—was as valid as the song was good, whereas Peewee believed it made no difference if a song was technically "good" or not; if it didn't challenge established boundaries, it was pretty much worthless. Believe me, it took a long time before we could say it as succinctly as I just did, and it would take years before we found a way of meeting in the middle. The other important result of that talk was that I was "allowed" to sing my own song at our next show at the Mudd Club, though I still had to compromise on the arrangement, letting Peewee make it more of a "beautiful mess," as he often described our sound. Even so, a number of people came up to me afterward and said, "I liked *your* song. You ought to sing more." It was mostly girls who told me that, and Peewee, irked, rechristened me "Bobby Sherman" after a teenybopper idol from the early seventies. I hated that. Good looks weren't especially desirable back then, not in underground-music circles, where most people practiced the aesthetics of ugliness. For a while I tried to starve myself, going for the acceptable "wasted" look, and I usually kept my hair buzzed short, though I stopped dyeing it shortly after we moved to New York. Peewee and I both began to retire the official punk uniform. He alternated between his motorcycle jacket and antique suits bought at thrift stores like Cheap Jack's, while I took to dressing in army fatigues to the point where panhandlers used to address me as "Sarge." I also wore a lot of bowling shirts, which were big in the East Village in those days. But so was anything working-class and retro. As for Peewee, he sometimes wore spats—the only person I ever knew who did that.

 We played at the Mudd Club on January 25, 1983. I know because I've still got the flier. It features the famed photo of JFK Jr. as a three-year-old saluting his father's casket. Peewee designed it. He designed most of our fliers, running them off at his copy-shop job (which is what eventually got him fired). He left it to everybody else to post them, and that meant me, since Anthony lived in Queens and worked full-time, and Terrence was too busy with school. We played two more shows after that one, and Peewee threw up beforehand both times, just as he had at the Mudd Club and all the shows prior, and I sang the only song people seemed to like. I was working on Peewee to let me sing more when, one night that spring, he threw another tantrum in practice, berating Anthony, who stood and said, "That's it. You can find somebody else to eat your shit. I fucking quit." Then he calmly started dismantling his kit, and Peewee shrugged and said we'd start looking for a drummer first thing in the morning, and Terrence said, "Yeah, you'd better start looking for a bass player too." He was likewise sick of dealing with Peewee. All kinds of gripes he'd secretly nursed came spilling out, and Peewee loudly counterattacked, and Anthony was lugging his drums to his van, and I stood there in a daze thinking, "My whole life is ruined! For the second time in a row! And I'm only twenty years old!" It really seemed that dire at the time. Peewee was shooting up and telling everyone he met he was a junkie, and I thought he *was* a junkie—I didn't realize he'd never gotten addicted—and who was going to want be in a band with a known junkie? Why did *I* want to be in a band with a known junkie? And what was I going to do now that I had no band?

But shortly after that Peewee had a health scare (I'll explain later) that frightened him so much he swore he was done with his "junkie" phase. Besides, we had a lot of work to do. We were going to start a new band. We weren't going to call this one the Widowmakers, though. We'd both grown to hate that name, since, among other things, we thought it sounded too metal. Then one night Peewee shook me awake and said he'd just come up with a great name: Scratch. I said, "*Scratch*? I don't know, man."

"No, it's perfect. It came to me in a dream, and I've been sitting here thinking about it for the last ten minutes, and first of all it's a noun and a verb both, so it's active and passive at the same time. It's—you know, it's something a cat does, but it's also something you find on a record. And Old Scratch is a nickname for the devil, so that kind of gives it a hidden menace, and it's also something you put together with bits and pieces of whatever you've got—you know, like baking a cake from scratch. And that's us. We're the bits and pieces of the Widowmakers, and anybody we play with from now on is going to be left over from some other band. We're not dealing with any more amateurs! We need some *old* people like Robert Quine of the Voidoids. That's what's so cool about Richard

Hell. He's always been a big image guy, you know, but then he gets some bald guy with a beard who looks about fifty years old—and that's what *we* should do. We've got to get some people with brains, because, I'm telling you, I am never going to be in another band with a moron like Anthony as long as I fucking live!"

And he rambled on and on, so that finally I said Scratch sounded fine to me. Anything to shut him up so I could get some fucking sleep.

"SCRATCH" HAD AT LEAST ONE OTHER CONNOTATION Peewee never underscored that night. Because all that putting-something-together-from-whatever-you've-got was textbook punk philosophy, though in certain ways we'd both moved beyond all that. It wasn't just a matter of shedding the costume. Peewee came to think that to call yourself a punk was not to truly be one, since punk was against all rules, including the rules that went with being "punk." In other words, he was *so* punk, he wasn't a punk anymore. Of course, his desire to make original music played a key part in his developing outlook, yet if you'd told him his music wasn't punk, he would've said, "Why? Is there some rule that says it can't be?" So there was still some flexibility about it, while I for one took pride in calling myself a punk, since I felt I'd paid the price and then some for the privilege of doing so. And that was just as true of the kids in the hardcore scene, and I admired them for it, while at the same time I could certainly see why Peewee had pulled away from them. They were like a tribe with, yes, too many rules, and that was clearly evident in the music, which for the most part all sounded the same. I liked a few hardcore bands—Negative Approach, Iron Cross, Really Red—just as I liked the manic energy at A7 and, later, at those Sunday matinees at CBGB's; but the kids were so cliquish, and there were never that many girls at hardcore shows, and so much of my life in those days was about getting laid. I even got laid at that midnight-to-eight security job. It was at a girls' dormitory, and sometimes when my boss told me to make my rounds, I'd run upstairs and grab a quickie with a chick named Robin and come back a half-hour later and say, "I made my rounds!" That's what led to my departure: somebody who lived on Robin's floor ratted me out.

But I was glad about it. I was young and living in New York. Who wanted to work all night with so much to do? Downtown club life was exploding. Every other week there was some hip new place you had to go, from Area to the World to the Milk Bar to, especially, Nell's, which, when it first opened, may well have been the most exclusive club on the planet. But I never had a problem getting past the doorman, and I racked up a lot of conquests at that place, including a red-hot Parisienne who worked as an au pair for Louis Malle and Candice Bergen. I met countless famous people. One night Peewee and I were at Kiev at three in the morning, and we spotted Allen Ginsberg eating by himself a few tables away. Peewee pulled up a chair and talked to him for at least an hour. Eventually I joined them. We also met Gregory Corso at Café Orlin; Andy Warhol at the Palladium; and one day we were walking around midtown, and Peewee said, "Hey, it's Norman Mailer!" and ran right up and talked to him too. I was a huge fan of Mailer's by then. I must have read a book a week, everything from Cervantes to Céline to Chekhov to Nabokov to, yes, Norman Mailer. I almost *had* to do that in order to speak Peewee's language, but also being well-read was fashionable in those days, or at least it was in Manhattan. People read on the subway, they read in coffee shops, they read while waiting in line for movies. And that was something else I loved about New York: you could get a great film education, what with all the art houses. There was Cinema Village, the Bleecker Street Cinema, the uptown and downtown Thalias, where we saw one great movie after another: *8½, 1900, Blow-Up, Breathless, Solaris*. Of course, it goes without saying that we saw almost every important band of the day, and some I saw repeatedly, including the Misfits, Ramones and Pogues. (I once got thrown out of a Pogues show at Maxwell's for slugging a guy who'd groped my date. That wouldn't be the last time I was thrown out of Maxwell's!) I also saw Mission of Burma two or three times, including what was supposed to be their last show, and I can't even count the number of times I saw Sonic Youth—but that's kind of a sore subject, since certain people accused us of ripping them off. It wasn't true, though I have to admit that Scratch and our later band, Superego, did sound a little like Sonic Youth circa "Death Valley '69." (Scratch likewise had a song about Manson called "Creepy Crawly.") Peewee *hated* that band. He used to say they'd ripped *us* off, which of course was completely ridiculous. And then there were these kids from the South someplace who called themselves Rude Buddha, and that was one band we both liked. It's a shame nobody remembers them. They had a girl singer who'd flounce around in Day-Glo dresses and let it rip in a voice so shrill it sounded like a banshee with menstrual cramps. But it was perfect for the kind of music they played.

And then there was Minor Threat. Peewee was *insane* about Minor Threat to the point where we once took a Greyhound to D.C. to catch one of their last shows at the 9:30 Club. I wasn't nearly the fan he was, but I have to say they put on a great show, and to this day I have a lot of respect for Ian MacKaye. There was a tremendous sense of warmth about that guy, and even at twenty you could tell he'd never do anything that violated his sense of integrity. He never has, so far as I know. Peewee once referred to him as "the saint of the Potomac." Yes, I think he might be.

But for me the greatest band of their time was, hands down, the Replacements. They'd take the stage drunk off their asses, and they didn't give one *fuck* what you or anybody else thought; they were going to do things *their* way. Peewee considered them a so-so bar band at best, but I still say Paul Westerberg wrote some of the best songs of the eighties: "I Will Dare," "Skyway," "Unsatisfied," to name but a few. I just wish he'd been a nicer guy. I tried to talk to him once before a show, and let's just say he was no Ian MacKaye. Bob Stinson, on the other hand, was one of the nicest people I ever met. But I continued to like the Replacements even after Westerberg shitcanned Bob and released those later big-label records written off by most as forty-proof crap.

Finally, there's one other show I'd like to mention. One night I went with Peewee and Terrence and Terrence's then-girlfriend to a club called Interferon. This must have been in the spring of '83, since I know it was right around the time the Widowmakers broke up, and Terrence's girl had a friend who was in a band called Pillow. That was the band we'd gone to see, but first we had to suffer through the opening act: two gay dancers and a short girl singer with big, dramatic eyes. They lamely danced to a drum machine before the singer sashayed up to the mic and said, "If you don't know *this* song, you're *nowhere*, man." Then she started screeching in a helium voice along to the drum machine, and we all kind of looked at each other as if to say, "Wow, self-delusion sure is something, huh?"

Well, two years later that girl was the biggest pop star on the planet, next to Michael Jackson, and hailed as some sort of fashion genius, even though she dressed like every other girl in the East Village. I think that's when I knew there was never going to be a revolution or, anyway, not the kind we craved.

ALL DURING THAT TIME, PEEWEE KEPT GOING through lots of phases. He lost interest in Captain Beefheart. Then, for a while, he talked about Throbbing Gristle. Then it was Can and Crass and Savage Republic. Then, for maybe a month, he decided he should know more about classical music and logged a lot of time at the Lincoln Center Library, going through its vast record collection, just as he later did during his blink-of-an-eye interest in jazz. He had a Spengler phase, an Orson Welles phase, a photography phase, and that long phase, lasting for at least a year, in which he thought he might be infected with the AIDS virus. When we started fooling around with heroin, AIDS was known as "gay cancer," and nobody mentioned that you could also get it from shooting up. Then it *was* mentioned, and Peewee found a swollen lymph node on his neck, which happened to be one of the symptoms. He was constantly feeling that thing, asking others to feel it too, and several times a day he'd take his temperature, and if it was running even slightly above normal, he'd say, "Oh my God, I've got the virus! Jason, if I die, *please* make sure my parents know it wasn't because I got fucked in the ass." He claimed he'd never shared needles, but maybe he'd sat on one at the shooting gallery without knowing it, or maybe a mosquito had bitten Nelson, who was looking kind of sick, and come down to our place and had a go at us. He drove me fucking nuts! Eventually I became so paranoid I went off and got tested, something he was afraid to do, and the results came back negative, and that gave him the courage to take the test himself. His results also came back negative, but he always held out the possibility that the test was wrong; so that phase—the hypochondriac phase—was apt to return if he so much as sneezed. And there was a chess phase, and a Schopenhauer phase, and a Baader-Meinhof phase, and at one point, during his Minor Threat phase, he went Straight Edge, giving up drugs, booze and sex. (The third he'd all but given up already, but not by choice.) I knew that wouldn't last. He was smashed in a matter of days. His "growth" phase, on the other hand, lasted for months. That started not long after he turned eighteen and noticed he'd gotten taller, and, encouraged, he researched herbs that were supposed to stimulate growth, and our apartment became a virtual laboratory, with him brewing teas and me drawing lines on the wall to mark his progress. He grew quite a bit, in fact, though I'm sure it had nothing to do with those herbs. He eventually reached maybe five-five, but his frame was so small, he still looked roughly the same. And there was a Guy Debord phase, and a Russian history phase, and a French Theory phase, and right before he died, there was a phase in which he was finally getting serious about making movies, and that's one phase I think might've lasted. And there were many others—so many it's hard to remember them all, especially since they always overlapped.

But there were two phases, aside from the one about AIDS, I found particularly grating, and the first of those was the "right-wing" phase. I hated Ronald Reagan, just as I hated Jesse Helms, that scumbag senator from my home state; and Peewee also hated Reagan, or at least he did when I first knew him, but at some point during the '84 election, he suddenly announced he was voting for Reagan. He said he couldn't see voting for Mondale, whose running mate was a "New York slumlord," or at least her husband was. Plus he liked Reagan's hard-line stance against communism. The irony was, he was meantime going through a Che Guevara phase. Naturally it did no good to point out the contradiction. I tried, but he said, "Hey, I'd never call Che Guevara some kind of great thinker. I like the *idea* of Che more than Che himself. Communism is the worst thing there is, and if you don't believe me, just walk up to the East Village and talk to the first Ukrainian you meet. *They'll* set you straight. But, no, these leftist intellectuals want to ignore the poverty and genocide and everything else. How much evidence do you fucking need it's not working?! And it's *never* going to work. But, no, it hasn't been applied the 'right way' yet. And Marx didn't know the first thing about biology, and do you know how they're trying to compensate for that? They're trying to 'fuse' him with Freud. Who was *another* moron. But, no, they're going to make this Marx-Freud milkshake, and that's going to solve everything. And these are the same people who sit around talking about how 'stupid' Reagan is. Well, he may be stupid, but he knows one thing they don't: he knows communism is *evil*."

"Well, he's pretty evil himself. He *hates* people like us. He's anti-drugs, he's anti-pornography, he's cut off funding for the arts—"

"Hey," I was shouted down, "if you're a *real* artist, you don't *want* the government to fund you! Who wants state-sponsored art? *I* don't. And do you honestly think for one second if Reagan cracks down on drugs or pornography it's ever going to go away? Of course not! It's just going to go underground and get even stronger! And it's *better* that way. Because I don't want to live in some happy-face world where everything transgressive gets the *Good Housekeeping* treatment. Otherwise it's like, 'Hey, I think I'm going to go smoke some crack while I beat off to porn,' and nobody even blinks. No, I want people to go all sorts of colors and threaten to take my kids away. So I really *approve* of all this crackdown stuff. I'll take even more of it, as a matter of fact!"

"So how about being poor? Would you like some more of that?"

"Wow, you've really become a New Yorker, haven't you? You ought to go hang out with Thurston Bore and Kim Boredom. They'll agree with every last thing you're saying. And that goes for all those lame so-called rockers at the Holiday too!"

He'd tipped his hand. He would never have talked about voting for Reagan in North Carolina. Now that he was surrounded by like-minded people, he had to find a way to set himself apart. And that he did. Our bass player, Giancarlo, quit when Peewee started praising Reagan. Other people screamed at him—and I mean full-on screaming. I was screamed at myself by Giancarlo's boyfriend: "How can you be in a band with a known *fascist*?! How can you be *friends* with someone like that?!" It reached the point where I once posted a flier at Café Orlin for an upcoming show, and a day later somebody had ripped it down. Then I put up another flier, and the next time I saw it, somebody—possibly Giancarlo's boyfriend—had scrawled BOYCOTT FASCIST BANDS across the front. And sure enough, when we played that show, which we did without a bass player, almost nobody turned up.

But did that stop Peewee? No, it made him worse. He covered his guitars with Reagan stickers, and the night of the election, after he'd cast his black-hearted ballot, he walked all over the East Village with a Reagan button as big as a coffee lid pinned to his leather jacket. I was with him that night, and some girl—a gutter punk unknown to us both—walked up and spit on him. Later, at St. Mark's Bookstore, I noticed Susan Sontag, who noticed Peewee and gave him a dirty look. Peewee said, "Did you *see* that? Susan Sontag gave me a dirty look! Yeah, I ought to give *her* a dirty look after some of the shitty books she's written!"

Shortly afterward I told him I was leaving the band. Even aside from the Reagan business, it wasn't going well. Our first drummer got hit by a cab as soon as he joined, paralyzed from the neck down. Our second drummer was lured away by another band, and Giancarlo was our second bass player—the first quit when he could no longer tolerate Peewee's outbursts. He took off minutes before a show at Kenny's Castaways, forcing us to play without him, and later that night somebody stole my first guitar, that gorgeous Fender Mustang I'd bought in North Carolina. I broke down in public tears when that happened. And then, musically, things weren't getting much better. Scratch was a lot like the Widowmakers, except I had more say when it came to my songs. Some of our stuff was straight-ahead punk in the vein of ROT and, increasingly, post-punk Replacements, but it was mostly more of Peewee's "beautiful mess," with his signature tempo changes and offbeat tunings. And, yes, it was good that I was finally getting my fair share of mic time, but we practically never played, we spent so much time trolling for new members, and I *loved* playing. That was the only thing that made it worthwhile: the shitty jobs and living in that senseless-killing neighborhood and the countless problems brought on by Peewee's tantrums and stage fright. I think that's one reason he was always trying to force people out: it gave him an excuse not to perform. And I figured, when I told him I was quitting, he'd say, "Fuck it, go ahead. You do your thing, I'll do mine."

But to my surprise, he begged me to reconsider, saying I was like a brother to him and he couldn't imagine doing the band without me, and if this Reagan thing was making me that upset, he'd never mention his name again. (And he never did, except to criticize him.) I said, "Well, look, if I stay, I don't want to look for a bass player. Now it's just you, me and Gareth"—that was our drummer—"and I think that's all we need."

"Yeah, but without a bass, we're not going to have enough bottom end."

I knew he was going to say that. We'd had this discussion more than once. But I thought we sounded better without a bass, and adding one meant having to stop again to break in a new member, and if we kept losing momentum that way, we were never going to get anywhere. But, really, where was that? That was another problem with Scratch: our goals were never pragmatic—or Peewee's weren't. I had some leverage at that point, so Peewee agreed to keep it a three-piece, and so we remained for maybe two months. And then one night he came home in a state of great excitement to say he'd just met this incredible girl who played bass, and that's what led to the demise of Scratch and the year and a half Peewee and I went without speaking. He was in love, and I more or less followed suit, and together we entered the "rivals" phase.

⌒

NOW, OBVIOUSLY, BY THEN WE'D BEEN RIVALS for quite some time. We each had our own vision of the band, and also by then I'd soaked up enough knowledge so that I could pretty much hold my own when it came to debating him. Yes, he'd trained me a little *too* well. Plus, whereas I got along with most people, he put a lot of people off, always trying to shock them, or sometimes shocking them without trying, and that made for problems with girls. He was always pining after one girl or another, and every so often he'd get lucky, but for the most part he scared them all away. A few times I tried to coach him. I told him to stop saying "fuck" every five seconds and to make his intelligence work for him and not against him. I mean, talking about Marx-Freud milkshakes or the Spengler model of history wasn't the best bait for getting laid. No, I said, he should talk about music; he should talk about movies—but even that might come out like: "Steven Spielberg ought to be guillotined! He ought to be drawn and quartered! Do you have any idea the *damage* that guy has caused? It took American film fifty years to finally grow up, and then *he* comes along with, 'Oh, let's all be children again! Let's all cry over a cute little alien with Christ-like healing powers!' What's with all this Christ shit? He's a fucking *Jew*!" That's something I once heard him say to a girl who'd just told him *ET* was one of her favorite movies, so naturally, within seconds, she was looking pretty shellshocked. Then I thought I'd show him by example how it was done, and unfortunately I did it *so* well that she was hanging all over me, and afterward Peewee called me a narcissist who just had to prove I could take that girl away.

"No, man, I was trying to help you."

"Oh, yeah, you're so magnanimous. Now, why don't go call one of your many concubines, and I'll go home and jerk off. You won, okay? You're a stud, and I'm a fucking eunuch!"

But, actually, I wanted him to get laid almost as much as I wanted to get laid myself. I was sick of hearing him bitch about it. So I couldn't have been happier the night he came home from Save the Robots and said he'd just met this amazing girl who was really smart and liked all the right bands—and she also liked *him*. Why, they'd talked for almost two hours! And get this, she played bass, and he knew he should've conferred with me and Gareth first, but he'd pretty much asked her to join the band. I said, "Whoa, wait a minute. I'm glad you met this girl, and I hope it all works out, but you don't want somebody you like in the band. What if she rejects you? Are you still going to want her in the band then? And you haven't even heard her play, right? How do you know if she's any good?"

"Because. I've got a *feeling* about this girl. I don't know why, but I'm sure she's the one for us. And it can't hurt to try her, right? Let's just bring her in and try her out, and if she's not right—and I *know* she will be—we'll just say thanks but no thanks, and that'll be it."

On and on he went. Finally I said, "Okay, I guess we can *try* her. But nothing is official till me and Gareth have a say." He wasted no time in calling this girl, whose name was Laura, to invite her to our next practice; and when I finally got a look at her, I wasn't impressed at all. She was as plain as a bar of soap: tall and skinny, with a dirty-blonde bob she kept shaking out of her eyes, and a face so pale and shapeless it looked like a bleached-out sock puppet. But then we gave her a taste of Scratch, and she jumped right in, backing the drums with pocket bass and none of the busy fretwork I loathed with a passion. (I still do. I prefer bass as pure percussion instrument.) Plus she really did seem to like Peewee—one of the few humans with a vagina I'd ever met who didn't flee or wilt after spending a handful of minutes with him. Plus she praised a couple of my songs, which didn't exactly hurt, since I was always trying to stack the band with people who'd take my side. That was how I ended up as quasi-co-frontman—everyone else insisted—though Peewee likewise tried, and usually failed, to stack the band to his own advantage. So after Laura left, we had a meeting, and the vote was unanimous: she was in. Then Peewee and I took the train to Manhattan from our practice space in Greenpoint (it was actually Gareth's loft), and he talked about Laura the whole time, dissecting every nuance of her every move and word. He asked what I thought, and I said, "Well, I can tell she likes you, but

I'm not sure if she likes you *that* way. But remember: no matter what happens, you're going to be cool with it." And he rolled his eyes like the whole thing had been decided long ago and said, "Yes, Dad, I'm going to be cool with it."

At any rate, Laura was in, and that lifted Scratch to a whole new level. She had a lot of ideas on ways to improve things, and Peewee was so besotted with her, he didn't give her grief like he always had with me; no matter what she said, he'd say, "Wow, Laura, that's a *great* idea. Yeah, let's do *that*." We started rearranging all our songs, and I got to do mine more the way I wanted, but also something else started to happen: Peewee and I learned to collaborate. Before then, he'd tell me what to do, and I'd do it reluctantly, still trying to sneak in what I *wanted* to do; and as I gained more power in the band, I'd tell *him* what to do, and he'd comply with even greater reluctance, meantime trying to subvert me. I liked riffs, and he liked noise, and the two were locked in a battle for supremacy. But with Laura, for the first time, we truly played *with* each other instead of *against* each other. I found ways to bracket riffs around his racket, and he in turn filled my riffs with noise. So, more and more, the halves of the band were coming together, though it was still raw at that stage, and I wouldn't see the full payoff till later, in Superego. We would tape ourselves at practice and go home and listen and say, "God*damn*, we're good." And the first show we played with Laura, at a club in Chelsea called Danceteria, was the first time I'd heard people say they really enjoyed us, and not just isolating a song here or a part of a song there. And that was really important to me. Because I didn't want people to just like *me* (which they didn't always, by the way), I wanted them like *the band*—and I really wanted them to *like* us, as opposed to Peewee, who thought it was good if people got annoyed or threw up their arms in confusion. To him that meant we were onto something new, something fresh, something nobody had ever heard before. Still, even he was pleased to finally hear a few compliments for a change, and for weeks afterward he went around saying, "We *killed* them! We blew them the fuck *away!*" Which was a bit of an overstatement, but no question, compared to the usual, that show had been quite a success. And it was all because of Laura. She was a goddamned miracle worker, that girl!

So, finally, everything was falling into place. The band was getting better, and I can't tell you what a relief that was. I had a lunchtime job tending bar at a Wall Street restaurant, which, as those things go, wasn't bad at all; and I was regularly seeing a gorgeous girl, a part-time model and modern dancer whom Peewee nicknamed "Yes," since he claimed that was all he ever heard her say. Even with me she was quiet to the point of catatonia. Not that I gave a shit. All she had to do was sit there and I'd drool all over myself. Yet the more time I spent around Laura, the more I wished I had someone like her, someone who wasn't all that pretty but actually had a brain. Maybe Yes had a brain—it was hard to say for sure—but there was never a doubt with Laura. She had a great gift for repartee, so that anything you threw at her, she'd throw it right back with a sly and biting curve; and even though I fought it, I found myself developing a crush on her. I was fairly sure it was mutual. I used to catch her staring at me, and noticed that she'd light right up whenever I came around; but that was something I was hoping Peewee hadn't noticed himself, since I had no intention of acting on it. I knew how he felt about her. He could hardly say a sentence in which the word "Laura" didn't figure at least once, and they were practically dating by the time we played at Danceteria. Peewee told me they routinely made out (something Laura later disputed), but at some point she sat him down and said, "Look, Bernard, I think you're a great guy in so many ways. But we're in a band, and if we sleep together, it's just going to mess everything up. Besides, you're nineteen and I'm twenty-four, and I can't see it working." I heard this story from Peewee and Laura both; and according to Laura, Peewee cried when it happened; and according to Peewee, she'd implied that the *real* reason she didn't want to sleep with him was because she really wanted to sleep with *me*. He asked if I knew she felt that way. I denied it. After all, she'd never *told* me so. He said, "Well, have you been encouraging her? Have you been seeing her behind my back or something?" And I told him I would *never* do something like that, and it was true, I never would. He really had nothing to worry about.

But it was too late. Because now he had it in his head that I was trying to steal Laura, just as I tried to steal every girl, just as I'd been trying to steal the band ever since the late Widowmaker days. Actually, the last was somewhat true, but now that we had Laura, there was no need to steal the band; it was finally starting to work. And then, overnight, it wasn't. He proceeded to do what I was afraid he'd do, what he promised he never would, taking out his hurt and anger on the music. If I so much as looked at Laura or she looked at me, he'd stop in the middle of practice and say, "I hate this fucking song! I don't know why we had to change it! It was fine the way it was!" He wanted to go back and undo our new arrangements, as if to remove Laura's taint from them, when a few weeks before he couldn't stop talking about all the improvements we were making. Sometimes he'd storm out of Gareth's loft and not come back, and once, apropos of nothing, he threw his guitar across the room, narrowly missing Laura and almost hitting an antique lamp Gareth's grandmother had left him. At least those two weren't living with the guy! He punished me at home as well. I started avoiding the apartment, spending more time with Yes, but sometimes I *had* to go home, and when I got there, he'd give me the silent treatment or force me into a no-win argument over penny-ante nonsense such as who owed more on the gas bill. And I kept hoping this phase would pass, as most of his phases usually passed; but as the weeks wore on, he showed no signs of letting up, and Laura was making noises about quitting. I asked her to stay as a favor to me, and she promised she would, but one day she called me at work and said she couldn't take it anymore; she was done with the band.

"Wait," I said. "Don't be rash. Let's talk it over first."

That night we got together at the 23rd Street Bar and Grill, right up the block from her place, and, man, I did everything but fall to my knees and kiss the soles of her feet to get her to reconsider. I didn't really have a lot of ammunition except to emphasize how brilliant I thought Peewee was, how I knew he was hard to put up with, but despite all that, I was convinced he was going to do something great one day, something the world would never forget, and I wanted to be there when it happened. And I wanted Laura to be there too. And she listened, and here and there I almost thought I'd won her over, but then she'd shake her bob and say, "But it really doesn't matter how brilliant he is. Nothing is worth this kind of abuse. Besides, he's not what I'd call brilliant when it comes to music. Why don't we start our *own* band? I'm sure Gareth would be willing to join us."

"And a few months ago I would've. But not now! Something is happening here, I can feel it! And, yes, right this second he's not cooperating, but I know him. It'll pass. And he'll move on to something else, and I'm not going to lie to you, that'll drive you crazy too, but the important thing is, the music will get better. That's what really matters here."

"Yes, but without him the music would be even *better*. We're propping him up, but he doesn't seem to realize it. And I know he's your friend, but you can't let that stand in your way. You've got to get out from under his shadow—for your own good!"

I'm not sure how long this went on, but at some point I realized it was hopeless. She was quitting the band, and there was nothing I could do to stop her. So I said, "Well, look, if *you* quit, then I'm going to have to quit too. Because we're just going to go back to the same old thing, and I can't do that now that I've had a taste of something better." Then she reached across the table and squeezed my hand and said, "I'm *so* glad to hear you say that. Don't you feel better? Don't you feel like an enormous weight's been lifted off your shoulder?" And at that moment that *was* the way I felt. We decided we should speak to Gareth right away, and ran downstairs to the pay phone, where Laura called him up and said, "Gareth? I'm here with Jason, and we have an announcement to make. We're starting a band without Bernard, and we want you to come with us." I was standing beside her whispering "What's he saying, what's he saying?" and she opened her eyes wide as if to say, "He's in!" Then she passed the phone to me, and I said, "Well, Gareth, welcome to the new band!"

"God, I was hoping something like this would happen. When do we start? Does Peewee know?"

And with that I felt my first pang of guilt. I felt like a thief, conspiring to rob a sleeping friend of his last fifty cents. Plus I'd never stopped to consider how my living arrangements were going to be affected, since I couldn't very well go home and say, "Well, Bernard, we're starting a band without you," and expect to remain in the same apartment. I told Gareth to keep it quiet for the time being and hung up and walked upstairs with Laura, who now assumed the role of therapist I'd been forced to play for her and Gareth for weeks. She said I shouldn't concern myself with Peewee's feelings, since, after all, he'd never been concerned with ours; and in terms of where to live, she said, "Well, I guess you could stay with me till you get your own place. But, Jason, please don't make it very long. We both know it doesn't work to live with somebody you're in a band with." We never discussed the spark between us, though it was obvious we both felt it. I walked her to her door at 23rd and First, and she hugged me, really tight, and said, "It's going to be great. You'll see. We're going to be the best band in New York City." And with a great big hard-on, I said good night and tore myself away.

All the way from 23rd to Rivington I walked home, just dreading the showdown with Peewee. I talked out loud, rehearsing approaches, and sometimes it came out angry, like "Fuck you, you little fucker, it's *my* band now," and sometimes it came out sensitive, like "I don't know what to say, man. I tried, you know? And you promised you weren't going to let your feelings for Laura get in the way, and you broke that promise. It's the best thing for everybody, don't you see?" But then I got home, where I found him glowering as usual, and I thought, "I don't have the energy to deal with this right now. He's such a lunatic, he'll either attack me and I'll have to hand his ass back to him, or else when I'm out of the house, he'll fuck up my stuff. So I'm not going to tell him till *after* I've moved out." I planned the whole thing for days, collecting boxes and arranging to borrow Gareth's truck. Then one morning Peewee went to work (I think at the time he was doing telephone sales, for which his gift of gab suited him), and I called in sick at my job and went up to the roof, where I'd stored the boxes, and started packing. Gareth's truck was in the shop, or something, so I called for a van, which showed up around four o'clock, and the aging hippie driver helped me move my heavier stuff. The apartment seemed sad without it. I had a last look around and dropped an envelope on Peewee's futon with some money for the rent (I figured I owed him that much) and a note explaining that I was leaving the band, and so were Gareth and Laura. I remember the note was on the sensitive side, saying I was sorry it had come to this, but I still believed in him and hoped that one day we could try again. I also remember driving to the storage place (since I couldn't keep everything I owned at Laura's) and telling the hippie driver about the band, how this girl and I had sacked my best friend and stolen the drummer, and he said, "That's some cold-ass shit, man." Then we drove to Laura's and rang her buzzer, and when she buzzed us up, she looked even paler than usual. I said, "Are you okay?"

"No, I'm not. I just got off the phone with Bernard, and he said some very terrible things."

"Like...?"

"Like he's going to buy a gun and kill me, *that's* what. *And* you *and* Gareth and then *himself*! He was out of control! I've never heard *anyone* talk the way he did! Do you think we should call the police? He threatened to *kill* us!"

Oh, I told her, he's just blowing off steam—but secretly I wasn't so sure. You never knew with Peewee! Meantime Laura was so shaken, just gray with worry, I was afraid she was going to say I couldn't move in for fear of starting more trouble, and where was I going to go then? But it was just the opposite: with me there she seemed to feel safer. She and the hippie helped me lug my stuff upstairs, and at some point we heard the phone ring and a loud click following the beep on Laura's machine. So there was Peewee. Then Laura started freaking again, so I said, "Let me try something," and called Terrence and asked if he couldn't go over and talk some sense into him, and, to my surprise, he sided with Peewee! He said I'd stolen his girl and his band; I'd left him with a $450 apartment on Rivington Street, and who was going to split a single room with a total stranger in a neighborhood as bad as that? He left me no choice, I said. I ticked off a list of my many grievances, and Terrence was and is a fair-minded guy, so in the end he said he'd try to reason with Peewee. Then I called Gareth to warn him that Peewee was on the warpath, but it turned out they'd spoken already, meaning Gareth had received his personal death threat, and he wanted no part of our band or any other; the whole soap opera had completely worn him out. I didn't even try to talk him back, since I could certainly sympathize. (And only a few weeks later, I would *really* sympathize!) I hung up and said, "Well, we've lost Gareth," and there was a terrible mood at that point. All that we've-got-a-new-band stuff from a few days before seemed like a chimera. We moped and milled and second-guessed till, finally, I said, "Let's just get drunk and forget about it. I've been through some bad shit in the past, and you don't think the sun's going to rise in the morning. But it does. It's all going to look better tomorrow."

So we walked a few blocks to the spot where the coup began, the 23rd Street Bar and Grill, and tossed back the liquor, and things looked better instantaneously. Laura said she knew a drummer to replace Gareth, and she also knew a second guitarist, since we both wanted a four-piece. Then the subject turned to us, which, again, was something we'd always sidestepped. I don't remember much about it, I was so drunk, except this sort of "Wow, you like *me*? Well, I like *you*!" and next thing I knew, we were making out. A few times we stopped to say, "Oh my God, what are we *doing*? We can't do *this*! We're in a *band*!" Then we'd make out all over again.

So we went back to her place and did the great deed, and the whole time the phone kept ringing, even at four in the morning, followed by a loud click as soon as the machine answered. It was as if, a mile downtown, he knew exactly what was happening and was trying to somehow stop it. And for weeks afterward he would try to find other ways to stop us, such as threatening to sue if we played any Scratch songs and reconciling with his parents in the hope that they'd pay for a lawyer. But the Scratch days were definitely over, and when I think about that name now, I never think of the meanings Peewee listed that night he woke me up to propose it; I think of two others I don't remember him mentioning. The first is a verb meaning to throw something away: *scratch* that. The second is a noun meaning a matter of no importance: a mere *scratch* as opposed to something worse or, anyway, bigger than it might have been.

AS FOR DOCKSIDE HOOKERS, the band I formed with Laura, there's really not much to say, since we'd already hung ourselves by the same rope that strangled Scratch: the almost-always fatal twine of personal feelings and music. Plus it turned out she wasn't nearly as together as she seemed to be; she was actually a secret basket case, just chronically insecure to the point where I could hardly make a move without stirring up some major drama. It's a phenomenon I've seen countless times: you meet a woman who seems cool and strong and full of good sense, but all that goes flying right out the window the minute you start fucking. And what made it especially difficult in Laura's case was that she had all sorts of problems with the way she looked, and no matter what I said, she found it hard to believe I'd chosen a plain Jane like her over a looker like Yes. She was constantly policing me for signs of a wandering eye, and there was a girl in the band, a friend of hers, and Laura was jealous of her, as she was jealous of every girl, so she fired her on some pretext; and after that drama she brought in a male friend who was a lousy drummer and a snotty fuck, and there was a lot of drama about that too, since if I didn't like him, then maybe I didn't like any of her friends, and if I didn't like them, it surely shed light on my opinion of *her*. Plus, even though she was terrific when it came to arranging a song, she had no talent whatsoever for writing one, and I'd been hoping she could help me come up with some new material. Not that I took Peewee's lawsuit threats (all passed on through Terrence) remotely seriously. I thought it was just hilarious, actually, that he'd try to pull a rock-star move like that one. But I didn't feel those songs reflected me anymore, and that was what I wanted this band to be: the sum of everything I'd learned. So I tried to write with Laura, and when that didn't work, she got upset; and she got upset when I criticized her friend's drumming; and she got upset when I suggested we come up with a better name than Dockside Hookers—that was her idea, obviously. I was hoping things would improve once I'd gotten a place of my own, but they never did. We stitched together about five songs, not including our cover of New Order's "Leave Me Alone," and played a single show at CBGB's before I reached for my ripcord. I didn't want to think about being in a band. I was sick to death of the whole thing.

So, for about a year, all I did was live. And it's funny how I always speak of Peewee's phases when I had so many of my own, but he had a way of pulling me in so that his phases became mine as well. But this phase—the Upper East Side phase—was mine exclusively, and was probably, aside from the Superego days (and even then), the best time I ever had in New York City. I was essentially living in a frat house, in a big apartment at the corner of 86th and Second with a stockbroker I'd met at my bartending job and a law student he knew from college, and all their other college buddies, most of them Catholic guys from Upstate, were constantly stopping by and sometimes crashing for days. There was a German restaurant right downstairs where the owners sold us imported beer for practically nothing, so we often stayed drunk around the clock. Those Upstate Catholics can sure put it away, brother! And you might think, being an artiste from the Lower East Side, I'd have trouble fitting in, but, nope, I got along fine with everybody. Those guys were all jocks, and that was a side of myself I'd half-suppressed while living with Peewee, since, as I've said before, he never cared for sports. But those uptown guys were passionate about sports; we were constantly watching games on TV and going to Shea or Yankee Stadium; and often, on weekends, we'd hit the Great Lawn of Central Park to challenge other yuppies to pickup games of football. And, yes, they were yuppies, my roommates, or at least that's the way they would've been characterized in the East Village, but I saw them more as red-blooded guys with white-collar jobs who were fun to be around—much more fun than most of the ghouls who lived south of 14th Street. And they weren't stupid, my roommates. They knew something about art and music, and we'd make the occasional downtown run for a taste of exotic club life; and I think, living with them, I started to realize just how seriously I'd fallen out of step with the rest of my generation. Because if you're going to talk about history in the kind of sweeping terms Peewee did, or, for that matter, most people do, I don't think the eighties will ever be regarded as a great time for bohemians. That wasn't the thing to do then. What you were supposed to do was get a real job and work like a maniac and, hopefully, become very successful so that, later, when you got married and had kids, right on schedule, you could buy a nice house in the suburbs and consume and accumulate and retire in comfort. That was the plan almost everybody my age seemed to have, and to this day most of them have stuck to it to the point where I don't think the eighties stopped when the eighties ended; I think those trends only intensified, so that by now nobody's a yuppie since *everybody's* a yuppie. Those values don't even stand out anymore, they've become so ingrained, and I'm sure I'd share them if I'd never met Peewee. Punk rock had saved me. It also estranged me. Not that it was too late. I was twenty-two when Dockside Hookers broke up, and I knew that one day I was going to have to get serious about life, but the thing was, I had no idea where to begin. I still read and saw movies and went to shows—impractical interests, all—and that was fine for now, just as being drunk all the time was fine too, but what was I going to do in a few years' time when I wasn't so young and still had no idea what I wanted to do? It was too scary to think about. So, for the most part, I tried not to. I just drank and got laid and played sports and worked as a bartender; and every so often I'd head downtown alone to hang out with Terrence. That's another funny thing: how I continue to think of Peewee as my best friend when, by now, I've known Terrence for twenty-some years, and he was much more like me in certain ways. He was somebody else who started off with grand ambitions and at some point realized they were never going to pan out, though in his case it wasn't a matter of bad breaks but plain old-fashioned laziness. He loved movies, but he didn't want to go the trouble of making them. No, he mostly wanted to get wasted and play with his computer. (In fact, he was the first person I knew who owned a PC.) And at that time he was just beginning to question the whole thing, and we'd talk about it and he'd shrug and say, "Fuck it. Let's go buy some coke or drop acid or something." Meantime he was still in touch with Peewee, as I wasn't, so he acted as a kind of go-between. I remember once I dropped by, and he said, "Guess who just left here not five minutes ago? That chair's still warm from where he parked his ass on it." I said, "The ass on top or the ass on bottom?" And he laughed and said, "Jesus, you guys are like a couple of queers. Why don't you kiss and make up? You know you're dying to." Then he told me the latest news, and, man, Peewee always found a way to hold your interest, even when you were having nothing to do with him. First he moved to Williamsburg, Brooklyn, which in those days was more dangerous than Rivington Street, if such a thing was possible, so the rent was even cheaper. Also, of course, he'd reconciled with his parents, who'd put him back on the payroll on the condition that he see a shrink. He'd railed against psychiatry since I first knew him—modern-day phrenology, he used to call it—but I heard he liked this new shrink, and he supposedly told Terrence he was making a lot of important "breakthroughs." He'd also fallen madly in love with a German girl named Monika, an avant-garde theater performer, and not only had they gotten married but afterward they'd taken a long trip to Europe, where Peewee had considered remaining, only to decide, no, he wanted to stay in New York after all. So now he and Monika were living in Williamsburg, and Terrence showed me their picture, and, God, it was fucking hilarious: this girl had Peewee beat in the height department by a good half-foot, and her head looked like a big blonde pumpkin, while he, of course, had a face like a ferret mask designed for tiny tots. Terrence described Monika as "crazy, but not the way he is. She's just in kind of a fog all the time, and when she talks, I have no idea what the fuck she's talking about. It's not just the accent. She's just out there, man."

"Well, look who she's married to. Jesus Christ, I can't believe he's *married*! And she's *German*! I wonder what his parents think about *that*!"

"I think they're pretty happy about it. I don't know if it's Monika or the shrink or what, but the only times he gets really hyper is when we're talking about you. He's so happy you're not doing well! I mean, I tell him you're doing just fine, you know, but he says, 'Oh no, I know him. I know he feels bad about that band, I just know it. He always thought *I* was the problem, but now he knows he's got problems too.'"

"Fuck it. Who cares what he thinks?"

But I did, and I knew it. He was always in the back of my mind. It was hard to even read the paper without wondering what he'd have to say about this story or that one. I could speculate, but I knew I never had it right; where I thought he'd say one thing, he'd probably say something else, something I could never have imagined if I'd furrowed my brow for weeks. But in terms of Dockside Hookers, I knew exactly what he'd say, and that was the one reason I tried to make that band work even after it became obvious it was all in vain: I knew he was waiting for me to fail, and when I did, I knew he'd go around gloating about it. And the terrible thing was, he was right: I *hadn't* been able to succeed without him. And now he was going to take his whack at me. That was another bit of news I picked up from Terrence: Peewee's anti-Jason grudge band. He'd even named it for me, though I had no idea what an "egonaut" was till Terrence spelled it out for me: "You know. Jason…? Greek mythology…? The Argo…?"

"Oh. Jesus fucking Christ. Why doesn't he give it a rest?"

"Well, that's just one meaning. An 'egonaut' is a consciousness explorer, whatever the fuck that means. Plus it means 'ego not,' get it? No egos in the house."

"Yeah, let's just see him pull *that* off! He's only got an ego the size of the Empire State Building!"

At any rate, just as Peewee had been waiting for me to fall on my face, I now waited for him to fall on his. I tried not to show my hand. I was always casual when I asked about the band; and Terrence was no fool, he knew what I wanted to hear, but all he knew was what Peewee was telling him; and Peewee, of course, was no fool either; he knew Terrence was the pipeline to me, so all he gave was glowing accounts of terrific practices where life among the Egonauts was peace and harmony; great leaps of creative brilliance. He'd found a new partner through Monika, some guy named Lucien who was writing half their songs, and this Lucien was supposedly *so* great Peewee was letting him split the frontman duties. I lost it when Terrence told me that. I didn't care how much Peewee was supposed to have changed, I couldn't imagine him being that compliant with anybody, and Terrence agreed, since, after all, he'd been in a band with Peewee himself. Then it was finally announced that the Egonauts were making their big debut, and Terrence went off to see them, and the next day I called him, fully expecting a bad report, but instead he said, "You know what? They're not bad at all."

"You're kidding."

"No, they're actually pretty good. And that Lucien guy really is doing half their songs, and—how do I describe their sound? It's kind of like Scratch except it's more...coherent, I guess you'd say. There's a little more melody, a little more for people to hold on to."

"And they all get along?"

"Well, it *looks* that way. But, then again, Lucien's kind of a cipher. He doesn't say very much. He just kind of sits there looking depressed."

"Of course he looks depressed! He *is*! He's in a band with Peewee!"

"Well, I don't know. It looks like it's working to me."

And I thought, "Jesus Christ, Peewee waits for *me* to leave, and *then* he decides to get his shit together." But I was sure it wouldn't last. "I bet they're broken up in a month," I thought; but a month later they played again, and Terrence said the same thing: they weren't bad at all. I kept pressing him for details, and he said, "Look, I don't know what to tell you. You ought to see them for yourself. And I think he *wants* you to come. I think he's really curious about your reaction."

"Yeah," I said, "maybe I'll go next time." But I didn't mean it. I didn't want to have to witness Peewee's success, not even on such a tiny scale, and so much shit had gone down, I couldn't imagine the two of us being in the same room without a little blood being shed. We hadn't exchanged a single word in a year and a half. We'd never even seen each other.

One night in the fall of '86, I was downtown with my roommate Joe (the law student), and after getting completely smashed, we went to grab a slice of pizza at Stromboli's at the corner of St. Mark's and First Avenue. We were eating outside, both so drunk we could barely stand, and at some point I looked up and saw a little guy with Caesar bangs and Captain Kirk sideburns walking toward me. He was holding hands with a big blonde chick wearing a long black cape, and for just a second I thought, "What a weird couple," and then I realized the guy was Peewee! He was looking straight at me, and I tried to read his expression, but, being so hammered, I couldn't; and they got closer and closer, and right as they were about to pass, Peewee said, "Hey, Jason," with a nonchalant nod. I did as he did. I said, "Hey, Bernard," as nonchalantly back. Then he and Monika (since, of course, that was who the big blonde was) kept walking and I watched as they faded into the shadows of First Avenue. It was so surreal I almost felt like I'd dreamed the whole thing. I turned to Joe and said, "*Man*, that was weird."

"What was weird?"

"That guy I just spoke to? That's the guy I used to be in a band with."

"What guy?" He was so drunk he'd never seen Peewee or heard me speak to him, which further made me wonder if I really had. Even so, I called Terrence the next day and said, "Guess who I ran into last night?"

"I know, I know, he called me too. Jesus Christ, you guys are predictable!"

"So what'd he say about it?"

"He said you were eating pizza with a yuppie and you looked like you were going to throw up."

"Well, not because of him! Let's get that straight right now! And it's just like him to throw a brick at Joe just because he's not some cool downtowner with a groovy haircut and a German art chick hanging off his arm!"

"Jason, what the fuck is wrong with you? What, do you *want* trouble? Bernard wasn't throwing any 'bricks' at anybody. He said he was glad you two had finally seen each other, and he was really impressed with how cool you acted. And he wants to talk to you, and I gave him your number, and now I'm going to give you his. Because this has just *got* to end, and this is your chance, so don't fucking blow it."

Then he gave me the number, and I thought about calling, and once even had the phone in my hand, but then I thought, "No, if he really wants to talk, let him call *me*." And Terrence was getting really impatient with the whole thing, so that the next time the Egonauts were playing, he called me and said, "Okay, this is the deal: Bernard has personally requested that you come. And I want to make this absolutely clear: you *have* to fucking go. Because you know you're curious, and I've had it up to here with this baby fucking bullshit you guys keep pulling. And it's mostly coming from *you*. So if you don't go to this show, I'm going to—man, I don't know *what* I'm going to do, but if you ever say the word 'Peewee' again, I'm going to punch you in the fucking mouth!"

And that wasn't Terrence's style at all, to say something like that. So I said, "Okay, okay, I'll be there," even though the Mets were in the middle of the World Series, and, being completely obsessed with it, I knew it might present a conflict the night of Peewee's show. I just hoped the game that night didn't go into extra innings, but of course it did. I was uptown glued to the TV with my roommates, thinking, "Gotta go, gotta go," but this was Game Six; if the Mets lost this game, that was it, they'd lose the Series after a season as one of the most indomitable teams in baseball history. (The Red Sox had won three games already.) Then, in the bottom of the eleventh inning, Mookie Wilson hit a routine grounder, what should have been the final out of the Series, and Bill Buckner let it roll through his legs, allowing Ray Knight to score the winning run; and, man, that apartment exploded with cheering and yelling. It was a fucking miracle, and I was so caught up with the celebrating I forgot all about Peewee's show. Then I remembered, and nobody else wanted to go downtown; they wanted to stay uptown and get knackered. That was what I wanted to do as well, but, because I'd made that promise to Terrence, I ran out and hailed a cab; and all the way downtown there were people in the streets, pumping fists and jumping on cars, a victory party just this side of St. Patrick's Day. Finally we pulled up at a bar in the East Village—and that's something else I can't remember, the name of that place, though I know it was somewhere around 13th Street and Second Avenue and there was a big window through which you could see almost the entire bar. And this brings up an aside. Peewee kept a journal for most of the time I knew him, and after he died, Monika packed up most of his things and took off with them; and for years I tried to get in touch with her and never could, and so much of my life is in those journals, so many details I know I've forgotten, and since Peewee never had need to write me a letter, I don't own a single sample of his writing apart from his lyrics. And by now I'm sure Monika's moved on with her life, so I don't know if she still has those things, or, if she does, how much they still mean to her; but if by chance she should read this book, I hope she'll get in touch with me. Because I'd like a copy of that journal, and I'd also like a copy of that script I was writing with Peewee right before he died. Thanks, Monika.

 The show was in progress when I walked inside. It was a small place, with maybe fifty people in the audience—quite a lot for a band like that one—and I recognized a few old friends, including Terrence, but it was mostly people I didn't know, including Monika, who was hanging out by the side of the stage with a guy you could tell on sight was a German art fag. I stood in the back, not wanting to make Peewee nervous, and the stage was only a foot off the floor and a few bodies were blocking my view, but here and there somebody would step aside, so I mostly saw just fine. There was a sense of celebration in the bar too, a number of people wearing Mets or Red Sox caps (and at that moment I loathed anyone wearing a Red Sox cap), and a great cheer followed every song; and not that the band wasn't good—it was—but I felt like the Mets fans at least would've cheered just about anything that night. I could tell Peewee had come some distance musically since the last time I'd seen him. There were hints of the old Scratch disjointedness, but, just as Terrence had said, there was a little more melody, a little more for people to hold on to. Also—and this was something Terrence *hadn't* mentioned—there was a lot more fuzz, a lot more feedback, and I thought that was a definite improvement over Scratch, just as Lucien was a far better drummer than Gareth. Peewee didn't strike me as nervous or spastic at all; he seemed much more in control of himself; but then this was the first (and only) time I'd watched him as part of the audience, so he might've appeared that confident for some time already without my being aware of it. At one point I remember thinking, "You know, maybe I *was* the problem all along. Maybe I brought out all the wrong things in the guy. But I wasn't doing it to fuck with him. I just wanted the band to be great." Then there was a long pause while Lucien climbed out from behind his kit, and he strapped on a guitar and took over as frontman for a couple of songs, and I thought, "What the fuck was Terrence going on about? He doesn't seem depressed at all!" He had hangdog features that gave him the look of a natural downer, but he certainly didn't play like one. I thought his songs were the best so far. As for Peewee, I thought he was pretty good too; and, no question, the Egonauts were leagues ahead of Scratch, or except for that time with Laura; but, overall, I still wasn't blown away. Which was definitely a relief.

But then there was another long pause while Peewee climbed out from behind the drums. (He'd played them on Lucien's songs.) I was looking for something to talk about later, some kind of constructive criticism to offer, so I thought I'd suggest they find a more efficient way of switching off, the crowd having grown restless during the gaps. Then Peewee strapped on his guitar and glanced around the crowd with his hand cupped over his brow, and I had a feeling I was the one he was looking for, and of course I was right: he spotted me and said into the mic, "You're here! Hey, that's the guy who broke up my last band! Now everybody please form a neat, orderly line and go over and beat the *fuck* out of him!" And every head in the place, just about, swiveled to look at me, and some people laughed, and I laughed too, even though I thought he was half-joking at best. I gave him a little salute, and he saluted me back and said, "How you doing, brother? I got something for you. One-two-three-FOUR!" And, bang, he started scratching away on his guitar, a frantic squealing distorted sound, Lucien heavy on the kick drum behind him, and I thought, "This is for *me*? What the hell *is* this?" Then Peewee started screaming:

> *I've stood in many poses*
> *I've stood on my head*
> *And begged you to like me*
> *And what did I get?*
> *Slings and arrows*
> *A knife in my back*
> *A smile that hides*
> *A plan of attack*
> *And what's my crime?*
> *Just being alive*
> *Just lifting back the veil*
> *Where the good folks hide!*

So this was Peewee's cover of "Banished." It barely sounded like the original. It was his own version, off-kilter and oddly tuned, but he was rocking out like I'd never seen him before, like I'd never seen anybody before—a holy roller, a spinning top—and when he sang it looked like the veins on his forehead were going to burst open, like his whole head was about to explode. And that *sound*: it was so raw and so nasty, so out of this world; and Lucien was *pounding* those fucking drums, so that I bobbed my head till my neck started to hurt, and, glancing around the room, I saw lots of other heads bobbing too. *I didn't want it to ever end!* Then Peewee jumped off the stage and collided with the audience, at one point disappearing altogether, and I pushed through the crowd to the last place I'd seen him, and there he was, lying on the floor, eyes shut tight, legs kicking, hips fucking air, still scratching away on his guitar, still making that piercing noise. People were staring down like, "Holy shit, what's happening with this guy?" and then, as if pulled to his feet by a witch doctor directing his movements from afar, he charged back to the stage and grabbed the mic for the next verse. He sang it right to me, no longer playing the guitar but jabbing his hand in the air, fingers like a pistol, and sometimes he pointed them at me, and I thought, "Jesus Christ, he's using one of my favorite songs to get back at me!" But it wasn't just that. He was "shooting" everybody else too, and meantime he'd changed the words of the chorus so that it wasn't "I'm BANISHED!" but "You've VANISHED!" And it went on and on; he added at least three minutes to what had originally been a two-minute song, once again playing the guitar till he snapped it off and raised it above his head like Moses with the stone tablets and slammed it down on the floor. And he slammed it again, and he slammed it again, and the neck broke off, and he picked up the body and threw it down and jumped up and down on that. Debris was flying off the stage, and people stepped back, out of the line of fire, and even the other band members—the girl bassist and the male second guitarist—were cowering with their mouths hanging open. Only Lucien participated in the destruction. He knocked his drums to the floor and threw them and kicked them; he kicked them wide open and ripped the ruptured skin off with his hands. And when there was nothing left but the buzz of the amps, Peewee collapsed on the floor of the stage. He didn't move, and for a moment I didn't either. I think that was the single most electrifying display of rock & roll power I ever saw (but didn't participate in) till many years later at the Fold in Los Angeles. I had goosebumps. Then I walked outside and stood by the door, speechless. It was as if I had to be alone for a few minutes, and only later did I fully understand why. Because what I'd experienced inside wasn't just music. Something had died and something had been born in one fell whack.

BUT, OF COURSE, I HAD PERSONAL FEELINGS in the matter. Not many others felt the way I did. After Terrence walked out and found me, I told him it was the greatest thing I'd ever seen, just about, and why hadn't he mentioned Peewee was doing stuff like this; and he said, "I never saw him do it before. And it wasn't *that* great. It's pretty passé, don't you think? We already *had* the Who." Terrence was hardly what I'd characterize as a typical East Village hipster, but, still, that was exactly what you heard after any show, no matter how good. Nobody ever said, "Oh my God, my whole life's been changed forever." It was always, "Yeah, they were okay," followed by a blasé comparison to another band. That was especially true if you were speaking to somebody with a band of their own. Outside the hardcore scene, it was very important to be aloof and arty, and that giving-yourself-up-to-the-moment stuff almost never happened, and when it did, you could bet your last nickel it wouldn't get *too* crazy. No, for that you had to turn to out-of-staters like the Replacements or the Butthole Surfers. But as much as I loved both those bands (the first especially), I always had the feeling they were just kind of kidding around, whereas with Peewee I truly felt it was a life-and-death matter. He'd topped them both as far as I was concerned, and I said as much to Terrence, but I was dreading speaking to Peewee, since it was clear he still had a lot of resentment toward me. Besides, I was so fucking jealous! So I lingered by the door, and people kept walking outside, and the ones I knew would stop and say, "Hey, what's going on? Got a new band? No? What'd you think of these guys?" Again, very few seemed as impressed as I was, and I'd check out those people I didn't know, but it was hard to tell how they felt, what with so many looking pleased in a general way on account of the Mets. I watched through the window as Peewee talked in a corner of the bar to his fellow Egonauts and some other people, including Monika; and then somebody pulled up in a station wagon, and the whole band but Peewee started lugging out the gear. That's when I met Lucien. Terrence introduced us, and I shook his hand and said, "Man, that was great."

"Thanks," he mumbled.

"So were you planning on ripping shit up?"

He shook his head.

"It just happened?"

He nodded. I was starting to see why Terrence had described him as morose. He said practically nothing while staring at you with deep-set eyes that made you wonder what the fuck he was thinking. Finally I managed to extract a couple of actual sentences from him. I said, "You guys are going to have to replace an awful lot of stuff," and he said, "I don't even want to *think* about it. And it looks like we fucked up the floor a little, and that cocksucker manager's refusing to pay us. He's trying to make us pay *him*." By then the bass player and second guitarist were standing beside him, and they said, "Well, we're not paying *anything*. You and Bernard are the ones who did it, and we're not going to pay for something *we* didn't do." Then they walked off in a huff, and Lucien gave an "Oh, brother" roll of the eyes and walked off behind them, and I watched through the window as Peewee kept talking to some guy in the corner (who, I now realized, must be the manager) till he and Monika and the German art fag all moved to the bar. I knew I was going to have to say something at some point, so I walked inside with Terrence, and the second Peewee saw me, he stood and gave me a hug. Which was definitely a first, let me tell you! And he said, "So?"

"It was incredible."

"You really think so?"

"You can ask Terrence. I've been standing outside telling everybody it's the greatest thing I ever saw."

"Get out of here!"

"No, it's true. You see? I always told you we should be more like the Replacements. But you did them one better. *That's* the kind of show we should have been doing the whole time!"

"Yeah, well, it's going to cost me a pretty penny. But never fear. I'm rich! You know I'm married now, right? And Monika's father is a vice president at BMW. Isn't that right, baby?"

"Yes. This is true, yes."

Then I was formally introduced to Monika, who was every bit as weird as Terrence had said she was, as weird as she looked. With her unblinking eyes and unchanging smile, she appeared to have undergone shock therapy. Peewee and I spoke for a few minutes, mostly confirming a few things passed on by Terrence. I told him about Dockside Hookers, and he told me about making up with his parents and seeing that shrink (though, to me, he claimed it made no difference) and also a bit about his travels; but every time we got going, Monika would interrupt with some non-sequitur like, "I think the Tasmanian Devil is the best character in all the cartoons!"—stuff that made no sense at all—and Peewee would break off to speak to her. It was like they were in a world all their own, their own private language and everything, and Monika kept smiling with those button-like eyes, reminding me of Raggedy Ann or one of those girls in ABBA. Peewee seemed exhausted, or maybe this was the big change Terrence had been telling me about, since all that maniacal stage behavior seemed to belong to a different person entirely. In fact, that whole exchange was sad in the sense that we'd been as close as grunts in the trenches, and now it was as if we barely knew each other at all. Plus I felt like a lowlife for eloping with Scratch, and I apologized for the pain I'd caused, and Peewee said, "Fuck it. It was my fault as much as yours. I was *trying* to make you quit. You and Laura both." Still, that was as deep as we got that night; he stood a minute later and said, "Well, look, I'd love to hang out, but I should really be helping with the equipment. But why don't we get together later this week?"

"Sure, okay. You've got my number, right?"

"Yeah, but don't you have mine?" Then Terrence said, "Here we go again," and Peewee laughed a bemused laugh unlike anything I'd ever quite heard before and said, "All right, I'll call you. Or why don't we just make a time right now? Let's say we get together next Saturday. Maybe I can come up to nosebleed country. I don't think I've been that far uptown since I was twelve years old." Then he and Monika and the art fag all walked out of the bar, and I turned to Terrence and said, "Man, I can't believe it! You know what's happened? He's become a *man*!"

"See? All that horseshit was over nothing."

Then he and I went barhopping, and again, half the town was out celebrating, and it really did feel like there was some kind of special magic in the air. I took a cab at the crack of dawn to the Upper East Side, where the whole crew was passed out, and I went to my room and picked up a guitar and wrote a whole song in maybe ten minutes, lyrics included. That was practically the first time I'd touched a guitar since Dockside Hookers. Then the Mets won the Series and I wrote a song about that, and I wrote a song about the jealousy that had torn apart Scratch called "Beneath Us All," and I wrote a song about Yes called "Hair Shirt." (I sorely regretted dumping Yes, who refused to take me back.) Now I know I was preparing an audition, but at the time I wasn't sure why I was doing it, except I felt so inspired. Peewee called on Saturday morning to see if we were still on. We were, I said, and he rode up on the subway and walked in the door and said, "Jesus *Christ*, you live in the middle of nowhere! How do you *stand* it all the way up here?"

"Shut up and have a seat. I want to play you something." We were the only ones there; my roommates were off having breakfast, which for them was usually liquid. I played him the new songs I'd written, and he sat and listened, not saying much, looking distracted the whole time. Finally I finished, and he said, "That's all from the band with Laura?"

"No, this is from last week. I'm just *shitting* it out! I'm writing songs in my *sleep*!"

And with that he abruptly stood.

"Let's go for a walk," he said.

"Where?"

"Anywhere. Come on, I can't take this place. It smells like dirty socks."

I was really annoyed when he said that, and I was also irked by his cool response to my songs, but I kept it to myself, not wanting to start a new fight. We walked downstairs and up 86th Street toward Central Park, and practically the first thing he said outside was: "So how'd you like my cover of 'Banished'? Were you surprised about that? I bet you think I played it just to give you the finger."

"Well, that's what you were doing, right?"

"Not really. I was going to play that song if you showed or not. I've been going through this whole Rule of Thumb rediscovery thing."

"Oh? What brought that on?"

"I just started to realize how right they were about so many things. It really hit me after I got to Europe. That was the first time I'd been since I was a kid, and I had a memory of everything being really different, but then I get there and it's worse than this place. I mean, London—their big thing is 'warehouse parties' where they play 'acid jazz' in these abandoned dumps, and they think it's so daring when the police come along to break it up. And France—you don't even want to *know* what they're listening to in France. They *hate* rock & roll. It's like Maurice fucking Chevalier, except it's disco. And Germany—that's the worst of all. It's all this electronic shit, only not interesting like Kraftwerk or Einstürzende Neubauten; it's just this awful pop shit, and when people get up to dance, they move like fucking robots. It's not like they're *trying* to, that's just the way they *dance*. Honestly, even my fucking mother can move better than they can! And it made me think about 'Lockstep,' you know, that Rule of Thumb song where everyone in the whole world is going to end up looking and thinking just the same. And that's true—I really think that's starting to happen—but there's also this whole other meaning to that word, which is you literally can't even move, you're so out of touch with your animal self. And I think that's why those Europeans can't respond to live instruments: because the robot in *them* can only respond to robot *music*. And after I got home, I started listening to that song and all the others, and, man, that guy was really on to something.

Like 'Artificial Pussy'—I think that's happening too. Just the other day this friend of Monika's said, 'You know, I'll be so happy when science figures out a way you can have a baby without having to carry it around for nine months.' She basically wants to grow a baby in a fucking Petri dish! And, you know, Lucien never gets laid, never. He just rents porn and jerks off all the time, and Monika's been trying to fix him up, and he always says no, it's too much trouble. And I started to realize there must be a lot of people like Lucien out there. Because, you know, they shoot most porn on video now, and it's so cheap to make there's just reams and reams of it, and I think the more there is, the more tempting it's going to be for people not to fuck. They're just going to want to watch *other* people fuck."

"So, what, you're down on porn now?"

"Yeah, you know what? I really kind of am. After I got with Monika, boom, I had no use for it anymore. And what I'm starting to see more and more is this sort of Plato's-cave world, where people mistake shadows for the real thing, and that's all I think pornography is: a shadow. And, you know, Monika's just great, and I can't wait for you to get to know her, because I really think you're going to love her as much as I do. I mean, obviously, we don't want another Laura situation. We don't want that, do we?"

"We don't, no."

"But the thing is, even though Monika's terrific and we get along just great, I've got to tell you, it can be really hard sometimes. I mean, she's got her foibles and I've got mine, and there's cultural barriers, and she's six years older and blah-blah-blah. But the thing is, it's *real*. I really have no desire to improve things, because whatever faults she's got and whatever faults I've got, that's what makes us human. But then we'll hang out with one of her friends and she'll be talking about some guy she likes, and it's like, 'Well, he's great except for this and that, and this and that.' And you start to think, 'She doesn't like this guy at *all*. She likes some *idea* she's got, and that's it.' You know, it seems like every time I look through a magazine, there's all this stuff in there about 'relationships' and how to make them work better. I mean, if I have to hear that word one more time—'relationship'—I think I'm going to kill somebody! Because I don't think most people want 'relationships' at all; they want a robot that'll do whatever they want. They're just like Lucien:

they don't want any trouble. And that's what feelings are: trouble. It's to the point where if you sat a lot of people down and said, 'Okay, you have two choices: you can feel a whole lot, and sometimes it's going to be great and sometimes it's going to be really painful, or here's your other choice, you're not going to have the lows but you're not going to have the highs either,' I honestly think that's the one most people would choose. Especially people *our* age. We're the absolute *worst*. I mean, don't you remember how we always used to talk about the revolution?"

"It was mostly you."

"Well, I was wrong! I have no trouble admitting it. When you're wrong, you're wrong, and I was definitely *wrong*! But I'll tell you this much: we never had a chance. Because for that kind of thing you need leaders, and who the fuck did *we* ever have? I mean, Ian MacKaye—he should have been *huge*! Instead he—what?—runs some little hardcore label down in D.C.? Give me a fucking break! And Jim Cassady—okay, he's older than us, but what the fuck did he mean by pulling that whole vanishing act? Did you notice I changed the words to his song?"

"Of course."

"Because it pisses me fucking *off*! And, okay, he probably OD'd—and I hope he fucking did! Because it's just inexcusable otherwise. What, you're going to put out a few records hinting what you *could* do if you felt like it, and then turn around and say, 'Oh, gee, guess I changed my mind. Guess you guys will have to wait for somebody else, because I'm washing my hands of the whole thing.'"

"Yeah, but, you don't know *what* he was thinking. When did *he* ever use the word 'revolution'? I never saw it anywhere. You're the only person I ever knew who talked about it, and I always thought you were full of shit."

"Well, it doesn't matter anyway. We're fucked! We're only the most boring generation since the Middle Ages. I thought there were a lot of people out there who felt the way I did, but all they think about is shit they can *buy*. And you know what? *That's* the revolution. Yeah, I really think there was one, but it wasn't the one I had in mind. Corporations—they're running the world now. That's something else I realized in Europe: there *is* no Europe. There's no America either. There's just these giant multinationals that are nations unto themselves, and they're going to keep going and going till you've got a McDonald's in the middle of the

Sahara and a David's Cookies in Siberia. And, all right, on the surface maybe it's not so bad if camel jockeys eat Big Macs. But when all you eat is food that tastes like cardboard, it kills your idea of what food can be. And it's the same way with music and movies and everything else. That's all cardboard too, or ninety-nine percent of it is, and people are so used to that crap, they resent the real thing. You know what I feel like sometimes? I feel like one of those people trying to hold off the zombies in *Night of the Living Dead*. And you know how *that* turned out! *Everybody's* going to be a zombie by the time it's over. It could even happen to *me*!"

By this time we were in Central Park, a gorgeous fall day, the leaves red and orange and yellow; and we walked and walked, and talked and talked, or mostly he did. He said he and Monika had an "open marriage" in which they were free to sleep with other people, and a couple of times they'd shared their bed with other girls. It was "weird," he said, not nearly as exciting as he thought it would be, and there was something so funny about that, to hear him talking like a jaded roué. We also spoke for a long time about Terrence, about whom Peewee was "worried," since it was starting to look like he was never going to amount to much of anything. At one point he compared him to Lucien, saying that Lucien was apathetic too, but he at least had an excuse: his brother had committed suicide, and later, while attending school in Madison, Wisconsin, Lucien had suffered some kind of "nervous breakdown" and decided in the aftermath he was moving to New York and dedicating his life to music.

"And he was just like us," Peewee said. "When he first got here, he barely played. And, man, he may have a lot of problems, but in terms of the band I've got no complaints. He's like Brian fucking Jones! You could put a *tuba* down in front of him, and after an hour he'd be playing it like an expert! And you saw the way he was the other night, right? I started ripping the place apart, and he jumped right up and joined me. I wish the other two were like that. *God*, what a couple of drags. They're just the most miserable people. Honestly, man, I don't know why I bother. I think about all these other things I want to do, all these movies I want to make, and a band—it's nothing but fights. And, you know, I really wouldn't mind if it's over the right things, but it's always, 'I don't *wanna* practice, I don't *wanna* play it like that, I don't *wanna,* I don't *wanna.' You* were never like that. You always gave a hundred and ten percent, brother. You were wrong most of the time, but that's a different subject entirely." And here we both laughed, and then he paused, and I'd had a feeling for some time that he was building up to something, but I was sure it didn't pertain to music, he'd seemed so oblivious to my songs. But then, as we stood watching the kids on the Central Park Carousel, he said, "Look, I'm going to propose something, and I think I know what you're going to say, but I want you to hear me out. Those songs you just played me—they're pretty good. They're a little too *clean* for my taste, but I think they're some of the best things you ever wrote. And I think you ought to come down to Williamsburg, and let's try them out—just you, me and Lucien—and if we like the way it goes, I think we should start a band. Because it's really not working out with Sam and Allie, and I've finally got somebody really good with Lucien, and if *you* came in—man, it makes me *cum* to think how good we could be! And if one of us feels like it's not there, we'll just say, 'Okay, we tried and it didn't work out,' and that'll be that. But I definitely think we should *try.* Otherwise I'm just going to hang it up, and, you know, I really don't want to right now. I feel like I'm just getting started."

So, of course, I was overjoyed. I said, "I can't believe you're saying this! Sure! Of course! I would've said something the other night, but I thought you'd laugh in my face!"

"Are you *kidding* me? I was *waiting* for you to say something! That's the only reason I wanted you to come! I was hoping to lure you back!"

"So when do you want to do it? Right now? Let me go back and grab a guitar, and we can do it right this minute!"

But suddenly all the excitement drained from his face.

"Goddamnit," he said, "we *can't.* Lucien really trashed his drums the other night. But maybe he can borrow some, right? And if he can't, fuck it, I'll steal one of Monika's credit cards and buy him some new ones!"

Then we went charging out of Central Park, and basically, by ten that night, Lucien had a brand-new kit and the new band had written its first song. And when Peewee raised the question of what we were going to call ourselves, I blurted out the first thing that ran through my head, which was Superego, and he said, "Great, perfect, we're Superego." I said, "Are you sure? Maybe we should think it over for a few days."

"No, it's right on the money. We both have giant egos, and super is what we're going to be." And he was right: we really were stellar. There were times when I'd describe us in all sobriety as one of the best fucking bands on the planet, though none but a handful knew who we were.

BUT DON'T TAKE MY WORD FOR IT. You can always hear for yourself. Even though the one record we made has been out of print since its first and only pressing, there are a number of collectors and specialty stores selling it over the Internet. It goes for eighty-five bucks, the last time I checked, I guess because it's so rare; so if you're interested, it's called, simply, *Superego*, and it was released in 1987 on our own label, Cell Kit. But since I doubt most people are curious enough to shell out eighty-five bucks for a one-shot record by a short-lived band, I can still give you a very good idea of how we sounded, because there's a song called "Caterpillar" by the band Unwound, which, the first time I heard it years later on KXLU in Los Angeles, I thought for a second it *was* Superego, it sounded so like us. It's got the same menace and sense of frenzy, of something threatening to splinter out of control but still held together by a strong melody. Also, like so many Superego songs, there's a tempo change halfway through, and the singer has a tone to his voice that reminds me a lot of Lucien's. I wonder if they ever heard us? I'd love to think it's more than coincidence, though I'm sure that's all it is. I mean, we never tried to sound like Sonic Youth, but somehow we did. Those guys were really sophisticated, with their Glenn Branca and all that. We just kind of bumbled down the same road. We also sounded a bit like Pussy Galore, and some claimed to hear a little Jesus and Mary Chain, I suppose because of the fuzz. But in the end I think we found ourselves; we had our own unique sound. And that was how we sprang out of the womb. It took us no time to develop, we meshed so perfectly. And though this is a gross oversimplification, since we all swapped roles within the band, often literally, you might say in Freudian terms that I was the superego, the structure guy; and Peewee was the id, the fountain of chaos; and Lucien was the ego, mediating between the two, though never in terms of resolving conflict, since, at least musically, there *was* no conflict. No, Lucien was the key architect of the Superego sound, with his love of reverb and heavy, busy drums; and his ear was so keen that Peewee and I followed his every suggestion. Yet, very quickly, we all developed a psychic understanding, so that fewer suggestions were needed. I would *know* as we worked out a song that Lucien wanted to slow the tempo, before he'd said a word, and Peewee would know *I* knew, and lo and behold, the song would slow. Even when we wrote songs individually, it was if the others were somehow contributing, though many of our songs were collaborations, including the one that came out of our first practice. We were fooling around with "Hair Shirt," my song about Yes, but it soon evolved into something else, and finally the last trace of the original riff had given way to a better riff. Then Peewee stepped up to the mic and started yelling a stream-of-consciousness monologue about the old days on Rivington Street, and it fit the song so perfectly that, later, when we talked about lyrics, I said, "You know what? Let's not write any lyrics. Every time we play it, Peewee can get up and say whatever he wants, and that's the song." Of course he *loved* that idea, so even though we called the song "Rivington Street," he almost never mentioned Rivington Street later. On the track we laid down for our record, for instance, he rants about everything from the 718 area code to Oliver North to the beauty of Brigitte Bardot in *Contempt*, only to scream out as the song closes, "Jim Cassady, where the fuck *are* you?" That was the G-rated version. At shows he could say things so confrontational that, once, at the Continental Club in Buffalo, he was attacked by a musclehead who rushed the stage; and when I tackled the guy, his buddies jumped in, slugging me so hard I literally saw stars. I thought for sure the manager was going to pull the plug, but, no, the bouncers bounced the muscleheads, and, bruised and bleeding, we finished the show and went *especially* crazy at the end. We did our standard closer, "Vanished" (formerly known as "Banished"), and I broke a guitar I'd borrowed from Shock Corridor, the band we were touring with (I'd broken my last guitar beyond repair the night before in Rochester), and, man, were they pissed about *that*! But they should have known what was going to happen, no matter the promises we'd made beforehand. We couldn't help ourselves! And that was another way in which we were different from most other bands of our time: we fucked shit *up*! It was one of our trademarks, I suppose you might say. And we did it because that was how we felt—it was the only way to express the kind of ecstasy that overtook us at shows—but also Peewee and I especially were alarmed at the way things were developing in the national music scene, which seemed increasingly focused on "entertainment" and less on music as a vital, dangerous art form. We were trying to bitchslap some life back into things! Half our songs were wake-up calls to the living dead. There was "AWOL" and "Don't Forget to Breathe" and "Calling Che Guevera." There was a song called "Wounded Knee," about the death of the primitive spirit, and another song called "Take Me," which I'll get into in a minute. Plus we had personal songs, such as "Keeper of the Gate," which Peewee wrote about Monika, and "Contradiction Man," which I wrote about Peewee, and "Hippie Heaven," Lucien's song about Madison, Wisconsin and everything he despised about it. (Curiously, though, he didn't sing it. I did. We always turned the mic over to the voice that best suited a given song, just as we took turns at different instruments. We had to, otherwise we would've come up short when a bass was needed or Lucien was singing. He refused to sing and play drums at the same time. It made him think of Don Henley, he said.) And with almost no exceptions, everything we did rocked the fuck out, and there wasn't one song in our collected works I didn't think was top-notch and couldn't recreate this minute if I picked up a guitar. They're tattooed on my brain forever.

But, then, Superego performed more than all my other bands put together, and then some. In the year and a half we lasted, we must have done at least 100 shows, and that's including the month we lost after Lucien fractured his wrist. And of those 100 shows, I'd say only twelve took place in the metropolitan New York area. That's because, beginning with our first show, at the Pyramid Bar in January 1987, we started getting banned. It happened at the Pyramid when a kid standing by the stage got brained by a flying cymbal, and though he was cool about it, the Pyramid people were not. Then we got banned from Maxwell's in Hoboken (our favorite local venue), and from CBGB's (in a sense, the band's birthplace), and later from yet another place I can't recall the name of; but it was near Times Square—a Middle Eastern bellydance joint that, on certain nights, doubled as a rock club. But that stopped not long after we played there, and I always wondered if we were the reason. That was the night Peewee jumped on somebody in the audience, causing him to drop his beer, and a song later I fell in the broken glass and gushed blood all over the audience, not to mention the manager, who was on his way to shut us down. I barely had any idea I'd been injured, I was so into it, but there was a nice sliver of glass lodged inside my forearm, and the trip to the emergency room to have it removed was as costly as it was painful. At any rate, that show was possibly the reason those Arabs stopped booking bands and returned to bellydancing full-time, though all I know for sure is: "You will never play here again! You are very sick boys! Sick in the head!"

But we were getting used to that, just as we'd long since gotten used to cold or lukewarm reactions from the audience. And with Superego the reaction was the best it ever had been, and there were a few people, such as my Upper East Side roommates, who'd rave about us, but we thought everybody should be raving, and we knew in New York that was probably never going to happen. So very early on, right after our second show at an East Village dive called Sophie's, we basically decided we weren't going to put up with the snubs anymore. Our attitude was: "Fuck these jaded New Yorkers and their too-cool-for-school bullshit. Let's go play for the hicks. People must be dying for some good music out in the boondocks!" It's a wonder we'd never thought of that before, but, then, we'd never thought of trashing our gear till Peewee spontaneously discovered it. We called other bands we knew who'd toured and said, "What towns do we hit? How do we go about this?" and Peewee and I booked the tour ourselves in his apartment in Williamsburg, using stolen credit-card information to foot the phone bill. (Let's just say my bartending job had its fringe benefits.) We rented a van and invited Shock Corridor to come along to split expenses, and for three weeks that spring we drove as far west as Columbus and as far north as Montreal and back to the city by way of New England, and it was just incredible, the reaction we got. Now, obviously, if we'd been laconic art rockers of the kind so many people in the East Village aspired to be, it would've been a whole other story. But we weren't laconic and we weren't ironic; we got our fucking hands dirty, and the grittier the venue, the more people loved our stuff. You'd have your drunken jerks here and there, guys who'd try to pick fights (as if we didn't have plenty of those in New York!), but mostly we couldn't get over how generous people were. Total strangers would come up and say, "Need a place to crash? You can stay at my place, no problem." They'd feed us and drive us around to parties, sharing their drugs and booze, and set us up with girls who wanted to fuck us like we were Bruce Springsteen or somebody. They even wanted to fuck Peewee! And I had moments playing that, even at the time, I knew I'd never touch again, moments that bordered on beatitude, they were so overwhelming. To this day I'm not sure where it came from, since, only a week into things, I was already starting to feel run down. We all were. I mean, you're cooped up in a van for hours on end, and you hardly ever get a good night's sleep, and you're eating the worst food in the world, or sometimes you're so broke you eat nothing at all, so tempers are short, and there are certain people you really want to strangle. And the van is constantly breaking down, and everybody fights about how to fix it, and you're late and can't find the venue, so you stop at a phone booth to call for directions—or at least you did in those days—and nobody's got a goddamned quarter. Then you find the place, and you're treated like shit by the management, and you *feel* like shit because your clothes are dirty, and you stink from the sweat of last night's show if you never got to take a shower, and there's a good chance you never did with so many people competing for the bathroom wherever you find yourself crashing. Then you donkey gear from the van to the venue, and hardly anybody is there to see you, and you start getting shitfaced since drinks are on the house, and the sound guy is usually some geeky prick who thinks he knows everything and gives you lip when you question his expertise. Yet somehow, come show time, something would come over me, come over all of us, even Lucien, eerily quiet (more quiet even than Yes!), not to mention Peewee, who, if he'd ever been stymied by nerves in the past, sure wasn't stymied now. And we didn't care if it was four people (and once it was, and all four worked in the joint) or 300 (which was as many as we ever played for), we always gave everything we had. And chances were, at the end of the show, we'd break a few things, including some belonging to the venue, and that would bring on the wrath of the manager, and all we could do was shrug and say, "We're a rock & roll band, what do you expect? That's what rock & roll is."

"Who the hell do you think you *are*? You're going to tell *me* what rock & roll is? Well, let me tell *you* something: I've run this place fifteen years, and I've had some of the *giants* come through here, and I've never had *anybody* come in and pull the shit you punks just pulled!" By that, of course, he wouldn't mean "punk" as we knew ourselves to be; he'd mean it in the original sense of pissant petty criminals. Then we'd try to get some money out of him, if we possibly could, and that was practically nothing, since, even if he decided to pay us, we knew we were getting shortchanged. Then we'd break down the equipment and drive all night to the next town or head off with the person who was letting us crash, and, after drinking till five or six in the morning, everybody would claim his spot on the floor and wake up stiff-necked a few hours later and do it all over again. So, yes, it was really exhausting. But what made it all worth it was the chance to perform, and also those people who'd come up afterward and say what we wanted to hear: we'd changed their lives in some way. We'd made a difference. Maybe it was just a small difference, but how small was the lamp that burned down Chicago? And if we heard the slightest hint that somebody was holding themselves back from starting their own band, we'd do for them what Jim Cassady had done for us: we'd tell them to go for it. I still think about some of the people we told that to. I wonder if they took our advice. I wonder if they now regret it. And if that's the case, what can I say? We never said it would be easy. We ourselves weren't aware of how hard it could be—not really, not yet.

At any rate, we returned to the city, bedraggled but triumphant, and told everybody we knew we'd been worshiped like the gods we thought we were. There was nobody in that town who could shine our fucking shoes as far as we could see. That was another reason Shock Corridor hated us: they were Little Leaguers, and we were a goddamned All-Star team. We had it all, baby. We could write, we could play, we could put on a show you'd still recall in geriatric diapers. Hell, one of us could even sing. (That would be me.) And what *didn't* we have? We could beat you there too. Every instrument, cable and cabinet we owned was demolished or damaged in some way. We were broke, and in two cases (and one of those would again be me) we didn't have jobs to come back to, since we'd quit them to tour in the first place. Plus we had no record. After five years of playing in four bands apiece, neither Peewee nor I had ever managed to put out a single record. And whereas in the past it had been murder trying to get Peewee to help with the promotion side of things, or apart from designing fliers, now he decided we *had* to get a record deal, and we weren't going to settle for some rinky-dink little SST or Dischord release; we were going to court the fucking majors. Because, as he pointed out, it was very expensive being in our band, what with all the broken equipment, and we'd gotten too good to be, simply, the cult band we'd set out to be. No, he said, we *deserved* to reach as many people as possible. Which were my sentiments exactly.

So we all went back to our comparatively dull lives in New York, and I got a new job as a barback and moved into Peewee's building in Williamsburg. I couldn't believe how little I paid. My room was tiny (it was formerly a pantry, off to the side of the kitchen), but who cared about that when I was only paying $200 a month? Plus Lucien was one of my roommates, and I knew he'd be easy to live with (though the lesbian sculptress leaseholder was not); and the neighborhood looked like Warsaw circa 1945; and Monika claimed the building was haunted; but, again, who cared? Peewee and Monika lived right upstairs, and our practice space was two blocks away, so, in addition to everything else, it was very convenient. We immediately set about booking another tour with a band called Demon Rum, this one crossing the entire country, and Peewee especially went to work on scaring up some label interest. And this is one of those things I don't think I'll ever understand: why no one approached us even to turn us down. Or, actually, that's not quite true: we did get turned down twice. Through Peewee's dad, we spoke to someone at William Morris about management, but we knew that was doomed anyway. Come back when you're stahs! Then, when we realized we weren't getting anywhere fast with the majors, we sent a demo to Dischord, and Ian MacKaye personally wrote us a letter to say sorry but Dischord only put out records by D.C. bands, so he was sending back the demo. Still, thank you, Ian MacKaye, all these years later, for being a human being as everybody else was not. We heard nothing from nobody, and I can remember at least two occasions when word filtered back that some A&R person had definitely been in the audience, and I still don't get how somebody could've seen us and not at the very least come up afterward and said, "You guys are really interesting, and I wish there was something I could do, but unfortunately I'm working for very conservative people who wouldn't know what to do with you." That's the only reason I can think of that we never got approached. Plus we lacked the credentials of, for instance, the Replacements, who, by the time they signed with Sire/Warner, had released four records on independent labels and, thanks to a lot of nationwide touring, had already amassed a huge cult following.

At any rate, right up to the end, we kept trying to attract interest from those people. We even wrote a song about it, the aforementioned "Take Me," though the lyrics were such that I'm sure none of them got the message, or if they did, it only made them keep their distance that much more.

> *I'm a whore*
> *I'm a whore*
> *I'm a dirty little whore*
> *You're the master*
> *I'm the slave*
> *Let me make a decent wage*
> *Let me fill your dirty coffers*
> *At your dirty little store*
>
> *Take me!*
> *(You'll rue the day!)*
> *Stake me!*
> *(Or so you say!)*
> *Make me!*
> *(I won't obey!)*
> *Break me!*
> *(I'll break away!)*

This was obviously written at a point of frustration. (And those parenthetical bits, by the way, were my backup shouts to Peewee's lead vocal.) But we also intended the song to be open-ended enough so that you could read any number of meanings into it. Maybe it sounds like we were ambivalent about getting signed, but I don't think we were. We were beating the labels to the punch. You don't want us? Fine, fuck you, we don't want you anyway. I would like to think if we'd kept going we would've gotten some attention at some stage. We would've *had* to, since we just kept getting better and better. Meantime we kept writing more and more songs, and that meant our old songs weren't going to get played as much, and an important band like ours surely had to preserve its catalog. That's why we decided we couldn't wait anymore; we had to make a record right away. So, first, Peewee went to his parents and pleaded for money, and eventually his dad said he'd give us $500, but that was it—not a penny more! Then Monika (who was a perfect angel, right up there with Bob Stinson as one of the nicest people of all time) volunteered to do some pleading of her own. This is something else I've often thought about in the years since: she called her father in Munich and told him that Peewee was dying from brain cancer and there was some kind of miracle drug she'd have to fly to Mexico to get, and altogether it was going to run $10,000 to save her beloved's life. Peewee and I were right beside her when she made the call, and we didn't understand a word she said, but even so we couldn't get over how convincing she was. She cried real tears and everything! And, sure enough, Daddy Deutsche Marks wired her 10,000 big ones, and we booked ourselves some studio time at Sear Sound in midtown, recording fourteen songs in two days, and then we took the masters to a pressing plant in Cherry Hill, New Jersey, and *voilà*: instant record. Afterward we had enough money left over to throw ourselves a release party *and* buy a van *and* make a video, since we thought maybe—just maybe—if some of those A&R pigs could get a sense of our live show, they might finally express interest.

So on our next tour, which had us driving as far west as San Antonio, Peewee brought along a 16mm movie camera, and our roadie shot the shows, and Peewee shot everything else: the crash pads, the greasy spoons, the American landscape just before it gave way entirely to an endless expanse of strip malls. We developed the film back in New York, and Peewee and I cut the video at NYU film school, thanks to some help from Terrence. We'd long since decided that "Contradiction Man" had breakout potential, since that was the song most remarked upon. I don't know why so many people preferred that song to others I thought were far better. In any case, that was the song we chose for the video, hoping the MTV people would like it enough to give us a call, but of course they never did. Still, it's a first-rate clip, in some ways reminiscent of Beat photographer Robert Frank, and thank God I've still got a copy, since it's the only footage of the band in existence, at least as far as I know. Meantime those cutting-room sessions are another great memory, the way Peewee and I worked so well together, the band telepathy kicking in. We would take breaks and go out for coffee, walking around the East Village really fast like a couple of speed freaks, plotting out the future. Even working on such a tiny scale, we were thinking like the Beatles must have thought at the time they were forming Apple. Superego wasn't going to be just a band. No, we'd go multimedia. We'd release records by other bands on our own label—maybe some of the ones we spawned on tour—and we'd publish books and produce movies that Peewee would direct. And me—what could *I* do? Well, maybe being

Bobby Sherman, I'd be the star, ha, ha. But, no, I could do other things. I could do anything! We shouldn't even wait; we should start writing a script *right this second!*

So we did. Probably we wouldn't have, except that Lucien broke his wrist when a Marshall stack collapsed on top of him and suddenly we had a month to wait till the cast came off. I remember the exchange that inspired the script. One night I was up at Peewee's place, and Monika, who was fascinated by vampires, said, "If you meet a vampire, what would you do? Kill it or let it live?" Peewee and I both said, "Kill it, of course! We'd drive a stake through its fucking heart so fast it wouldn't know what hit it!" And Monika said, "Why, because it will kill you first? What if it's the only one in the whole world? Like the last—what do you call the tiger with the long teeth? Would you still kill the tiger with the long teeth if she's the only one left?" Then Peewee got this *eureka!* look in his eye, and next thing I knew, we were working on a script based on that premise: vampire as saber-toothed tiger. It began with a scene in which a beautiful vampire was on a moving train, famished for blood, and she picked up a guy in the lounge car and took him back to her cabin, where she all but killed him. Later, bleeding to death, he chased her through Penn Station and out to the street, where he collapsed and died. As we had it, this vampire was the last of her line and a great musician who'd studied piano with, for instance, Chopin (that was how long she'd been around), and she was being stalked by a religious fanatic who'd exterminated all her relatives. (In our story vampirism was passed along genetically and not through infection). There was another character who was in love with her, and he wasn't sure what to do: help the fanatic destroy the monster who preyed on humanity, or save the great beauty who was not only the last of her kind but a great artist to boot. We ourselves had no idea how it was going to end. But almost every night for a month I went upstairs to Peewee's place, and we'd pace and smoke and take turns sitting at the typewriter, trying to figure out the story. And it was during one of those sessions that something bizarre happened, something I still don't know how to explain, unless I buy into Monika's belief that our building was haunted, or Peewee's explanation, which was stranger by far. We were in his kitchen one night, working away, and even though it was February and the heat was turned up, the room suddenly got cold, and I had the sense that something or somebody, other than Peewee, was looking at me. Then it felt like an icy hand kind of lifted up my shirt and raked its fingers over my back. I thought I must be hallucinating, but then I locked eyes with Peewee, who said, "Did you *feel* that?" And I nodded, and he said, "Do you know what it was? Death. *Death* just came into the room with us." Which only disturbed me that much more, because it really did feel like Death. It was the eeriest thing I ever experienced, the only time I felt anything remotely like it; and if that accident hadn't happened a few months later, I probably wouldn't mention it. But since it did, it seems a lot more relevant after the fact.

SO HOW DO I DO THIS WITHOUT FALLING APART? For a long time I avoided the subject altogether, even when I was past the grieving stage, since I still felt so fucked up over it. I felt angry and guilty and full of questions I knew I would never have answered. Yes, I was right there when it happened, but all I know is what I read in the police report, what I was told the other two survivors had to say, and both were drunk, and one especially you couldn't trust anyway. As for me, I blacked out. Just as I don't remember much about the fight with Mark Powell, I remember almost nothing about the accident that killed Peewee and two others besides and almost left me an amputee. There was a time in the months afterward when I considered seeing a hypnotist to recover any memories I might be squelching, but I finally decided, no, maybe it's better this way. Maybe the blackout happened after I'd seen things so horrific that something in me wisely shut down, taking with it the moment of impact. That was the moment I wanted to recover. The rest I didn't.

So the critical part, when if one thing had gone just slightly differently, is lost to me. I do have some thoughts as to what may have happened, but this is all I know for sure. It was April 1988, and we were about a week from finishing our fourth tour, which more or less followed the same route as the tour before that one: a swing south to Texas and along the Gulf Coast and up the Atlantic seaboard, with our final show scheduled for City Gardens in Trenton. We were traveling with the same band we'd taken with us last time, these wild kids from the Lower East Side by way of San Antonio who called themselves Helen Keller Drunk. Musically they weren't very interesting, just your basic psychobilly band, shades of the Cramps, but they put on a good show, full of props, such as the sequined jockstrap the frontman, Hunter, wore on top of his trousers, and a knife-throwing bit the drummer, Clay, was sometimes allowed to perform. They were the perfect tour companions, really fun to be around, and as opposed to Shock Corridor and Demon Rum, everyone got along without a hitch. We laughed all the way to Texas, but then somebody caught the flu and passed it on to everybody else, so for about a week you had seven guys in a van (our roadie, Todd, being the seventh) puking and coughing and hacking up snot. At one point we had a snot beauty contest: everybody had to blow their nose and cast a vote as to whose snot was prettiest. I forget who won, but no matter; we couldn't afford to cancel a single date, and after a week everyone had gotten better except for Peewee. He had the worst case by far, so congested he barely sounded like himself, and of course, whenever he got sick, he always assumed the worst. He moaned and groaned and griped so much I wanted to kill him. We got to my hometown (we hadn't stopped there last time around; I wasn't sure it was a good idea) and had dinner with my parents at a Big Boy restaurant, and that was pretty tense. I mean, it was fine, nothing happened, but they'd always hated Peewee, and I was afraid he or somebody else was going to slip up and cuss or talk about drugs or pussy, so for me that meal was nerve-racking. My parents were on the fence about seeing the show. I told them not to bother. I knew they wouldn't approve. But my brother Scott showed up (my brother Keith was away at college), and he was seventeen at the time, and we tried to sneak him inside the club, but one of the bartenders got wise and sent him on his way. Three or four punk kids were hanging around outside. They were decked out in dog collars and Doc Martens and so on, and we'd seen quite a bit of that kind of thing all across America—punks in the boondocks, punks in towns twenty blocks wide—but this was different; this was my hometown. We asked if people gave them shit, and they said, "Well, sometimes, but not *too* bad." How times change! We crashed at my grandmother's house after the show, and the next day my parents called to say that Scott had come home sick from drinking, and, true to form, they were pinning the blame on me. I said, "I had nothing to do with it! And I knew you guys were going to pull something like this! I wish we'd never played here!" I wanted to hit the road right that minute, but we couldn't; my grandmother was cooking us lunch. She loved those guys from Texas! She told Hunter, "Honey, if I was twenty years younger, you'd have to watch out for *me*." Meantime Peewee looked and talked like he was going to die. This wasn't the flu. No, it couldn't be. Everybody else had gotten better and he was still sick—there must be a *reason* for that. My grandmother lived right behind a hospital (with a graveyard right in front of her!), and she told him he should see a doctor, but he cried poorhouse. Fair enough. We could barely afford gas. So, after lunch, my grandmother gave us some money and I walked with Peewee to the hospital, and it took forever for a doctor to see him. I knew it was nothing serious, and we had a show that night in Virginia Beach, and it was getting later and later and I just wanted to get the fuck out of that town. Finally a doctor saw him and said he had a mild respiratory infection brought on by the flu. He should be fine in a couple of days, he said; but Peewee said, "Look, I've had this thing for a week and I'm still not better. And I'm in a *band*, and we've got *shows*, and can't you give me something for it?"

So the doctor prescribed antibiotics, and then we had to wait at the pharmacy for at least an hour. Everybody was pissed. I wasn't the only one. Then he finally got his fucking prescription, and the label said something like, "Do not drink alcohol while taking this medication." And he didn't. We just made that show in Virginia Beach, and he never drank a drop. The same the next night in Richmond. The same the next night in Charlottesville. We played at a club called Traxx, and I wish I could say something astonishing happened, sort of a big, grand finish as seen in *The Buddy Holly Story*, but, no, it was nothing extraordinary. We were fine and smashed things up a little, but there were only about twenty people in the audience (it was a weeknight: Wednesday, April 13th, to be exact), and by then we'd been on the road for three weeks, and Peewee was still getting over the flu; so, overall, even though we gave it everything we had, there really wasn't a lot left. But one small detail about that night: instead of finishing with "Vanished," we did a relatively new song called "Full Metal Erection," just to shake ourselves up, and it didn't work nearly as well, and I remember some talk about that after the show: "Let's never do *that* again." And we never did, of course. That was the last song we ever played.

At any rate, we started breaking down the equipment, and two girls we'd been talking to earlier walked up, one with sandy blonde hair, the other a pretty brunette. The brunette had seen us the time we played in Charlottesville, and she obviously must have liked us; she'd come to see us a second time and brought along a friend. Both had Southern accents and that feathered hair you saw so much in those days, cut in wings and blow-dried away from the face. Both had attended the University of Virginia (or I know one of them had), and both were curious about life in New York, and I had a feeling we were about to get lucky and remember saying as much to Peewee when we were putting our stuff in the van. However, I'd overlooked the Hunter factor. He didn't wear a sequined jockstrap for nothing. He only got more ass than a sultan, and during the brief time we'd been outside, he'd swooped down on the blonde, who was clearly smitten. It must have been about 12:30, and we all hung around the bar, drinking beer, though Peewee abstained, as he had all night, and at some point the blonde (whose name, I think, was Holly) volunteered to let Helen Keller Drunk crash at her place, while the dark-haired girl (whose name was Betsy) said Superego could stay with her. We always tried to arrange for more than one crash pad if we possibly could, otherwise it was seven guys sharing a floor and, chances were, a single bathroom.

I'd sort of assumed that Betsy was interested in me—I was, after all, Bobby Sherman—but it turned out she was far more interested in Peewee. They broke off by themselves, talking in a corner, and I remember glancing over at one point and thinking, "Man, look at that. He's come so far with girls. He's got her practically hypnotized!" (As much as I liked Monika, I never saw any problem with Peewee fucking around, since that was part of their arrangement. Their affection was genuine, but they married primarily for visa reasons.) Meantime our roadie Todd had broken off with Lucien, and I had a feeling I knew why: Todd was having problems with his girlfriend back in New York, and Lucien, being so quiet, attracted confessions, and the romantic sort especially bored him shitless. Sure enough, I walked over and found Todd talking about his girlfriend, so I sat down to give him the benefit of my tremendous insight, allowing Lucien to escape. Todd and I went through a pitcher of beer, and at some point I looked up and saw that almost everybody else was gone, and I walked over to Peewee and said, "Hey, did Lucien take off with Hunter and those guys?" And he said, "Yeah, he was pretty beat, so we'll take Todd with us." So here's the first of those quirks where somebody's life got saved and somebody else's got snuffed out, and all because of a chance decision, something nobody thought twice about at the time. I drank some more with Todd, and around quarter to two the lights flipped on and Peewee and Betsy came up to the bar and said,

"You guys ready?" and we all walked out to the parking lot to Betsy's car. (Helen Keller Drunk had taken the van with them.) I could tell Betsy was a little drunk, but I wasn't concerned, since we were constantly being driven around by drunk people and nothing had happened so far. Her car was an old Volkswagen Beetle, a heavily oxidized yellow, and she unlocked the passenger side, and Peewee folded the seat back and said, "I call shotgun." Those are the last distinct words I remember him saying: "I call shotgun." They *would* have to be tinged with violence. Of course I was much bigger than he was, but I got in the back anyway, since he was the one Betsy seemed to like and so it made sense for him to sit up front with her. Todd also got in the back, on Betsy's side of the car, and that's what cost him his life and no doubt saved my own. Then Peewee and Betsy climbed in, and the radio started blasting as soon as she turned the key, and she peeled out of the parking lot, and that's when I realized she wasn't just a little drunk; she'd gone the distance. She was doing fifty at least on residential streets, at one point running a red light, and I remember sharing a look with Todd, like, "Wow, I hope she doesn't live too far away." I tried to find my seatbelt, which was buried beneath the seat, and Betsy was talking to Peewee but the radio drowned out their voices, and suddenly the car stopped without turning off and Peewee and Betsy both got out, and I watched as they ran past each other in front of the car, all lit up by the headlights, and Betsy got in the passenger seat and Peewee took the wheel. I shared another look with Todd just then—a look that said, "Oh *no*, not *this*." We both knew what a bad driver Peewee was. Not that he drove too fast or took unnecessary chances or anything along those lines. No, it was just that, first of all, he had no experience; he'd only recently gotten his license after repeatedly flunking the test, so determined to pull his weight on tour. But he never paid attention when he drove; he was very easily distracted by his own thoughts, or else he'd sit there running his mouth while fucking with the tape deck or radio dial. Then the van would start drifting; he'd be halfway in the next lane of traffic without knowing it till other drivers honked and swerved, and he'd slam on the brakes in a panic and everything in the van would tumble forward; and if you said anything, he'd turn around to defend himself, once again losing control of the van. That's why we almost never let him drive us *anywhere*. Only in our most desperate moments, when the designated driver was nodding off and everyone awake was shitfaced, did we let Peewee take the wheel, and even then he typically only lasted a few minutes before we assigned the job to somebody else. We were safer by far with a drunk driver, and I'm sure Todd was thinking as much that night. I certainly was. And Peewee? He undoubtedly figured that, since he was sober and Betsy wasn't, she was better off navigating; but I just wish, before making that decision, he'd consulted with me, because I know if he had I wouldn't be writing this. *He had no idea what he was doing.* He'd never driven that car before; he'd never driven those roads before; and the last song I remember hearing was Duran Duran's "The Reflex," and I can't help but wonder if that wasn't a factor too, Peewee thinking, "What a piece of shit," and taking his eyes off the road to switch stations and a second later seeing a pair of headlights moving rapidly toward him, and that was it: all those lives destroyed because of bad music. But since my last memory of being in that car is of trying but failing to dig out my seatbelt, I'll never know for sure. I know the other car was driven by a man named Clayton Page, that I know. And I know he'd been out celebrating a friend's birthday, and I know his wife, Anne, was with him; and according to her, he was driving much too fast; and according to the police report, he had a blood alcohol content more than twice the legal limit. Clayton Page told the police that Betsy's car was in the middle of the road and he swerved to avoid hitting it, but he was contradicted by his own wife, who said it was *their* car that was in the middle of the road and *Betsy's* car was the one that swerved. The police, who analyzed the skid marks, inconclusively sided with the wife. Still, there's no disputing that the cars briefly sideswiped; and though the Pages, who suffered no injuries at all, both said they didn't see Betsy's car slam headfirst into that tree by the side of the road, they definitely *heard* it. "It sounded like a bomb had gone off," Anne Page stated in the police report. (My lawyer later told me she filed for divorce shortly after her husband plea-bargained on numerous charges and got twelve years in the state pen.) So, again, since I'm working without witnesses, I have to speculate; and I think what probably happened is that Peewee, being a poor driver and possibly distracted by the radio, saw the Pages' car coming at him at high speed and panicked, causing the cars to sideswipe, and afterward went, "Oh my God, we've had an accident!" and let go of the wheel, allowing the VW to veer out of control, and, bam, it's wrapped around a tree. And that's why, even half-drunk, *I* should have been driving. Because I'll never forget something my dad once told me: "If you ever have an accident, just keep driving till the car's come to a complete stop. Don't panic, don't let go of the wheel; *just keep driving.*" It's also possible that, after hitting the Pages' car, Peewee was injured in some way so that he *couldn't* keep driving. Or maybe the brakes locked. Or maybe Betsy panicked and grabbed the wheel, making matters worse. But I don't know, and I never will. When the VW hit the tree, Betsy was thrown straight through the windshield, killed instantly, so there goes that witness. And the front of the car, especially on Peewee's side, folded and flattened, crushing Peewee, who was likewise killed instantly. Plus the roof caved in and shaved off the top of his head, just as part of Todd's head was shaved off, though he lived for a few days on life support, all but dead already. I likewise got a nice gash on my head. I'm still not sure what kept me from flying through the windshield like Betsy, except that I must have been hampered by the passenger seat or Todd fell in such a way as to block my exit. I'm also not sure why, except for some fluke or law of physics, I was mostly hurt on my right side, when the main impact of the crash took place to my left. I never spoke to the Pages, who were advised by their lawyer not to contact me, just as I never spoke to the paramedics, who were gone by the time I regained consciousness in the emergency room an hour or so later. I remember feeling like I was in a wind tunnel with voices kind of slipping around me and what felt like a blanket covering my face, and the more I tried to see through the blanket, the more it seemed to evaporate, and finally it was all gone and I saw people in scrubs staring down at me. I tried to raise my head but couldn't: my neck was taped to a gurney. My clothes had been cut off; my head and arms hurt; I felt an intense pressure in my lower right leg. I asked where I was, and a plump white nurse stroked my face and very lovingly, actually, explained that I'd been in a bad car wreck. She asked if I remembered anything, and of course I didn't. It took me hours—all the time I was being prepped for surgery and the sedated morning after—to reconstruct the minutes before the accident, so that even now I'm not sure if all I just wrote, all those memories of being in that car, are things that really happened or things I partly invented in my need to recall *something.* I asked the nurse if I was the only one who'd survived, and she said no, there was somebody else, she didn't know his name, but he was in worse shape than I was. Then an elderly black attendant came in and snipped off a silver cross my mom had given me on my twelfth birthday, and he put it in the palm of my hand and closed my fist around it and said, "He was really looking after you tonight, wasn't He?" I only wore it because I liked the way it looked, but I guess it's true what they say about atheists in foxholes, because I clutched that thing and prayed to a god I didn't believe in that Peewee wasn't dead. And Todd was a great kid, and I'm so sorry, Todd, I was pulling for him and not you, but if you'd been me, I'm sure you would have done the same. My leg was pulsing like a gunked-up heart on the verge of rupture; and I was in shock, but shock doesn't mean you don't feel pain, it means you feel it less; and there were curtains all around me in that tiny room, and people kept pulling them back to ask questions about my insurance and where it hurt and whom they should call; and I wanted to call Lucien and the Helen Keller guys, but I didn't know how to reach them, so I said to call my parents, and even though I couldn't remember the first thing about the accident, I could recite my parents' number without a pause. X-ray machines were dragged in and dragged out; and somebody stitched up the cut on my head, as well as various other cuts; and I clutched that cross and prayed and prayed that Peewee was alive. Then this fat pig of a cop pulled back the curtains and strolled in with a clipboard, and he also asked what I remembered, and I told him I was in a band and we were on our way to somebody's house after playing a show, and that was all I knew. He said, "So you'd been drinking, right? What else?" I said, "Nothing else. I just had some beer, that's all. And one of us didn't have that, and I think—I think he was the one driving." Then he glanced at his clipboard and said, "Bernard Mash?" And I said, "Yeah, that's him. Is he alive?" And he asked if I was a relative, and I lied and said I was, and very casually, just business as usual, he said, "Sorry." That's how I learned my best friend was dead: some fucking cop, resentful he was working the graveyard shift, a janitor at the scene of an accident where a New York freak had met his just deserts, tossed it off like nothing. I could tell he didn't believe Peewee had been sober, and oddly, at that moment, that was all I could think about: I wanted to make sure he did. I never mentioned Peewee's shoddy driving. Not that I was trying to cover it up. I couldn't bear to think the accident was Peewee's fault in any way.

But later I did start to blame him. I still blame him. But I can forgive him now as I couldn't for the longest time. It took days to grasp that he didn't exist anymore. How could somebody as vital as Peewee not exist anymore? Meantime, with so many things happening, it was like

I couldn't fully reflect on it. There were problems created by my lack of insurance, and daily visits from Lucien and the Helen Keller guys (who stuck around for as long as they could and openly mourned as I could not), and Todd's parents asked to speak with me—they'd immediately flown to Virginia to keep vigil. I could barely look at them. I'd been wishing it was their son who was dead and not Peewee. He died soon afterward. There, you got your wish. Are you happy now? And there were phone calls from my family and Monika and Peewee's parents, and Lucien or Clay or Hunter or Justin (the other guy in Helen Keller Drunk) would have to hold the phone to my ear, since my left arm was in a full cast and my right forearm had literally been snapped in two. I spoke to Terrence and Joe and the Upper East Side guys, and Laura found out and called to say how sorry she was, and I got a few calls from the lesbian sculptress, very unpleasant, in which she basically said yeah, it was terrible I'd had this accident and everything, but I still had to pay the rent, otherwise she as the leaseholder was going to have to find a new roommate. But that was the last thing on my mind. I couldn't even walk. Again, I'm not sure how it specifically happened, but I'd shattered my right tibia and developed what's called compartment syndrome, meaning there was a lot of internal bleeding that was drowning and killing the muscle, and once muscle dies, that's it, there's no bringing it back. So I could easily have lost that leg if the paramedics hadn't promptly shown up (alerted by a nameless someone woken by the sound of the crash) and rushed me to Martha Jefferson Hospital, where the preppie-seeming surgeon sliced away the skin on the front part of my leg and vacuumed out the blood and bone fragments, allowing the muscle to breathe again. Then he removed some bone from my hip and used that to fuse my tibia back together, and, after closing me up, he screwed a contraption into my leg: a kind of metal Tinkertoy set called an external fixator. Plus I had a foot-long rectangle of skin shaved off my left thigh and grafted onto the skinless part of my shattered right shin, stapled there till the graft could take. A piece of plastic was pressed over the donor site, making it look like a bloody steak at the supermarket. It burned like a motherfucker too—the worst pain I was ever in. As for my right arm—the arm that was broken in half—that was pieced back together with metal plates and likewise got a small skin graft to cover the gash where the bones had popped through. My leg and that arm were both in traction, so I couldn't move or sit up for over a week. It took even longer before I had a bowel movement. Or maybe that came first. It's hard to remember.

But I can never forget when it fully, finally hit me that Peewee was gone. It happened the first time I was allowed to sit up. I'd been warned that, after lying flat for so long, I might feel dizzy at first, so I remember the nurse raised the bed very slowly. It was so strange, because all I was thinking about was, simply, how good it was going to be to finally sit up—no thoughts of Peewee, nothing about the accident—and yet the very second my head rose so that it was a fraction of an inch higher than the rest of my body, and with absolutely no sense it was about to happen, I burst into tears. The nurse and my doctor were standing by the bed saying, "What is it? Are you in pain?" and I kept shaking my head and crying. And I cried and cried and cried, so that, before long, they lowered me back down and gave me a shot that knocked me out.

IT'S CLEAR TO ME NOW, as it wasn't at the time, that I'd basically had a nervous breakdown. I woke the next day feeling like I'd fallen down a deep well filled with black water, and that was how it stayed for months to come. My parents drove up and checked me out of the hospital and took me home to North Carolina to recuperate, and I sat in my old room like a hostage, watching TV and stuffing my face. I must have gained twenty pounds. I could afford to. I'd lost that much due to the shock. I had an operation to take off the external fixator and got a cast in its place that covered my leg from hip to foot; and to give myself a better way to pass the time, I studied for my GED and passed the test, and so finally finished high school. My parents nagged me about the future. I wasn't going back to New York, was I? I was twenty-five, you know. It was time to start getting serious about life. They sent their fucking pastor to see me, and he suggested in so many words that my "hedonistic lifestyle" had brought about the accident. I thought he was right in a strange way. What did we do onstage? Smash things because it felt so goddamned good to smash things. Then Peewee pulled off the ultimate smash-up, and I found myself thinking about other rockers who'd died much too young—from Elvis to Eddie Cochran to Jimi Hendrix to Jim Morrison—and decided I wanted nothing more to do with it. Besides, when Peewee died, he took the band with him. I knew lightning was never going to strike twice. I'd been through years of squabbling and stolen gear and lugging amps and posting fliers for barely-attended shows and brutal tours in stifling vans, and for just a second it was all going to pay off, and then this? No, I couldn't go through it again. Lucien called, and I told him I was through with playing music, and he said, "That's not what Bernard would have wanted," and I said, "Fuck fucking Bernard! He fucking died on me!" And I cried all over again. But Lucien had joined another band right away, and he wanted me to try out for them when I came back to New York; and that fall, when the cast came off, I did go back and try out for Lucien's band, but they were kind of jazzy, not my thing at all, and besides, it felt strange to be playing with Lucien without Peewee. So I told him thanks but no thanks, and from that point on we started losing touch, and seven years later, long after I'd moved to California, I heard through a mutual friend that he'd killed himself. I really don't know much about it. All I know is what our friend told me. She said he'd eaten "some kind of plant," something poisonous, and he decomposed in his apartment for at least a week before somebody found him. He battled depression all his life, and suicide ran in his family, so maybe it would've happened no matter what, but I still wonder if the accident wasn't a contributing factor, if maybe, like me, he felt guilty for being alive. And through that friend and others from the scene in New York, I was always hearing about the sad fates of other downtown music people—suicides and AIDS and overdoses, or just plain poor and wasted—and that deepened my sense that rock & roll was inherently destructive, that there was something about the nature of the music itself that made for a no-win outcome. Yet for a number of months after I returned to New York, I continued to go to shows, unsure of what else to do with myself. I got another place in Williamsburg (I would've moved even if the lesbian sculptress hadn't kicked me out) and picked up another barback job, temping on the side. Plus, here and there, the Mashes slipped me money. They'd become surrogate parents, more or less. And that's how I got involved with Suzanne.

I realize I haven't mentioned Suzanne in a while, but for most of the time I lived in New York, she was always there in the background. She moved back as soon as she finished school and joined the staff of *Elle*, where she dashed off pieces along the lines of "Ten Ways to Make Your Boyfriend More Romantic," quickly scaling the editorial ladder. At first she acted like it was just a job, a way of supporting herself while she wrote serious fiction, but after so much time you could tell she really liked it. She got $200 haircuts and ate in three-star restaurants and lived in a brownstone on the Upper West Side—in short, she'd become a yuppie. Peewee thought she'd lost her mind, yet she was just as whip-smart as always, and still very loyal to her brother. When he and his parents weren't speaking, she acted as a go-between, trying to forge a reunion; and when he and I weren't speaking, she cut me off as well. Then, after we patched things up, she came to Superego shows, sometimes bringing her uptown friends—that was always good for a laugh. It nearly killed her when he died. Only Monika seemed to take it worse, and at some point during the summer Monika had moved back to Europe, and despite many efforts to get in touch with her, we never spoke after she called me at the hospital. Lucien told me she was so shattered she wanted to sever ties with everything related to Peewee. And I hope it worked. I really do.

At any rate, spending so much time with the Mashes, I suppose getting involved with Suzanne was inevitable. There'd always been a spark between us, going back to the old days in North Carolina, but for most of that time she had a boyfriend, and besides, I wasn't about to try anything with Peewee hanging around. She also looked a bit like him, which was off-putting to say the least, and even though she was only five years older than I was, I felt like a kid by comparison. Looking back, I *was* a kid; yet once we fell in love, none of that seemed to matter. We would talk four and five times a day, and that's not including the pillow talk, the talks at breakfast and dinner. I spent more and more time on the Upper West Side, weekends in the Hamptons, and started dressing like I had in high school, in khakis and blue blazers. I came to like the kind of music she did. Tracy Chapman was a big favorite. It's amazing when I think about it now: I actually liked Tracy Chapman! But I could barely listen to rock & roll without thinking of death, and with Suzanne I felt alive again. We talked about marriage and having kids almost from the beginning. And I wanted kids—badly. That way a small part of her brother could continue to live.

Yet, for all that, I was still confused. What was I going to do with myself? I couldn't keep on working in bars. I couldn't keep on temping. Then I had the strangest idea: I thought about becoming a cop. I knew from temping I wasn't the office type, and I pictured myself at crime scenes, piecing things together, and thought I might have a good mind for that kind of thing. But, mainly, I think it was something else. I'd been harassed so many times by cops, even after I left North Carolina. It happened constantly on tour: they'd see those New York license plates and stop the van and search it, or else they'd shut down shows or hang around the parking lot, just waiting for an excuse to make an arrest. It's a wonder they never did—especially with *our* band! So I guess I thought by becoming a cop myself, I could somehow right their wrongs, the same way a kid who's lost a parent on the operating table wants to become a doctor.

Fortunately Suzanne talked me out of it. Thank God she did! I was so mixed up that, without her, I might well have gone forward. Her advice was to take some classes at City College and see what, if anything, clicked; and that's what I was planning to do, when, in the summer of '89, my grandmother died. I was devastated all over again. First Peewee, now this. Suzanne and I rented a car and drove down for the funeral, and a few weeks later the will was opened and I learned my grandmother had left me $100,000. She'd recently sold her house to the hospital behind her, which was looking to expand, buying up all the houses on her block and knocking them down as soon as the owners died or vacated. So now I could I pay off my medical bills (and my parents too, since they'd shelled out quite a bit), and after all that and taxes, I was left with thirty grand. But more was on the way: later that summer I received a settlement offer from Clayton Page's insurance company. That's something else that was going on at the time: I'd filed suit against the Pages, with Peewee's parents as co-plaintiffs, and so there'd been depositions and investigations and so on, and I gather the insurance company was afraid we'd go to trial and so made an offer of $500,000. The Mashes were inclined to hold out for more, but I thought about it and talked it over with friends and family and said, "Look, I don't want this thing to drag on forever. I think we should take the offer."

The Mashes ate the legal fees out of their half of the split. I told them not to, but they insisted, leaving me with close to $300,000, including what remained of my inheritance. I'd shattered my leg but landed on my feet. I could live off that money for the rest of my life if I made some wise investments. I could go to college and learn a profession. The profession, of course, had yet to be decided, but I pictured myself in plush surroundings with Suzanne and our kids, including the one we would surely name Bernard.

Out of hardship, ease. Out of punk, respectability. The lure is always strong, and so concludes the career of many an aspiring rebel.

But the very first thing I wanted to do was travel to Europe. I was always so jealous of Peewee and Suzanne and their time spent abroad. Now I could afford a trip of my own. Suzanne was too busy with work to join me, but she knew there was a lot I had to sort out, and she thought travel would do me good. And so that fall I flew to London, and from there I hit Paris, Berlin, Rome, Barcelona. I loved Barcelona: beautiful women, friendly people, bullfights and late nights, those astonishing buildings by Gaudi. One day I visited La Sagrada Familia, climbing one of its steep towers, and there at the top, with Catalonia spread out for miles at my feet, I had an epiphany: I wanted to make movies. It suddenly seemed so obvious. Movies were the only thing I'd ever loved as much as music—not just seeing them but working on that video with Peewee; helping out on Terrence's student films at NYU. I was so inspired I ran back to my *pensione* and called Suzanne with the news: I was going to be a filmmaker! Wasn't that exciting?

But it wasn't—not to her. She out and out disapproved. Hadn't I heard her father's war stories about Hollywood? Didn't I know how disgusting that place was? I said, "Who's talking about Hollywood? I'm talking about making movies." Same difference, she said; *everybody* who made movies ended up in Los Angeles, and she hated that place, and she hated film people, and I had no real experience anyway. I said, "Well, I had no experience playing music before I started a band. And I've got all this money, and I'm sure that's enough to make a movie. I mean, look at Spike Lee. How much do you think he spent on *She's Gotta Have It*? I bet less than *I* have."

"Jason, I hate to say this, but that's *blood* money. You're going to take money you got for my brother's *death* and use it to make a *movie*? And what about your grandmother? Do you really think she left you that money so you could turn around and *waste* it?"

"Hey, how do *you* know it's going to be a waste? Don't you have any faith in me? Besides, people die, you know? *Everything* dies. And I want to make something that's going to *last*."

Well, we talked about it that day, and we talked about it when I got back, and she had her father speak to me, as well as some writer who worked at *Elle* who'd gone out to Hollywood and come back to New York with his tail tucked between his legs, but I still couldn't stop thinking about it. I already had a sketch for my first feature, which, to my mind, would fill an overlooked gap. I'd never seen a truly good movie about rock & roll, except for documentaries like *Gimme Shelter* or maybe *This is Spinal Tap*—and the latter almost didn't count, being a parody. (For that matter, I never thought *Spinal Tap* was as gut-wrenchingly funny as the whole world seemed to regard it.) And, yes, I was really down on rock & roll at that moment, but it was something I knew, just as I knew about life downtown, and most of the movies I'd seen about that seemed no less false. I wrote a script in less than two weeks, building the story around the Laura love triangle and Peewee's "junkie" phase, as both unfolded in the aftermath of a disastrous, aborted tour. So, even though the chronology was scrambled, it was mostly based on fact, and a bit moralistic, I'd say. There was definitely the sense at the end of it that being in a band was bound to conclude in one of two ways: dead like "Midge," the character inspired by Peewee, or lost like my alter ego "Brian." I showed the script to Suzanne as I wrote, and she tore it apart like the would-be novelist she was: this scene was too long and this one didn't pay off; there was too much emphasis on this character and not enough on that one. She wasn't trying to help me, she was trying to discourage me, but in fact her comments substantially improved the revisions. Eventually, when she saw how determined I was, we struck a deal: I could make *this* movie, but, after that, I could never make another one. I know, it sounds crazy. It *was* crazy. But I complied, trying to please her, and went off to make *Sick to Death,* the one movie I was "allowed" to make, and pretty much had the time of my life. Not that it wasn't difficult. Everything ran more than I thought it would: film stock, lab costs, equipment rentals, locations. Casting was a bitch as well. I asked Clay from Helen Keller Drunk to play "Julian" the drummer, and he turned out to be a total natural—one of the best things in the movie, as a matter of fact. I also got lucky with the girl who played "Eve" (Laura), but that took a lot of looking. But finding somebody for Midge was the hardest of all, and the guy I settled for was *not* that good, and—wouldn't you know it?—he was the one person in the cast who went on to make something of a name for himself. He did a sitcom in the early nineties, and afterward I used to see him quite a bit on commercials. What a fucking moron! I had to teach him how to pronounce "schizophrenic." At least he *looked* intelligent. As for Brian, I had somebody else picked out for that part, but he landed a play on Broadway a week before we started shooting, and I thought, "Fuck it, I'll just do it myself." All four of us had been in bands (two still were), and we mostly played Superego songs, and we weren't nearly as good as the real thing, but of course who could be? Terrence helped out, bringing in friends from NYU, including Renata, the cinematographer, who was *such* a happening chick, even though she did mess up an awful lot of shots. But she had the right spirit, and besides, her mistakes no doubt contributed to the verisimilitude. I haven't talked to her in over ten years. And that goes for almost all my friends in New York, except for Terrence and my friend Joe, the lawyer, and Spike, my other roommate from the Upper East Side, who now guides rock climbs near New Paltz, New York. He had a small part in *Sick to Death,* and sorry, Spike, but you were terrible! But that was true for most of the bit players. The ones I'd lined up were always flaking on me, so I had to grab the first person I saw. And we had sound problems and continuity problems and transportation problems and every kind of problem you could possibly think of, short of somebody dying, and that almost happened too, thanks to our genius electrician. People would go off to do other things—somebody would get a job on another movie, or their band had an out-of-town show they just *had* to do—so that a year after principal photography, I was still grabbing shots. Which further inflated the budget. I was lucky to be left with twenty grand by the time I had an answer print.

Still, I've never regretted making that movie. It had a lot of flaws, but I nailed the central thing I was trying to capture: rock & fucking roll! And over the final shot, as Brian walks in the rain realizing his whole life is shot to hell, there was Jim Cassady singing "Raft at Sea." He could (and can) still be heard as the shot faded to a title card that read:

FOR BERNARD MASH
1965-1988

That dedication later led to some awkward moments. Strangers would sometimes ask me about it, wanting to know if it related to Midge, and even with close friends I had trouble talking about Peewee. That's another reason I think it was so important that I make that movie. I dealt with the first big trauma of my life by writing songs like "I'm a Motherfucking Man." I dealt with this one by making *Sick to Death.* And I wanted to go on making movies. Yes, I did. I'd found my calling, or so I thought, and meantime I was having serious doubts about Suzanne—in fact, in some ways I see her as a symbol of all that was wrong with America at that time and the time since. She had brains, talent, influential parents—every advantage a person could have—yet all she finally aspired to was a safe life with a husband and kids and, probably one day, a house in the suburbs. One of her best friends lived in Greenwich, Connecticut, and we spent a couple of weekends there, and Suzanne couldn't get over how "beautiful" it was. Me—I fucking hated that place. It reminded me of my hometown—which, by the way, Suzanne had liked as much as she did Greenwich. And what was it she liked about *me*? Of course we shared that bond with her brother and a few things besides, but in retrospect there was something else. I'd met a lot of her exes, all of whom were average-looking, and I used to notice that when she got me around her friends, she'd show me off as if to say, "Look what *I've* got." So I think she saw me as a kind of trophy, not to mention a good sperm donor. Speaking of which: was it really a good idea to mix my DNA with Peewee's? Maybe the world wasn't ready for the Antichrist! And what kind of mother was Suzanne going to make? I was having some doubts about that as well. Her friend in Greenwich had a kid, and you would have thought that brat was Baby Moses, the way its parents slobbered over it. That was the parenting style of a whole generation, apparently; all over New York I saw kids throwing fits and their doting parents indulging them. Besides, I had plenty of time for having kids, but I was already getting too old for a film career. Hard to believe but true. When *Sick to Death* went to Sundance, I was approached by Cy Parker after the second screening, and he was clearly disappointed when he asked my age and I told him twenty-eight. Still, he expressed interest in signing me. Just one catch, though: I'd have to move to Los Angeles.

Fortunately Suzanne wasn't around for that talk. She'd flown back to New York after the first screening due to some problem at work. Then I flew back myself and told her I might have to spend some time in California to meet with distributors. I had to lie about it. What if Cy had been talking smack? I snuck off and wrote my lovers-of-the-future script, taking it with me when I went to Los Angeles, and by God I fucking sold it. But there was a catch to that too: now I had to level with Suzanne. I was signing with an agent and moving to L.A., and she was more than welcome to come with me, but I really wasn't ready to get married and have kids; and, man, you have no idea, the scenes that went on, the crying and accusations and the guilt she laid on me. I'd used money I'd gotten from her brother's death to *betray* her! What would *he* say if he could see me now? She had me feeling so bad, I was on the verge of calling Cy to say I was staying put.

But one night, in the middle of all that drama, Peewee came to me in a dream. It really felt like a visitation, the dream was so vivid, and yet he barely looked like himself. He seemed bigger, and his face was older, and his hair had a strange metallic quality, like a skullcap wig made of steel bristles. I started to tell him what was going on, but he already knew all about it, and he said, "Jason, you can't worry about Suzanne. She's going to be fine, and you've got to do what's right for *you*. It's what *I'd* do." Then I woke. I was immune to Suzanne's histrionics after that. Her brother, or at least my conjuring of him, had given me the strength to make the break. And over the years I've had similar dreams, though that was the only one in which I remember him specifically advising me. I'll be walking around North Carolina or the East Village or some exotic locale such as I've never seen in waking life: fantastic cityscapes, half-ancient, half-futuristic. And sometimes he's there at the start, or sometimes I'll run into him, or sometimes I'll be talking to somebody else who'll transform into Peewee right in front of my eyes. And at first it'll be great—we'll be talking about the old days, or we might start writing a song—but then I'll realize something isn't quite right, and finally I'll know just what it is.

"Hey," I'll often say at that point, "you can't be here. You're dead." And sometimes he'll vanish; I'll turn around and he's not there anymore, and I'll spend the rest of the dream trying to find him. And other times, if I mention he's dead, he'll act like nothing has changed, talking away like he did in life or working on a song that somehow remains unfinished.

Three...

I see the future
It's like a footprint

The Sleepers

I WAS DREAMING OF DISASTER WHEN THE PHONE RANG. I've always had such dreams, even before the accident: Noah-like floods and mushroom clouds; smart tornadoes that seem to know exactly where I'm hiding. It was a few nights after that odd encounter with Jim Cassady in Rancho Cucamonga, and at first I thought the ringing phone was mine—a "Gotcha!" call from a twister, perhaps. Then Irina reached for her cell, which she'd left on the floor beside my bed, and from her first words I knew it must be David. The late hour was another clue: in Prague, where he was prepping his movie, the day had begun. I had to wake up early to work a temping job, so Irina took the phone to another room, and maybe a half-hour later she came back to bed and said, "Jason? I did it. I told David I'm leaving him."

I'd dozed back off while she was talking on the phone, but I shot up on the spot and said, "You *told* him? I thought you were going to wait till you saw him in person!"

But she wasn't going to see him now, or not in Belgrade as planned. He was flying to London for an emergency casting session, and he wanted her to meet him there, and she was *not* going to do it.

"Every Christmas it's the same thing," she fumed. "I have to go to London and sit around with his boring family, and I hate it. And he knows very well I told my mother I'm coming home, and she *loves* David, and this is how he treats her. And I know he's got the movie, but it's been this way our entire marriage. And I'm sick of it. And I told him so. I said, 'I think I need a break from this marriage—or what you *think* is a marriage. I think, when the movie is over, I'm going to get my own place and live alone for a while. And I'm *not* going to London, and if you want to fire me from the movie, fine, I'll just go to L.A. after I see my mother and get my own place.'"

"So what'd he say to that?"

"He said, 'No one is firing you. And I think you *should* get your own place. You've got it very good, but you don't seem to realize it. Maybe this way you'll find out.'"

She was very pleased with herself, when to me it seemed like a half-measure. She'd made it sound like a temporary arrangement, omitting any mention of us. Yes, she said, but she thought it was better this way: David was fine with separating, but if he knew there was somebody else, he'd go off the deep end. Besides, she could always tell him when the movie was done, and she didn't want to think about it right now and so spoil her fun with me. That was a great time for both of us, actually. Those two weeks, from the night I picked her up at Jim's place to the day she left for Belgrade (or, technically, Budapest, since at that time you couldn't fly directly to Belgrade due to NATO sanctions), were two of the happiest I ever spent. I'd come home from work and find her waiting, sometimes with dinner she'd cooked herself, and the food was always great, and she was never less than great company. She didn't talk about mundane shit as had so many of my exes; she knew things about history I didn't, things about Byzantium and the Ottomans, odd facts about World War II. She had a passion for art and games of all kinds, and taught me how to play backgammon, which has got to be the greatest board game ever invented, and sometimes when I was about to pass up a good move, she'd nod to the one I *should* be making, and from there I'd go on to kick her ass good, though it was usually the other way around. Once, as we were about to play, she said, "Okay, this is the game that decides who's smarter, women or men," and after destroying me completely, she said, "Well, I guess that decides it." Yes, she could be funny too! And she was really curious; she wanted to borrow half my books and listen to every rare record I owned; and she loved it when I told her stories, especially those concerning Peewee. She thought he looked "adorable" in the pictures I showed her, she thought the video he directed was "brilliant," and she responded so much to the songs he sang on the Superego record, I felt impelled to point out my contributions to every last one of them. Yes, I got a little jealous! And that was the one thing that bothered me: that here was a girl so astonishing in every way, I was always going to feel jealous, even of someone who'd been dead for years.

But, of course, she had a problem herself, being a shameless flirt. But was that really her fault? The night she did her final performance of

Forever and a Day, I suffered through it a second time and tagged along to the cast party, where every guy in the room seemed to have a crush on her. But who could blame them? And how could she not feed off it? She was only human, right? And I couldn't interrupt with, "Hey, gentlemen, we observe a three-foot rule around Irina; get any closer and I'll cut your fucking balls off," since she felt "funny" about people knowing we were together before she'd informed David. Officially I was an old friend from New York, so I had to keep my qualms to myself; and later, alone, I vented, and she said I had to start trusting her, I had to realize there was nobody else and never would be; what we had could last a lifetime. And *how* did she know? Because she felt afraid of me; I made her feel things she'd never felt before and it scared her. Which, as I've said before, was the way I felt with her.

That cast party was one of very few times we left the house. Another was the Serbian Christmas party thrown by her friend Milan. He'd invited us separately, of course, and I walked in to find her surrounded by guys, including her cousin Bora; but he was safe, and so were the others, since she'd mentioned many times that she could never be with another Serb. Yet, in a strange way, she was *with* another Serb. I'd long resented the sense of apology I was supposed to feel about my masculinity, as American culture then dictated. But the Serbian guys I met that night were proudly full of swagger, much like me. And I realized something else that night: I realized why Irina had been so nuts about *Sick to Death*. Because at least twice, talking about movies, one Serb or another would rave about Jim Jarmusch, and both the writing and the visual style of *Sick to Death* owed a great deal to Jarmusch's *Stranger than Paradise*. Sure enough, I later asked Irina what she thought of Jarmusch, and she went to pieces, saying *Night on Earth* was one of her all-time favorites. So there you go, Jim Jarmusch, you're a big hit in Serbia. Even Irina couldn't explain why. She said she personally liked his sense of humor. She also liked mine, and she loved what she regarded as my "brutal" honesty, and sexually we couldn't have been more compatible. So many lookers are duds in the sack, as if they think their beauty alone is enough to satisfy; but Irina was intensely sexual, which is likewise a Serbian trait. They're more like Latins than Europeans. Believe me, they've certainly got Latin tempers, as I would eventually discover in a major way!

But just then it was bliss. And all too soon she had to leave, and I drove her to the airport, and we both got weepy along the way. We weren't going to see each other till the beginning of February or possibly longer, depending on how the shoot went. She'd asked David for separate accommodations when she got to Prague, but he told her it was an extra cost the movie didn't need, and besides, he was renting a big apartment where she'd have her own room. Plus they didn't have sex anyway. They were just friends, she kept telling me, that was all they were now. And right before she boarded her plane, I took off that silver cross I'd been wearing the night of the accident and slipped it around her neck.

"If it ever brought me any luck at all," I said, "I want it to be yours." And that was true, but all the same, I'd just been around pussy-hustling Serbian guys—and though, again, she claimed she didn't like Serbian guys, there were bound to be a few exceptions. And the Czechs—what the hell were *they* like? She was also going to spend a little time in Hungary, and even the *Serbs* said the Hungarians were the biggest sex fiends in Europe. And David concerned me most of all. It's always easy to sleep with an ex, no matter how finished you think it is—especially if you happen to be living together.

So to ward off all those evil spirits, I gave her that cross. Then we kissed one last time, and I watched her walk off, and suddenly something hit me: since when has a cross stopped anybody from fucking? It certainly never stopped me!

THE DAY AFTER IRINA LEFT, I LEFT TOO. I flew to New York and took a cab to Terrence's place on East 11th Street, and literally the minute I got there, we started drinking. I buzzed him, and he came downstairs and said, "Let's grab a beer at Telephone," which was a bar a block away. We didn't even put my bag upstairs first. We went to Telephone and had a few beers, and, once we'd taken care of the bag, we continued from one bar to the next till we found ourselves near Rivington—and, holy shit, there were clubs and shops and even a McDonald's where there used to be nothing, and kids walking around without a care in the world. And why shouldn't they? It was perfectly safe. Even the building where I'd lived with Peewee—the one with the fifth-floor shooting gallery—had now been gentrified. I could tell because, through the windows, I saw the same camp shit hipsters used to have in the eighties: lava lamps and love beads and "ironic" photos of squares. Jesus, why don't you new kids come up with an aesthetic all your own? Not that *we* were anything special. Peewee had it just right when he called us the most boring generation since the Middle Ages. But the Middle Ages lasted for centuries, and our replacements were just like us except even *more* boring, even *less* inclined to rock the boat, so the Middle Ages II could easily last as long as the original. Kids kept filing past us with their blank faces in this bland setting that used to be so exciting; and I asked Terrence why they bothered to live here, since, for all the money it took, it was just another city, and he said, "Oh, they're so busy spending Daddy's money I don't think they realize." Good old Terrence! Who cared if New York wasn't what it used to be if I could hang out with my oldest and dearest friend? I told him about Irina, and he told me he'd just started seeing a girl named Emily, and he'd naturally procured some smack for the occasion, which we smoked at dawn, and the world was a fine place indeed.

But a few hours later Emily showed up and the good times instantly ended. She took one look at me and Terrence, both hung over, and decided this wouldn't do at all. No, I was dangerous. I was trouble. I wasn't the kind of friend she wanted for Terrence. She made plans to keep him busy the whole time I was there, and he let her—that was the thing that killed me. He'd only flown me 3000 miles to hang out, and once I got there, it was: "I'm having dinner with Emily and some friends of hers. Want to come?" And a couple of times I went as asked, but Emily would freeze me out while pretending she wasn't doing it, and her friends were equally phony, and every time I brought up the old days, she would change the subject, since that was a part of Terrence's life she knew nothing about and didn't *want* to know, it was all so frightening. Couldn't he see how bad she was? But I wasn't about to say anything, even though he sensed my disapproval and got peevish over the dumbest shit, so that I tried as much as possible to keep out of his way. One night I had dinner with my former roommate Joe, who was pretty much the same as always, except now he had money. Another night I went alone to a show in Williamsburg, and talk about a changed neighborhood! I was in shock! And then there was something else I did, which I wrote about to Irina on the last day of the twentieth century, and since I've always saved my correspondence, here it is:

Angelface:

I tried writing last night, but apparently I fucked up something on Terrence's computer and it didn't go through. He's got the whole thing laid out in a very elaborate way, and I guess I clicked on the wrong icon or something, but he came home and threw a whole little shitfit. Tonight's the big night, and it looks like we're going to a party friends of Emily's are throwing – some idiotic thing that costs fifty dollars to get into. I know exactly what it's going to be. There used to be a lot of those parties when I lived here – yuppie moneymaking enterprises. Terrence says I'm being cynical, and I told him cynical is just another word for right. [...]

Yesterday I saw Peewee's parents. This was the first time in eight years, since I broke up with Suzanne, and I wasn't sure what to expect, but they sounded thrilled to hear from me when I called them and invited me right over. The apartment hasn't changed at all, but they've both aged considerably. Peewee's dad has leukemia and looks like he's got one foot in the grave, but he's a resilient guy and a little bitter, I'd say. He wrote a new play he's trying to get produced, but nobody's interested, and it looks like he's coming a little unhinged in his forced retirement. He and Peewee's mom gave me a lot of shit for disappearing on them the way I did. I told them I felt guilty about the way things ended with Suzanne, but they said they always thought I was too young and wild for her anyway, which they never once said all during the time I was with her. Apparently she's now preparing to adopt an orphan from Romania and she's going over soon to pick it up, and they both hinted they have some reservations about it, like they're afraid she might get stuck with a lemon. They asked if I had a girlfriend, and I told them I did, that I was ecstatically in love as a matter of fact, and they asked what you were like, and I said you were Serbian, which they took to mean you were a Bosnian refugee who'd been raped in a concentration camp. Emily also seemed to think Serbia and Bosnia are one and the same – do you run into that a lot? I also told them

I'd recently met a punk rock guy Peewee and I used to idolize, and even though he's now seriously fucked up, he remembered having met Peewee at once, but that didn't go over the way I thought it would. I don't think they like to think of the music side of Peewee's life, when, as he once told me himself, if you'd cut his veins open and put his blood under a microscope, you would have seen little electric guitars floating around instead of blood cells. But here's the big thing they laid on me: they said that some teacher who'd taught Peewee in the fifth grade had recently been arrested for molesting his former students, that several had come forward after all this time, and they wanted to know if Peewee had ever mentioned anything about this guy. He never did, but it's obvious they're still looking for something or someone to blame his "behavior problems" on, and now, at last, there's a scapegoat. Peewee had so much rage in him, I wouldn't be surprised if somebody *did* molest him, but I asked Terrence what he thought and he said he seriously doubted it, so I give him the final word in the matter. But I guess nobody will ever know for sure.

Terrence has now come home and walked over to check that I haven't fucked up his computer again. He's making me nervous [...] so I guess I'll send this off. I'm being a very good boy, except for doing some controlled substances the other night. Oh, and I've become a chronic masturbator. You're never out of my thoughts for a single second. I had an incredible dream about you, and I'd tell you about it, but Terrence is saying he has to use the phone. Which reminds me: send me your cell phone number over there and I'll call you as soon as I get to LA. Okay, have to run.

Love you MADLY!!
J.

The party I attended that night turned out to be exactly what I thought it would be: a lot of losers who'd coughed up fifty bucks lamely trying to get their money's worth. I didn't have fifty bucks to throw away, so Terrence paid for my ticket, just as he paid for everything on that trip, which I'm sure caused tension as well. He did start to act normally the night before I left, but I suppose my imminent departure put us both in a good mood. I was actually happy to get back to L.A., where I found this waiting in my inbox:

Beloved,

I wish you had told me about your dream!! I spoke with David for a long time today. He just fired the location manager and he was upset because [famous British actor] has turned him down and now he will have to push back for a week so he can find somebody else. I asked if he would please not tell people we are married when I come to Prague because I don't wish them to know that this is how I got the part and he blew up and said of course everybody knows and I am so difficult these days, I don't seem to understand the pressure he is under. So you see it's a good thing I didn't tell him about us, it would just make everything worse. I'm having a great time in Belgrade. My mother is so great, it makes me sad that I don't see her so often, and my brother is great, also, but also very terrible!! I can't wait for you to meet them and, also, my friends like my friend Milica. I told her about you which was good for me as I haven't told my other friends. It removed some of the pressure, I think. For new years we went to a big party at my friend Dragan's house. He has a big apartment, very old and beautiful, and I saw many old friends and a few people I don't like so much, also. (Is this OK? I speak much better than I write!!) It's very strange to see where the bombs have fallen. It's very precise. You see they didn't make many mistakes but I'm afraid many innocent people died just the same including a friend of my brother. This is the depressing side of life here but I try not to think about it so much and just have fun which is what most people my age try to do. We don't have Christmas the same day you do, it's on the 7th January, but I think I will miss it because I have to go to Prague for wardrobe and make-up tests. But David said I can come back to Belgrade for a few days after I finish which is good because we celebrate two new years here, the one everyone does but, also, the Orthodox new year on the 14th January. Another reason to celebrate, like we need any more!! […]

I'm writing this from Dom Omladine. It means Youth House, they have an internet café here. I don't have my new mobile number with me but I will call you in a few days to give it to you. I'm being good, too. I love you so much, Jason, I think being away from you convinces me more than ever. I didn't tell you but I stole one of your dirty T shirts that has your smell on it and this is what I wear to bed at night.

XXXXXXXX

⌒
•

THEN, FOR ABOUT A WEEK, THERE WAS NOTHING. She didn't call and didn't write, so I figured she must be in Prague or wrapped up with the holiday in some way and couldn't spare the time. Avatar called to offer me a job writing episodes for a softcore TV series, and while I wasn't exactly enthusiastic, I had to admit it beat temping. It was cold and rainy, and I felt so lonely I'd take unnecessary trips to Pioneer Market just to be around other people. One night I went to the Silverlake Lounge to catch a few bands that could've billed themselves as sleeping pills, and though Scott Sterling wasn't around, it made me think of that night at Jim's: was Buddy in jail or what? I was still thinking about it the next day when I realized Jim's number was probably still on my caller ID. It was. I never thought I'd get him. I thought I'd get his mom instead, intending to hang up as soon as she answered, but after a couple of rings, there was Jim, sounding more groggy than drunk. I had to remind him who I was, of course. I said, "It was the same night Buddy came by? With a beautiful Serbian girl? Well, I'm the one who came to get her."

"Oh, right," he said, "you're that *big* guy." Which is something I always find a bit weird, how people always seize on my size. Half the time I forget how big I am. But I told him that was right, I was the big guy, and he apologized for being so spacey; I'd caught him in the middle of writing.

"That's funny," I said. "I'm writing something myself."

"Oh? What's that?"

"Some stupid TV show. You don't want to hear about it."

"You're a screenwriter?"

"No, a director. Screenwriting is—it's just something I do every once in a while to pick up a little money. My version of flipping burgers."

"Yeah, I'm real lucky I don't have to do stuff like that. My mom—she made some investments for me, so that's what I live on now. And she owns the house outright, so there's no rent. You met my mom, right?"

"Yeah, she threw us out."

"Oh," he laughed. "Yeah, she throws a lot of people out. She's good people, though. She's been through a lot. Well, I guess we've *all* been through a lot."

"Some more than others."

"You know, I'm not too sure about that. When I was in high school, I used to work at a grocery store, and the guy I worked for, my supervisor—I couldn't stand him. He was a real prick, kind of a John Wayne type—I even slashed his tires one night, I hated him so much. And then, years later, I was talking to a woman who used to date him, and it turned out he had two dicks."

"You're kidding!"

"Yeah, he pissed out of one and came out of the other. And she said he was really torn up about it. So that really taught me something. Everybody suffers. Even the pricks among us."

"Well, in his case, it was *two* pricks."

"Yeah," he laughed again, "I guess you're right."

I couldn't believe how talkative he was, how normal. Like I say, he sounded groggy, but he chatted away from the get-go like he'd known me forever. I asked if the police had ever caught up with Buddy, and he said, "Yeah, but I dropped the charges. He's a real blowhard, you know, but we go so far back, and I know he's suffered a lot. I mean, Gary's dead, and he's got kids and ex-wives, and he just can't put the music thing down. I'm not really sure he's all that dedicated, you know; he's just one of those people who's always got to be on a pedestal. That's why he's still got problems with me: because in our band, *I* was the one on the pedestal, if you can call it that."

"Well, you were sure on a pedestal to *me*. It's hard to believe I'm talking to you right now."

"Really? Why?"

"You changed my whole life. But I told you that."

"You did?"

Then I reminded him how I'd driven up when I was eighteen to see his band at CBGB's with that kid who'd been smoking the cigar, and he once again recalled meeting Peewee right away.

"Oh my God," he said, "that kid! That kid was something else! What's *he* up to now?"

"Dead."

"Oh, I'm so sorry to hear that." He really sounded broken up too. He asked when he'd died and if it was drugs, and I said no, it was twelve years ago in a car crash.

"That's so sad," he said, "so sad. You know, back in the old days we used to play sometimes with these kids from Long Beach—Rhino 39, they called themselves. And their frontman was a kid named—what was his name again? It's right on the tip of my tongue. Anyway, he was a real talent, that kid, and he got killed too. Car crash. Seventeen years old. I think. He was just about to graduate. It happened that spring."

"Rhino 39—weren't they on Dangerhouse?"

"Hey, you know something? I think they *did* put out a record on Dangerhouse. We did too, you know."

"Of *course* I know. Man, that was the one! That's the thing that got me into punk rock. We used to cover 'Banished' in my old band."

"Ha!"

"Yeah, that's what we used to close with. I've got some recordings of it somewhere. We were going to put it on our record, but then we decided to stick with original stuff. But I'd love to hear what you think of it. It doesn't even sound like the same song."

Then we talked for a while about music. His interest in new bands surprised me. He raved about the Monorchid and Bedhead and Sleater-Kinney, calling their frontwoman, "that girl, whatever her name is," the best punk singer he'd ever heard. I asked how he knew so much about recent music, since, according to Buddy, he never left the house, and he said he listened to it all the time on the Internet.

"That's funny," I said.

"Why? What do you mean?"

"Well, so many of your songs were anti-technology."

"Oh," he laughed. "Yeah, that was really a lot of posturing on my part. I didn't know what I was talking about. I was reading a lot of writers like Burroughs and Ballard and Phillip K. Dick, and I thought it sounded smart to talk about those things. I wasn't the only one. Devo—that was their whole shtick, just about. And there was this band called the Mutants—they had a whole futuristic outlook. But they kind of played around with it, whereas we were—I was—much more black-and-white about it."

"Yeah, but you were right in a lot of ways. Don't you think the world has gotten more dehumanized?"

"Not especially."

"Well, you know, I just got back from New York—I used to live there—and it's changed like you can't believe. I mean, even when I lived there it was getting pretty gentrified, but it's gone way beyond that now. It's like a giant shopping center, fast food and chain stores everyplace you look. It's not as bad as L.A.—not yet—but it's getting there pretty damn fast."

"Yes, but how does that amount to 'dehumanization'? What's dehumanizing about it?"

"Well, maybe that's the wrong word. But there's a sameness about it, you know? A uniformity."

But he said that was a small price to pay for the convenience such stores provided. He understood what I meant—it was corporate and so on—but if you needed something in the middle of the night, you could always find it, and that kind of convenience was something your small-time entrepreneur couldn't provide, lacking the resources. I said, "Yeah, but don't you think people make too much over convenience? They used to get along fine without it."

"Did they? I think a lot of people *died* because of inconvenience. Now, granted, a hamburger probably isn't going to save your life, but you might need a prescription at three in the morning, and where are you going to get it? I think you might feel pretty grateful for a Sav-On drugstore at a time like that."

"I see your point."

"It doesn't sound like it."

"Well, I don't agree. Because to me it's one step forward and two steps back. I mean, the family doctor—didn't they used to drop by in the middle of the night? They used to make house calls, right? Well, they stopped doing that a long time ago. Plus the whole system has gotten so impersonal, there's a good chance you don't even *know* your doctor."

"So you have to know him to get good treatment? You can't even *compare* medicine these days to the way it used to be. Things are so much better it's not even funny. And sure, okay, it's more impersonal, but how can it not be with so many people running around?"

In fact, he continued, overpopulation itself was proof of the triumph of modern medicine. Women used to die in childbirth as a matter of course, he said, but these days that almost never happened, at least not in first-world countries like this one. Plus people were living longer; he'd just read the other day that the average lifespan would soon expand to 120, that scientists had figured why we age and how in theory to stop it; and meantime there hadn't been a worldwide plague in years already. I mentioned AIDS, but he said, "I don't count that. You can't even compare AIDS to the bubonic plague or the flu outbreak during the First World War. They wiped out huge numbers of people practically overnight, and AIDS has only killed a few million over the last twenty years."

"Well, maybe we *need* a good plague. Maybe there's too many people in the world."

Then I heard him take a drag on his cigarette—he'd been doing that constantly since he picked up the phone—and he said, "Would you still feel that way if it killed somebody you loved?"

WE SPOKE FOR A REALLY LONG TIME THAT DAY, maybe as long as two and a half hours, but at some point he started drinking, so that by the time we hung up, he could barely recall what he'd said five seconds before, much like that night with Irina. He said for a number of years he'd been off drugs and booze both, but then his agoraphobia took a turn for the worse, and alcohol was the only halfway effective treatment he'd ever managed to find. He wasn't so admiring of modern medicine once the subject turned to agoraphobia. He'd seen countless doctors, he said, and taken countless medications, but none of it relieved his panic attacks, and now he was basically housebound and could only go places he knew really well, and even then he might freak out unless his mother went with him. In fact, he said, if his mother went with him, he could go lots of places, but since she was seventy, there weren't a lot of places she wanted to go. Fine by him. There weren't a lot of places he wanted to go either, and he had plenty to keep him busy around the house. Yes, he told me, he still wrote poetry as well as music, and he claimed to have made "dozens" of records he'd never released, though he declined to play me samples. Music sounded terrible over the phone, he said, and besides, I might not like his new stuff, which he described as "introspective"—far more so than *Tinderloin*. I told him it made no sense to write music if he wasn't going to perform it, and he said,

"Well, come on, it's hard to leave the house, let alone go onstage. It was always hard. Even in Rule of Thumb I used to have panic attacks; I just didn't realize that's what they were. I'm sure that's why I got on heroin. Well, it's not the only reason. Everybody *in* Rule of Thumb was on heroin by the time we broke up. But I think I was always an agoraphobic; it just took a while before it reached the point where I couldn't do anything."

"So why don't you post a few songs on the Internet?"

"Yeah, I've thought about doing that. But I don't think anyone cares what a fat old fuck like me is up to."

"You might be surprised. I was trying for months to track you down, you know, just because I was always curious about you, and I heard some pretty wild stories about what you've been up to."

"Ha!"

"No, I really did. People have got you joining cults and living in Atlanta, and—oh, you'll like this!—one person said you had a sex-change operation and you're racing cars as a woman."

"Jesus Christ, really? I never raced cars as a *man*." Nor had he ever lived on the street. I told him somebody had claimed to see him dressed in rags and begging for change on Hollywood Boulevard, and he said, "Yeah, somebody else told me that. I don't know where people come up with these things. There were times when I was crashing on sofas, but I was never *homeless* homeless. And I never panhandled, not even when I was a full-blown junkie."

He was amazed that people still talked about him. He was amazed that I'd seek him out. I mentioned the ads I'd run and the private detective I'd considered hiring, as well as my talk with his old friend Michelle, and he said, "Oh, *her*. I hope you didn't sleep with her. She gave me gonorrhea."

"Really? She told me she used to go out with Gary, but she never said anything about you."

"Yeah, she went out with both of us. She gave us *both* gonorrhea." Then he recounted a few stories about Michelle, none too flattering, but that was the only bad word he had to say about anybody. He called Irina, for instance, the most beautiful girl he'd ever seen, and he asked a lot of questions about her—the kinds of questions he would like to have asked when she came by with Buddy, but he'd been so blown away by the way she looked, he could barely bring himself to look at her. He also asked about my own music and the movies I'd directed and where I was from and so on, and said I sort of reminded him of somebody, though he couldn't place whom. He said that more than once before his mom started yelling for him to come and eat, and he barked, "I'll be there in a minute!"—several times, in fact—and muttered, "The old battle-axe," same as last time, and also like last time: "Don't you love it when people say that?" I had the sense that he could've spoken forever—not because we were particularly simpatico, but because he was so starved for company, he would've spoken to anybody. And it was fine till the last half-hour or so, but then he started repeating himself while bickering with his mom, so I told him I had to go. But before I did, I gave him my number and encouraged him to call. Not that I had any interest in making that movie, the one I'd vaguely planned about ROT. That all stopped on the windy night I drove to Rancho Cucamonga and shook the hand of Eddie Brown: the misfit Jim had been prior to his self-reinvention and was again now. And I liked Eddie Brown. He struck me at the time as a gentle soul, but all the same, I still wanted to meet Jim Cassady. Over the last few months, with Irina's help, I'd started thinking more and more as I had in my early twenties, as Peewee had just before he died in the middle of his "ROT rediscovery thing." And if he could do it, and I could too, then why couldn't Eddie Brown?

I THINK IT WAS LATER THAT NIGHT when I finally heard from Irina. At two in the morning she called to say that, yes, she'd been in Prague, where she'd gone for a few days for a fitting, and now she was back in Belgrade to spend the Orthodox New Year with her family. She'd stayed with David in Prague, she said, in a two-bedroom apartment near Old Town Square he'd rented for the length of the shoot. She claimed she hadn't seen much of him, but she'd seen a lot of Astrid, who was designing the costumes, and Astrid had actually been nice to her, so, obviously, she must know about the breakup. And Prague was so beautiful, and Belgrade was so ugly by comparison, and she'd met some of the other actors, who were "intimidating" but friendly as well. So it was a good report all the way around, and everything seemed fine on the surface, but somehow she sounded a bit stressed. I asked if anything was wrong, and she paused for quite some time and said, "Well, I'm not sure how to tell you this, but I'm a little…late."

"Oh."

"Yes."

"Uh, how late are you?"

"Well, my last period was almost two months ago. And I've been this late before, so maybe it's nothing, but I don't think so, Jason. I've got a really bad feeling about this."

"Well, it's easy to find out, right? Don't you guys have those do-it-yourself pregnancy tests?"

"Of course we do," she snapped. "We're not *that* backwards."

But a second later she apologized. She was really irritable, she said, and she didn't know why; she'd cried all the way back from Prague for no reason, and she looked just *awful*. I said, "Well, that doesn't mean you're pregnant. It sounds like you're depressed."

"But I'm *always* depressed, and it's not like this. My God, what's wrong with me? I tell David I don't want a child, and then I get pregnant by someone else!"

"Well, you don't know you are, yet. First you've got to find out."

"No, I know. I know what the answer's going to be, I just know it."

Then she cried, and I sat there feeling completely helpless. I kept telling her it was better to know than not to know, that it was going to prey on her mind a lot worse if she didn't, and waiting for her period to kick in wasn't going make her less pregnant—if, in fact, she was. Finally she said she'd buy a test at the pharmacy and call me as soon as she got back so we could get the results together. Good, I said, I'd be waiting. Hours passed, and I paced and wondered what the hell was keeping her. Finally, at maybe six A.M., the phone rang, and without even saying hello, she said, "Well, I was right. Congratulations. You're a father."

"Oh, fuck. Why didn't you call me before you took the test?!"

"Because. My friend Milica came over, and I'm glad she did. We had a long talk, and I don't feel good, but I definitely feel better than I would have."

In fact, she sounded remarkably composed. *I* was the fucking wreck. I asked her what we should do. "I guess I see a doctor," she said.

"And it's not going to be a problem?"

"No, it's very easy here. You just make an appointment, and that's it."

"So should I fly over or—?"

"Oh no. You couldn't even if you could afford it. It's very hard to get a visa. So don't worry about me; Milica will take good care of me. She's the only one who knows."

It really stung, that remark about affording it, but I knew she was right. Even so, I told her I'd send her some money, but she said I couldn't because of the sanctions. Besides, it wasn't that much: only about 300 in Deutsche Marks.

"Deutsche Marks?"

"Yes, we use a lot of Deutsche Marks here. The dinar's so low, you know. And three hundred is—in dollars it's about a hundred and fifty. So don't worry, it's nothing; I can pay for it out of my 'allowance.' This is another thing that bothers me. David is going to pay for me to get rid of someone else's baby. I can't *wait* to have some money of my own!"

"So are you going to tell him?"

"Oh no. He'd never forgive me. Never. Maybe one day I will, but not now. That's the *last* thing I need."

"Well, I guess you know best. This is—I've never been in this situation before."

"Never?"

"No. You'd think I would've, I was such a slut for all those years, but unless I got somebody pregnant without her telling me, it never happened."

"And how does it make you feel?"

"You know, I don't really think it's hit me yet."

"Yes," she half-laughed, "I know just what you mean."

Then, because I felt somebody should bring this up, I asked if she wanted to keep it. I wasn't sure how we could pull it off, I said, but if she really wanted to, I was sure we could work something out; and she said, "Well, thank you for saying that. But I don't see how I can. I haven't left David yet, not completely. So, no, this is definitely not the right time."

Then she asked me to say something to boost her spirits, so I told her a few jokes, and she laughed at some, and some she didn't get at all. And that was pretty much how that conversation ended: with me trying to explain a joke she didn't get. Then she said she had to go, that she was running up quite a bill, and I told her I loved her, and she said she loved me. And the next time we spoke it was all over.

SHE DIDN'T WANT TO TALK ABOUT THE ABORTION ITSELF. She just said there were no complications, and it wasn't nearly as painful as she thought it would be. But she sounded tired and *very* depressed, though she tried to make light of it, talking a lot about the movie and the terrific wardrobe Astrid had put together for her. She said she could hardly believe it when she saw herself in the mirror at the fitting in Prague, that she looked like a Hollywood star from the 1940s. That was when the movie was set. It was a Holocaust drama about a Polish family hiding Jews in their attic, and Irina played the daughter who rats the Jews out. She was fucking this Nazi, see, except you never really saw them together, and all she did in the meantime was clear the table and say, "I'm going out for a little while," till finally, at the end of the movie, you learned where she'd been going. I'd read the script and thought it was okay—nothing special—and that was Irina's opinion as well; but she'd never had a movie part nearly this big, and she was hoping it would lead to bigger parts. And, frankly, I was hoping it wouldn't. I think, deep down, I was always hoping she'd fail, because, first of all, I thought she showed no talent for acting, and regardless, I considered her much too special to waste her life that way. Actors are some of the dumbest people on the planet—even dumber than musicians, which is saying a lot. Plus it took her away from me. And that raises a matter I didn't altogether realize till after the abortion: I think I *tried* to get her pregnant in order to keep her close. It wasn't a conscious decision, but I remember pulling out late on at least one occasion, and why would I do such a thing if I wasn't secretly hoping to knock her up? Something in me was deeply pleased when she told me I'd succeeded, just as I was later crushed when she decided to abort. I knew it was the so-called right decision, but that's rational talk. Emotionally, I was fixed on what might have been. I kept thinking of something Suzanne had said when she was trying to talk me out of getting into filmmaking: that even if I had all the success in the world, I'd wake up one day and feel awfully empty if I never had kids. And of course I *wasn't* successful, and I *did*

feel empty, and the girl I loved was so young and ambitious, it might be a very long time before she was ready to have kids. I even wondered if I shouldn't have stayed with Suzanne after all; but that was just a passing thought, the way you can always look back at your life and think, "If I'd just done this and that instead of this and that, I might have been happier." Yet I knew and know I *wouldn't* have been happier. I might have been more comfortable, given her parents' money, but nothing comes from comfort but the fear of losing it, and that's exactly where my generation made its big mistake. Yet *dis*comfort's no good either. There's just no winning, is there? Do it one way and lose your soul; do it the other and lose your livelihood. You guys who run the world, you've got all the bases covered.

But I couldn't burden Irina with such thoughts. Instead I shared them with Jim. I called him one day to get it off my chest, and since he had nothing better to do, he listened, all the while puffing on countless cigarettes and slurping lots of beer. I'll tell you, hearing all that, I had to question my own bad habits. I was never much of a smoker, but I sure was knocking back plenty of booze, even after losing my best friend to a drunk driver. (In fact, for a number of years after the accident, I cut back considerably.) But what the hell else was I going to do? I practically never saw people. Even when I went out to see bands, I could never find anybody to go with me. And I asked Jim how he stood it, being alone so much of the time, and he said, "Oh, it never bothered me that much, not even when I was a kid. I never had much need for people." Which I took with a huge grain of salt, since he was so obviously such a lonely guy. Even so, I asked him why it was.

"I think," he said, puffing and slurping, "it's because I can always predict what they're going to do anyway. As soon as I meet them, I figure them all out, and nothing they do surprises me."

"Really? For me it's the opposite. I may *think* I know, but people always find a way to surprise me. Especially women."

"Oh, I don't know. Women like to think they're so mysterious, but I know what's going on. I know what they're thinking every minute."

"Oh yeah? Let's have it."

"*Nothing.* They think about their clothes, their hair, their weight and their boyfriends, and that's it. You can ask my mom. She worked around nothing but women for forty-some years, and she'll tell you the same thing."

"Yeah, well. I sure hope you like fucking your mom."

I thought that might piss him off, but all he did was laugh.

"Yeah," he said, "too bad I don't! I can't *remember* the last time I got laid! I think the last time it almost happened was—God, when was that? Three years ago? I met this woman on the Internet—she lived in San Bernardino—and we were carrying on this whole thing, you know, lots of sex talk. Finally she decided she wanted to meet, and I warned her I wasn't the prettiest guy in the world, but she said that didn't matter; she loved me for my mind. Yeah, she loved me for my mind, all right! She walked in here and took one look and practically *ran* out of this house!"

"Yeah, well. I've been pretty hard up myself."

"What are you talking about? You come over here with—what's that girl's name again?"

"Irina."

"Good God, you don't *know* what I'd give to have a girl like that! I was afraid to even look at her!"

"I know. You told me."

"So? What are you crying about? That's what I don't like about kids your age: you're all a bunch of crybabies."

"I'm not a kid. I'm thirty-seven years old. Irina—*she's* a kid. And I'll tell you, boy, before her there was a *serious* fucking dry period, and who knows what's going to happen after she goes? I mean, I *hope* she never does. But, you know, I'm twelve years older than she is, and one of these days she's going to look up and wonder what she's doing with this ugly old man."

"So? By then you might be tired of her."

"I doubt it. I mean, talk about unpredictable! It's never a dull moment with that one."

"Yeah, I had somebody like that once."

And he told me about Cybil Disobedience. He didn't mention the name right away, but I was sure that was the girl he meant. He said he used to be with this flipped-out chick who was insanely jealous—not so much of other women as Jim's creativity.

"She wanted to be an artist in the worst way," he said. "And she *was* an artist, that's what's so funny. It just didn't manifest itself in the usual ways. I'd write a poem, you know, and it made her so mad I could do something like that and she couldn't, she'd rip it up. One time I did a reading and she stood up and heckled me—my own girlfriend! And she slept with nearly all my friends. Buddy fucked her, Clint fucked her—I think they all had a go at one time or another. But I never left her, because she was never boring, not for a single second, and also at that time I was really intrigued by self-destruction. All my heroes were really self-destructive, you know, and I was trying to emulate them, and this girl—she was like my cheerleader. We were always talking about killing ourselves. We used to read up on it—different methods and all that—and we had a pact where one of us wouldn't do it unless the other did it too. And then she broke it."

"How so?"

"Well, first she cut her wrists. But maybe it was taking too long that way, or maybe she lost her nerve, so she took my belt and hung herself. And I was in the next room when it happened. I was asleep. I'd gotten really wasted the night before, and by the time I woke up, she was blue and stiff as a board, her tongue hanging out, blood all over the place. I can't even tell you how terrible it was. And this was only a few days after Darby killed himself. You know who that is, right? Darby Crash?"

"Of course."

"Yeah, Darby and I—we weren't exactly friends, but there was kind of a bond there, because he was somebody else who didn't like performing. He couldn't do anything unless he was drunk, just like me. And he was always saying he was going to kill himself, and I was too, so whenever we saw each other, it was like, 'Still here, huh?' And then he actually did it, and I don't know if there was some connection—if that sparked something or—you know, I really don't know. I mean, Cybil wasn't all that friendly with Darby either. And the thing was, I thought I knew about death, because my father died right in front of me when I was sixteen, but that was just a heart attack. There was no blood or wounds or that kind of thing. But Cybil—it was so terrible I never talked about suicide again. I mean, I'm *still* trying to kill myself, but not like that. I'll just drink and smoke till I get cancer or drop dead of a heart attack, and that'll be that."

"So why are you trying to kill yourself?"

"Well, what's there to live for? My life is over. I'm not being a crybaby; that's just the way it is. My life's been over for years already. I'm just a body taking up space—too *much* space."

"Well, yeah, but what are you doing with yourself? It doesn't *have* to be that way."

"Sure it does. I've been on every medication they could prescribe for me, and I still get these fucking panic attacks. I can't go anywhere, and even if I could, where would I go? There's not a woman in the world who'd touch me with a ten-foot pole, and who can blame them?"

So I said if that wasn't being a crybaby, I didn't know what was—he could fill the Grand fucking Canyon with all the tears he'd just shed—and he said, "Well, maybe you're right. But that doesn't mean I'm not right too. I know what I am. I used to have a lot of delusions, but not anymore. And it's not like I ever stopped being productive. I probably get a lot more done than you do. That's one advantage to being celibate: you can really get a lot accomplished once you cut sex out of your life or sex does it for you. It's kind of a good thing in a way."

So, once again, he was saying the opposite of what he'd said years before, in his song "Artificial Pussy." I asked if he realized that, and he said, "Who cares? Besides, that wasn't a song about celibacy; it's another anti-technology song. I was saying—you know, I was saying that one day people would all be voyeurs instead of procreating. But I didn't know what the fuck I was talking about. People are fucking just as much now as they were back then."

"Well, I haven't exactly checked the stats. But, you know, Irina was telling me in Serbia it's really unusual to have more than one kid—two at most. And in France and Italy it's less than that—in fact, if this keeps up, Italy won't exist in two or three hundred years. The land will still be there, but it won't be Italians living on it. And the same thing is going on with middle-class Americans. They have one kid, maybe two, and that's it."

"So? That's how many kids they have. That doesn't mean they're not fucking."

"But doesn't that kind of prove your point?"

"What point?"

"The one you made in 'Artificial Pussy.' You were saying people should just be animals, right? They should let it rip. So, if they're having less kids, it can only be one of two things: either they're not fucking so much, or they're using more birth control. And birth control is a kind of technology, so in the long run the song is right."

But we were rapidly coming to the end of his "good" time, when he was still lucid enough to conduct a conversation. He said he couldn't quite follow my argument, so I repeated it, and he burped and said, "Well, I don't see why you think there's less kids being born. Yeah, maybe white people aren't having that many, but the spics and niggers are shitting them out like there's no tomorrow."

⌒

SO HE WAS A RACIST. Peewee's grandiose explanations for Jim's lyrics, or anyway the lyrics of that one song, now stood revealed as total bullshit. He definitely wasn't trying to be funny, and I felt so foolish for having been duped all those years ago, I brought it up the next time we spoke, and right away he started splitting hairs.

"Well," he said, "I wouldn't call myself a *racist*. To me that's somebody who advocates separatism or hurting people for looking different. Well, that's definitely not me. When I was a kid, I was beaten up by black kids for being white, and later on I was beaten up by white kids for being a punk rocker. So, you know, I really understand what discrimination means. But I'll say this much: I don't think it's happenstance that the most developed countries are white. That's not the way I want it to be; that's just the way it is. So maybe, if you've got to call me something, you could say I'm a reluctant racial chauvinist."

"Nah, I'll just call you a racist. 'All the most developed countries are white.' Yeah, that Japan, boy—they're whiter than fucking sugar!"

"Oh, come on. *We're* the inventors. Asians knock off whatever we do, and they do it really *badly* too."

"What are you talking about? *We're* the inventors? I mean, the Chinese—they invented gunpowder, right? And silk and pasta—that comes from them. And the Egyptians invented beer, and the first written language comes from Mesopotamia, and the Arabs—weren't they the ones who came up with the concept of zero?"

"Yeah, and what have they done since?"

"That's not the point. The point is, we've taken just as much from other people as they have from us. It's all a big melting pot."

But he said we'd done the most with it, I had to give him that, and I said it wasn't true. Just look at rock & roll, I said; that was a synthesis, right? It was a European song form fused with African rhythms. Well, the last part didn't come from white people. But he kept on splitting hairs.

"Actually," he said, "it's hard to say *who* started rock & roll. For every Bo Diddley, there was a Carl Perkins or a Wanda Jackson. And, by the way, I'm not sure if you're aware of this, but a big part of punk was removing black influences and taking it back to something pure white."

"Bullshit."

"Sorry, but it's true. I think it's very obvious if you listen to the music. And blacks were doing something similar with their own music: weeding out the white parts—the rock & roll part—and reinforcing the soul. You'd have to go back to Jimi Hendrix to find the last black rock star."

"Well, there was Bad Brains—"

"Oh, they're just a footnote, like me. Besides, they started out punk and started getting more and more reggae. And who was their audience? White kids. There's practically no such thing as a black punk rocker. I think I knew two the whole time I was involved. It was a really fascist movement in a lot of ways, all that black leather and short hair. And the way kids were acting—beating people up and vandalizing—that was Hitler Youth stuff. Now, in the beginning, it wasn't like that. It only attracted freaks. But then we started getting these right-wing beach people up in Hollywood, and they were really violent, those kids. That's when I started getting nervous about performing."

"Why? They sound like your kind of people."

"Oh, not at all. To me it was like theater, you know, but those beach kids were literalists. They thought if you sang about breaking things, that really meant you should break things. And unfortunately we did have that one song, which I wish I'd never written, and they'd come up to me and say, 'Right on, man, I hate niggers too.' Which really disgusted me, because that wasn't what I was going for at all."

"Then what *were* you going for?"

"Well, it was just a *song*, you know? Like I say, black kids used to beat me up, and I had some resentment about it, so I was saying, 'This is the way I feel sometimes.' But it wasn't the way I felt every second of the day. I felt like if there was one place to express that kind of thing, it was through art. I still feel that way. I wasn't trying to incite racism; I was just kind of unburdening myself. That song—it was almost like Tourette's syndrome."

"Oh, come on, you *knew* what you were doing."

"Yeah, I was trying to make art. I was never interested in politics or trying to control people. Now, there were others in the scene who were very interested in things like that. Like Darby. He wanted to rule the world, that guy. And I know after I got out of it, punk got very political, but I think that was a big mistake, all that strident moralizing. But, come on, it's just music. Music doesn't change the world. It can change your mood for a couple of minutes, but name the band that toppled a government."

"So who's being literal now? Sure it doesn't happen directly, but music changes *people* who change the world."

"Like who? Who's president right now? You think he was ever a big music guy? Yeah, I know, he plays saxophone, but that's got nothing to do with the kind of leader he is. And I bet you couldn't point to a single important leader who was ever a big music person. Art changes artists. No one else."

"Well, it sure changed *me*. I certainly wasn't an artist before I got into punk. I'm not sure if I'm an artist now. It's not something I think about much. I just do what I do, you know? But before punk, I didn't even do *that*. So if music could take someone like me and turn me around, I'm sure it could do the same for lots of others. And it does."

"That," he said, "is a really puritanical point of view. You're giving it this whole utilitarian spin, like if all music does is give you pleasure, it's not enough. No, it's got to *change* people. And what is it supposed to change them into? Artists? Yeah, that would be just terrific, a whole country full of artists. Who'd collect the trash? Who'd scrub the floors or fix the sink?"

"Hey, there's no law that says you can't do both. How do *you* know what the trash man's doing? He could be making all kinds of art with the stuff he collects. And even if he's not, I think he could benefit from something that really moves him. I mean, everything out there's so trivial. Like, you know, I work in the movie business, and I can count on one hand the people I've met who really have something to say. And it was the same way when I was doing bands, and even now I'll go out and hardly ever catch anything worth listening to. I mean, just last month I saw an incredible band, one of the best ever, and do you know what happened when they started playing? People turned around and left."

"Well, there you have it. Didn't you just say people would get more out of life if they were exposed to good stuff? But they don't want it, and they never did. And why should they? They've still got to work and go home to their families. I think in the long run it's really damaging for most people to have some kind of artistic revelation. It makes them want something they can never have anyway. So it's better for them, and it's better for everybody else, if they stay home and watch TV. Otherwise society would stop functioning altogether."

"So is that why *you* stay home? You're trying to help society function?"

"In my own way, yeah. That's what anarchy is all about: cooperation. I'm doing my part by keeping out of the way."

"You're joking, right?"

"Look," he said, sounding a bit pissed, "I don't know what you want from me. I told you before: I'm agoraphobic. Besides, I've got no interest. I've been out there, I did my thing, I don't give a shit anymore. The world is the way it is, and whether I sing a few songs or publish a few poems isn't going to make the slightest difference."

I disagreed, pointing again to myself as proof. I would never have led the life I had if I hadn't heard "Banished." That song had effectively freed me. And I was just one person, but maybe later, when my band covered "Banished," that song had freed someone else, who in turn had freed another person, and on and on. Small changes added up, I said, and for years I'd been too withdrawn to care, but more all the time I realized how important it was to try and make a difference. Then, very snidely, Jim said, "*What* difference?" And with that I exploded.

"Do you even *know* what's going on out there?! No, I don't think you do! You may *think* you know because you're sitting in front of your TV or computer, but that's like getting a postcard from Spain and thinking that means you've been there! Well, I've been to Spain, and it's not a fucking postcard! And I don't leave the house that much myself, and when I do, I can't *believe* what the fuck is going on! People have no curiosity, they get bored in two seconds flat, they can't even reflect the right way. I mean, if you took someone like, I don't know, Henry James, it wouldn't make a lick of sense, all those subtle ways of thinking. And maybe that's just the way things are, maybe that's evolution, but you could've said the same thing a hundred years ago. I mean, Lenin—he could have said, 'You know, there's really no point, getting rid of the czar. People starve, it's a fact of life. Nothing you can do about it.' And, yeah, maybe what he put up wasn't much better, but that's not the point. The point is, you can always take that passive attitude and find reasons to hold it up."

"And which band did Lenin sing for again?"

"The Beatles. Yeah, I was waiting for that one! But I think you're wrong. Music makes a *big* difference in people's lives. They get married to it, they get buried to it, they even used to fight fucking battles with music playing in the background. And the sixties—you could say everything that went down in the sixties was tied to music in a very intimate way. *That's* what punk was trying to revive. I mean, why am I even telling you this? You said the same thing yourself!"

"When?"

"Twenty years ago. You want me to read it to you? I've got the interview right here on my computer. And I don't care if you *have* changed your mind, you were right *then*, and you're wrong *now*. You specifically talked about rock & roll getting banned or sanitized, and the same thing happened with hip-hop. It took years for hip-hop to get played on MTV, and do you know why? Because white people didn't want their kids getting infected with black music. And, by the way, hip-hop practically *is* punk rock as far as I'm concerned. It's the only interesting thing to happen in pop music since punk got its dick cut off. That's what white people always do: they chop the dicks off everything, and the pussies too. And then you talk about how great we are! Yeah, we're the best! We're so fucking terrified of nature, we've got to destroy it every chance we get. It's like two hundred years ago, killing the Indians and stuffing them in corsets and dragging them off to church. And we're still doing it, except now it's Backstreet Boys and *ER* and *Jurassic Park*. That's the *new* church, and everybody's got to join. If we could find a way to get polar bears to watch *ER,* we'd do it. And don't think we *won't!*"

I sounded more like Peewee than Peewee! And I really wasn't sure why I bothered, except I wanted to kill Jim and this was second best. And maybe he had a point here or there—maybe the Japanese *were* imitators, and maybe blacks *didn't* come up with rock & roll, or at least not by themselves—but none of that really mattered, since, true or false, everything he said was rooted in fear. It was all another lock on his cage. And he liked it in there, that was the thing. Because it was *safe*.

So I gave him this big speech, and I should've known it wasn't going to make any difference, and of course it didn't. He said I was so "parochial," so "bourgeois," that I was just like punk kids he'd known in the past who were so *bored*, and instead of trying to fix the problem inside themselves, which was all they *could* fix, they had to fix the whole world; *everything* had to change just so they wouldn't feel bored anymore.

"That's all punk rock ever was or ever will be," he said, "a way for kids to stimulate themselves. Nobody else. Just them. It's just masturbation, that's all it is."

"Well, you're sure an expert when it comes to masturbation."

Then he paused so long I thought he'd hung up. But he hadn't. He said, "You're really an asshole, you know that? You know who you just reminded me of? Buddy. That's just the kind of thing he'd say."

"Hey, I thought he was a good guy. He suffers, right? Doesn't everybody suffer?"

He didn't have much to say to that. On the other hand, his "good" time was just about up.

Beloved,

I don't have time to write as much as I would like. I have a very early call time tomorrow for one of my bigger scenes. I'm very nervous because the other actors are so good and they do it so fast, in one take sometimes and David always makes me do it several times. It's very embarassing [*sic*]. I like the English actors a lot. They're very funny and tell good stories, there's always a lot of gossip in the make-up room. I think this is the only thing holding David together, he has the English to make him feel at home. The schedule is a mess and we'll do stupid things like shoot at one location and have to leave because someone didn't do their job and shoot someplace else and then go back to shoot at the first location a second time. Chad is a big problem, too, he tries hard to show he's as good as the English. He argues with David all the time, he can't do one thing without the postmortim [*sic*] as David calls it. Astrid is still very nice to me. I went to a club with her on Saturday night and she talks all the time about her problems with men. There is some guy she started seeing before she left and she's worried that he won't be there when she comes back. She mentioned you the other day and this gave me a chance to hear what she had to say about you. She said you were very good in bed (I almost died when she said that!!) but you would make any woman you were ever with very unhappy. I asked her why she said that and she said you didn't know how to be intimate and you were bitter because your career isn't going the way you want. But she did say, twice, you were good in bed and it made me very jealous to know she knows some private things about you which I know, also.

I'm not enjoying Prague so much as I thought I would. There are a lot of Americans but I like that because they're much more interesting than the Czechs. I find them very boring although a lot of the girls are very pretty. They're blondes who dye their hair black so they have black hair and blue eyes and good skin, many of them. Maybe we'll visit together one day and you can tell me what you think. I'm still very sad about what happened in Belgrade. I think about it all the time but I go to the set even when I'm not working and that helps. I may have to stay longer than I thought but I don't know yet. Milica has called about visiting but I think she may have a problem with her visa. Nebojša [Irina's brother] would like to come, too, but he can't because he hasn't done time in the army and they won't let you have a passport until you've done time in the army.

Well, this is all my news. I will try to phone you in a few days, it's hard with David around. He asked me to stay on for a while even after my part is finished but I told him I don't think I can stand Prague any more and I want to come back and get my own place. Think of me tonight!! That's when I'll be doing my big scene!!

Miss you!!!
XXXOOO

WHEN I FIRST STARTED TALKING TO JIM, I was always the one who called, but he soon started calling me. It got to be an everyday thing. During the day he was usually coherent, and that was our time for debate, but at night, being drunk, he'd speak more personally. Many times I wouldn't pick up past a certain hour, knowing what I was in for, but even then he'd leave long, rambling messages. Once, in the middle of leaving a message, he passed out and snored till the recording cut off. Another time he got in a fight with his mom, so I was left with a minute and a half of "Go to bed" and "Go to hell, you battle-axe." I offered to play it back for him so he'd know what he sounded like, but he said he *knew* what he sounded like, and I'd sound the same way if I lived with a "crusty old bag" like her. At the same time, he clearly loved her. She was one of his favorite things to talk about! He said she was originally from Oklahoma and was one of those Steinbeck Okies who moved to California in the mid-thirties and, once there, used to work as a movie extra to supplement the family income. Later, he said, she went to hairdressing school, working briefly as a "beautician to the dead," meaning she'd coiffed cadavers, and later still she worked at Twentieth Century-Fox before opening her own beauty salon in Hollywood. This was after she married Jim's dad, who taught high-school history and was possibly, Jim thought, agoraphobic, since he never left the house, except to work. It was a very unhappy marriage, Jim said, and when he was three, his brother, two years older, drowned in a neighbor's swimming pool, and when he was sixteen, his father had a fatal heart attack—he was just sitting and watching TV when he suddenly died—and through every bit of it, his mom was the bravest person you ever saw. Then she met her second husband—"that halfwit Martin McDaniel"—and moved from Burbank to his place in Rancho Cucamonga, and a few years later he died as well, which made Jim her only living relative (unless you counted that dog, whose name was Benji). Then she retired and sold her salon for a lot of money—not because the business itself was worth so much, but the real estate sure was—and even though you'd never know it to look at her, she had a great head for business, and thank God she did. Where would he be without her? She'd put him through several programs to get him off heroin, and whenever he found himself without an apartment, he knew he could always stay with her. He spent half his life at his mother's house after ROT broke up and he was cohabitating all over L.A. with a succession of girlfriends who invariably kicked him out. At one point he left town altogether, heading to Alaska to work as a fisherman; but come on, he was no fisherman, and his co-workers were some of the meanest sons of bitches he ever met. So it was right back to Southern California, or, as he referred to it more than once, "the tar pit." He never liked it, he told me repeatedly, not even as a kid, and he still hoped to leave one day, but knew he never would. He envied me for having lived in New York. He'd always wanted to live in New York, especially during the ROT days, and he tried many times to get the band to move, but the others were all dyed-in-the-wool Californians who would never consider it.

Those were my favorite talks: the ones about the band. That was where I always tried to steer things, and since he'd talk about anything to hear himself talk, I never had to steer very hard. He told me countless great stories, not just about ROT but other important bands from the scene at that time—the Weirdos, the Gun Club, X, the Screamers—as well as giving me the inside scoop on the origins of various ROT songs, including "Banished," which he said he'd written in response to certain scenesters who'd reviled him for not being punk enough. But that was ridiculous. Why, he practically invented punk, he and Buddy and Gary. When they started ROT, there *were* no punks, except for the ones in New York, and even the Stooges, their biggest inspiration, had stopped putting out records. Well, yes, the Doors were also a big inspiration, but only to him. Oh, the struggles he used to have, trying to sell his bandmates on songs like "The Coldest Beer in Town," songs full of "Morrison fag poetry shit," as Buddy used to refer to it. Yet the longer the band lasted, the more Jim's songwriting was moving in that direction, while Buddy was moving more into roots rock. It was a wonder they'd lasted as long as they had, between their musical differences and Jim's panic attacks (which at the time he didn't realize were panic attacks) and also, of course, the heroin. They had to fire their first bass player, Clint Cancer, when his habit became too much for the others to bear, and a few years later he fatally overdosed. And that was Gary's fault. *He* was the one who first brought heroin around, and if Buddy said otherwise, Buddy was a liar. Buddy was worse than a liar. After Cybil died, Jim wrote a cycle of songs to help himself heal, including "Raft at Sea," and he was going to record them all by himself, but then Buddy got involved, insisting they also record some of *his* songs, so what should have been a Jim Cassady solo record became an ROT record after all. He and Buddy had fought for years over its minuscule profits, which Buddy claimed Jim had stolen from him; yet in spite of all the drama surrounding it, Jim regarded *Tinderloin* as the best thing he'd ever done, and he was clearly pleased when I said the same thing. In fact, for all his griping about the old days, he obviously missed them. He was constantly reminiscing about his former girlfriends, a number of whom had turned tricks, and Cybil had been a dominatrix to boot. He *loved* talking about that. He said she had one client, a TV actor, who used to give her a laxative, and either she'd shit on his face or, if he couldn't mess himself up, he'd slide beneath a glass table while she squatted over the top so he could watch all that chocolate milk come gushing out of her brown eye. But, wait, there's more! When he *could* get messed up, he'd not only have her shit on his face but rub it in like suntan lotion, plus doodle with it, writing words like "shit" and "fuck" over clean parts of his body. But that was nothing, Jim said: Cybil had another client who used to have her beat his ass to the point of leaving blisters, after which she'd pop them and feed him the pus.

But that wasn't the kind of sex *they* used to have. No, he told me, they had sex the *normal* way. And what about me and Irina? What was *our* sex life like? He asked me that many times, and no *way* was I going to answer, no way in the fucking world; the thought of Cybil popping blisters was nothing compared to the idea of Jim jerking off to thoughts of Irina. Jesus Christ, I had so many reasons not to like that guy. And yet I was never quite sure just how genuine his more outrageous talk was. We were always debating the merits of punk, and I was pro and he was against, so certain things he may have exaggerated to put me in my place, like "Yeah, you may *think* you're so punk, but I can out-punk you any day of the week." Plus, in his sober moments, he gave me food for thought. For instance, so what if I was bored with American culture? There were cultures that had barely changed over the course of centuries, but you didn't hear those people complaining. But I was a white, middle-class, American male, and as such spoiled. I thought I had a right to live in exciting times, only, unlike so many others, I knew the times were lackluster. But were they, really? Yugoslavia, for example, with its recent wars, certainly hadn't lacked excitement, but, according to Irina, all it did was tire people. They were dying for some boredom. Boredom was like paradise to them. Also, as Jim routinely suggested, it was a great time for technology and scientific breakthrough, and I had to admit he was right. An injury like the one I'd suffered in the accident might well have resulted in amputation fifty years before, but my leg had been saved. Meantime, in untold smaller ways, I benefited from technology every day of my life. I could send mail to the other side of the world with a push of a button, and see any movie I wanted to see whenever I wanted to see it, and drop a record and not have to hear pops and hisses the next time I played it. Peewee lived long enough to hear CDs, but he was an analog purist. Digital sounded so *cold*, he said. But I had two copies of our record on vinyl, and one was scratched, while the other I never took out of its sleeve. I did remove the factory wrap, since at some point that starts to shrink, but now it just sat there in its looser-fitting plastic cover—something I could look at but never play, otherwise that copy might get scratched as well.

So, yes, I could see there was progress. But all those conveniences dulled the mind and the senses with it. I don't think Jim and I were the only ones leaving the house less often. I think there's a lot more of that kind of thing, and to me that partly explained why contemporary America seemed so lifeless. Even football now seemed lifeless. Those guys were so pumped up on steroids, such a bunch of oversized lab rats, the human element was missing completely. A similar thing was happening with women. With Irina gone I was renting lots of porn, and practically every actress (so to speak) had basketball breast implants and either no pubic hair at all or a thin stripe so precise it looked like a fuzzy band-aid. Plus you could tell most of them worked out, and I've never liked girls with muscles. Fortunately Irina was nice and soft. She used to wax before we got together, but that was to please David. Me, I loved a hairy pussy; and I told Irina she could stop waxing, and I would've told her to stop going to the gym, except she was so lazy about that kind of thing I never had to. And, yes, she was a freak of nature who could eat whatever she wanted and never gain a pound, while I was forced to go on gym kicks every so often to work off my gut; but Irina told me she *liked* my gut. She thought it was "honest." She liked my receding hairline for the same reason.

So we were both rare in that we found imperfections attractive, whereas, judging from the media—and I realize that can be deceptive—most people wanted robots. There could be no fat, no body hair, nothing unique except for tattoos and piercings—and how unique is a form of "self-expression" practiced by half the population? Talk about fascism!

But Jim said that was all just fashion. He said eventually people would tire of the robot look and return to something more natural, and after so much time I would tire of that too. I said, "Well, women didn't use to shave their legs and armpits, and once they started, they never went back."

"And aren't you *glad*?"

"Well, yeah, I'm glad about *that*. But the pussy—it's perfect the way it is. I mean, if you've got hair going up to the navel, sure, break out the clippers, but otherwise leave it the way it is. There's something animal about pubic hair, you know? I don't want to fuck a baby. I don't know, maybe *that's* why people like it. We're all like a bunch of kids these days."

"I know *I* am."

"Me too. And that's another reason I wish Irina had kept that baby: it might have forced me to grow up. It's about fucking time! You know, you reach a point where you accumulate so much knowledge and it's weird not to pass it on. It's like there's a missing dynamic."

"Well, there's more than one way to pass it on. You can do it biologically, or you can do it through art."

So here was our running art debate. He as a person who refused to share his art, who felt it didn't matter in the first place, would argue a second later how important it was. At least I was consistent: I *knew* it wasn't important. In the world of progress Jim kept pushing, art didn't exist anymore. Not true, he said. Art and design were the same thing, and since everything man-made was designed in some way, you couldn't separate the two—a car was art, a stove was art, and so was a blank sheet of paper. But to me that wasn't art. I knew, of course, that you could take any object and separate it from its context and say, "Okay, this is art, and there's no way you can tell me otherwise," but I'd seen a lot of that crap in New York, and you were basically given two ways to respond: you could "get it" and prove how *kewl* you were, or you could *not* get it and prove yourself a rube. But both were dead ends as far as I was concerned, and that equally applied to what was coming out of the mainstream. To me art was something that made you think and feel at the same time; but the "high" conceptual art embraced by the educated was all shallow thought, while the "low" popular art loved by the simple was all shallow feeling. So, no, there was no such thing as art anymore, and to that Jim once said, "Well, there's always you, right? You're the only one who's got it right."

"Hey, I never *said* I had it right. I'm just as shallow as everybody else. How can I not be? I'm a product of my time. And the new kids are worse! So I don't think there's anything they're going to produce that's not going to be shallow, and I reject that as art."

"So does that mean red isn't red anymore? Was the old red better than the new red? And what about the human voice? Can people not sing as well as they used to, or is that a thing of the past too?"

"You know what? You tell me. You've supposedly got all these records you've been making. Why don't you play me one?"

"I told you already: I don't want to play it over the phone. It doesn't sound right."

"Yeah, right. Why don't you cut the shit? There's no records, and you know it."

But he insisted there were. And after so much of this, I said, "Okay, why don't I drive out there one day? Would you play me one then?"

"Sure."

"And you're not going to run away before I get there? You're not going to say you're too hungover or make some other excuse?"

"No, no. Any time you want to come is fine with me. You know I can't go anywhere."

So, because I was writing at the time and could pretty much make my own schedule, I asked how the following day sounded. I knew I had to get there before he'd started drinking, so I suggested noon, and he said, "Couldn't we do it a little later?" We eventually settled on two, and since I was certain he'd have nothing to show me once I got there, I told him I'd bring a copy of my movie and a tape of my band playing "Banished." And he said that all sounded fine to him.

I HEARD HIM TELL HIS MOM I WAS COMING, but I still had visions of her throwing me out, so I bought her some flowers before leaving Echo Park. Then I followed Jim's directions to Rancho Cucamonga and this time found his place without a hitch. It seemed different in daylight. The house itself looked exactly as I recalled, but there was a tall wall of purple mountain looming up behind it that couldn't be seen at night. I rang the bell, and right away the dog started barking. Then Jim's mom answered the door and glanced at the flowers and said, "Who are *they* for?"

"You."

"Why?"

"Well, last time I was here it was pretty late. So just so there's no hard feelings..."

She obviously didn't trust charm, this woman. But she took the flowers anyway, inviting me inside without inviting me, and yelled, "Eddie, your friend is here!" and left me alone in the room. The dog stayed behind to bark at me, and I said his name in a short, terse voice—*"Benji!"*—and he shut up for a second, giving me a look as if to say, "I don't know who the hell you are, but if you say my name like that, maybe I shouldn't be barking, huh?" Then, in a state of confusion, he went back to doing it, and I leaned down to pet him, and once he'd let me, he wouldn't let me stop. I'd made a pal for life.

Then Jim walked into the room, wobbling like a bowling pin about to drop. His eyes were bloodshot—he'd just gotten up—and he wore stained gray sweatpants and a T-shirt so big it was practically a dress. I stood from petting the dog, and he said, "Good God, Jason, is that you? You look like a cop!"

"I *am* a cop."

"Yeah, I don't doubt it! Jesus, how tall *are* you?"

"Six-two."

"You're taller than that."

"I just look that way."

"Are you Irish?"

"Irish and English."

"Yeah, you look Irish. You remind me of that actor—what's his name? He was in that movie—the one where everything blows up?"

Well, that was sure slimming it down! He never did think of it. He noticed I was holding a videotape and asked what it was. My movie, I reminded him, and I gave it to him, and also gave him the tape I'd made of Superego; and he said, "Great, let's go have a listen. Hey, Mom! Mom, we're going to my room to play music!"

"Don't play it too loud!" she yelled without reappearing; and I felt like I was ten years old and visiting a new friend from school. Then I followed Jim down a short hallway to a door that was slightly ajar, and he pushed it all the way open, and, Jesus, it was a totally different world back there. The walls and ceiling were painted black, and there were shelves packed with books and magazines, and still more shelves were crammed with CDs and LPs. He had not just one but two computers on a desk beside his unmade bed, just as he had two mini-amps stacked in a corner, and two guitars sitting on stands: a cheap acoustic and a late-model black Jaguar. I told him I had a Jaguar myself, but red, and he said, "Yeah, I used to have a lot of guitars, but I pawned them all for drugs. I held on to one, but it goes out of tune so easy, I picked up the Jag as a backup."

"Yeah, we used to buy a lot of guitars at pawn shops. We broke a lot of equipment—it was part of the show—and there were so many junkies on the Lower East Side, the pawn shops were full of great gear going for nothing. One time I picked up an Elektro for fifty bucks."

So that kicked off an equipment talk—real geek stuff—and at some point he went to his closet and hauled out his other electric guitar: a seventies Vantage with a wood finish. He'd already started playing my tape, and at first he barely seemed to listen, but then, out of the blue, he said, "You guys were pretty good. You remind me a little of Sonic Youth."

"Oh, man, we used to hear that so often! And the thing is, my friend Peewee just hated those guys!"

"Why? They're a great band."

"Oh, he was just jealous. Everybody always talked about them, and we could barely get people to *see* our shows."

"Is that you singing?"

"Can't you tell?"

"Nice voice. Sounds kind of bluesy."

"Yeah, I used to get that too."

Then "Banished" came on, and he *really* listened, and halfway through he said, "Wow, you really did something different with it. You even changed the words."

"Yeah, that was a whole generational comment we were trying to make. I wish you'd gotten to see us live. We'd go fucking nuts when we did that song!"

"Us too. God, it's so funny. It's hard to believe I wrote that thing. It's got so little to do with me now."

"Well, let's hear some new stuff."

Later, he said. First he had some things he wanted to show me, and there was certainly a lot to show: that place was a regular museum. It was less the room of a man in his forties and more the room of a teenaged boy—a room on a spaceship, maybe, that's headed for a two-year orbit and so it's been packed with everything the teenaged pilot will need to keep himself entertained. He had a lot of men's magazines from the sixties and seventies, and he pointed out girls he used to jerk off to, including one with tits like fleshy fire hydrants—he'd written some of his first poems about that girl. He also had a lot of old comic books, including these things called *Classics Illustrated*—comic renditions of great novels—and some of those were worth something now, or so he'd learned online, and if they'd been worth something twenty years ago, he undoubtedly would have sold *them* for drugs. And then there were things that, even at his most desperate, he would never have *considered* selling, he valued them so highly. One was a book by Bukowski and signed by the poet himself after a reading Jim had attended. Another was a copy of *Howl* with a personal note from Allen Ginsberg. He used to be friendly with Ginsberg, he told me now for the first time, when he was in ROT and Ginsberg was singing for another punk band in San Francisco. I said, "I didn't know he did that!"

"Yeah, what were they called? Was it...? No, can't think of it. Anyway, they weren't very good, but it was still *Ginsberg,* you know, and I was so enamored of the Beats, I'd let him think he could blow me just to keep him talking. Very nice guy. Bukowski—he seemed like kind of a prick, but Ginsberg was a real sweetheart."

"Yeah, I met him myself one time."

"Really. He must have loved *you*."

"He liked both of us. I met him with Peewee, and he did come on a little bit, but not in a sleazy way. He was just like you said: really warm, really approachable."

Meantime my tape was still playing in the background. I asked him to take it off and play his own music, and he said he would, but he didn't. He just went again to his closet and took down a cardboard box packed with more stuff: fliers and zines and clippings of the band and photos of old friends and girlfriends, including Cybil. She was Asian, which was something else he'd never told me, and he lingered especially over one shot of her lying topless in bed. God, he kept saying, she was so beautiful, and it seemed like he wanted me to say it too, so I did, even though I didn't find her attractive at all. Then he stood and said he was going to get a beer, and I said, "Hey, you told me if I drove out you'd play me some songs!"

"And I'm going to."

"When?"

"As soon as I get a beer."

But even after he returned from the kitchen with a couple of beers—the second was for me—all he did was show me more stuff: drawings he'd drawn and notebooks filled with lyrics and high-school yearbooks with photos of himself and Buddy and Gary. And it was all very interesting, but I was sure it was smoke and mirrors; I was sure he had nothing to play for me and never had. Finally I said as much, and he said, "No, I do. But it's very different from Rule of Thumb, very, and some of it's not complete, and you know how it is with works in progress. If you don't like it, I might develop a block."

"Oh, come on, just *play* it. I'm not going to say anything."

Then he sat at his desk and turned on one of his computers, but every time he clicked on a file, he'd click it off a second later. Not that song. He hated that song. He hated that one too. Then he clicked on something and turned away, as if he couldn't bear to see my reaction, and I heard his voice count off through the speakers and, a moment later, an acoustic guitar and his singing voice, which now sounded a bit like Leonard Cohen's. The fucker had gone folkie on me! Yet, in a way, I wasn't surprised at all. It was a natural progression from the gentler sound of *Tinderloin*; he'd just slowed the tempo and stripped away everything but the essentials. And it was fucking beautiful; his gift for melody had improved with time. That song was every bit as good as the best of Nick Drake, who's the king of acoustic music, or maybe that's Elliott Smith. And the lyrics were beautiful as well, and they vaguely told a story of a man who walks the streets at night to peer through windows and so catch glimpses of family life denied him. The lyrics weren't complete—in some spots he was clearly improvising—and before the song had finished playing, he clicked it off and said, "Pretty corny, huh?"

"Are you out of your fucking mind? It's great!"

"You really think so?"

"Yes!"

"You're not just saying that?"

"No! You ought to put it out right now! Even if you never finished the words, that thing could break your fucking heart!"

And suddenly he was brimming with confidence. He had a lot of ideas on ways to improve it, he said. For instance, he wanted to add some bells; and he played the song a second time, and whenever he came to a spot where a bell would go, he'd make the sound with his voice—"Ding!"—and he was dead right: it would've sounded great. Then he played me other songs, all very similar, all with haunting melodies, and most about lonely people at night. One was called "Fluorescent Light," and for that he wanted backing vocals but using a different voice. He asked if I'd do it, and I said, "Me? I don't know, man. I haven't sung in years."

"No, all you'd have to do is hum. Here, I'll show you what I mean." Then he played it again, asking me to hum along, and once again he was dead right: it really added something. He said he'd like to record me, and he set up a mic and gave me some headphones. A few takes later we listened to the playback, and I said, "You know what this could use? You know those chiming guitars on 'Raft at Sea'? You ought to add something like that in there."

"Well, let's try it out." Then he plugged in the Jaguar and tried to play "Raft at Sea," and here he'd written the fucking thing and couldn't remember how it went. I could. I took his guitar and tried to work out a variation we could use on "Fluorescent Light," and he picked up the Vantage, playing along, and soon we were jamming away. I hadn't done that in over a decade, and, man, was it satisfying. How could I ever have left music? And I could see he was loving it too. Oh yes, you stubborn fuck, it was written all over your fat white face, which suddenly didn't look so fat anymore. No, for as long as you played, it was positively beautiful.

Then his mom knocked on the door and said she was back from the mall with some KFC. Jim asked if I was hungry, and I was; so we went in the dining room, where his mom had put my flowers in a vase in the center of the table, and she was actually nice for a change. Jim had told her quite a bit about me. She knew about Irina, the fact that she was married, and said I should really watch myself, what with that and her being an actress.

"I know all about *them*," she said. "I used to do hair at Fox."

"Yeah, Eddie mentioned something about that."

Like him, she liked to gossip. She told me some funny stories about the stars she used to work with, including Marilyn Monroe, whom she described as "not really *there*, you know what I mean?" She said she used to dye Jim's hair, back when he had some, and he said, "Fuck you," and she said, "Now, Eddie, you know that's not nice." But she didn't seem bothered by it. How could she be? She heard it every day of her life. And Jim was wolfing down that chicken like Henry VIII, and the dog was having a feast as well, gobbling up the table scraps Jim's mom kept feeding it. No wonder it was so fat! No wonder *Jim* was so fat! Both he and his mom had cigarettes burning at the table, and both were drinking beer; and usually by this hour Jim was either drunk or halfway there, but tonight he wasn't, and I realized why: he was having too much fun. We went back to his room after we finished eating and jammed some more, and he wasn't kidding about the Vantage: every fifteen minutes he had to stop to retune it. Then he broke a string, and by then it was at least ten o'clock, and I told him I should go, but he kept trying to stall me, just as he'd do on the phone. He showed me still more stuff, including his poetry, some of which he read out loud, and I liked one poem so much I asked him for a copy, and, flattered, he went to his computer and printed one. The title probably explains my enthusiasm. The poem was called "The Only Living Witness."

> For just a second
> there's the sound of laughter.
> No voices before or after.
> Just a short burst
> as if a ghost had told a joke
> as it dealt a final hand
> of midnight poker.
>
> A leaf is crushed
> by a foot without a leg.
> A car drives by without a driver.
> A dog owned by nobody
> barks at a shadow
> it never saw.
>
> It only happened
> if somebody says it did.
> But who can that somebody be?
> I am the only living witness
> listening at this hour.
> And lost inside its thoughts
> my head never heard
> the sound my fingers made
> as they were typing out these words.

THEN HE STARTED PLAYING RECORDS. Not records he'd made himself. He wanted me to hear some new stuff by other people, and some older stuff too, including a kind of Portuguese folk song called the Fado. That Fado singing was phenomenal, almost like opera, something the singers must have trained for years to do. By then it must have been midnight, and once again I said I should go, but he said, "Hey, weren't we going to watch your movie?"

"Yeah, but you can keep that tape and watch it later."

Well, somehow I ended up watching it with him. His mom watched part of it with us, and she talked the whole time, going, "Is that the same girl? She doesn't look the same. Her *hair's* different." It drove me fucking nuts! Jim kept telling her to shut up, and finally she went to bed, and once Jim had heard himself sing "Raft at Sea" over the final shot and credits, he said he was blown away. What a talent I was! He had no idea. Now he had something he wanted to show *me* (naturally), and he went to his bedroom and came back a few minutes later with a video of Rule of Thumb playing at San Francisco's Mabuhay Gardens in 1978. It wasn't done by amateurs. Apparently there used to be a company that produced a slew of similar videos, so the show was shot with several cameras and sometimes intercut with, for instance, footage of Russian soldiers goosestepping as Jim sang "Lockstep," or, during "Big Sur," home movies of the California coastline shot in the fifties through the windshield of a moving car—an oddly poetic juxtaposition. And I thought the band was outstanding; I was finally seeing ROT as I hadn't at CBGB's all those years before, and here was Jim in his prime: pre-Cybil, pre-junkie, 100 pounds lighter and all his hair intact. It was so sad to go from that to the aging marshmallow beside me. Then the video finished and Jim got us a beer, and by then it must have been four in the morning, and the old lady was shouting for him to go to bed, and he shouted back and so on. He tried to get me to stick around for another beer, but I said, "No, man, I've really got to go," and he walked me to the door and said, "Damn, Jason, I'm *so* glad you drove out. I can't remember the last time I had so much fun!"

"A lot better than talking on the phone, huh?"

"I feel like I really got to know you."

"Same here."

We promised we'd do it again sometime, and I got in my car, and all the way home I thought about this tour of his life he'd taken me on, and, basically, I was back to liking him. He really had been prolific during his "missing" years—not quite as prolific as he'd made himself out to be, but, no question, he really had something to show for himself. And he'd been so alive when he was playing music, and he'd written these gorgeous songs and poems, and it was obvious he was dying to share it all. And I wanted to help him share it—but how?

Well, a few nights later I had dinner with my friend Paul Bertolette at a French restaurant called Frères Taix. It's an old place in Echo Park, with private rooms where businessmen held (and perhaps still hold) company get-togethers, and a large bar area with three TVs affixed to the walls, each tuned to a different sporting event—*une touche pour les Américains stupides.* Paul was always going there. He had a regular night with friends from the movie business, and every so often I'd join him, though his friends bored me. They were all postproduction types who jabbered about movies from a tech-geek point of view, and they always sat at the same table beside the bar and ordered the same food: the ten-dollar bistro steak, with calamari beforehand and pineapple sherbet for dessert. And this night was the same as any other—endless talk of Avid crashes and telecine transfers and CGI—when I looked across the room and saw a scrawny kid setting up a PA beneath the main television. I asked Paul what was going on, and he said, "Oh, they're trying to attract a younger crowd, so they started doing a music night." Then the lights dimmed and the kid sat behind the mic with an acoustic guitar and performed a bleeding-heart song, and practically nobody was there, and the few who were weren't listening. Paul and his friends left as soon as he started playing, but I hung around and watched the whole set, as well as a set by a second kid who got up and played still more acoustic songs that weren't a fraction as good as Jim's. Almost nobody showed up to see him, and, as with the first kid, those who did barely paid attention. I sought out the manager and asked how he went about booking musicians, and he said it was open mic: all you had to do was sign the list and a spot was guaranteed.

I drove home and called Jim and told him all about this place. It was the perfect way to start over, I said—he wouldn't have to audition, and nobody came or cared—and he said, "Well, I can't do that. I can't even leave the house. You know that."

"Yeah, but you leave the house sometimes."

"Only when I'm with my mom."

"Well, she can come too. And I'll drive, how's that? In fact, if you want, I'll play *with* you. I mean, I haven't played in a long time myself, but this place—it's almost like playing by yourself."

But he said he couldn't possibly do it, that he'd freak out for sure; the worst panic attacks he ever had came when he used to perform. I said, "Yeah, but that's exactly why you should do it! If you can get up there and play one song—"

"But I can't."

"No, you just *think* you can't. I just saw you the other day, and I don't think you realize how much you love music, and for someone like that—it's not *right* to shut yourself away. Are you going to do this for the rest of your life? You're only forty-five years old! And weren't you just telling me that people are going to start living to a hundred and twenty? That's an awful lot of time to fill."

"Oh, that won't be a problem. Not in the shape I'm in."

"Yeah, and whose fault is that? And by the way, man, your mom is really getting up there. What are you going to do when she dies? Or what if she gets sick and you have to take care of her? It's going to happen, you know. How are you going to take care of either one of you if you can't even leave the house?"

"Oh, I'm not worried about that. She'll bury all of us."

"And what if she doesn't?"

"Well, then, she won't. But I don't see what that has to do with me playing in some French restaurant. I mean, thanks for the thought, but no thanks."

So, fine, be an ostrich. I don't give a fuck. Yet the next time we spoke, *he* was the one who raised the subject of playing. He said he'd been listening to the recording we made, the one with me humming, and it sounded so good, and he'd found our jam so inspiring, and he wished he *could* get up and play, but he knew he couldn't.

"It's hard to explain to somebody who's never had a panic attack," he said. "It's not just feeling nervous. You really feel like you're going to die, and you almost wish you would, it's so terrifying." I thought, "Well, maybe he's right," and after we hung up, I went online to research panic attacks, and Jim's description was borne out by every firsthand account I read. People mentioned palpitations, vertigo, a sense of impending doom. One site said the only thing that worked was years of therapy, and a second site discounted therapy in favor of medication; but Jim had said numerous times that he'd tried both, and neither had worked. I also read a personality profile of the kind of people prone to agoraphobia, and it sounded like Jim: overthinkers who responded to stress like children, and who typically relied on a sole caretaker to help them get around. In Jim's case that was his mother, of course, but what was *she* getting out of it? But wasn't it obvious? There she was, seventy years old, with no apparent friends and no family, apart from Jim, so as long as he stayed an overgrown houseplant, she knew she was never going to want for company. It explained her rudeness to Jim's visitors, rare though they were. Yes, she eventually warmed to me, but she'd been so cold when she opened the door, so frightened somebody was going to take her baby away from her. She'd even attacked Buddy with a chair! How could Jim live with himself, having a seventy-year-old woman fight his battles for him? He couldn't. So he drank and smoked, and she drank and smoked alongside him, and basically tended to his every need in order to keep him close. Yet every single site I came across agreed on one thing: this disorder was definitely treatable. It might take a while, and you might never fully recover, but a lot of people did and went on to lead satisfying, productive lives. One site promised results relatively quickly, and I liked what it had to say: you had to "welcome" the fear; you had to be willing to pass through it and come out the other side. That's what I'd done when I started driving after the accident. I'd tense every time I climbed in a car, knowing the damage a car could do, but I *made* myself drive and gradually came to relax; and Jim's problem was that nobody was making him do a goddamned thing, least of all his mother.

I sent him a link to that website. He didn't respond, so I called him and yelled at him, and *that* produced results: he called back a few hours later to say, yeah, he checked it out, but he'd done all that stuff, and it never got him anywhere. I said, "Well, it doesn't happen right away. It's like they say on the site: it happens one step at a time."

"They don't know what they're talking about."

"What do you *mean*, they don't know what they're talking about? That site was put up by former agoraphobics! And they've got a book and tapes and a support group and a whole program."

"It's just a scam, that's all it is. It's just a way to pry two hundred bucks out of desperate people."

"And you're not desperate?"

"I'm fine."

"You are *not* fine, you fucking idiot! You need help! And if you're too cheap to spend two hundred dollars to get it, *I'll* fucking pay, how's that?"

"Why would you do something like that?"

"Because. Your band meant a lot to me, and I had a great time the other day, and maybe if you get better, you won't call me so fucking much. I mean, don't get me wrong. It's been very entertaining in a lot of ways. But I think you need other people in your life, not just me, and I don't care how 'predictable' you think they are; the way you're living is unnatural. So I'm going to go online and send for that shit, and when it comes, you've got to promise you're going to use it."

"I can't let you do that."

"Well, I'm fucking doing it."

"No," he said, "*I'll* send for it. I know it's a waste of money, but I guess it's like you say: it can't hurt to try."

Then he said he had something to play for me. He'd never once played me a song over the phone, but now he did, and it was based on the jam we did together. I'd co-written a song with Jim Cassady! I wish Peewee could've heard it. But, then again, he'd have been so jealous.

Beloved,

Yesterday I wrapped. It was so nice, everyone clapped for me, but I don't think I was very good. David says I'm fine and he'll make something in the editing I'm happy with but I think next to the other actors I'm going to look terrible!! But I've learned a lot by watching them so that's good. It hasn't been easy because Chad and David have been fighting a lot and David is very tired, I think this movie has broken him. He still wants me to stay and I think I will for a couple of days because I've made friends with so many people on the crew. I want to see my family before I go and then I'll have to go back to Prague to fly to LA. My friend Maja has written to say she needs a roommate so I think I will probably move in with her. She lives in Hollywood near the Scientology mansion and Bourgeois Pig. There is always a lot of activity there and I know Maja's apartment so I think this will work out very well. I'm not so happy about returning. Although I don't like Prague so much I know it's better than LA and I think after a week it will hit me where I am. But I'm starting a new life so this is exciting and I want very much to see you, of course!! I wish you didn't have to make such difficult choices in life. I like things about Belgrade but there's no future there and I don't like LA but that's where all my chances are. Why can't the two come together?

I will write or call you as soon as I know when I'm returning. I should know soon. I'm going to the production office now to sign some things and find out what can be done with my ticket.

XXX

ALL DURING IRINA'S STAY IN PRAGUE, I spoke with her on the phone maybe five times. They were brief conversations for the most part. She couldn't talk with David around, and I couldn't because of the cost, so we sent a lot of e-mails, and those grew shorter as time went on, but I knew she was busy, and there was nothing in the tone of her writing or the sound of her voice that made me think she might be fooling around. I didn't want to come out and ask, wanting to show how trusting I could be, and she always told me she loved me and missed me, and so convincingly I never had a reason to doubt her. I did note her apprehension about returning to L.A., but if I'd been in Europe, I knew I would have felt the same way. The last e-mail she sent was the one above on March 5th, and maybe a week later the phone rang and I saw the word PRIVATE on my caller ID. I picked up. "Surprise!" she said.

"You're back?!"

"Yes, last night."

"Why didn't you call me?! I would've driven out to the airport to pick you up!"

"Well, it was so late, and the production company had a car waiting, so I just went home and slept. And this morning—oh my God, there's so much mail! It's going to take me days to go through it all. And my cat—I don't know what's wrong with her. I think I'm going to have to take her to the vet."

"So when am I going to see you?"

"Well, Maja just called, and she wants me to come over to talk about the apartment. I wrote you about that, yes?"

"Yeah, sounds perfect."

"So that's what I'm supposed to do right now. But I can come to your place as soon as I'm done with her."

I told her that sounded great, I couldn't wait to see her, and she said she couldn't wait to see me. I showered and shaved and straightened the house, counting the seconds till she got there. Then I heard footsteps coming up my stairs, and there she was. She'd cut a few inches off her hair and rinsed it with henna, whereas I'd loved it the old way, but who cared about that?! She flew into my arms, and I held her and kissed her and said, "Goddamnit, don't you *ever* go running off to the other side of the world again. Not unless I'm with you."

"I know, I know. I feel the same way."

She'd brought me a present: a bottle of Yugoslav brandy called *šljivovica*. We opened it and toasted her homecoming, and she sat on my lap in the living room and showed me snapshots she'd taken on the set. Here was the gaffer, very funny guy. And here was Astrid, and here was the cameraman, and here was David on the brink of a nervous breakdown. Poor David. And there were pictures of the cast, and pictures of locals recruited as extras, and pictures of Irina in makeup and costume, looking almost like Gene Tierney. But there were no pictures of Belgrade, and I was curious about that place; I wanted to see what her friends and family looked like. Oh, she said, she had stacks and stacks of Belgrade pictures she could show me later. There were also no pictures of her apartment in Prague, as I pointed out, and she said, "You know, I thought I'd taken some, but I guess I didn't. It was really beautiful, but it drove me crazy."

"How so?"

"The pigeons. I mentioned that, didn't I?"

"I don't think so."

"Well, out in the hall there was a broken window, and these pigeons would fly in and make this noise. It sounded like an old car, you know, like the engine won't start, this '*whirrrr, whirrrr.*' And it was really loud, and sometimes I had to work till five in the morning, and the next day I'd be trying to sleep and those pigeons were out in the hall making that noise. And then I realized what it was. Because every time I saw them, it was always two, and one was always chasing the other, and I realized that was the male and the other was a female, and that noise—it's something he does to impress her. That's why it's so loud. It's like, 'See what a big noise I make? See me strutting around? Don't you want to sleep with me?'"

"Like a guy in a band."

She laughed. "Something like that."

"So you want me to make a big noise? Should I strut around?"

"No, I think you've impressed me enough."

Then we started kissing again, and she slipped off to the bathroom to insert her diaphragm—can't forget that! She was pensive after we made love, and told me what she'd told me many times already in e-mails and over the phone, that it was hard being away from me, especially after what she'd been through in Belgrade. She was still having dreams about that. In one of them, she recounted, she was walking down the street when she saw a deformed person begging for change.

"This is something you see in Belgrade," she said, "soldiers without their legs asking for money. So I went to give him something, and then I realized he was a child, *our* child, and as soon as I thought that, he reached out to grab me and wouldn't let go. He kept trying to say something, but he couldn't, there was something wrong with his face; and I kept trying to get away, but it was like I was paralyzed."

"Sounds horrible."

"It was. I must really feel guilty, to have a dream like that. You know, the day I made the appointment, I was standing on the street and this woman with a baby came up beside me, and he was so cute—I just wanted to eat him, he was so cute! And I hadn't been thinking about what our baby would look like, but then I did, and it made me feel so bad, you know. Here was this child I was going to get rid of, and I was never going to know the first thing about it."

"I had thoughts like that."

"You did?"

"Of course. I never dreamed about it, but sure, I wondered what our kid would be like. How could you not?"

Then she started crying. She was so sorry, she said, and I told her it wasn't her fault, she'd done the right thing, but that wasn't what she was sorry about. Oh yes, she was sorry about that too, but there was something else; and all at once, saying it so fast it took a few seconds to fully sink in, she told me she'd been sleeping with David for the last few weeks.

"I'm sorry," she sobbed. "It was just one of those things, you know? I was depressed, and David was having all these problems with the movie, and—I don't know—it just happened."

"Nothing 'just happens' if it happens more than once. You should've told me right away!"

"But I was afraid to! I was afraid you'd say it was over! And I love you, and I don't love David—not *that* way. I just needed somebody, you know?"

I literally felt like I'd been stabbed in the heart. I *knew* she was going to do something like this, and she'd gone ahead and done it after all that talk of trust and her sexless marriage and David being *much* too preoccupied with the movie to pay any attention to her. What they'd done sexually was almost beside the point. No, what really hurt and angered me was her sweet talk on the phone and her e-mails with their Beloveds and Miss yous and XXXs, while the whole time she was sleeping with somebody else, and then coming back and getting me in just the right mood before letting me have it. Guess what? I've been sleeping with David for the last few weeks. But I don't love him, not that way; I just *needed* somebody. What the hell was that supposed to mean? And when I asked her, she stabbed me again. She'd badly wanted to be with me, she said, but I hadn't been there.

"But I *offered* to fly out, and you told me no. And—what?—that gives you the right to fuck somebody else? I felt bad too, and guess who *I* had for company? My hand, that's who. I didn't go off and have an affair."

"But, Jason, I was too depressed to think the right way! And David was falling apart, and we just have this history, you know?"

"Uh-huh. And where was I?"

"You were here," she said, baffled.

"No, in your *head*. Where was I in your *head*? How could you call me and write me all that shit when you were sleeping with that guy the whole time?"

"But I meant every word of it! I *do* love you! He wanted me to stay longer, but I didn't. I'm here with *you* now."

"Yeah, and so's your diaphragm. Did you take *that* with you?" Which was something that suddenly came to me, and as soon as I said it, she was caught off-guard, so that I could see it on her face: busted! She knew I'd seen it too and fumbled through an excuse. It just happened to be in her purse, she said. She hadn't taken it with a plan in mind; it was simply a habit.

"Well," I said, "you didn't have it the first time we slept together. You didn't have it that night at the motel either."

"Yes, but I usually do. You know that. I had it every other time."

"Yeah, because those other times you knew something was going to happen."

"Yes, but I thought—I don't know *what* I thought, but I definitely didn't think I was going to sleep with David. He knows I'm leaving. He's known it for months."

"But you *haven't* left him. Not really. And I bet even after all that, you never even told him what's going on, did you? You slept with him and never told him you're sleeping with somebody else who got you pregnant. *If* that was my kid."

"Of course it was yours."

"Well, how do *I* know that? If you lied to me about all this, how do I know everything out of your mouth isn't a lie? I don't know, maybe you're too young. Or maybe you've been playing games with other people so long you think you can play them with me. Well, you can't. I'm not David. I'm an American—the old-fashioned kind of American that doesn't fuck around!"

"Oh yes, you've never done that. After some of the stories you told me!"

"That isn't the kind of fucking around I mean. And don't you try and turn the tables. You get on the phone right this second and tell David what's going on. And I mean *everything,* Irina. You burn your bridges with David, and maybe then I'll forgive you."

"Thank you so much, Your Highness."

"So I guess that means no."

"*Yes*, it means no! I'll tell him when I think it's the right time. And you have no right to tell me what to do!"

"And I never did before now. You told me to trust you, and I did, and this is what I got for it. And you know *why* you don't want to burn your bridges? Because you don't want to leave him, and you never did. And you know what else? I bet even if you called him and told him about me, he'd take you right back. That's why you don't want to leave him: because you know he's always going to let you get away with *murder*."

Then she got out of bed and snatched up her clothes and started getting dressed. That was another horrible thing about that fight: we were both naked, with all the body parts we'd just used to make love stripped of any power to excite. Plus she was wearing that cross I'd given her. I told her I'd love to be alone with her and David sometime, that maybe then I could figure out what their deal was, and she said, "There *is* no deal. We're finished, but you don't seem to believe me."

"Then *make* me believe you."

"No, I told you before, I'm not going to do that. I tell you things, things from the heart, and you twist them around to make me look *awful*. You have no idea what I went through. You never had to lie there while some—*machine*—sucks a baby out of your body. I'm never going to forget that sound as long as I live. I really get away with murder, don't I? Well, I *didn't*!"

Then she started crying again—in fact, she fairly collapsed—salty tears, trembling hands, the works. And I'd long since realized I'd *tried* get her pregnant, so to sit there taking the high ground—I felt like a hypocrite to do it. I went to her and tried to calm her, and, sobbing, she pushed me away. Then she finally let me hold her, and somehow we made love all over again.

THEN WE TALKED. We talked for hours about us and the abortion and everything she'd done with David. The first time she described as a kind of mercy fuck, though she didn't use that expression. She was trying to console him after an especially difficult day on the set, and while she was racked with guilt about me afterward, she also felt strangely relieved, a sense of life returning to her, a sense of solace. From there, she said, it was hard to say no when he came to her again. It had nothing to do with rekindling her feelings for him. No, she swore, it was just the opposite, as if every time they made love she was secretly saying goodbye. And now in that way her goodbyes had been said, and she promised she would tell him about us as soon as he got back, though in certain ways she was dreading the consequences. For instance, her car was technically his, so she'd have to return it to him and buy a car of her own. In fact, she wasn't going to ask him for any form of settlement, which I thought foolish and a sign of character both at once. We also discussed her moving in with me, but she thought that was rushing things; and we even talked about having kids, though not for a few years. In the past she hadn't been sure if she wanted kids; now she knew she did, though I pointed out that dream of hers was like saying any child she had with me would be some mutilated bum holding her down in the gutter. She said, "Oh, Jason, it was just a *dream*. And I had *other* dreams." And she described another one in which we'd been married on a cloud so green it looked like a field of clover—that was optimistic, right? All she wanted was to be with me, she assured me again and again, and now she was going to prove it.

Well, the next day she went off to feed her cat (whom she jokingly called Fufica: it means "little bitch"), and she came back and said, "I've been thinking. David's going to be gone for at least two weeks, and I can stay at his house for free, and if I move in with Maja, I'll be spending all that money for nothing." I said, "What, you're not going to move now?"

"No, I am. But maybe I should wait till the beginning of April."

It sounded like she was trying to stall for different reasons altogether, but she swore she wasn't; and just to make good and sure she moved, I told her I'd help—in fact, I insisted. I drove her around for a couple of days, collecting boxes, and she called a Serbian friend named Uroš, who owned a pickup truck, and he and I moved the heavier stuff to Maja's place near the corner of Franklin and Bronson. The apartment itself was less than beautiful, with beige walls and snot-green carpeting, but Irina's room was spacious and sunny, and Maja struck me as a likable girl who'd probably make a good roommate. She knew about us, but she was sworn to secrecy, since, again, Irina wanted the whole thing kept quiet till she'd broken the news to David, afraid he'd learn through gossip. Plus she was afraid of looking like a slut. She really had a thing about that. Almost every time we fought (and we would soon be fighting a lot), that was something bound to come up: "Are you calling me a whore? Are you calling me a *sponzoruša*?" I guess so many people had implied she was one, it was kind of a sore point. After all, she'd raced a rich guy down the aisle within days of her twentieth birthday and barely worked since. Plus, of course, she was a notorious flirt.

In any case, except for Maja, she didn't want people knowing. Yet at least one person was already starting to get suspicious. A few days after moving to Maja's, Irina threw a housewarming party, and it was mostly Serbs, including Milan, who at one point took me aside and said, "What is going on with you and Irina?"

"Nothing. We're just friends, that's all. Why?"

But he wouldn't say if he'd seen or heard something. He just smiled a wise smile and said, "You know, Irina—I love her very much, but she plays her game with men, you know. She does this for a long time with me, but then I realize nothing will happen. And she does this with many others—some right here."

I couldn't help myself: I asked if she'd ever slept with any of them.

"Of course not," he laughed. "This is her game, you know. She makes you think she will, but she never does. She is very faithful to David. I don't know why she pretends she is leaving him. She'll go back to him in the end, you'll see."

And it worried me, but at the same time it didn't. Because she *wasn't* faithful to David. On the other hand, she hadn't been faithful to me either, but I had to believe that was all the past. And, yes, she'd hesitated before moving out, but she *had* moved out, and everything aside from her lapse with David just screamed she loved me. And, frankly, there were times when I wondered why she did. She could have had any man she wanted, but she'd chosen *me*. Yet I also knew we had a lot in common. We were both reflective people who were likewise spontaneous—typically, it's one or the other. We'd both had lives marked by tragedy; we had similar taste in art and music; and, no question, we had great sex—in fact, I would later decide that was *all* we had in common. Stubborn, stormy, moody, and driven: those words could equally apply to both of us. Then again, we were both romantics; but where I almost always went for broke, Irina hedged her bets. That's where the fissure lay.

But it was finally a mystery, whatever it was that brought us together. We came from such different worlds, but that was never a problem, just as I never felt much of an age difference. Maybe that doesn't speak so well for my level of maturity, but if growing up means what most people seem to think it does—collecting cobwebs in a state of complacency—I'll stay young and immature, thanks. Besides, Serbs didn't seem as judgmental about age as most Americans do. At Irina's party there were people as young as sixteen and as old as fifty, but they all mixed easily, and after midnight one of them broke out a guitar, and the whole crowd but me sang Serbian folk songs. Even having been a musician for six years, I'd never once seen a real-life, non-church sing-along. But I think such things used to happen all the time. I think that's why families used to make a point of owning a parlor piano: that and the dining room were the two places where everybody came together. And now families often eat in shifts, and nobody shares the same songs, except for the national anthem, and most Americans don't know the words to that anyway, past the first few.

ONCE IRINA GOT BACK FROM PRAGUE, there were no longer so many talks with Jim on the phone. Most of my free time was taken up with her, but I had no reason to worry about Jim, who'd found a new way of keeping himself entertained. I could hardly believe it when he told me this, but he'd actually spent 200 bucks on that agoraphobia program, and though he shrugged off their recovery book and the self-hypnosis tapes that went with it, there was one part of the program he liked a lot: the support group. Apparently, as soon as you joined, you were put in touch with others in the same area with the same problem, and if you'd just had a panic attack, or you felt like you were going to, you could call one of them to commiserate. But that wasn't *all* that might happen. It turned out women especially are prone to panic attacks—housebound women; women who don't get out to meet men but still have certain needs, if you see where I'm headed. That's right: Jim was having phone sex with agoraphobic chicks. He had two semi-regular partners, I was told, but his favorite was a freelance writer named Nancy, who ranked herself an "eight" on the program's ten-point scale of recovery. (Jim ranked himself a "two.") He said she was divorced with a teenaged son, and she was obviously sort of a "square," but he'd impressed her so much by reading his poetry, she now wanted to meet him in person. But no *way* was he going to let that happen. She'd take one look and no more phone sex. Besides, he was afraid to see her too.

"I think she's fat," he said. "She won't send me her picture and she's mentioned being on a diet a couple of times, so I think we're talking Godzilla here."

"Well, come on, you're not exactly Brad Pitt. And you never know. She might *like* fat old fucks who don't have a job and live with their mother."

"Well, even if I wanted to meet her, I couldn't. She lives way over in Atwater Village, and there's no way I could get there without having a panic attack. I *told* you this program was a bunch of bullshit."

"Well, it worked for Nancy. How'd she get to be an eight?"

She wore a rubber band, he said. Every time she went out, she always had one around her wrist, and if she felt any of what the program called pre-panic panic—or PPP—she'd reach down and give it a snap that shocked her system, or something, and the panic went away. She'd encouraged Jim to wear one too, but he said that wasn't necessary, since he no longer *had* panic attacks. I know, it confused me too; but the way he explained it, he'd arranged his life in recent years so that all triggers of potential attacks had been eliminated. I said, "Well, how do you know you're still agoraphobic? Maybe you're cured and you don't even know it."

"No, I've been through this before. I'll think I'm better, and then I'll go out and something will happen to cause another attack."

"Well, so what? Why don't you go out tomorrow someplace you've never been before and see what happens? Without your mom, I mean. Or, here, why don't I drop by this weekend and take you someplace?"

But of course he told me no, so I dropped the subject. A little later, however, I happened to mention that Irina was now living in Hollywood near the Scientology mansion, and he said, "Oh, I used to live around there. That's where I lived with Cybil. God, I haven't been around that neighborhood in years." And the second he said that, I thought, *Of course! That's where it started, right there!* Because he'd mentioned many times that it was in the final days of ROT when he'd gotten so nervous he could barely perform, and by no small coincidence, that's when Cybil had killed herself. Plus I remembered something from my own past. I'd lost consciousness at the time of the accident and so recalled nothing of the site. I used to have nightmares about that place. I saw it stacked with body parts and burning wreckage; bloody zombies stumbling around. Then, after my grandmother died the following year,

Suzanne and I drove to North Carolina for the funeral, and she insisted on stopping at the scene of the accident, and it was really nothing: a few bland houses on a woodsy stretch of road and a stump where the offending tree had stood. (My lawyer later told me the tree had been removed not because it was badly damaged but, rather, in deference to the awful night it symbolized.) Birds sang. Lawnmowers hummed. A feeling of peace came over me. We gathered some flowers and left them there, and I drove away feeling I'd turned a corner, as indeed I had. The nightmares stopped. I gave myself permission to enjoy life, as I hadn't fully before. And I was willing to bet Jim had *never* been back to the building where Cybil had killed herself, not since the day he found her dead, and if he ever did go back, it might spark a new beginning for him. I was very sure of myself, very excited by the plan that now came to me. I knew Jim would never comply if I mentioned what I had in mind. I just said I'd drop by on Saturday, and maybe, if he wanted, we could drive to L.A. afterward and have dinner with Irina. He was noncommittal—he'd have to see how he felt on Saturday—and then I ran my plan past Irina, who wanted no part of it. She said she was repulsed by Jim and couldn't understand why I'd waste five seconds on him, except she also knew why: I was trying to bring back Peewee, as if a guy as "creepy" as Jim was any kind of substitute for a "beautiful soul" like Peewee. And, do you know, it was such an obvious thing, but until she said that, I had honestly never considered it. Not that I think she was altogether right. I think I had a number of motives per my dealings with Jim, and so far as they concerned Peewee, it wasn't a matter of bringing him back, it was more a matter of settling a debt. He and Jim had a few similarities—the stage fright, mostly—but Peewee had become a bold performer by the time he died at twenty-two, and here was Jim, now in his forties and still struggling with the same old crap and wasting his talent because of it.

    At any rate, Irina refused to have Jim over. Not that I was going to let *that* stop me. I drove out to Rancho Cucamonga on Saturday, and it was all very much like my previous visit: Jim and I jammed, his mom served junk food, and the whole time he barely drank, he was having so much fun. I knew Irina wasn't going to be around—she and Maja had theater tickets—but I told Jim she was expecting us for dinner, and having thus lured him into my car, I was going to drive him around Hollywood till he pointed to the building where Cybil joined the ages, and a big catharsis later, he'd waste his talent no more. He seemed open to going when I got there, but then, around seven o'clock, I said, "Come on, let's hit the road," and he looked like he'd just found a cockroach in his candy bar and said, "I don't think I can do it."

"Of course you can. It's just Irina's. And I'm driving, and we really aren't going to stay that long. We'll just have a bite to eat and come right back."

"Yeah, but she makes me nervous."

"Oh, come on, she's just a girl. And she's really excited about seeing you again, and you don't want to disappoint her, do you?"

Well, it took quite some doing, but he finally agreed to go. First, though, he wanted to change his clothes. His mom was in the living room watching *Wheel of Fortune,* and I told her I was taking him to my girlfriend's place, bracing myself for the shit sure to come. But there was no shit. In fact, he took so long to get ready, she started yelling for him to hurry up! So what do you know about that? I might have the old bag all wrong! Then he finally walked out in the same clothes, except for a pair of shoes (he'd been barefoot before) and a long, dark raincoat like something out of a film noir. He walked right past us on his way to the kitchen and came back with a beer and sat and drank it. I said, "What are you *doing*? We've got to go!"

"I've got to have something to drink first."

But as soon as he finished that beer, he went to get another. I said, "Come on, man, you can have all the beer you want when you get there."

"I'm not going."

"What do you *mean*, you're not going? You just told me you were! Do you know how long I've been waiting here? If you weren't going to go, you should've just told me!"

His mom said the same thing, but all he did was stand there. I gave up. I fairly stomped to the door and turned to give him a final look of disgust, and he kind of sighed and said, "Well, okay. If you want me to go that bad, I'll go. But let me get something for the road." Then he went to the kitchen again, followed this time by his mom, and I heard them talk for a couple of minutes, but I couldn't make out their words. I was afraid she'd changed her tune and was now trying to get him to stay; but then he returned alone with his pockets bulging with cans of beer and followed me out to the street. My car seemed to sink a foot lower the second he climbed inside. Plus he lit up right away, and I've got a thing about smoking in the car, and his B.O. was inescapable in a small, confined space like that one. But, hey, at least he was going. He barely said a word at first, and I drove carefully to keep him calm, but he'd also started drinking beer, so I drove carefully for that reason too, not wanting to attract the attention of a kindly cop. We got on the freeway. I asked how he was holding up. Well, he said—surprisingly so. He loosened up and talked more. I told him about Irina, how she'd slept with her husband after swearing she wouldn't, and even though things were fine right now, at times I wondered if I was deluding myself. "Well, of course you are," he said.

"Thanks."

"No, I mean love. Love is always a delusion. It's almost a drug in a way. That's what I liked about heroin: it felt like love but better. I mean, at least heroin's dependable."

"Yeah. It dependably kills you."

"Not always. And I think love's a lot more dangerous than heroin. I think more people have probably died because of love than all the drugs and wars and diseases there ever were."

"Including Cybil?" I wanted to ask. But I wasn't about to bring that up. He might start getting suspicious. We got off the 101 at the exit on Cahuenga, and I knew from my conversation with his old friend Michelle the previous year that he'd lived with Cybil somewhere close to that very exit. Sure enough, as we passed Argyle Street, a block or two away, he rubbernecked for a look at something, all his many chins flapping around. But he didn't say anything, and I didn't ask. This had to be handled just right. I drove to Irina's place, where I looked around and said, "That's funny. Her car's not here."

"Are you sure?"

"Yeah, she usually parks right there. Here, let me go see if she's in." Then I got out and rang the buzzer, putting on a whole show, and came back and said, "Man, this is so weird. I wonder where she went?"

"She probably just ran to the store."

"Yeah, you're probably right. Let's just wait till she gets back. I'm sure it won't be very long."

So we sat in the car while he drank and smoked, and soon he gave me exactly the lead I was hoping for. He said, "God, it's so weird, being back here."

"Oh, right, you used to live around here, didn't you?"
"Right by the freeway, yeah. We passed it a few blocks back."
"So how'd it look?"
"The building?"
"Yeah."
"I couldn't see it that well. I could see the top, but that's it."
"You want to go back for another look?"
"No."
"You're not curious?"
"Maybe. But I still don't want to go back."
"Why not?"
"I just don't."
"Well, maybe you should. I mean, I was just in New York, you know, and I went back to the building where I used to live, and I couldn't believe how much it's changed. I rang the buzzer, and the new tenants let me come up for a look around, and we had the greatest time. I was telling them how dangerous it used to be, the junkies and all that, and we all kind laughed about how safe it is now. It was one of the best things I did the whole time I was there."

All of which was a lie. Still, he didn't take the bait. I asked if he was afraid to go back. There was nothing to be afraid of, I said; it was just a building, and it might be good for him to go back.

"How could that possibly be *good*?" he snorted.

"Well, maybe there's something you're holding on to because you think it's still there. But it's not. That was a long time ago."

"Well, I don't care," he said emphatically. "There's some places I wouldn't mind seeing again, but that's not one of them. The worst moments of my life were spent in that place."

I let it drop. Already it seemed I'd said too much. He was acting a bit tense suddenly. I waited a few minutes and said I was starting to worry about Irina and wanted to find a pay phone to call her on her cell. (At the time all I had was a land line.) I started my car and made a left on Franklin, passing a store called Mayfair Market, which undoubtedly did have a pay phone, as Jim now suggested, but I acted like it was too late to turn. A few blocks later we came to a gas station, and Jim said, "They might have one," but I told him I knew they didn't and kept driving. We weren't that far from Argyle, and I was going to hang a right as soon as we got there, pretending to turn around, and hopefully, when he saw the building, he'd notice there was nothing threatening about it and suggest we stop, and maybe we *could* buzz the tenants, who'd buzz us up. But who the fuck was I kidding? Nobody was going to do that in this day and age, and even if they did, how did I know a stop at that place was a step in the right direction? It might even make him worse! The more I thought about it, the more ridiculous my scheme seemed, and Jim was so tense that *I* got tense and blurted out the dumbest thing I could've said. I said, "I hope you're wearing your rubber band."

"What did you say?"

"Nothing."

I could sense him staring at me; I could practically hear the wheels of his mind grinding away, but I kept going while I tried to avoid his eyes. Then we passed another gas station with a goddamned pay phone in plain sight beside it, and he said, "There's one," but I told him I'd tried it before and it didn't work. And we were almost there, maybe two blocks away, and his head was spinning this way and that when he suddenly said, "What do you think you're doing?!"

"Just trying to find a pay phone."

"No, *I* know what you're doing! I know *exactly* what you're doing! Stop the car!"

"I can't stop the car! I'm in the middle of traffic!"

"No," he said, clutching his chest, "you've got to stop it right now! I'm having a heart attack!"

"You're not having a heart attack."

"Yes, I am! I'm having a heart attack! I'm going to die! Oh my God, I'm going to die!"

And I looked over at him and, Jesus Christ, it *did* fucking look like he was going to die! His face was sweaty and sickly white, and for someone as sickly white as he was already, that's saying a lot. He was gasping and groaning with bugged-out eyes, and of course he only smoked two or three packs a day and drank at least a dozen beers, and his father had died of a heart attack when he must have been about Jim's age now. So it really seemed like Jim was going to follow suit, though I tried to assure us both he was only having a panic attack. But he said, "No, it's a heart attack! You got to get me to a hospital right away!" The closest hospital I knew of was in the opposite direction, at the corner of Sunset and Vermont, so, losing my head now, I hit the brakes and pulled a U-turn in the middle of traffic. Horns blared, tires squealed, cars swerved out of the way. I don't even want to think about how close I came to killing us both, not to mention a few others, but at that moment I thought I'd all but killed Jim already. I said, "Hang on, man, I'll have you there before you know it!" and hung the first right I could while he clutched his chest and leaned forward as if about to drop. I could sense a pair of headlights bearing down behind me—it seemed I was being tailgated—and I came to a red light I couldn't run without T-boning another car, so I stopped, and a second later I heard a voice say, "What the fuck, dude?" and turned and saw a hostile-looking white guy staring in through my window. He was just standing in the middle of the street, and I realized he was the one tailgating me—I must have cut him off a few blocks back—so right in the middle of everything else, it looked like I was going to get into a fight. I said, "My friend is having a heart attack and I've got to get him to the hospital right away!" and he looked past me and over at Jim and said, "Oh, sorry," and turned and walked back to his car. Then the light changed and I zoomed to Sunset and made a left—I think I ran the light that time—and a few blocks later Jim said to stop the car. I said, "What do you *mean*, stop the car?! We're almost there!"

"No," he said weakly, "it's just a panic attack."

"Are you sure?"

"I think so."

"Well, let's not take any chances!"

"No, pull over for a second. You're just making everything worse."

So I pulled over, and we sat as he sweated and breathed hard. We were both trying to recover. I hadn't been that scared in years. There was an Arby's restaurant a block ahead, its big glowing cowboy hat lighting up the street, and I asked if he wanted to get something to eat, but he shook his head. What he really needed was a place to lie down, he said, and I told him I'd take him to my place, which wasn't that far away. I got on the freeway and apologized, explaining my dumb idea, but he said little back, as if he couldn't spare the strength. We got to my place, and as soon as he climbed out of the car, it rose a foot taller. Then, inside, he collapsed on the sofa and sank it. He asked for a beer. I gave him the last one I had. I turned on the TV. He watched it with a blank face. I asked if he wanted to call somebody from his support group. No, he said; but I gave him the phone anyway, and a few minutes later he dialed a number and I heard him say, "Nancy? It's me. I just had a ten." I figured he might like some privacy, and I also knew he was going to ask for another beer, so I drove to the store and bought a couple of six-packs. He was still on the phone when I got back a half-hour later. Except now his mood had changed. He was laughing a dirty-old-man laugh, so obviously he and Nancy must be doing their usual sex thing. I didn't care—not as long as he didn't whip it out in front of me. I tried to keep out of his way while he sat and drank and talked on the phone, and it got later and later, and I still had to drive him home. Finally I said as much, and he told Nancy he had to go, but they still went on talking. A half-hour later I said something again, and he held out the phone and said Nancy wanted to talk to me.

"She wants to talk to *me*?"

He nodded, and I took the phone and a brassy voice burst my ear with: "Jason? Why don't you bring him over to me? I can drive him home."

"Are you sure? It's pretty far away."

"No, it's fine. I want to talk to him some more, and this'll give me the chance to do it. I'm sure he could get better if he really wants to. He's just got to make up his mind that's what he wants."

"I couldn't agree more."

She gave me directions. Atwater Village was close to Echo Park. I told her we'd be there in fifteen minutes. Then, the second I hung up, Jim said he wasn't going. I said, "Well, why'd you put her on the phone with me?! Why'd you let her give me directions?!"

"Because she wouldn't take no for an answer."

"Well, now she's expecting us. Let's just go. She's just going to drive you home."

"No, she's just saying that. She wants to get laid, that's all she wants."

"And that's *bad*?"

"Well, it's not going to happen anyway. She'll take one look at me and slam the door. And she'll probably stop calling me, and I probably won't *want* her to call—not if she looks the way I think she does."

Well, I wasn't about to press the point—not after what I'd put him through. I asked if he wanted to call her to say he wasn't coming, but he said, "No, she'll just bug me to come over. I'll call her tomorrow."

He went to take a leak, as he'd done a number of times during his marathon conversation with Nancy. (For that matter, during my own marathon phone conversations with Jim, I was constantly hearing the sound of his stream and a flushing toilet afterward.) Then he came back and started going through my record collection, asking if I could play this record or that one, but I knew if we started that, I'd never get rid of him. Fortunately he discovered he was running out of cigarettes, which I hadn't thought to buy at the store, so I didn't have to push him to leave. He packed his pockets with beer, and after he'd again sunk my car and we'd bought cigarettes down the street, he said, "Hey, let me show where I used to live." He meant his old place on Avon Street. It's funny; unlike the building in Hollywood, he was eager to go to Avon Street, even though he had bad memories associated with that place as well: his girlfriend at the time had a born-again ex who'd beaten him up. I drove him over, curious, and he pointed to a tract house that now had toys in the front yard. Then he remembered that Dangerhouse Records used to be in Echo Park and said he'd show me where, and even though we eventually found the street, he never could identify the house. He was already half-drunk by the time we left my place, and he was still ripping beer in the car, so that, next thing I knew, he was talking about going to Nancy's place. I said, "I thought you didn't want to go!"

"Go where?"

"Nancy's!"

"Oh, I don't want to go *there*. You think I should?"

"Well, *I* would if I were you."

"Then fuck it, let's go!"

As I say, he was fairly drunk. I hadn't brought the directions, so first I had to drive back to my place to get them. By then it was so late I figured Nancy had given up and gone to bed, but when we found her house in Atwater Village, the lights were still burning. The house was a small adobe with a red tile roof and a tan Volvo station wagon parked out front; and even though Jim had helped to navigate in his drunken way, he looked around and asked where we were. Nancy's, I said.

"Nancy's? I don't want to go to Nancy's!"

"You just told me you did!"

"When?"

"A half-hour ago. Come on, we're here now. Let's just go inside. If you don't like her, you don't like her. It's no big deal."

"And you'll come with me?"

"Of course."

"And you're still going to drive me home?"

Well, actually, half the point of taking him over was to save myself the trouble. But just to get him out of the car, I told him we'd only stay for a couple of minutes and I'd drive him home straight afterward; and I didn't think he was *ever* going to get out, but he finally did, and just before we knocked on Nancy's door, I glanced at him and thought he was probably right: she probably would slam the door the second she got a look at him. But she didn't, and that wasn't such a good thing as it turned out, but I'm getting a little ahead of myself.

NANCY WAS AT LEAST FIFTY and a far cry from Venus: short and, yes, thirty pounds overweight, with a body that reminded me of a frozen chicken's and thinning hair you could tell she dyed. But she was also warm in a Jewish-mother kind of way, and if she was disappointed by Jim, she certainly didn't show it. She welcomed us right inside, apologizing for the messy house, when to me it looked like she spent half her life with a mop in one hand and a Dust Buster in the other. Naturally Jim lit a cigarette right away, without asking first if she minded, and she rushed off to find him an ashtray. You could tell she wasn't used to entertaining smokers. Nor could you smell her cat—a really fat cat that looked like it never went outside and knew it never should, otherwise all the other cats would kick its ass good. The cat was agoraphobic itself, in other words, when at first glance Nancy seemed perfectly healthy—as brassy in person as she'd been on the phone. I even joked about it. I said, "Your cat seems more agoraphobic than you do." And she laughed and said, "Well, he's certainly very neurotic. But you know what they say about people and their pets."

She had a great sense of humor, and she talked a lot—as much as Jim usually did, but now he turned to stone. I knew what he must be thinking—she wasn't much to look at—but what did he expect? Irina? Besides, I thought they were perfect for each other: two fat agoraphobics with problem hair and pets that looked just like them. Plus, as I say, they both liked to talk. Nancy told me her whole life story, practically, from her childhood in Florida to her college days at UCLA to her years as a freelance journalist. It sounded like she'd specialized in the kind of fluff Suzanne used to dash off for *Elle*—lifestyle tips and so on—but then she married and had a kid, and by the time she was ready to go back to work, most of her contacts had moved on, and she couldn't sell a piece to save her life. Then she had a nasty divorce, including a child custody battle, which was when her panic attacks started, and those eventually reached the point where, being housebound, she was forced to let her son live with her father. (They'd since moved out of state.) Afterward she squeaked by on alimony and picked up work as a closed-captionist, transcribing TV shows for the deaf. She started out working at home, she said, but then she got offered a full-time position with great benefits, and since that required going to an office, she had no choice but to get better. Like Jim, she'd never had luck with conventional therapy, and as for medication, she didn't want to rely on that; if she beat this thing, she wanted to know she'd done it all by herself.

"It's really a decision you make," she said. "It's just like the program says: you have to *face* the fear. You really have to welcome it."

That comment was aimed at Jim, of course, but he didn't respond. He just sat there, drinking beer and smoking, and every time he stubbed out a cigarette, Nancy would grab the ashtray and rush off to empty it, talking all the while. Finally she said something that brought him to life. She mentioned that she wanted to write a book one day about all she'd been through for other women dealing with the same "issues," and Jim said, "What's the point? Nobody'll read it anyway. Nobody reads *anything* anymore." It's funny how he always stuck to that. Even in the late seventies he was saying the same thing: that nobody read and literature was dead, and you could make movies or you could make music, but it was pointless trying to write. But Nancy said people did so read—she read all the time—and if that was what Jim thought, then why did he write poetry?

"Oh," he said, "it's just a habit. I'd never force it on anybody else."

"You forced it on me," I said.

"Yes," Nancy laughed, "he forced it on me too. But I'm glad he did. I thought it was *wonderful!*"

"What do you know? You think Rod McKuen is wonderful."

"Rod McKuen *is* wonderful. You and my friend Miles, you're exactly the same. You know why you don't like him? Because he's popular."

"He's not popular. You're just old."

"And you're mean. Jason's a lot nicer than you are, and he's *gorgeous* too. Why don't you go and leave him here with me?"

"Oh no, I want to watch."

Hey, guys, leave me out of this! But they were having a great time, zapping each other back and forth, and even though Jim was smashed, he gave as good as he got. I figured now was the perfect time to make my getaway—if, that was, he'd let me. I yawned and said it was late—I could barely keep my eyes open, it was so late—and Nancy told me to run along; she'd drive Jim home in the morning. Jim, of course, looked panicked on the spot and said, "Jason's going to drive me." But Nancy said, "No, it's too late for that. Stay here tonight. It's a good thing to break up your habits. Believe me, I know." Then she walked me to the door, obviously eager to see me go, and I glanced back at Jim, who looked like a five-year-old on his first day of school and Daddy's just about to leave him behind. But there was an itch I needed to scratch: I ran to my car and raced to Irina's, hoping to find her awake. She was, and so was Maja, and both were acting a bit strangely. It seemed they'd just had a spat on account of Irina's own neurotic cat, Fufica, whose constant coughing and sneezing was driving Maja crazy. I sympathized. Fufica slept at the head of Irina's bed, and all night long she'd hack and gag and spray us with snot. Apparently she was fine before Irina went to Prague, so I thought it was psychological: her way of saying she didn't much appreciate Irina's globetrotting. Either that or she missed David.

I was sure I'd hear from Jim the next day, but he never called. I figured he might be pissed at me for leaving him with Nancy; but then it got to be a few more days and he still hadn't called, so I called him and got his mom, who was foaming at the mouth. She said she had no idea where Jim was; she hadn't heard from him since he left with me. Where had I taken him? What had we done? If he was back on drugs, she wasn't going to put up with it for one second, no she was not; she'd throw him out in a heartbeat and don't think she wouldn't. I told her he was probably still with a lady friend and promised to have him call her, and she said, "See that you do," as icy now as the first time I'd met her.

I didn't have Nancy's phone number, so I drove to her house, where nobody came to the door. I was concerned myself at that point. If something bad had happened—if Jim had flipped out or actually had a heart attack—I'd feel partly to blame. I left a note on the door, and an hour or two later he called me.

"Where the hell have you been?" I said.

"Here."

"Doing what?"

"What do you think?"

And he told me in vivid detail—*much* too vivid. He said the first night he was too drunk to do anything, but the next day Nancy woke him with a blowjob, and she was quite the blowjob expert. She used to fool around with chicks in college, and he'd never met a lesbian yet who couldn't suck dick—all that rugmunching was great practice. Plus she used to fuck black guys—*that* was pretty intimidating. We all knew how hung *they* were. In fact, in the shape he was in, it wasn't so easy to fuck, but Nancy hadn't had sex in a long, long time, so no complaints from her. Afterward she'd taken him to lunch at the Glendale Galleria, and he actually hadn't had a panic attack. At one point he felt kind of strange, but he tried that rubber-band thing, and did I know what? It worked.

"Well, there you go," I said.

"Yeah, and I've been walking around the neighborhood while Nancy's at work, and it's really okay. Guess where I was when you came by? Having lunch up the street. All by myself. And, you know, I've always had these periods where I'll get better, and then I'll have a setback, but I've got to tell you, right now I'm feeling better than I have in years."

"You're welcome."

"Yeah, I guess I do sort of owe it to you, don't I?"

Sort of? Trying to help Jim help himself was like trying to bathe a cat! But I didn't want to rub it in. As a matter of fact, I gave most of the credit to Nancy. I told him he ought to drive to Vegas and marry her, and he said, "Oh, I'd never do that. You can tell she's had a kid. It's like sticking your dick in a mayonnaise jar."

"Oh, Jesus, man, would you shut *up*? You're lucky she even likes you!"

"I know. She's a sweet old Jew. And I've got to say it feels so nice, having actual human contact. I'd forgotten what that even feels like."

Then I told him he should call his mom, that she was bouncing off the walls, and he said, "Fuck her." I said, "Come on, I thought she was good people. And you're going to have to go home at some point. You don't want to piss her off."

"Oh, she's going to get pissed off no matter what I do. That's why I haven't called. The minute she finds out I'm seeing somebody, she's going to get weird."

"She already knows."

"Oh, you told her. Shit, I wish you hadn't done that."

"Well, I had to tell her something. She had you back on drugs again."

"Oh well," he half-laughed. "I guess if things get too bad, I can always move in with you."

"Guess again," I said.

HE CALLED AGAIN A FEW NIGHTS LATER. He was back at his mom's and said she was barely speaking to him, she was so pissed off about his disappearing act, and she'd also been rude to Nancy, who'd insisted on coming inside. Poor Nancy! His mother accused her of being a drug dealer and threatened to call the cops. It was a bad scene, he said, and he realized now he had to get out, and Nancy had proposed that he move in with her. I told him it was way too soon for something like that, and he said, "Well, just the other day you said I should marry her."

"Yeah, but I was just kidding. It's a really serious thing to move in with somebody." I suggested he search the apartment listings in the *LA Weekly*, and he said he would, though he still thought his best bet was Nancy. She really understood what he was going through, he said, being agoraphobic herself, and this way he wouldn't have to wait, and later, after he'd gotten better, he could find something else. That was what I found so encouraging: he didn't talk like he *might* get better, he talked like he *would*, and even though it was fairly late when he called, he wasn't drunk. It was the rubber-band miracle, the miracle of getting laid. Life itself seemed miraculous at that moment. Irina was back and had her own place; Project Jim was proceeding nicely; and I was happily unemployed with reason to think I might be about to sell a screenplay for a substantial chunk of change. Back at the beginning of the year, I'd gotten a call from Paul Bertolette, who told me about a producer friend of a friend of his who was looking for an action project he could make for nine or ten million. I wasn't expecting much after years of similar calls—friends with so-called leads—but I gave him a copy of *Landmine*, which he said he'd pass along to his friend; and months later, right around the time Jim met Nancy, the producer called to say he liked the script and wanted to meet to discuss it. The one sour note was he turned out to be German. I've always had a problem with Germans, Monika being one of the rare exceptions. The rest are so bland and blasé it almost makes me think they embraced Hitler out of the sheer shock that one of their own could ever be so animated.

At any rate, I met with this guy, whose name was Horst, and he was about as German as they come, with blond hair and wire-rimmed glasses and a face like a sunburned greyhound's. He'd produced a few movies here in the States and lots of television back in Europe, but now he was looking to become a director because "Ei em so goot fiss see ahctohs, you know; seh know Ei em sehr friend," and *Landmine* struck him as a good way to get started. Still, he had a few problems with it. He found the ending "so sad, you know; Ei font see happy inding fere effreebaudee fills goot!" Plus it was set in Africa, and "its not so issy shootink en Ahfreecah, you know"; and there was also no romantic interest, and "sis is see sing sat meks all see movies grett, see luff." But *Landmine* was hardly what I'd call love-story material. It concerned a group of American mercenaries trapped in a minefield with the insurgents they're fighting, and after joining forces to find a way out, they end up fighting all over again. But Horst wasn't interested in buying the script unless I wrote a part for a good-looking woman, just as he wanted me to shift the action to South America and give it a happy ending. He basically wanted a page-one rewrite, which I was supposed to do without payment. I knew he was loaded—we met at his house in Beverly Hills—and I tried to shake him down for something, but he couldn't be moved. First, he said, I should write, and if he liked my changes, we would "tock about see money." Yes, we fucking *would* talk too. If it ever came to an offer, I was going to call the biggest agency in town and get some hotshot bloodsucker to do my talking for me. And, no question, I'd find one. The two words agents like most are "easy" and "money," particularly in that order.

Irina thought I was crazy to work on that script. She'd never liked it, and loved, for instance, the rock & roll western I'd never gotten around to finishing, but I told her if I sold *Landmine* I could use the money to write twenty rock & roll westerns. Hell, I might even be able to fund the shoot myself. But not long after I met with Horst, I got a call from my friends at Avatar, who wanted me to come up with a new idea for a kiddie flick, they'd done so well with the last one. This wasn't a paying job either—not yet—but since they were the only production company that regularly hired me, I couldn't risk potentially estranging them. So suddenly I was working on two projects for no money when I got a letter from the state of California demanding immediate payment of $900 in back taxes or they'd levy my bank account. The check I sent all but wiped me out, so I called the temp people, who found me work way out in Canoga Park; and practically my first day on the job I was on my way home when I felt my gears slipping, and I knew what that meant: the transmission was on its way out. I couldn't afford to have it fixed, and there was nobody I could borrow from except Irina, and I had too much pride to ask. Besides, she was having problems of her own. She finally took her cat to the vet and learned that Fufica had some kind of incurable disease called rhino-something-or-the-other, which meant she was going to spend the rest of her days gagging and sneezing and spraying us with snot. Apparently she could linger for years that way, and Irina wouldn't hear of putting her down. I know. I suggested it. But she'd dragged that poor animal all over the world, from Belgrade to Paris to New York to Los Angeles, so that losing Fufica would be like losing a part of herself. I said, "Baby, I know it's hard to hear, but she's just a cat. And look at her! She's miserable!"

"No, it looks worse than it really is. She's not in pain. The vet said it's just like having a cold."

"Yeah, but it's a cold that's never going to go away. And she's driving Maja crazy."

"So what am I supposed to do? Kill my cat just because Maja doesn't have any patience? Maja needs a boyfriend, that's what *she* needs. And she doesn't have to take care of her. I will. I always have." And that was true in a way. But she did travel a lot, which was how Fufica had gotten sick in the first place: some limey friend of David's had been feeding her during the shoot in Prague, and apparently she disappeared for a couple of days and returned with a permanent cold—just leave it to a Brit to fuck things up! Speaking of which, David got back and stopped by Irina's apartment shortly afterward to bitch about the movie. It seemed he'd just seen the rough assembly and everything was all wrong, and he was so depressed, Irina couldn't bring herself to tell him about us. She would, she said, but not right now. She likewise got depressed, since she'd been counting on that movie to put her on the map, and even though David had told her she was fine in the fucking thing, she refused to believe him. She was very sensitive about her acting at that point. The shoot in Prague had shaken her confidence, so that every time she auditioned, she'd seize on the slightest comment as proof that she was never going to work again. And what if she never did? That was another concern: how was she going to support herself? She'd made something like fifteen grand on David's movie, and I told her she could stretch it for quite some time if she kept herself on a tight budget, but she said she had credit-card bills, and it cost a lot to call her family, and also, of course, she had to buy a car—at this rate she'd be broke in a matter of weeks! Then some Serbian friend of hers who was line-producing a low-budget movie offered her a job as a script supervisor, and even though she had no experience at that kind of thing, she told him yes. I warned her about it. I knew the kind of hours she'd be working for next to no pay, but she wouldn't listen. She had a job—a *real* job. She was finally going to prove to all doubters that she could get along with no help from David. She was thrilled for the first few days; but the novelty of waking at five in the morning to work as a lowly script girl soon wore thin; and I was right, the pay was awful; and it was also frustrating, having to sit there and watch other people act. Then her agent called about the lead in a movie, and the part sounded perfect—the character was European and everything—but the audition was scheduled for the middle of a workday. No problem, I told her. Just find somebody to fill in for you.

So she called around and found somebody, and the night before the audition I coached her. I tried to get her to relax and not slip into that grand thing she did when she acted, speaking in that stilted voice. Plus she slowed things down and became weirdly kind of *small*. And she was making progress—every time she did the scene, she got a little better—when suddenly, out of nowhere, she threw her script across the room and said, "I give up! Look at me! I've been taking classes for years, and I'm still just awful!"

"No, that last time wasn't bad at all."

"You're just saying that."

"It's true. But, you know, if you want to be good, you've got to work hard."

"But I *have* worked hard. And every time I watch TV, I see girls *much* worse than I am, and *they* work. What am I doing wrong? Is it just the accent? Are my boobs not big enough? What *is* it?"

Well, she wasn't average, that's for sure. It's true she wasn't much of an actress, but I'm not convinced that's much of an asset anyway. Talent is threatening to those without it, and that's ninety percent of the industry. The bland cast the bland, reflections of themselves; and that equally applies to beauty and sex appeal. Hence the many dickless wonders onscreen; the cheerful, synthetic women passed off as "sexy." And I do think Irina's accent cost her points, but not in the way she thought it did. Foreign beauties weren't as welcome in Hollywood as they'd been in times past. The current trend called for homegrown androids along the lines of Britney Sprears. As I've said, I never thought Irina should act in the first place, but I couldn't tell her that, not with her confidence running so low. I just tried to build her up as best I could, and the next day she went to audition, and that night I could see at a glance she had nothing good to report.

"They barely looked at me," she said. "I read the scene and they said, 'Thank you very much,' and that was it. And I thought I was really good."

"Well, that's what really matters."

"Yes, but I still didn't get it. Then, a few hours ago, the production manager called and said I was fired."

"From the script girl job?" A sigh and a nod. "Why?"

"Because. The girl I got showed up an hour late. But that's not the *real* reason. I talked to Jovan, and he says I 'socialize' too much. But I *didn't* socialize. I just tried to do my job, and people kept coming up to talk to me, and now they act like it's *my* fault."

Translation: she was getting hit on. Good God, you practically needed a gun to be with that girl! She said she didn't care about the job per se, but she'd been fired after working a week and a half—not exactly the best omen. Plus she was again faced with the question of how to support herself when her money ran out. How about waitressing? No, a good waitressing job in L.A. was almost as hard to find as an acting job, and even people she knew who'd been doing it forever were constantly getting fired. How about temping? No, she was a hunt-and-peck typist, and she saw what temping did to me—no use *both* of us being in bad moods. She needed something where the hours were flexible so that next time an audition came up she could run right out; and actually there *was* such a job, but she refused to consider it. I'm referring to modeling.

We'd discussed it several times already, but she always said what she told me now: she'd rather starve than go back to that. She loved the travel involved, but it was otherwise hateful comments by ugly people who made her feel like a piece of meat. I said, "Well, what about your art?"

"Oh, Jason, I can't make a living at *that*."

"There's ways."

"Yes, but I don't have any training. It's just something I've always done, you know, and I'm not even sure I'm very good. People *tell* me I am, but that's because they're amazed I can do anything at all!"

Her hope at the time was that David would cut her performance in a way that made her look better than she really was and, through that, she could still get work as an actress. She always maintained that was all she cared about, just being a working actress, but I think—I know—she also craved celebrity; she just didn't want to be a *stupid* celebrity. Yet I never really minded these bitch-and-moan sessions, which weren't as frequent as I'm no doubt making them sound. Besides, between my tax problems and temping and working on two scripts at once, I wasn't always such a joy to be around, and she pointed out something interesting. She said, "Maybe April's not your month." She was and is a believer in things like that, and do you know what? April's the month Peewee got killed, it's the month I got kicked out of school, it's the month Peewee stabbed that kid and we fled that night for New York. Plus two of my bands broke up in April, and it's also when I had that awful breakup with Suzanne. I'm not saying bad things haven't taken place in other months, but for whatever reason, April's been especially difficult. And yet I was born in December, so that must mean I was conceived in April, though I sometimes wished I never had been, the way my good luck always turned bad.

JIM MOVED IN WITH NANCY a week or so after he raised the possibility. She insisted, he said, whereas she later said it was *his* idea, but no matter; they were living together, and every day for a week he called me up to invite me over. I'd suddenly become so busy it was hard to make the time; but one night on my way home from work, I got off the freeway in Atwater Village, and when Jim came to the door, I couldn't get over how good he looked. He was dressed like a bum, like always, but his eyes were clear and his face had color, and to me it looked like he'd dropped a few pounds. He had, he said. He was walking all over the place, and as a matter of fact, he'd bumped into somebody from the old days who was going to help him get a job at a recording studio. Then he led me to his room—what used to be Nancy's son's room, but now he'd made it his office. He'd moved maybe a third of his stuff from Rancho Cucamonga, including his computers and most of his gear; and there on a stand beside his other guitars was a brand-new Martin—a present from Nancy, he said.

"What, is it your birthday?"

"No, she just gave it to me. We were having dinner up by the Guitar Center the other night, and I told her I always wanted one of these things, and she went in and bought me one. Isn't it beautiful? It's handmade, you know."

"Yeah, a friend of mine used to have one. Damn, that must have cost five hundred bucks!"

"Yeah, well, I sure earned it. She's horny as all get out. Did I tell you she's a lesbian?"

"You did, yeah. But I don't think fooling around with girls in college makes you a lesbian. I had a girlfriend who did that, and she *definitely* wasn't a lesbian."

"Yeah, but Nancy's got lesbian fantasies. She told me about them. I wish one night she'd bring another woman over, but I know she never will. She's got no friends at all. She calls the people she works with her friends, but they never come over."

I asked where Nancy was, and he said, "Work. Her company does one of those dating shows, and they've got some kind of deadline. You'd never think the deaf watch dating shows, but I guess they must."

"Well, don't the deaf date too?"

"Do they? I always think of the deaf as voyeurs. Now the blind—I hear they're *really* something. Buddy used to fuck a blind girl, and he said she was one of the best he ever had. I guess, if you can't see, you've got to make it up in other ways."

Then he played me a new song. It was a fine song, but I wouldn't say it was better than the songs he'd played me in the past, as he seemed to think it was, as if his having written it someplace other than his mom's automatically made it superior. Then he played another song and a song after that, and soon I was on the Jaguar, and he was on the Vantage, and for at least an hour we jammed away. I should have been home writing, but I couldn't help myself; it was almost like playing hooky, like a nice little holiday in the form of music. Then I glanced up and there was Nancy, home from work, and she looked better too, I thought. Unlike Jim, she hadn't lost weight, but her face had that same healthy glow. Jim and I broke off jamming, and she said, "Oh, please don't stop! It's so nice to come home to somebody playing live music! I didn't even know you played, Jason!"

"Of course. How do you think I know this guy?"

In fact, she knew nothing of Jim's punk past. She knew he'd been a musician, of course, but she seemed to think he'd always been a solo performer who specialized in the acoustic stuff she was used to hearing him play. She loved that. She thought he sounded like James Taylor. Jim groaned and said *"Please,"* and she laughed and said, "Oh, he can't stand it when I say that, but I think it's a compliment. I used to have the biggest crush on James Taylor. And you know who else I like? Paul Simon. You know, a couple of years ago, when I couldn't leave the house, I really got hooked on *Oprah*, and one season she had Paul Simon do her theme song, and it was so *wonderful*! I even called the show and asked if there was some way I could buy it, but they said I couldn't. I don't know why. It would've been the biggest hit!"

The babbling had begun. Man, could that woman talk! She asked if I could stay for dinner, but I told her no, I was supposed to eat with my girlfriend later; and she said, "Oh yes, Eddie told me about her. She's Bosnian, right?"

"Serbian. But close enough."

"Well, I'd love to meet her. Maybe one night we can all have dinner. We're always looking for places to go. I think it's very important for Eddie's recovery to go out as much as possible. And mine too! I'm still not completely there, you know!"

Then I had another of my brilliant ideas. I told her about Frères Taix: how on Saturday nights people played the same kind of music Jim did, and nobody came, and it was the perfect way for somebody like Jim to get his feet wet. Nancy thought that was a *wonderful* idea, but of course she thought lots of things were wonderful. Jim, meantime, got tense on the spot and said, "I can't do that!"

"Sure you can. And I'll play with you if you want me to."

"Yeah, but I'm not ready."

"Well, you sure sound ready to me. Don't you think so, Nancy?"

"I certainly do!"

I suggested we make a date for Saturday night. Jim said, "Well, maybe we can have dinner, but that's *all* I'm going to do. If you try to make me play, I'll get up and leave!" I said, "How am I going to *make* you play? No, we'll just eat and watch the show. You'll see what I'm talking about." Nancy asked if I'd bring my girlfriend, and I said, "Well, she's kind of shy, but I'll see what I can do." I never thought Irina would agree to go, and sure enough, she refused. She'd recently lost that script-girl job and said she felt bad enough without watching Jim eat. I said, "Look, it's just for a couple of hours. And he's really changed, and if you could hear the kind of music he's making, you'd see why it's worth it." Finally, at the last minute, she relented, calling to say she'd meet me at the restaurant; and I drove to Frères Taix, where Paul Bertolette was chowing down on bistro steak with his techie friends—their Saturday-night ritual, as I've said before. I stopped by their table to say hello, still chatting when Irina walked in, and, man, she looked fucking stunning. I remember she was wearing a black dress and pink sweater, and for whatever reason those colors brought out the best in her, but even so she had a kind of psychic switch that, once pulled, transformed her from your basic pretty girl to the most beautiful thing you ever saw. I could almost forget the way she looked after months of acclimation, but every so often she would pull this switch and blow me the fuck away. Paul and his friends were slack-jawed, eyeballing her and looking at me as if to say, "*She's with you?*" Not that I could say she was, since, again, she was paranoid about people knowing her business. She knew Jim knew—how could he not?—so that was okay; and Paul likewise knew about her, though she wasn't aware of it. I introduced her, saying, "Guys, this is my friend, Irina Sekulić," and one by one they said hello—or they *tried* to say hello. It made me love her that much more, to see the effect she had on others, and I wanted badly to kiss her—that was the least of what I wanted to do!—but I wasn't allowed to, not in public. We got a table and ordered a bottle of wine, and thirty minutes late, our dinner companions arrived. Nancy had decked herself out with a smear of lipstick and long earrings that looked like chandeliers stolen from Barbie's uptown condo; and Jim—well, he was the usual nightmare in that dark raincoat he always wore in public, as if it somehow made him invisible. Plus he and Nancy were both sporting the very latest in rubber-band fashions. Jim shook my hand while glancing wildly around, as if he half-expected some kind of special forces team to parachute from the ceiling and force him at gunpoint to sing. In fact, the first thing he said was, "Where's the stage?" I said, "There is no stage. It's early; they'll set it up later." Nancy, meantime, met Irina, saying, "Oh my God, you're *gorgeous*! Jason, you never told me how *beautiful* this girl is!" Of course that went down well with Irina, so she warmed to Nancy right away. She was even nice to Jim. You would never have guessed she felt about him the way she did, she was so sweet and charming, but he barely noticed, he was so busy draining the bottle of wine. Then we ordered a second bottle, and he asked for a beer on top of that, and Nancy said, "Eddie, *please* don't have any beer. Wine and beer don't mix." But he got the beer anyway, meantime hogging the wine, and at first he spoke only to me, leaving the women to chat with each other. It drove me crazy! I kept trying to follow what Irina was saying, but I couldn't with Jim demanding my attention; and then he finally loosened up after so much drinking and told a few stories, most of which I'd heard before, and the halves of the table were joined in listening; but even then something weird was going on. I'd noticed a little tension between Jim and Nancy a few nights before, but this was different. It was as if they'd been fighting on the way over, and, knowing Jim, I wouldn't have been the least bit surprised: *I don't want to go; I'm not going; why are you trying to* make *me go?* Then he went off on a long tangent about music: how at the time he started Rule of Thumb music was so bad; it was the seventies and rock & roll was practically dead, and all he wanted was to make it relevant again. But then disco came along, and he knew it would never happen. After that, he said, popular music was split in two: people danced to disco, and rock & roll was something they *listened* to. He said something similar had happened with jazz, that people used to dance to jazz before rock & roll came along, and afterward jazz became a listening-only experience. He thought that was the mark of decline: the minute music stopped being party music, it was on the way out. I'd never heard this speech before, and he was actually fairly eloquent. Even Irina seemed intrigued. Then Nancy said, "Well, I don't think the seventies were all that bad. I had a great time, and I thought the music was *wonderful*!" And Jim fixed her with a withering look and said, "Nancy, you've got the worst fucking taste." It was awful! Nancy tried to pass it off as a joke, but you could tell she was hurt, and Irina gave me a look as if to say, "Yeah, he's really a lot better, isn't he?" But Jim was just getting warmed up! When the menus came, Nancy said she was tempted by the clams, and Jim said, "I just bet you are." A baseball game was playing on TV, and when a black guy came up to bat, Jim said, "Look, Nancy, there's one for you!" He also asked, loud enough for Nancy to hear, if I thought she looked like Gertrude Stein. Actually, she sort of did—that was the awful part!—but it wasn't just Nancy; he later managed to offend my friend Paul, who'd come up to our table to say good night. I introduced Jim, explaining who he was, and Paul said, "Oh, right, you know my friend Michelle, don't you? Michelle Calderon?" And Jim said, "Oh, *her*. I hope you're not sleeping with her. She gave me gonorrhea."

"Well," I said, "nice seeing you, Paul! I'll call you in a couple of days!" He was a nice guy, but he had a bad temper, and I didn't want him to kick Jim's ass. That was *my* job! And the next time Jim went outside for a smoke, I went with him and said, "What the fuck do you think you're doing?"

"What do you mean?"

"You talk shit about my friend's friend to his fucking face? You insult Nancy with my girlfriend sitting right beside her? Are you out of your fucking mind?"

"Insult Nancy? I didn't insult Nancy! When? How?"

So now he was going to act like he didn't remember. Or maybe he *didn't* remember; I was never sure about that. It's true that the more he drank, the more his memory started to go, but even very drunk, he could sometimes recall things I couldn't, such as Peewee smoking that cigar outside CBGB's almost twenty years before. He likewise had no trouble recalling the dose of gonorrhea he'd supposedly picked up from Michelle, also dating from twenty years before, but now, like magic, his mind was a blank. What? How? *I* didn't do it. And, okay, let's say that's possible—some things you remember, and some things you don't; and everybody's got their own set of synapses, and no two rigged in exactly the same way—but even where memory fails, you're still accountable. But Jim was *never* accountable. He had more excuses than hairs on his head: he was drunk, he was scared, he was going to have a panic attack—and the attacks, by the way, never seemed to come on unless they were needed. Nancy later said they were a way of trying to control things, and she would know. On the other hand, Nancy was fucked up in her own right. Sure, she was lonely and all that, but I think she *liked* being treated like shit. Well, she partly did, and that was something I didn't quite realize at the time.

At any rate, I took Jim to task. I ran down a list of all his gaffes, and then he magically remembered and said, "Well, I was just kidding around. Nancy knows that. We talk that way all the time in private."

"Well, it's not just you and Nancy right now! And I had a hell of a time getting Irina to come tonight, and *she's* not enjoying it, I can tell you that right now."

"I'm sorry. What do you think I should talk about?"

"The weather. I don't give a fuck. *Anything* so long as you're not fucking with Nancy."

Then we went back inside, and for a while he behaved himself. Our food came, and a couple of kids with guitars walked in, and one started setting up the PA. More kids appeared—many more than the last time I'd been at Frères Taix—and Jim kept knocking back wine and beer both, once again talking mainly to me, but now that was something I encouraged. Then Irina started talking about life in Serbia, which Nancy especially seemed to find interesting, and at some point Jim cut in with: "Hey, aren't there a lot of prostitutes over there?" And Irina had a thing about that, as I've said before, so she kind of froze and said, "Well, no more than here."

"Oh, there's got to be more. Weren't you just saying things are really hard over there?"

"Yes, but it wasn't always like that. Things were very good when Tito was alive."

"Yeah, but Tito's been dead for—what?—twenty years now. And you've been having all those wars, and there's always a lot of hookers during wartime—especially in a place like *that*."

Then *I* cut in. I said, "Would you mind explaining what point you're trying to make?"

"No point."

"Good. Then maybe you won't mind if we change the subject." And he looked right at me and read my meaning well: *Danger! Shut the fuck up! Your life is in peril!* After that he barely said a word. The lights dimmed, and we sat through half a set of some kid moaning his heart out. Yes, he came from Tennessee with a suitcase in his hand, he missed his sweetheart, he missed that sweet land. At least Nancy seemed to like it. Of course, as we'd all been informed, she had terrible taste; and Jim sneered every time she applauded a song; and Irina looked like a cat at the animal shelter, her eyes begging me to take her home; but I was dreading the lecture she was sure to give me as soon as we left, with its many complaints about Jim and even more I-told-you-sos. Still, there was no point in delaying the inevitable: I flagged down the waitress and asked for the check. Our half came to $100, which I considered a cheap price for a ticket out of hell. Then Irina stood and hugged Nancy, who whispered something in her ear, and Jim tried to talk me into staying longer, but I stonewalled him. At least the lecture outside was a brief one. I asked Irina what Nancy had whispered, and she said, "That you're a great guy and we make a beautiful couple. I don't understand it. She's so sweet, and he's a *monster*. Jason, you know I don't want to tell you what to do, but I wish you wouldn't see him anymore. I used to think he was creepy, but now I think he's *evil*. I really think he wants to hurt you."

"Oh, come on. Nancy's the one he was trying to hurt."

"Yes, but she's nothing to him. And you—he's jealous of you. Didn't you see the way he was looking at you? He acts like he likes you, but I think he hates you."

But I thought that was going too far. Sure, he might be jealous—that was possible—but that wasn't the same as *hating* me. Still, I was definitely resolved to keep my distance, at least for a while. The problem was Nancy. I had no beef with her, and the next day she called, and after thanking me for a *wonderful* night, she passed the phone to Jim, who said, "Nancy seems to think I owe you an apology. I'm not sure what I did, but whatever it is, I'm sorry."

"Man, you are something else! You don't know what you did, huh? You want me to *tell* you what you did? You spent the whole night fucking with Nancy. And you offended my friend Paul, and you offended Irina—"

"How? What did I say to her?"

"Oh, you *know* what you fucking said. You sat there talking about Serbian hookers when I'd just *told* you to watch what you said. And she doesn't want me to speak to you anymore, and, frankly, I can't think of one good reason to do it. I fucking knock myself out to help your ass, and *this* is how you repay me? And Nancy too. And don't tell me you were drunk—I'm not buying that one. There's no excuse for the shit you pulled!"

"Well, what can I say but I'm sorry? I was so nervous, Jason. I only started going out a few weeks ago, and I didn't know what to expect, and your girlfriend—she's really intimidating."

"I know, man, you've *told* me that. But that's still no reason to talk the shit you did."

"Well, I wasn't trying to offend her. You know, I've lived with hookers; it's just kind of an interest of mine. And I could tell she didn't like me the minute I got there, and you were acting nervous yourself, if you want to know the truth. Every time I said something, you looked at me like it was all wrong."

"It *was* all wrong."

"Well, I said I was sorry; what more can I do? I don't know. Maybe I just don't know how to be around people. It's never been easy. Most of my life I lived in my own world. I had no choice. Nobody cared about the same things I did, and even when they did, I always felt different. I mean, Buddy—we liked the same music, but that was the only thing we had in common. He used to beat me up, for God's sake! You're one of the few people I ever met I could actually talk to. And I'll tell you something: I feel like you're the best friend I ever had. I know I haven't known you very long, but that's the way I feel, and if you stopped talking to me, I don't know what I'd do. Even if you *do* drag me to French restaurants to make me listen to god-awful music."

And with that the tension broke. I laughed and said, "It was pretty bad, huh?"

"Oh man," he laughed himself, "we sat through the whole thing, and not one of those kids can write a song to save his life. And I thought you said nobody came!"

"Well, the last time I was there, nobody did. I guess one of those kids must have some pull."

"Yeah, well, I can't play there, that's for sure. But I'm open to something else. I really want to get back on my feet again, and maybe you're right: maybe if I can get up and play, it could really make a difference. But it's got to be the right venue, and that is definitely not the one."

Then he returned to the subject of what a great friend I was—how much he cared about me and so on and so forth—the sappiest speech you ever heard this side of the Grammys; and it surely says something about my vanity, not to mention his gifts as a con man, that I bought the whole thing. So, in the end, I forgave him, and that bought him the time he needed to figure out a way to express his appreciation big time.

THE NEXT GOOD NEWS I got before the end of that April was the announcement, from New York, that Terrence was planning to marry Emily. That was all he wrote in the e-mail he sent me—"Emily and I are getting married"—an office drone to the end, dashing off this life-changing news in a quick one-liner. I knew exactly what was going on. He was taking the path of least resistance, just as he'd done with filmmaking and the Widowmakers and everything else, including that job he'd worked since 1986, which was about how long he'd lived in the same apartment. Sure enough, I called him and said, "So you're getting married, huh? Whose idea was that?"

"Hers. But, you know, I'm going to get married sooner or later. And she wants to do it, so fuck it."

I tried to restrain myself but couldn't. I told him he was making a huge mistake, that Emily was going to cut him off from everything and everyone he loved, including me, and he said, "I know, she's fucked up. But they're *all* fucked up."

"Oh, that's a great attitude. Yeah, it's written in the stars, this one."

"Well, what do you want me to do? Snag a Serbian supermodel? We can't all be *you*, Jason."

"That's not what I'm trying to say, man. And this girl is going to make your life a nightmare. You've got a lot to offer. Don't sell yourself short."

But he always had, and he always would. Plus I knew at some point he was going to repeat what I'd said to Emily, and if she hated me now, she was *really* going to hate me then. Yeah, so long, Terrence. Nice knowing you the last two decades.

But the best news was yet to come. One day when I wasn't temping but slaving away at home on *Landmine*, Irina called to say that David was in the hospital. It seemed, a few hours before, he'd been in the cutting room when he'd somehow managed to scald himself with coffee. Apparently somebody had put a pot in the microwave to heat it up, and

David, not realizing how hot it was, had gone to take it out, spilling it and burning himself so badly he'd been taken to the emergency room at Cedars-Sinai, where the doctors were keeping him for observation. I knew as soon as I got that call it was going to have some serious consequences. Irina immediately went to see him and came by my place a few hours later and said it was just awful, that the left side of his body was covered with blisters, one almost as big as her fist, and his left hand looked like a lobster claw. She was very concerned, not just for David but the movie—what if the producers let him go? I said, "Oh, they're not going to do that. It's *his* movie. They might have to shut down for a few days, but that'll be it."

"Yes, but he's on painkillers—won't that affect his judgment? God, this movie is cursed! It took so long to get made, and the shoot was a mess, and now this!"

She was in a funk for the rest of that night. Her phone kept ringing with friends of David's, friends of *theirs*, and she'd describe his injuries in fretful detail and hang up to fret some more. She spoke for a long time to Astrid, which was strange to hear. They sounded like the best of friends. And as I listened, I realized exactly the consequences this was going to have. She was going to play it as a reason not to make that final break, which she'd been postponing anyway, precisely as David wanted. He knew what was going on. He lacked the facts, but he surely suspected, and she meantime was getting a taste of the working world after years of living like a princess and having second thoughts about leaving him. The next day she went to the hospital to see him again, and afterward she went to his fucking house and cleaned it for him. She didn't mention the latter till I saw her that night. She said that with his hands burned he couldn't clean the house himself, and as a matter of fact, he'd asked if she could stop by for the next few weeks to cook and clean and drive him around. I said, "He wants you to be his *maid*? And you're willing to *consider* that?"

"He doesn't want me to be his 'maid.' He's burned, Jason. He can't take care of himself right now, and he's willing to pay me, and you *know* I need a job."

"Well, not *that* job! Don't you see what's happening? He wants you to go on being his wife, except now he's going to *pay* you for it. And you don't have any *problem* with that!"

"Of course not. I'm a whore. Isn't that what you mean?"

As I've said, that always had to come up at some point. I told her *I* hadn't called her a whore, that was her own mind at work, and she really ought to look into de-complexing that complex of hers. She said, "Well, what else am I supposed to think when you act like I'm going to sleep with somebody for money? But I don't *care* about the money. He's my friend, and he's hurt, and I want to help him."

"Oh, really. Tell him about us. Tell him about us first, and let's see if he wants your help then."

"I can't do that. Not right now."

"Yeah, why did I have the strangest feeling that's exactly what you were going to say? And I bet you think it's so compassionate too. 'Poor David. He's in so much pain. I can't make him feel any worse.'"

"Jason—"

"I'm not finished yet. I've been really patient about this, and you *know* I have too. You didn't want to tell him at Christmas—I accepted that. You didn't want to tell him during the shoot—I accepted that too. I didn't even get mad when he came to your apartment! But then you start talking about going to his house every day—that's where I draw the line. You slept with that guy when you swore you weren't going to, and I don't want you around him—not unless you tell him about us. And if you can't understand that—well, I really don't know what else to say."

She stared at me and sighed. She understood, she said. She asked Astrid to look after David, and I thought, "Now, that's more like it. Astrid would *love* to look after David." She was practically like Jim's mom, the way she guarded that guy. I was surrounded by incest on all sides!

In any case, for about a week, Irina barely mentioned his name. *I* was the one who brought him up. I'd say, "Heard anything from David?"

"Nothing."

"Aren't you worried?"

"I'm sure he's fine."

Meantime she was a perfect angel—a little *too* perfect. Then one night on my way home from work I stopped at Jerry's Video Reruns, which, as I've said, was close to David's house. I'd been renting a lot of kiddie flicks to help me think up a story for Avatar—everything I'd pitched so far they hadn't liked—and I was just about to leave the store when I suddenly had the strangest feeling that Irina was with David. It wasn't simply a suspicion; it was something more: a certainty brought on by what I couldn't say. So I drove past David's house, and guess whose silver

BMW was parked behind his SUV in the driveway? I felt like stopping and smashing their windshields and spilling my guts when David walked out to investigate. Instead I kept going. I was supposed to see Irina later that night, and I wanted to hear what she had to say about this—if, that was, she said anything at all.

But she said nothing when she showed up at nine as planned. She'd picked up some Thai food, and we ate by my non-functioning fireplace, and I asked about her day and what she'd done, and she said she'd dropped off her headshot negative at the photo lab to run off some copies, and she was thinking of getting a new headshot, since the one she had made her look too young and blah-blah-blah. I was trembling, I was so pissed off, but I tried to hide it; and I must have thrown her five fucking leads, and she never came close to mentioning her covert visit to Lord Coffeeburn's Spanish castle. Finally I threw her the most blatant lead of all. I said, "You know, I tried calling you about seven o'clock and couldn't get through." And she was good, boy. She may have had trouble acting in professional situations, but in real life she was seamless. She said, "That's the second time today somebody told me that. Something must be wrong with my phone."

"I figured you were probably busy."

"No, just having coffee with Maja."

"Well, that's interesting. Because I just happened to drive by David's house, and there was a car parked outside that looked exactly like yours. But we both know it couldn't have been yours. You were having coffee with Maja." Then her face turned diaper-rash red, and she threw down her fork and said, "So you're *spying* on me! Is my phone tapped too?! You're like the secret police!"

"That's the only time it happened, Irina. Of course I *should* have been doing it the whole time. Who *knows* how many times you've been up there."

"One time!"

"Yeah, that's what *you* say. But I don't believe anything you say from now on. You obviously can't be trusted."

"No, let me tell you what happened. Astrid was supposed to do David's laundry, but something came up, and she asked if I could do this one thing. And that's all I did. I washed his clothes, and he showed me a rough cut of the movie, and that's all that happened. And the only reason I didn't tell you is because I knew you wouldn't understand.

But there's something else. I didn't say it the other night, but I'll say it now. I think it's very unreasonable for you to think I can never see this man. He was my best friend for six years, and I don't know if you noticed, but I've stopped seeing every American friend I have, because I know you wouldn't approve. This is what I did for you, and I know you didn't ask me, but I did it anyway. But I can't do that with David. He's the one friend I want to keep, and I am *going* to."

She said this in a great rush, dead serious, and when she finished, I told her, no less serious, that she could have me or she could have David, but she couldn't have both.

"But nothing happened! I don't know why you have to be this way!"

"Because you *lied* to me!"

"Yes, and every time I tell you the truth, you *punish* me for it. I can't pretend six years of my life didn't exist! Why can't you accept me the way I am?"

"But I *have* accepted you, and you still sneak around behind my back. And you won't tell that guy the truth when you have every chance to do it. Tonight while you were up there doing his 'laundry,' did you tell him then? Did you?" She covered her face and shook her head. "Well, there you go."

"Well, what *good* would it do? If I tell him, he won't want to see me anymore, and you still won't trust me anyway. Why can't you let me do this *my* way?"

Then she cried. It worked too, like it always did, my resolve starting to melt; but I couldn't let that happen. I told her I didn't understand why she didn't want to tell David, that if she really loved me as much as she claimed she did, she'd want to tell the whole world.

"I mean," I said, "I've told all my friends about *you*."

"Oh," she said with a look of horror, "that's just great." And to me that pretty much said it all.

OF COURSE SHE SAID I'D MISUNDERSTOOD, that she only meant she didn't want people knowing her business and repeating it to David, and I said, "Yeah, there goes your safety net." Then she said she couldn't stand it when I acted this way, that I was just like a Serb, and I said, "Well, fine, why don't you just run along? And don't come back till you've talked to David." That effectively ended the crying part of the episode: she jumped up, really mad, and threatened to leave for good. I said, "If that's the way you want it," and she stormed out, slamming the door so hard behind her it was a wonder the glass didn't shatter. I listened to her footsteps going down my stairs. I listened to her car start and drive away. I knew every last nuance of that sound. I could pick it out anywhere. I remained by the fireplace and tried to force down some more Thai food, as if by doing one normal thing I could prove to myself that none of this mattered, I wasn't upset, I hadn't just made a huge mistake. Already the doubts were setting in. But the more I reconsidered, the more confused I got, and suddenly I threw my plate across the room, sauce and noodles everywhere. Yeah, fucking brilliant. Where was *my* maid? And where was David's? Probably back at his place, I decided; and I ran outside and drove to Los Feliz, but her car wasn't parked in front of his house. Then I drove to Hollywood, but her car wasn't parked in front of her place either. Where was she? Who was she with? Was she fucking somebody else? I was going to wait around to see if and when she returned, but then she might spot me and accuse me of spying, and of course this time I really *was* spying, and worse than that, I was stalking her. So I kept driving with no destination; and the city seemed so lonely, which it always did, but now it seemed especially lonely, and I was dying to talk to somebody, anybody, I didn't care who. I passed Nancy's house, where the lights were still burning, and thought, "Don't stop. Jim can't help you. He doesn't know shit about a situation like this." But what did *I* know? Who was I to advise him or Terrence or anybody else, when my own life amounted to one disaster after another? I parked and knocked on Nancy's door, and she cracked it open, bleary-eyed, and said she was about to go to bed.

"Oh, I'm sorry. I was just in the neighborhood and saw the lights were on, and I know Eddie is usually up late."

"Well, he usually is, but not tonight." Then she opened the door a little more, and there he was, passed out on the sofa. He looked like a six-foot infant lying in its crib, like a giant cookie that's resisted baking. Nancy said she'd come home and found him drunk, and I asked if that happened often, and she said, "Well, yes, lately it happens quite a bit. He found some bar up the street, and I think that's where he's spending his days. I told him before he moved in he needed to get in a program, and he said he was going to. I suppose you know he used to be a drug addict."

"Of course."

"Well, *I* didn't know till his mother told me. I don't see how he's managed to stay off drugs if he's not in a program. I always thought if you had one addiction, it triggered all the others, so how can he drink and not do drugs? You don't suppose he is, do you?"

"Well, he never mentioned anything. And I used to fool around with heroin myself, and I never noticed any of the signs. But, you know, I've only been around him a few times. For the most part we always just spoke on the phone."

"Well, his mother seems to think he's back on drugs. And she thinks *I'm* the one who got him on them. Me! I don't even take drugs for *anxiety*, let alone *heroin*. That woman is *such* a nightmare! That's why I let him move in here. At first I said no, but then I met her, and I said, 'Sure, pack your bags!' She's the reason he's so screwed up. Well, I know she's one of them. She lost a child when he was a baby, and it was hard for me to let my son live with his father; I can't imagine what it would be like to lose a child altogether. And that's why she doesn't want to let go of Eddie: she doesn't want to lose him too. I can't even tell you how rude she was. Do you know what she said to me? She said I should stick to my 'own kind.' Well, you know what *that* means! She's an anti-Semite! And Eddie's made a few anti-Semitic remarks, and you just *know* that's where he got it from. Jason, honestly, he's one of the strangest people I ever met. He'll read me something or play something so sensitive I think I'm going to cry, and then he'll turn around and say something so shocking I can't believe my ears. And he's so smart and well-read—how can somebody like that be so *ignorant?*"

On and on she went, standing in the doorway, despite the hour, seizing the chance to bitch about Jim. He was messy. He was mean to her cat. He smoked, even though he'd promised to quit before moving in. And then there was the biggest "issue" of all: money. He'd likewise promised to get a job, and as a matter of fact, Nancy had tried to get him one as a closed-captionist, but he failed the grammar and spelling test. How could he do something like that? He was a *writer*, for God's sake!

"Well, I guess he *wanted* to fail it," I said.

"Yes, exactly, that's what I think too. And I know this girl that sells air purifiers. She's in the program with us—for agoraphobia?—and she runs the business out of her house, and I told Eddie that's what *he* should do, but he's never gotten around to calling her. I should call her myself! I could use one of those things, what with all the smoke in here! He keeps saying he's going to get some job at a recording studio, but every time I ask about it, he gives me some excuse. And I'm not worried about the mortgage—I can take care of that myself—but I don't think it's asking too much for him to chip in for food and utilities. And I realize he's doing things. I realize he's writing and working on music, and I think that's *wonderful*! But, you know, my friend Miles—we work together—he writes poetry too, and he's doing a reading next week and he was looking for some people to do it with. So I asked Eddie, and he said he would, and I gave some of his poems to Miles, and he just flipped! He thinks Eddie's great. And he is, you know. And Eddie—as soon as I told him Miles liked his poetry, he said—"

"He's not going to do the reading. Yep. That's him, all right."

"Well, I think he *should* do it. It's just like you were saying a couple of weeks ago: if he can get up there and take a risk, it's really going to help him. That's exactly what they teach in the program: whatever it is you're most afraid of, that's what you've got to do. I wish you'd speak to him, Jason. Don't tell him you spoke to me. Just call him, and if he says anything about the reading, tell him you think he should do it. He really listens to you. He's always complaining that you never call. Or maybe we can have dinner again. I know you may not want to after the way he acted last time, but I think he learned his lesson about that. And maybe you can bring Irina. I just loved her. She's a very special girl, Jason. You *deserve* someone like that."

Wow, thanks. But I said I'd give Jim a call, and she let me go. I'd worked up quite a thirst while standing on her porch for however long she held me prisoner, so I drove to the Short Stop, where I hit the bottle hard with my friend Thom, the bartender, and a couple of off-duty cops. I'd never told Nancy about the breakup, but I sure told them. I told them till five o'clock in the morning. One cop said I should get a gun and shoot that lying bitch, but Thom had met Irina and said he had a good feeling about her; he was sure she was going to do the right thing and tell her husband. It was too late to sleep by the time I got home, so I took a cold shower and drank two pots of coffee, that lethal substance, and drove to Canoga Park, where I worked in slow motion and called Jim during my lunch break. He knew I'd dropped by the night before. Nancy, like a perfect dumbass, had mentioned it. How was I now supposed to pretend I'd never spoken to her? But, as if making idle conversation, I asked Jim about the job at the recording studio, and he said, "Yeah, I'm not sure what's going on with that. The guy never called me."

"Have you tried to call him?"

"Yeah, but he never called back. Why?"

"I'm just curious. Didn't you tell me you were going to get a job?"

"Yeah," he said, "I'm going to get a job." But he sounded so nonchalant, and I was so tired and strung out because of Irina, I wasn't much good at hiding my annoyance. I said, "So when exactly were you planning on getting one? Next week, next month, next year?"

"Did Nancy say something to you?"

"No, I'd just like to know. I mean, you aren't the only one who got drunk last night. I did too, and I still had to go to work, and it's—what?—one o'clock and you're sitting around doing nothing. So maybe you can tell me what it feels like to be a big man of leisure."

"She *did* say something. God, that bitch can whine! I don't know what she's so worried about. I told her I'm going to pay her back everything she's putting out right now."

"Yeah, and we all know exactly how much your promises are worth. What's all this about a poetry reading?"

"She told you about *that*? What *didn't* she fucking tell you?"

"Hey, maybe if you hadn't been passed out on the sofa, you could've told me yourself. I didn't come by to speak to Nancy, you know. And if you don't want to read, you should never have told her you were going to."

"I never told her that! She asked if I wanted to *go* to a reading; she never said anything about *me* reading. But no, she's got to run off and give my poems to some stupid kid and act like I stabbed her in the back just because I don't want to do it."

"Well, why *don't* you do it? You're getting a free ride over there. The least you can do is read a few poems."

"Why? So Nancy can feel like some patroness of the arts? *She* doesn't have to read. She doesn't know what it's like!"

"Well, she sure knows what it's like to get up and go to work every goddamn day. Jesus Christ, man, how can you live with yourself? That woman's been nothing but good to you. She moves you in and feeds you and fucks you—and don't you *dare* fucking act like that's some kind of

343

chore. The minute you started getting laid, you took a turn for the better. And she bought you a goddamn Martin guitar, and for what? For you to turn around and treat her like shit? Well, I'm not going to let you do it. I'll kick your fucking ass, Eddie. I don't care about a poetry reading, but you're going to get out there and get a fucking job, you get me?"

"Well, it's only been three weeks. Jesus Christ, these things take time!"

Still, he promised he'd get one. Yelling at him was the only way I could get him to cooperate, and even then it wasn't foolproof. Honestly, there were times when I felt like his father, and I was seven and a half years younger than he was. But it wasn't as if I got nothing out of it. I was able to exorcize some of my grief about Irina and hung up feeling better. But there was still the rest of that day, and the day after that, and the days to come. I had to fight the urge to pick up the phone, to spy or stalk her. And I fought the urge successfully. But I yearned and pined, and hated myself for yearning and pining, and I hated Irina for *making* me yearn and pine. If only I knew she was yearning and pining herself. She probably was, my brother Keith told me. She probably wasn't, my brother Scott told me. But both said I had to stay strong; and Jim—yes, I ended up confiding in him as well, and he said it must be tough to lose a girl like that, but look on the bright side: at least I hadn't found her hanging in the bathroom with her wrists slashed open. Oh man, to compare his love to mine! But he probably wasn't far off, I thought. After all, she was surely back to fucking her meal ticket, burned or not. And I was going to cave, I was going to call her, I was dialing her number and hanging up before my number flashed on her caller ID and she could see how weak I really was. And then one night the phone rang, and I somehow knew by the sound alone it was going to be her.

"I miss you," she said right away.

"I miss you too."

"Can I come over?"

"As soon as you can."

She arrived a half-hour later, and I took her in my arms and said, "I'm sorry," and she said, "No, *I'm* sorry," and I said, "None of that matters, this is all that matters," and swept her off to bed, and the world was set right again. And then it was set wrong again. Because afterward she told me how she'd spent the last few days, and of course they'd mostly been spent with David. Oh, she said, she hadn't slept with him, she'd just dropped by his house here and there, and being around *him* had made her realize how much she missed *me*. I said, "I don't suppose you told him that." And she shook her head.

"Irina, why *not?*"

"Jason, *please* don't start this again. You just said it doesn't matter."

"But I don't understand why you don't just *tell* him. I mean, what do you *do* when you're with him?"

"We just talk. Mostly about the movie. He showed me the rough cut—I told you that, right?—and of course I'm just *awful*. I don't think I'll have any future at all when this thing comes out. *If* it comes out. It's so bad, Jason. It's like a left-handed drawing made by a right-handed man."

"Well, why can't you, when you're talking about the movie, just say, 'David, there's something I have to tell you,' and lay it on him. You're such good friends, he's bound to understand."

"But he won't. When I told I him I was moving out, he asked if there was somebody else, and I told him no. So if I tell him yes now, it's going to make me look like a liar."

"You *are* a liar."

"Thank you so much."

"Well, you are. When you don't tell somebody the truth, that's a lie, right? Especially when they *ask* for the truth. You should've told him then. It sounds like he was ready to hear it."

"Jason, you're *obsessed*. If I tell him or I don't tell him, it makes no difference. I'm here with *you,* not him."

"Yeah, but I feel like I'm cheating when I'm not! I don't want to have to sneak around so I don't upset somebody who's not even supposed to be there. I mean, do you know what you're doing here? You're *supplementing* him. It's like you like me for certain things, and you like him for certain things, and you're trying to make us into one person."

"Doesn't everyone do that?"

"No, they don't. *I* don't. And thanks for telling me I'm right. You've got my fucking head on his body. Or, actually, it's the other way around."

"That's not what I mean," she sighed. "I mean—suppose Peewee was alive. Wouldn't you want to spend time with him? Wouldn't you feel there are some things you could say to him you could never say to me? Well, this is how it is with me and David. We went places together; I can remind him of the guide we had in Egypt, and he knows just what I'm talking about. And nobody else does. And if I told him I could never see him again, or he said he never wanted to see me again, I'd lose all that."

"But you're *going* to lose it one day."

"Why? Because you say I have to?"

"No, because people lose things. I mean, look how much *I've* lost."

"Well, I've lost things too, you know. Do you know what I would give if, just once, I could hear my father say my name? And my family and all my friends back home—I never get to see them. I know all *about* loss, Jason. And I don't want to lose you, but I don't want to lose David either. Not his friendship."

"So what is it about me you don't want to lose? My dick?"

"Of course not. I don't want to lose *anything* about you."

"Yeah, but everything else you can get from him. That's the only thing he doesn't give you: sex. That didn't stop you from sleeping with him when you were making that movie, but you probably wouldn't have done it if I'd been there. I'm like a dildo. Too bad you can't pack me in your purse."

"That's the most ridiculous thing I ever heard!"

"Yeah, and how ridiculous do *you* sound? You want to have it both ways, and expect me to go right along with it. And I will. Because I can't *not* see you. I can try, but I know I'll fuck it up. So, fine, you can go up to his house and be his maid and talk about your Egyptian guides or whatever the fuck it is you guys talk about, and when you're ready for some dick, you can come down here, and I'll give it to you like nobody else. And you *know* I will too. So everybody gets just what they want. What do you think?"

"I think I'm going to leave," she said, and she started to get up, but I pulled her down and fucked her nearly comatose, and she was nothing if not encouraging. In fact, except for that night at the motel on our way home from Jim's place, the night I possibly got her pregnant, that may have been our best sex so far.

SO, PRETTY MUCH, I THOUGHT I had it all figured out. And I'm not trying to suggest my dick is *that* big, or I'm *that* great in bed; it all depends on your partner, and as I've said before, Irina was one of the best there was. And afterward she was all softness and sleepy-eyed sweetness, and she swore she'd tell David very soon, but guess what she had lined up the next time I saw her? She said she knew what I was going to say, but the fact was that Maja could no longer tolerate Fufica's constant sneezing, so she, Irina, was going to have to get a new place, and David was offering *his* place, and she'd look for a place of her own the whole time she was staying with him and blah-blah-blah. So inch by inch she was working her way back to David, and I could fight her about it, and did, but I knew even as the words left my mouth what a pile of shit it was. Like I'd told her already, I couldn't *not* see her; and one day I was sure she'd dump me altogether and find somebody else to keep her well fucked while David paid her bills and doused himself with hot coffee whenever she was in danger of wandering too far afield. Jesus, Jim's relationships with Nancy, Cybil and his mom combined were looking downright healthy compared to those two. And me—I was the sickest of all, playing out my role as David's stunt dick. Of course I could've told David myself what was going on, but I knew Irina would dump me the second she found out, and I wanted to hang on for as long as possible. God, I hated her. I hated her so much I loved her—or was it the other way around? Sex was the only pleasure I had. Every other minute was taken up with temping or warring with Irina or going from *Landmine* to the kiddie flick and back again, so that my brain started to feel like taffy. Three ten-year-olds meet a real-life unicorn and step on a bomb. Wait. A South American revolutionary peers though his rifle scope and spots a friendly bear. Then Avatar approved one of my pitches and cut me a check just big enough so that I could stay at home to bang out a first draft, but not big enough so that I could fix my transmission; amazingly, it hadn't given out yet. I also managed to finish *Landmine* and gave it to Horst, who read it quickly and said, "Fell, siss iss much bitter but fe still haff a few problems," and handed me 100 new notes. But I was close, he said, and he was confident that once I made these next few changes, we could finally "tock about see munny"; and I hoped and prayed that I could shake him down for at least 150 grand. Let's make a deal, God. What can I give You? You already got my first child. Wait, that probably won't work, not since You sacrificed Your own first child. But if You could bring Yourself to help an atheist in a very foxy hole, I'll take 150 grand, please. I figured with that much I could buy the fox. Oh, but she couldn't be bought, could she? She cared nothing about money. She wasn't a *sponzoruša*. Yet months later, after this whole fiasco had reached its gruesome climax, she *finally* admitted that money had been one of her main motives in sticking close to David.

Meantime, on the Jim-and-Nancy front, Jim had never gotten a job. What a shock, huh? But he was looking—oh yes, he was looking—and just to keep Nancy on the string, he'd finally agreed to read his poetry. Then, the night of the reading, Nancy called to say that he was backing out again. How was she ever going to face her friend Miles? She was going to have a panic attack—a really bad panic attack of the kind she hadn't had in a year and a half.

"Goddamnit," I said, "put his ass on the phone!"

"Eddie? Jason wants to speak to you!"

"Leave me alone!"

"No, Eddie, come to the phone! He's *waiting,* Eddie! Eddie, come here and speak to Jason!"

That's right, Mom, make Eddie speak to Daddy. But Eddie was a very bad boy. He didn't want to speak to Daddy, because he knew Daddy wasn't going to put up with his shit. So, to Mom, Daddy said, "All right, you tell him I am getting in my car, and I am going to drive to that place in a neighborhood I despise, and if I get there and he doesn't show up, I am going to drive right back and kick his fucking ass. And I have never been more serious in my entire life."

"You want me to tell him right now or after we hang up?"

"Right now, please."

Then she repeated every last word, absolutely verbatim, and I heard Jim say, "Okay, I'll go! But I'm not going to read!" I said, "I heard that! Tell him he *is* going to read, and if he doesn't, I'll kick his ass for *that!*" Then Nancy relayed my revised threat, and after Jim mumbled something I couldn't make out, she said, "He'll do it. Thank you, Jason. Thank you so much."

The reading was halfway across town at a place called Masquers Cabaret, not too far from the monstrous Beverly Center shopping mall. I battled traffic all the way there and parked about ten blocks away and walked back up, and guess who was hanging around outside on the sidewalk? No, not Irina. Not David either, but you're getting warmer. Give up? Astrid! Yep. For the first time since I'd seen her skating in my puke some nine months before, here was the lovely Astrid, who seemed strangely glad to see me.

"Well, look at this!" she said, as she waltzed up to give me a hug. "What brings you to *this* side of town?"

"I've got a friend who's doing a reading."

"Well, isn't that something. I do too."

That was why she was so glad to see me: she wanted to show off the guy beside her. He reminded me of one of Irina's retro friends: young, with dyed-black hair, and dressed in "ironic" bellbottoms looped with a white belt. Irina had said something about Astrid having a new boyfriend, but she never mentioned he looked like this. Still, you could tell he wasn't digging Astrid nearly as much as she was digging him. She was all over the guy, just like she'd been with me, but he was, like, a poet, man. In his heart he was, like, free and stuff. I shook his hand after he finally managed to reclaim it from Astrid, who asked what I'd been up to.

"Oh, just writing. And you? What's going on with you?"

"Well, I just got back from Prague. David's movie, you know. He finally did it, and I think it's going to be very good. But he had the most awful accident."

"Really."

"Yes, he spilled hot coffee on himself. It was terrible. He was in hospital for a couple of days. Oh, and he and Irina finally split up."

"You don't say."

"Yes, but it didn't last. She called him saying she made a mistake, and of course he took her right back. He's so forgiving, you know."

Well, thank you very much, Astrid. Never feel you didn't add something to my life, you definitely did. Now, if you'll excuse me, please, I need to hit the bar and kill myself with alcohol. Oh, you want to keep talking? Sure, go ahead. Irina is bad in David's movie, huh? He's cutting almost all her scenes and getting another actress to loop her lines. Wow, that sure is something, all right. Well, again, I really need to hit the bar, but I'm sure I'll see you later. Yeah, good luck with your reading, White Belt. You got yourself a fine lady there.

Inside, this place wasn't what you'd expect for a poetry reading. It was like a fake Paris bistro strung with white Christmas lights, but otherwise dimly lit. There was a small stage with a mic stand and stool in the center, and, beneath the stage, a number of tables were pushed together, a small candle burning in the middle of each one. Hipster kids were slowly gathering, but this wasn't their typical hangout. It was more the kind of place where gay waiters sang the score of *Gypsy!* for an over-sixty crowd. Yet the staff was mostly women: blonde actress types with StairMaster bodies and tanning-bed complexions. The bar was behind the stage, almost a separate room, and the bartender was another bronzed blonde who poured me a Jameson's and a beer chaser and charged me twelve bucks. But fuck it—let the suicide begin! I was on my second round when Jim and Nancy walked in, both looking like they had at Frères Taix: Jim in his raincoat, Nancy in lipstick and foot-long earrings. Both wore rubber bands, of course; and Jim was *not* looking wildly around as he had at Frères Taix, staring instead at the floor, and you could tell by his smell alone that he was blitzed right out of his marshmallow head. Nancy gave me a peck on the cheek and ran off to find her friend Miles, leaving Jim with me. I bought him a drink and asked him where his poems were. He patted one of his pockets.

"I think I'm going to vomit," he said.

"I think I am too."

"Why? *You* don't have to read."

"I got my reasons."

"My God, did you see all those kids? I feel like somebody's *grand*father!"

"Good. They're so used to each other, you'll be like the voice of authority."

"This is insane! Why am I doing this?!"

"Because you said you were going to. You need to stop making promises you can't keep. Besides, you're going to feel a lot better when it's over."

"No, I'm going to feel better when I vomit!"

Then Nancy came back with a scrawny kid I'd seen hanging around outside. This was Miles, the organizing genius. He asked Jim if he'd like to read first, and Jim said, "I don't want to read at all."

"He's just shy," I said. "Yeah, put him up first." Then Jim said no, and I said, "Yeah, go ahead. Get it over with." Miles asked how he wanted to be introduced, and Jim said nothing, so I said, "Just say he was a founding figure of the L.A. punk scene and the last reading he did was with Charles Bukowski." Then Miles' eyes got as big as quarters, and he said, "You did a reading with Charles Bukowski?"

"No," Jim said, "I didn't."

"He's just being modest," I said. "Say it."

"No," Jim said, "don't say it." Miles kept looking from me to Jim, and I said, "Say it!" and he ran out of the room.

"Why did you tell him to *say* that?" Jim said.

"Because. It's going to make everybody like you. Didn't you see how impressed he was?"

"But now they're going to expect something really big. I can't do this! I can't!" Nancy and I both told him he could, and he kept shaking his head while trying to light a cigarette. The blonde behind the bar said he'd have to smoke outside, but I wouldn't *let* him go outside, since I'd have to go with him, and I was obviously trying to avoid Astrid. He tried to get around me: he moved left, and I moved left; he moved right, and I moved right—a whole little dance going on. Then he stopped the dance and lit his cigarette, and the blonde said, "Sir? You really can't smoke in here. Sir?" But he paid no attention and she finally gave up, and then Miles came back and said they were going to start, and Jim just stood there smoking. He'd also started sweating. Miles asked if he was okay, and Nancy said, "He's fine. He's just a little nervous, that's all." Then Miles left again, and Nancy said, "Eddie, I think I'm going to go get a seat. Are you going to be okay?" He didn't answer, and Nancy was looking so nervous in her own right, I was afraid she was going to tell him he didn't have to read, and I was *determined* to get him on that stage. I told her to get a seat and save one for me, and she kissed Jim and told him to *breathe*, to float *through* the anxiety and all this programspeak. I said, "Nancy, he's going to be fine; just go!" and she tottered off to the main room on her frozen-poultry legs. You could tell they were dimming the lights in there, you could hear the buzz of the crowd; and Jim asked me to buy him another drink, but I said, "No, it's going to start. Just read, and I'll buy you all the drinks you want as soon as you're done." I felt like a fucking prison guard! But at least it kept my mind off Irina. Then I heard Miles' introduction on the PA in the next room. He said, "I just met our first reader a couple of minutes ago. He was a leading figure of the L.A. punk scene, and he used to do readings with *Charles Bukowski*! So everybody give it up, yo, for Mister Eddie *Brown*!" Then I heard a smattering of applause, and Jim stood there with his head hanging low, and I wondered what I was going to do if he refused to go onstage. Was I really going to hit him? Did it really mean that much?

But it never came to that. Suddenly he turned around and walked off into the darkness of the next room. I followed, watching as he bumped up the steps leading to the stage and collided with the stool, which was now in a circle of light. Then he plopped down on the stool and reached in his pocket and pulled out some crumpled-up pages that were folded in half and sifted through them for a good two minutes. An uncomfortable silence filled the room, but he kept sifting through his pages with trembling hands and a visibly sweaty face till, finally, when it seemed he had everything arranged just so, he announced the name of the first poem without looking up and started reading. His voice was flat, and a few times he stumbled over the words, yet he was somehow really magnetic up there. He wasn't in real life, not even when I first met him in 1981, but as soon as he got onstage, you couldn't take your eyes off him. He seemed naked and vulnerable, as if he were reading from his very soul, and his nerves were actually an asset. Here, you thought, was somebody who gave it to you straight, even though it cost him to do it. Then he finished his first poem and the audience clapped, and when they did that, he raised his head for just a second with the look, almost, of a wild animal waking in the zoo for the first time. His voice became more confident with the next poem. He stumbled less and played more with the words, stressing some and rushing past others, so that the poem had the rhythm and feel of music. People were literally on the edges of their seats, including Astrid and White Belt, whom I spotted near the back, and I thought, "Goddamnit, the motherfucker's got it! He's *always* had it! Why was he giving me so much shit? The guy is a fucking natural!" And he got better and better—every time he read another poem, he seemed more self-assured—and he also started talking between readings, at one point shouting out, "Somebody buy me a drink!"

"*I'll* buy you a drink!" Miles shouted back. "What do you want?"

"Anything so long as it's got alcohol in it!" That got him a laugh, and he said, "Yeah, got to love that alcohol. I've had some real visions getting drunk. Like, one time I saw Mr. Peanut. I swear to God, Mr. Peanut walked by, and he tipped his hat and walked right through the wall. And I heard him back there. I heard Mr. Peanut having sex! I don't know who it was with, but Mr. Peanut was getting busy, and, let me tell you, peanuts make some weird fucking noises when they're getting laid." That brought down the house—I saw a blonde girl almost fall out of her seat, she was laughing so hard—and Nancy's eyes met mine in the darkness. She was so proud of him. *I* was so proud of him. I *knew* that guy; he was my *friend*; he was the most talented person I'd ever known, except for Peewee and, possibly, Lucien. He read maybe twelve poems, including my favorite, "The Only Living Witness," and then he came to the finale, and I liked that poem so much I asked him for a copy later that night. It was set in my neighborhood and dated from the time when Jim had lived there himself, and that was partly what I liked about it, but I also appreciated the sentiments. I very nearly destroyed my copy a few weeks later, but I'm glad now I didn't. The title is written across the top in Jim's scrawl: "Song of the Open Freeway."

> From a distance
> like the distance of the cliffs in Elysian Park
> the two lines of car lights appear quite beautiful.
> They barely move at all
> and it's tempting to imagine what each set of bulbs represents.
> You think of Walt Whitman making lists of occupations:
> all those people who stand for different livelihoods
> and are headed home to families
> that are different but the same too.
> Maybe they're linked by the same radio station.
> Maybe it's a day when some news has broken
> such as the space shuttle exploding in the sky over Florida
> or the first reports of retaliation bombs dropped on Tripoli.
> And there down on the freeway
> everybody is listening to the same report
> with the same acute ear
> and feeling at the same time
> the same stakes and curiosity.
>
> Isn't it pretty to think so?
> It's as pretty as watching red and white lights
> like two long stripes on a great American flag
> that can only be seen from a distance.
> It's the same distance Whitman used for everything
> as he hovered a hundred years ago
> and saw too little to understand the strangers
> he claimed to love.

His midwives and prostitutes were ciphers.
His coachmen and blacksmiths and firemen
were as blank as raindrops
and part of the neverending sea of himself.
And America too:
that's what he tried to embody.

But if you were on the freeway in a car of your own
and not watching from a distance as he once did
you'd see the missing part of his vision.
You've already seen it.
Even if you're just passing through
you've looked through your window
which is rolled up to maintain a certain temperature
and seen that most of the windows in the right and left lanes
are rolled up too.
Most of the glass is tinted
so you can't make out the faces
and when you can
they're staring straight ahead
or at the cigarette they're just about to light
or glancing at their hair in the rear view mirror.
It's highly unlikely they're listening
to the same music
or the same deejay
or even the same helicopter report
explaining why they're stuck on Interstate Five
with fifty thousand other cars
they can't wait to lose.

HE RECEIVED THE RECEPTION OF A ROCK STAR. People actually stood to clap—maybe ten of all fifty present, but still. He thanked them and stood, tipping over the stool as he headed to the bar, and I ran back to meet him and shook him by the shoulders and said, "Man, that was incredible!" Nancy came back and said he was *wonderful*, hugging and kissing him, and even the bartender was full of praise. She bought him a shot, and Jim slammed it, meantime acting as if he had no idea how good he'd been, though I was sure he knew perfectly well. I heard Miles in the next room announce the next poet, and Nancy trotted off to watch, leaving me with Jim, whose modest act was slipping. Wasn't the poem about Whitman *great*? And how about the one about North Beach? That was a tribute to Jack Kerouac, in case I couldn't tell. Oh, I could? That was strange. There was a time when he used to imitate Kerouac quite a bit, but that was before he'd read better poets and learned how to write a good poem. All the same, he still had a lot of regard for Kerouac.

"I'll never forget," he told me, "the first time I read *On the Road*. I was fifteen, and for months afterwards I'd go to the Greyhound station and watch people waiting for the bus. I just thought it was so romantic, you know. They were *going* someplace, and I was stuck in Burbank. It was so boring back then. You ever watch *Laugh-In*? They were always cracking jokes about Burbank, and I used to laugh so hard! Then I decided I was going to be a big car thief, just like Neal Cassady, and to practice I thought I'd steal my dad's car. I didn't even know how to drive yet, but one night I took his keys and backed the car out of the driveway, and—bam!—I plowed right into another car. It was just a fender bender, you know, but my mom and dad came running out of the house, and I thought they were going to have a heart attack! In fact, a few months later my dad *died* of a heart attack, and I always thought that was the reason."

I'd never heard that story before. He was full of new stories, full of himself, and the more he drank, the louder and more effusive he got. I knew exactly how he must be feeling. I used to come offstage so revved up. It never left me tired; it was better than doing coke or speed, though I'd take any drugs on hand to enhance the high. Then, before I knew it, the reading was over and the bar was filled to capacity, and I was going to beat it before I bumped into Astrid, but she seemed to have gone home, and I was drunk and wanted to get drunker yet. Miles suggested we move to the cheaper bar next door, so we all walked outside, where Astrid and White Belt were hanging around on the sidewalk, and I ducked inside the place next door, hoping they wouldn't follow. I got a booth in the back, and Jim and Nancy and Miles and a few others joined me, and still others from the reading stopped by our table to compliment Jim. What had Miles meant when he called him a leading figure of the L.A.

punk scene? Who was he? What was the name of his band? And Jim was just glowing; he sat there like a mafia don, like the wise old man on top of a mountain climbed by pilgrims in search of the meaning of life. Then, to my horror, Astrid and White Belt walked up to pay homage to Jim; and Astrid tried to speak to me, but I kept saying, "What? It's too loud, I can't hear you!" Finally she and White Belt left the bar, and I almost felt like chasing after them to see if there were still more painful revelations Astrid could lay on me. But I didn't. I commiserated with Nancy, who now suggested, as she never had previously, that Irina might be too young for me. I had a feeling that was coming. Both my brothers had said the same thing, but I'd told them what I now told Nancy: Irina could be older than I was and still be afraid to leave her husband. That was the problem: fear. She'd tied the knot at twenty, and I was thirty-seven and, briefly, I'd been semi-engaged, and that was as close as I'd come to getting married. In other words, age was relative. There was a blonde girl eavesdropping across from us, the same blonde I'd seen laugh so hard at Jim's anecdote about Mr. Peanut, and she said she agreed with me, that she was seeing an older guy who wasn't nearly as mature as *she* was and blah-blah-blah, meantime giving me the eye. It's always that way. If you're single and jerking off, they leave you to it. If you're getting laid, they're interested. And it wasn't as if that girl would've needed to hear me talk about Irina to know I'd been privy to some top-shelf pussy. Chicks can sense that shit. I broke off with her and chatted her up for at least an hour. She was very cute and very stupid (an actress, what else?), and I was sure I could easily have fucked her that night, but, as it was, all I did was ask for her phone number. Might as well, right? I was soon to be single. Our party closed the bar; and I was so drunk Nancy said I should ride with her; and Jim was so drunk I had to help him to Nancy's car; and Miles was pretty drunk himself, spotting Jim on the other side. He was already proposing another reading. He told Jim he was almost as good as Bukowski, and Jim said, "Fuck that prick! I'm better!"

"Man," Miles said, "I just *love* this guy! Don't you just *love* this guy?" And just then I have to say I did. Jim's triumph, however small, effectively saved my life that night. It would've been the perfect note to finish things on. But I didn't realize at the time I'd shortly want to finish things—with Irina, yes, but not with him.

I couldn't face having to wake up and find a way back to my car. I drove home, and the next day Irina came over and said she'd never asked David to take her back; she *wasn't* back, and she couldn't believe I'd listen to a single word Astrid had to say. We had a terrible fight, the worst one ever, but there was nothing we said that hadn't been said before, and we ended up in bed, same as always. What a vicious circle! But only she had the power to end it, and so by way of forcing her hand, I called the blonde. I fucked her too. We had a few drinks at a bar called Jones, and that was all it took: she could hardly wait to get me home. And I could hardly wait to leave as soon as it was over. She had nothing, that girl. I could only get it up by thinking of Irina. Then I went back and told Irina, who exploded and said it was finished, exactly as hoped, and left my place in tears. I'd finally done it. I'd finally shed that lead jacket once and for all. But was I happy about it? Of course not. What *was* it about that girl? Why was I so in love with her? Honestly, there were times when I thought she'd cast some kind of spell on me, and a few days later she did something so bizarre it almost seemed to prove it. I'd gone for a walk in Elysian Park, the setting of Jim's poem, and when I got home, I went to put my key in the door and felt something on it, something that felt like hair. Sure enough, I leaned down and saw that somebody had wrapped strands of long dark hair around my doorknob. Yes, I wonder who *that* was? And why had she put it there? Was this some kind of witchcraft thing? I went inside and called her—she picked up right away—and said, "Irina, would you mind telling me what your hair is doing on my doorknob?"

"My what?"

"Your *hair*. I just found your *hair* wrapped around my doorknob."

"I don't know what you're talking about."

She kept on denying it. It wasn't *her* hair, she said; it must belong to my *new* girlfriend. I said, "She's not my girlfriend. And she doesn't know where I live, and she's a blonde and this hair is dark. And I only slept with her one time, and that was just to make you mad."

Finally, after much groveling on my part, she copped. She said she'd stopped by a half-hour before and, thinking I was refusing to come to the door while possibly banging somebody else, she'd yanked out a hank of her hair in a fit of rage and wrapped it around my doorknob. Sweet talk. Apologies. We sealed the deal with sex. Things were going to be very different from now on, she swore. She was going to have her own place within a week.

"But you don't *need* your own place. Just move in with me!"

"But it's not the right time for that. Look at us. All we do is fight. And I know it's not always going to be that way, and I want to move in when everything is good."

She always was a big one for the perfect moment, and by now I understand. I should've understood long before. I met Peewee at the perfect moment and so discovered punk. I met Jim at CBGB's at the perfect moment and so left North Carolina. Luck played a part, but there are states of mind that create or, anyway, lead to luck, both good and bad, and from there it's a matter of shrewdly using the possibilities opened to make for an ideal outcome. That, in a nutshell, was Irina's philosophy, or at least part of it; and despite her histrionics, she was very shrewd.

Still, for the moment, nothing really changed. She did start looking for her own place, and I looked with her, but there was always a problem with every place we saw. It was usually a matter of cost, since the L.A. rents were spiraling out of control. I hadn't realized it, I'd been living in the same place so long, but L.A. landlords were increasingly charging New York prices, and for what? In New York it almost made sense. It wasn't what it used to be, but it was still the most exciting city in North America. But L.A.? It was nothing but a giant parking lot. Then she found a studio in South Pasadena for $450 a month, and at first she was going to take it, and a day later she wasn't. She said it was a little too small and too far away; she could see herself stuck on the freeway when she really had to make an audition. Oh, and speaking of auditions, right in the middle of looking for apartments, she landed a part in a play. It was just a little non-paying fringe thing, like *Forever and a Day*, but she still got excited about it, and then the director let her go after a couple of rehearsals. I think he cast her hoping it was going to lead to romance, and when he realized it wasn't, decided to cast someone else. But she took it as still more proof of her lack of talent, and to make matters worse, David informed her that her role in his movie had been cut by half and he was hiring another actress to loop her lines, exactly as forecast by Astrid. He told Irina it wasn't her fault, that the movie was running too long and he needed to focus more on the main characters. Plus every time he showed the film to strangers, they asked why the girl who played the daughter spoke with a strange accent—was she supposed to be adopted or what? But they always said she *looked* great, and he was going to give her a tape of her cut scenes so she could put them on her demo reel. But what good would it do? They'd only show how bad she was. She was nothing. She had nothing. I said, "Hey, you've always got *me*."

"I know. And you're everything I ever wanted in a man, but I can't live *through* you, you know. I wouldn't want that, and I know you wouldn't either. I want people to realize I've got things to say, but I'm not even sure if I *do* anymore. All I've got is the way I look, and once that goes, I'm going to be left with nothing."

If only she could've been that dramatic when the cameras were rolling! And I loved that about her; I loved that whatever she felt, she really *felt* it, but I'd reached a point of emotional saturation. It wasn't just her, it was working on two scripts at once, and driving a deathtrap I couldn't afford to fix, and best friends announcing they were going to marry bitches who couldn't stand me, and alcoholic poet-musicians and their masochistic girlfriends who wouldn't stop calling—I'll get to that in a minute. And Irina was the only thing holding me together, but she was also the main thing tearing me apart. She was life, she was grief, she was breath, she was death. She couldn't even stay the night anymore; she had to run off like Cinderella by midnight, otherwise David might get suspicious. And what was funny was how much time we spent talking about that guy, and yet I never saw him. He was almost like a ghost, like Irina's imaginary friend she alone had the power to see, communicating all his sayings and doings. And then I finally saw him myself. It happened in June, Irina's all-important month, a week before her twenty-fifth birthday and the fifth anniversary of her supposedly-over marriage. And that June also marked the fifth anniversary of Milan's move to America, and he was throwing a party to celebrate, and Irina was going with David. Which meant *I* couldn't go. There was no way I could be in the same room with the two of them; but Irina said David never stayed late at parties, and if I came after eleven, she promised they'd be gone. I was really annoyed they were going together, but, after all, even if David stayed home, I still couldn't touch her in front of other people—definitely not *those* people. As far as they were concerned, she and David were still a couple.

The night of the party, I waited till 11:30 before leaving the house. Milan lived in Silver Lake, ten minutes away, and my transmission was acting up all the way there: I'd stop and start to move again, and for a second the car would balk, and then I'd feel it pop into first gear, fine till the next time I stopped. There was no place to park on Milan's street, so I drove around the block, looking for a spot, and there in front of me, maybe fifteen feet away, I saw a couple walking toward an SUV parked along the curb. The SUV was David's—I'd seen it in his driveway many times—so that must mean—my God, that was David and Irina! It's so strange that I recognized the SUV before I did Irina, but her back was turned to me, and it was at least forty-five minutes after she'd promised they'd be gone, so I wasn't expecting to see her. I stopped to watch as they kept walking. They weren't holding hands but they were obviously talking, and at one point Irina turned in profile to laugh, apparently at something David had said, and I could tell she liked him, when I'd always wanted to convince myself she didn't truly like him at all. He was wearing a sports jacket that must have run a cool thousand—real top-of-the-line stuff—and this was maybe six weeks after his coffee-burning episode, and after hearing so much about the extent of his injuries, I half expected to see a pus-covered monster; but, no, he was as handsome as ever. Then, when they got to the SUV, Irina walked over to the passenger side, disappearing from sight, and David went with her, apparently to open her door like a gentleman. (I always did the same thing.) A moment later he reappeared in my headlights, and squinting toward me, a presumed stranger, he held up a finger as if to say, "The parking spot is yours in one minute!" It was such a courteous gesture, and for someone like David, I knew it was meaningless—fine manners were part of his upbringing—yet I still couldn't help but like him for it. He seemed sort of fragile in my headlights—that squinting made him seem vulnerable—and I realized he wasn't a wraith standing between me and Irina; he was flesh and bone; he squinted like any other human being in the headlights of a car that could easily crush him. Yes, I thought about running him down for a second! He was the bane of my existence. And yet I barely knew him, and I'd never once considered his feelings in the matter. I didn't care if he loved Irina or not, and so what if he got hurt? He was hurting me by trying to hold on to her. But wouldn't I do the same if I were him? And how did I know I wasn't wrong by trying to pull her my way? I was so confused! I was doubting what I'd never doubted before and pissed at myself for doubting it, and pissed at Irina for not leaving when she said she would, and pissed at David for his classy manners while, at the same time, liking him for it. And I sat and watched as he got inside his SUV and drove off with the girl I loved, leaving me to park my car in a spot I wasn't about to take.

◠

AND NOW TO BRIEFLY BACKTRACK. Maybe a week before Milan's party, I'd gotten a call from Nancy—in fact, ever since the reading I'd been getting a *lot* of calls from Nancy. Jim had broken the toilet. He wouldn't look for a job. He'd gotten drunk and passed out with a pan still burning on the stove. She'd ask me to speak with him, and I would speak with him, but apparently the applause of fifty people had caused his head to swell to the size of a small planet and damaged his hearing to boot. Not even yelling worked. He'd yell right back or vaguely promise to make things right, and from there he'd talk about his "great" new poems or invite me over to jam. Then he'd kiss Nancy's ass for a couple of days, and during that time the phone wouldn't ring, but then it would again with: "Jason, Eddie's doing such-and-such, could you speak to him please?" Finally I told Nancy I was sick and tired of playing Daddy all the time, that she was going to have to take matters into her own hands and kick him out. But she couldn't. She *loved* him, don't you know. I said, "Nancy, that guy doesn't love you. He treats you the same way a pimp treats a hooker. He's nice, then he's mean, and he sits back doing nothing while you pay for everything." Then she went back like a perfect dumbass and repeated what I'd said, and Jim called to say I'd made Nancy upset. I said, "Since when do you care? What, you're Nancy's protector now? And I wouldn't have said a word if she didn't call me up to bitch every five seconds."

"Yeah, that's what she does, she bitches. But you don't have to listen to it. You know what your problem is, Jason? You've always got to be everybody's *savior*."

He was right: I did have something of a savior complex. I wonder if that related to the accident. Gosh, you think? What a mystery! But Jim, I now decided, couldn't be saved, or in any case I no longer had the wherewithal to make the effort. Nor was I going to help that dumb cunt Nancy, who continued to call, though I seldom picked up. Then one night around eight o'clock the phone rang, and, seeing her number on my caller ID, I let the call go to voice mail. A few minutes later I listened to her message, which she'd left in practically a whisper. Please, she said, *please* call her back; she was scared to death. She'd never sounded like that before, so I called, and, still speaking low, she said, "Jason, could you please come over? Eddie just tried to hit me."

"He what?"

And she told me the story. It seemed the day before she'd taken $200 out of the bank, and now she was missing fifty she knew she hadn't spent. In fact, she whispered, ever since Jim moved in, she'd noticed small amounts disappearing here and there, but she'd never wanted to think he was *stealing* from her. Now she knew he had been—there was no other possibility. So she confronted him, and he blew up and took a drunken swing at her, and she ran to her room, where she still was, and called me. She didn't want to call the police, since if Jim got arrested, he might freak out in jail or some hardened criminal might beat him up, and she couldn't have that on her conscience. At the same time he couldn't go on living with her; he was going to have to get out, and she was afraid to tell him herself. I said, "Okay, sit tight, I'm on my way," and started getting dressed. I was almost out the door when she called again to say he wasn't there anymore. I said, "What do you mean, he's not there? Where is he?"

"Well, he knocked on the door and said he was sorry, and I told him you were coming over, and he stormed out of the house. Wait, what's that? Jason, *please* get over here! I think he's coming back!"

But he wasn't at the house when I got there ten minutes later. Nancy said he'd probably gone to that bar where he'd taken to spending so much time—Club Tee Gee, it was called—so I told her I'd look for him there, but she was afraid he might come back while I was gone. Nor did she want to go with me. She didn't want to see him at all. I said, "Well, you're going to have to see him at some point. He's not going to do anything. I won't let him." Finally she agreed to go with me, and we took her car, since mine was fucked up, and drove a few blocks to Club Tee Gee. He wasn't there, but he had been. I described him to the bartender, who said, "Oh, him. He left about ten minutes ago." I asked if she knew where he might have been headed, and she said, "How would *I* know? He just came in and used the phone and left."

Still, since he'd left on foot, he couldn't have gotten far. We drove all around Atwater Village, checking restaurants and liquor stores, as well as more of the same in nearby Glendale—nothing. Who had he called at Club Tee Gee? That person must have picked him up. Nancy thought it was probably his mother or, possibly, Miles. It seemed Jim and Miles had gotten kind of chummy since the reading, and as a matter of fact, Miles was putting together another reading for the following week in which Jim was planning to participate. Then we drove back to Nancy's, where she called Miles to see if Jim had called him. He hadn't. I wasn't eager to call his mom, and neither was Nancy. She heated up some leftovers and analyzed Jim at some length while we waited for him to call or return, and she said she now thought I was right, that he treated her the same way a pimp treats a hooker. Weren't pimps control freaks? Well, that's what Jim was. In fact, most agoraphobics were control freaks: everything had to be just right, otherwise they couldn't function. On and on she went till two in the morning, and the phone never rang, and Jim never came back either. I was sure he must have found a way to his mom's, but Nancy asked if I'd mind crashing just in case. It was hard to say no with her looking so scared. She got me a pillow and blanket, and I tried to sleep on the sofa, but every time I dozed off, Nancy's cat would thump around and I'd wake thinking it was Jim. Finally I napped till I heard a sharp noise and saw it was morning. The noise was Nancy shutting the bathroom door. Then she walked out to the living room with her hair sticking up like pins in a cushion and said, "I guess you were right. He must have gone back to his mother's." There was only one way to find out: one of us was going to have to call.

So, while Nancy got ready for work, I did. She answered, and I said, "Hi, Mrs. McDaniel, it's Jason. Is Eddie there?"

"*Eddie*? You know Eddie's not here. He moved in with that—woman."

"Yeah, that's where I am right now. He left last night and didn't come back, so we thought he might be there with you."

Then she laughed a snippy laugh and said, "Well, I could've *told* you that was going to happen. Every time he gets on drugs, he does the same thing, running off and worrying people half to death. And I'll bet you he's going to call me and ask me to come get him. Well, I'm not going to do it *this* time. And *you*—I *trusted* you. I thought you were a *good* boy, but you had to take him over to that woman and let her put him back on drugs."

"But he's not *back* on drugs. Nancy's not that kind of person. And they had a fight last night, and he can't stay here anymore, and I think he's going to have to come back and live with you."

"*Oh* no!" she squawked. "I told him when he moved out I was done. I've been through this too many times already! Uh-*uh*! No more for *me*!" I said, "Mrs. McDaniel, you know you don't really feel that way. I know you still care about him, and I know he cares about you. I realize he doesn't always show it, but I'm going to have a talk with him about that. Honestly, you deserve a medal for the way you've dealt with Eddie. You're the only person who knows how to." I kept laying it on as thick as I could, and she wasn't responsive, or she wasn't at first; but then it was like the dam broke, and she ran down a long list of her many sufferings—her sore feet and arthritis and various other medical problems, not to mention running a business while losing a child and not just one but two husbands—and did I think *he* cared? No, he did not. She'd done so much for him—she'd gotten him off drugs and given him a home and even arranged it so he wouldn't have to work, seeing that he could never hold a job anyway—and where was the gratitude? There was none. All he ever did was run off to play "rock music" with "a bunch of lowlifes" and come back whenever he got in trouble. He was the most selfish boy she ever met. Why was he like that? Where did he get it from? Certainly not from her. She came from *good* people. I said, "Yes, and that's exactly why he needs to be living with you. You're a great influence!" We spoke for quite some time, and she never said she'd take him back, but I knew she would. She needed him. He needed her. How could I ever have convinced myself he was better off living elsewhere? He was like a genie I'd released from a bottle, and now I wanted to stuff him back and drop the bottle in the middle of the ocean, where, hopefully, some fish would come along and swallow it up, and then the fish would be swallowed by a giant sea beast, and so on. And she was the bottle and the beast both, yet I couldn't help but feel sorry for her. I hung up and told Nancy to give me a call if she heard from him; and then, at home, I grabbed some more sleep and, late that afternoon, started writing. Nancy called to say there was still no word from Jim, and she asked if I'd meet her when she got off work in forty-five minutes, afraid Jim would be waiting at the house when she got there. I said, "Nancy, I really can't keep doing this. I missed a whole night of work last night, and I've got to finish a script."

"Well, just do it this time, and I promise I won't ask anymore. If he's not there, I'm going to call a locksmith and have the locks changed."

So, once again, Jason the Savior couldn't say no. I drove to the house, where Nancy was sitting outside in her car, looking about as gray-faced as Laura had that time Peewee had called threatening to kill everybody in Scratch. She was convinced she'd seen Jim peer out the window, and she gave me her keys, asking me to go inside first and have a look. I opened the door. Everything was very quiet. I searched the whole house, checking closets and behind the shower curtain, and even got down on my hands and knees to look beneath the beds, where I thought I saw an enormous rat that turned out to be Nancy's cat. Then I walked back to the porch and told Nancy it was safe, and suddenly, as if she'd seen somebody rise up behind me, she went, "Oh my God!" I whipped around. There was nobody there. I turned back and said, "Why did you *do* that?"

"I'm having a panic attack! Oh my God! Oh my God!"

She slapped her rubber band. She fanned her face with her hand. Then she ran to the dining room and picked up the phone and punched a number, and I heard her say, "Carmen? It's Nancy. I'm having a ten!" I went to the bathroom to take a leak, and when I walked out a few minutes later, Nancy was still on the phone, looking like she'd just been shot.

"He's there," she told me.

"Who's there?"

"Eddie. He's at Carmen's house!"

Well, I'll be damned! Carmen was *another* of his agoraphobic phone-sex partners. He'd mentioned her a few times, and for all I knew, he'd been jerking off with her the whole time he'd been living with Nancy. I asked Nancy for the phone. She gave it to me, and I said, "Carmen? It's Jason. I'm a friend of Eddie's. Could you tell him I have to talk to him, please? Tell him I'm not mad, I'm not going to yell at him. I just have to talk to him for a minute." Then a woman with an accent said to hold on, and finally Jim came on the line, and as if we'd been playing a fun little game of hide-and-seek, which I guess to him we had been, he said, "You found me."

"Yeah, by sheer accident. How'd you get there?"

"I took a cab."

"Well, that was resourceful. I'm sure you realize you've upset a lot of people, right? We've been looking everywhere for you!"

"Well, I couldn't stay there. I thought you were coming over to beat me up!"

"Yeah, I *ought* to beat you up. Trying to hit Nancy. What the fuck is wrong with you?"

"Hey, you told Carmen you weren't going to do this. And I never tried to hit Nancy! She was acting like such a maniac, accusing me of stealing from her, and all I did was—"

But I cut him off. It didn't matter what the story was, I said; Nancy had reached her limit, and he was going to have to move.

"Well, if she would just—"

"No, it's all been decided. She's having the locks changed, and you're just lucky she called me and not the police. She still could, you know. And I spoke to your mom, and I think you're just going to have to go back and live with her."

"*What*? I can't do that!"

"No, it's fine. Unless you're back on heroin. You're not, right?"

"Of *course* not. But, Jason, I can't go *there*. Remember how you were always saying I had to get a life? Well, you were right. And I've made a lot of progress these last few months, and if I go back there, it's all going to be lost."

Not true, I said; it was all up to him. His mom didn't charge him any rent, and if he got a job and worked a few months, he'd have the money to get his own place in no time. In fact, I could *help* him get a job—a really good job I was sure he could work. I was supposed to direct a movie in a few months, and he could be the composer—what what a perfect fit! The movie was the kiddie flick, but I couldn't get Jim a job. Avatar was too cheap to pay for a composer, so I was always forced to use canned music. Besides, even if I could've hired Jim, I wouldn't have. I was just trying to con him, the same way he'd conned me and Nancy, and as soon as he coughed up Carmen's address, I was going to collect him and drive him to his mom's and sever all contact, at least for a while. The con worked, but I could also tell he *wanted* me to pick him up, since he wasn't too impressed with Carmen's looks, or as he put it: "Nancy's like Sophia Loren compared to this one." He had Carmen give me directions. Then I called Jim's mom to say we'd found him and I was bringing him back to her; and she said, "Well, okay. But if he doesn't shape up this time, I'm kicking him out for good." Yeah, right. Then I hung up and dealt with Nancy, who was jealous of Jim and Carmen. Jesus Christ! He'd mooched off her and stolen from her and even tried to slap her around, yet the minute she learned she had a rival, none of the rest seemed to matter. I said, "Do you want to be rid of this guy or not?"

"Yes, but—"

"But nothing! Now let's pack his shit and be done with it!"

So we did. Nancy had moved him to her place in a single trip, so his stuff easily fit the back of her station wagon. She let him keep the Martin, which I thought generous. Then, alone, I followed Carmen's directions to Boyle Heights till I came to a small house painted the same flat blue as the spiked iron fence surrounding it. I never got a glimpse of Carmen. Jim answered the door, smiling coyly like a second-grader who's been caught drawing dirty pictures. He knew what a bad little boy he'd been, running away from home. Now he wanted to make amends with Daddy. His mood changed when he saw that Nancy's car was packed with his stuff—I hadn't told him I was bringing it. He said I should have let *him* pack his stuff, especially his computers, but I said, "No, I was really careful," which I had been. Then, after he'd sunk the passenger seat, we hit the freeway, and he was talkative for most of the trip. He said one of Nancy's co-workers must have stolen her money, and he likewise insisted he never tried to hit her. He'd just been gesturing with his hands, he said, and Nancy was so hysterical she'd mistaken it for something else. He wasn't a violent person and never had been. That was part of the reason he abandoned punk rock, remember? Those right-wing beach kids who took over the scene—*they* were violent. But now that he thought about it, maybe they should have been. There was a lot to be mad about. There still was. Look at this place, with its back-to-back strip malls and fast-food joints. I was right: things were getting worse. Corporations ruled the world, and people were starved for something better, something that really moved them, and there was nobody there to give it to them. But maybe *I* could give it to them. I was so talented, you know, and such a great friend—I was the best friend he'd ever had. Yes, it was Grammy night all over again. What, did he have that speech memorized? Yet he seemed so sincere, and even as pissed as I was, it was hard not to find him engaging. On the other hand, everything he now said was something I'd said to him, and that was something Peewee had once said to me, and he in turn had picked it up from Jim, among others. And I was so tired, I was so sick and goddamned tired, and Jim wanted to talk about that bogus composing job, and I said, "Let's talk about it some other time. I'm pretty burned out right now."

"Oh?" he said. "Having problems with your girl again?" I thought, "Actually, the problem is *you*, motherfucker. But I'm taking care of that." He grew quiet as we got closer to his mom's place, and he walked inside as if ready for a fight, but she made his homecoming easy. You could tell she was glad to have him back, and that horrible dog danced for joy at the sight of Jim. We lugged his stuff inside, and afterward he tried to get me to stick around for a beer, but I told him it was getting late and I had to return Nancy's car. Then he walked me to the door and said he hoped to see me at his reading with Miles the following week. That's when I should've leveled with him. I should've said, "You know what? Lose my number. I can't deal with your ass anymore." But he'd gone along so peacefully, and I felt so relieved, and there seemed no reason to spoil a perfectly good parting for the sake of being honest. The genie was back in its bottle now. Unfortunately, I hadn't thrown it far enough.

HE LEFT ME SEVERAL MESSAGES over the next few days to remind me about the reading. It was scheduled for the same night as Milan's party, and that, again, was the night I saw David with Irina. After that I couldn't bring myself to go the party, driving home instead. I called Irina the next day and said I had to see her, it was urgent; and when she got to my place a half-hour later, I told her what I'd seen, and she said, "Yes, I saw you too. I'm sorry, sweetheart. I know I said we'd be gone, but David kept talking to Milan—"

"It doesn't matter, I really don't care. But you're going to have to make a decision now. If you want to be with David, be with David—I'll understand, I really will—and if you want to be with me, you know I'm yours. But you can't string me along anymore. I am seriously losing my fucking mind. I can't take another day of this shit, I can't take another—"

And with absolutely no sense it was about to happen, I started crying. It was almost like that time at the hospital when I sat up in bed and it suddenly sank in that I was never going to see Peewee again: one second I was fine, the next I was bawling. It wasn't the first time I'd cried in front of her—I'd done it that night at the motel when I told her about the accident, and I'd also gotten a little misty before she boarded her plane at Christmas—but this was different; this was big hot tears that almost seemed to burn my face and sobs like a goddamned baby. And she came to me and held me and said as she stroked me, "It's okay, it's okay, *shhhhhh.*" I cried on her shoulder, and she cried too, and the whole time she stroked me and said in a whisper, "*Shhhhh,* it's okay, it's all going to be okay." And when I couldn't cry anymore, when I was all cried out, I asked her what she wanted to do, and she said, "Well, I'll have to tell him, of course."

"No. You can't say that unless you really mean it."

"Of course I mean it."

"You promise?"

"I promise."

"You swear?"

"Of *course,* Jason. I was always going to tell him, but you never seem to believe me."

"And you'll do it right away?"

"Well, he's taking a break in a few days. They're changing to a new cutting room or something, and that should be a good time. At least he'll have a few days to get over it."

"And what are you going to say?"

"What *can* I say? I'm in love with someone else."

Then she wiped away her tears and mine too and said, "Oh, sweetheart, I'm *so* sorry. I knew it was hurting you, but not this bad. It breaks my *heart* to see you this way."

"What a pussy, huh?"

"Not at all. I think it's beautiful. It makes me feel so close to you."

I felt the same way. I felt closer than ever before, as if by crying I'd burned something away, and now I felt really clean. Maybe it sounds foolish, given all the broken promises along the way, but when someone you love is looking you in the eye and swearing she's going to do something, you really believe she's going to do it, no matter what's gone on before. Even knowing what an effective liar she can be, you believe. We were together the rest of that day and into the night, spooning on the sofa as we planned the days ahead. We agreed that she'd live with me till she got her own place, or maybe she'd never get her own place; maybe we'd get a bigger place for the two of us if living together went well. But everything was fine, everything was going to be okay; she might tell David as soon as she got home if she got the chance, and if she did, she'd call me. Then she left and I worked on the kiddie script till I managed to finish it, and drove a copy to the Avatar office late the next day and waited till they cut me a check. I put the check in the bank on the way home, and once it cleared, I could finally fix my car—it was just barely drivable. I tried to call Irina, and she didn't pick up, but she didn't always, especially after she moved back to David's; and most days we spoke for at least a few minutes, but sometimes we'd miss a day, so I wasn't too concerned. I worked on *Landmine* till I went to bed at dawn, and at some point I thought I heard the phone ring, but I wasn't sure, and, exhausted, I fell back asleep. I woke around noon and checked my caller ID, where I saw Astrid's name and thought, "That's weird. Why would *Astrid* be calling me?" Then I checked my voice mail and listened to her message, and this is pretty much how it went:

"You piece of fucking shit. You are the lowest, most disgusting piece of shit *trash* ever to walk the earth. You are *shit*. You are *scum*. I hope you die the most miserable, painful *death,* you piece of *shit*, you *scum*."

And then, of course, a loud click. It really had a good zip to it with that clipped accent of hers, and I stood there shocked out of my fucking skull. Believe me, I had no desire to listen again, but I did to see if I could pick up some clue as to what she was talking about; but, no, that was as much as she'd said. The only thing I could figure was that Irina had sat David down for the big talk, and David had told Astrid, who was mad at me for giving her brother horns. Except Irina had said she was going to call me as soon as she told David. And she never had.

I tried her again. There was still no answer. I left a message saying I'd gotten a *very* strange call from Astrid and to get back to me right away. Then I dressed and paced and waited. The phone didn't ring, so I went online to see if she'd sent me an e-mail. She hadn't. However, Jim had sent me an invitation to the reading that was still unopened in my inbox, and when I saw that, I was hit by the most horrible thought. I thought, "What if *Astrid* went to Jim's reading, and somehow they started talking, and *that's* how she knew about me and Irina?" What a disaster that would be! Jim knew things I was sure Irina would never tell David, and of course he loved to stress the most lurid details whenever and however possible: popped blisters, and pussies like mayonnaise jars, and blind girls who fucked bandmates. And Astrid would take whatever he said straight to David, and she would likewise stress the most lurid details to make good and sure he knew what a slut his wife was. Of all the ways for him to learn about us! Irina would be so upset! But it wasn't possible, you're jumping to conclusions, stop thinking about it right this second. But Jim did have an *awfully* big mouth, you know. He'd no sooner met Paul Bertolette than he'd told him his friend Michelle had given him gonorrhea; and once, by a fluke, he'd been in the same room as Astrid, and if her boyfriend had read this time too… But cut it out, stop it, this city was too big, word couldn't travel that way. It wasn't like I was back in high school. But maybe I'd never *left* high school. After all, the rich kids were still in power, and the mavericks were still pariahs, and people just loved to run their mouths—especially in *this* town. I paced and waited for the phone to ring, and then it did ring, and guess who was trying to reach me? Jim, that's who. I was almost afraid to pick up.

But I did pick up.

"Well, *there* you are," he said. "I've been trying to reach you for days. Why didn't you come to the reading?"

"Had to finish a script."

"Oh, right. Get it all done?"

"Yeah, but I'm working on something else now. So? How was it?"

"Well, it wasn't as good as the last one. It was okay, I guess. I read some new stuff, and that seemed to go over well. Nancy was there, she liked it. And Miles—he drove out to pick me up, and we got *so* drunk when it was over. I wish you'd been there. I think that's one reason it went so well last time, having you there."

"Yeah, sorry about that. So who else read? Same people as last time?"

"I don't know. I was at the bar for most of it. I watched Miles, and he was so bad I was afraid to watch the others. You know, the more I think about it, the more I think you were right. These kids got nothing. I was talking to a bunch of them after the reading, and they're so empty it's really kind of sad."

"And you don't know who else read? What about a guy with dyed-back hair who came up and talked to you last time."

"Dyed-black hair?"

"Yeah, about thirty? Kind of a good-looking guy?"

"Oh, I think I know the one you're talking about. He's in a band, right? And he's got an English girlfriend? Yeah, he was there. You know, I don't mind that guy. He seems kind of smart compared to the others. And her—has she got some tits or what? But I guess you know that."

"What do you mean?"

"Well, didn't you used to go out with her?"

Okay, stay calm, don't freak out, just find out exactly what they said. I asked, and he said, "Not much. She asked where you were and I said I didn't know, and that was it. I mostly talked to him."

"Well, you know I used to go out with her, right? She must've told you that much."

"No, I think *you* did. No, I remember now. Yeah, she said you used to go out and—did she dump you for somebody else? Does that sound right?"

"No, it doesn't. But I hope you didn't mention Irina."

"Did I? Yeah, I think we *did* talk about Irina. Why? Was I not supposed to?"

"Yeah, you could say that! That was Irina's husband's sister, okay? And he didn't know about us, and now he does, thanks to you!"

"Oh," he said, and I said, "Yeah, fucking *oh*! Now, what exactly did you say to her? Did you tell her I got Irina pregnant?"

"I don't remember."

"Yes, you *do* fucking remember! Don't you pull that shit with me! I need to know *exactly* what you said to her!"

"Well, she said—I think she said something about you and Irina. Yeah, she was the first one to bring it up. She already knew, Jason."

"No, she did *not* fucking know! Believe me, I would've heard about it if she did!"

"Well, she didn't seem upset about it. And I'm almost positive she was the first one to say something. Maybe she was suspicious, I don't know, but, like I say, she wasn't upset at all. There was nothing dramatic about it. It was just kind of small talk, you know? The whole exchange was really pleasant."

"Yeah, because you were telling her exactly what she wanted to hear! You fucking told her *everything*, and don't you fucking tell me you didn't!"

But he kept insisting he didn't remember what he'd said, that he was too drunk and they hadn't spoken for long, and it really hadn't seemed like that big of a deal. I said, "No, it's a *very* big deal! She fucking hates Irina, and she's going to make it look as bad as possible, and I'm never going to live it down! This is the worst goddamn thing you could've done! You could've taken a gun and shot me and it would've been better than this!"

"Well, *I* didn't know! And if you were really that worried I was going to say something, you should've been there to make sure I didn't."

"*What*? You mean this is all *my* fault because I wasn't there to babysit your fucking ass? Man, you've got balls of fucking steel! And you want to know *why* I wasn't there? Because I was sick and fucking tired of babysitting your ass! You're a grown fucking man—or no, you're *not* a man—no man would ever talk about another man's business to his ex-goddamn-girlfriend!"

"Well, you talked about *me*! Every time I turned around, Nancy was on the phone with you. And you told my mom I was seeing Nancy—"

"Yeah, because she thought you were shooting up! And you think I *enjoyed* talking to Nancy? I was just trying to help you work things out! And you would never have met Nancy in the first place if it hadn't been for me! I gave you a goddamn *life*, and all you ever gave me back was grief!"

"Well, I *told* you I was grateful. What do you want me to do, write it in blood? And I never asked for your help in the first place; you just came in and decided you knew what was better for me than I knew myself, when you didn't know the first fucking thing *about* me. You just had some picture in your head of what I was supposed to be, and every time I failed to live up to it, you'd tear me a new asshole. You think you're God, Jason. Well, maybe you need to stop thinking about saving other people and start thinking about how to save *yourself*."

Then I told him I'd done that already—I'd gotten rid of him, and that was a start—and he said, "Well, if that's the way you feel, I don't want to know you anyway. I had a feeling you were mad at me. Nancy told me you were, but I thought, 'No, that's not like Jason. If he's got a problem, he's going to say something; he's not going to just vanish.' Well, that just goes to show you. You think I fucked *you* over? Well, you fucked *me* over too."

"So, what, you decided to get back at me?! I'm not there to push your ass onstage, so you decide you're going to turn around and fuck up my whole life?!"

"Jason, you're out of your mind! I had no *idea* who that woman was! And I told you before: she already knew."

"No, I think *you* knew! I think you knew the second she said my name you'd found a way to hurt me! Well, you got me good, motherfucker! You really hit the motherlode!"

"Jason, do you even *hear* what you're saying? Why would I want to hurt you? I loved you! I loved you like my own brother!"

"No, you just *think* you did. You don't even know what love *is*, Eddie. Anybody that treats you good, you have to treat them like shit. You did it with Nancy, you do it with your mom, I bet you did it with Buddy and Cybil and everybody else. Anybody that really cares has got to pay, and do you know why? Because you hate yourself. You hate yourself so much you can't stand it when somebody actually *cares*. How could somebody care about a guy like *you*? So you've got to find a way to hurt them; you've got to find a way to make them hate you as much as you hate yourself, and *then* you can start to love them. I bet that's why you still love Cybil. She hated you so much she killed herself just to fuck you up, and what do you do? You *love* her for it."

I had no idea where any of that came from. It just popped out of my mouth. But I knew it was true, every last word of it; and when I finished, Jim spoke in a tone I'd never quite heard before, really nasty and full of contempt.

"Yeah," he said, "like you're an expert when it comes to love. You really think that little *Serb* loves you? Well, I feel really sorry for you if you do. She's just using you, but you're too blind to see it. And I hope I *did* fuck everything up. It'll be the best goddamn thing anybody ever did for you!"

"Well, you'd better pray that's not what happens! You'd better get down on your goddamn knees and *pray* it all works out! You don't even want to *think* about what's going to happen if it doesn't!"

"Oh, yeah? What's going to happen?"

"I'M GOING TO KILL YOU, THAT'S WHAT! I'M GOING TO COME OUT THERE AND CUT YOUR FUCKING HEAD OFF!"

And he hung up on me. Never in my life have I been as angry as I was at that moment—not even with Mark Powell, not even then. I smashed the phone against the wall; I broke that. I turned over the dining room table and threw chairs across the room; I picked up a halogen lamp and chucked it like a spear. Every single thing I could lay my hands on got thrown or smashed or broken. Then I punched a hole in the wall and hurt my knuckles so badly I had to stop. Everything was very quiet, and I looked around the room, which almost seemed to talk to me like a battered wife, saying, "*Please* don't hit me anymore, *I* didn't do anything." Luckily my computer was in the next room, otherwise I might have destroyed it. I'd totaled the TV with one of the chairs I'd thrown. Plus I no longer had a phone, so Irina couldn't call, and I had to speak to her; I had to speak to her right that second.

So I ran outside and drove down Echo Park Avenue to a liquor store called House of Spirits. There was a pay phone right outside it, and I parked and tried to call Irina, but she still wasn't answering. I left a message saying, "Look, I know what's going on, and I need you to call me so I can explain," and read off the number on the pay phone and paced around on the sidewalk. The June sun was beating down, and the light was blinding, and traffic kept rumbling past—buses and trucks and Mexican hotrods—and I was thinking so many things at once I was barely thinking at all, my mind was spinning, and mostly what I saw was bits and pieces: Astrid's smirk and Jim's big mouth and Irina warning me not to say anything, it might get back to David, and David himself a perfect gentleman standing in my headlights—would he really be such a gentleman now? And the phone didn't ring, and I thought, "Let's try her at the house." I never tried the house; I always called her on her cell phone and didn't even know what the house number was. But, here, I can get that from information. Yes, operator, I need the number for—what's David's last name again? Oh, right, it's a goddamned hyphenate. Yes, that's the one, thanks. Thirty-five cents, ring ring ring, David's voice, leave a message, beep. "Irina, can you hear me? If you can hear me, pick up. Okay, I'm waiting for your call, and the number is 213-663—" Wait a minute, what are you doing? You shouldn't do that! Now you've left your voice on David's machine! But calm down, stop it, it's all okay, it's all going to be just fine. And the sun was so hot, and the light was so harsh, and the traffic was so loud in my ears; and people kept pulling up in the House of Spirits parking lot and glancing at me as I paced in circles like I'd lost my mind. *Had* I lost my mind? Yes, I think I had. And the phone didn't ring, and my whole life was just waiting for the phone to ring; that was all I'd done since I'd come to this town, just wait and wait and it finally rings, and it's never what you want to hear: you've lost your agent, your movie's no good, she's pregnant, she's not, why didn't you come to the reading? And walking slowly toward me was a Mexican lady, seventy at least, with a plastic grocery bag in each hand, and so shriveled it was like those bags were weights and all that kept her from blowing away. She got to the phone and put down the bags and went to pick up the receiver, and I said, "Ma'am, I'm sorry, I'm expecting a call. Ma'am? *Senora? No habla telefon!*" But, as if she couldn't hear me, she fished for change and went to make her call, and I circled round and round and thought, "Jesus Christ, man, what are you doing? The guy knows, the jig is up, and maybe Irina *can't* call you, maybe he's holding her prisoner—there's no telling *what's* going on!"

So I jumped in my car and made for David's house, fifteen minutes away. It seemed like all the lights were against me—they kept turning red as I reached them—and every time I stopped, my car stalled before moving forward when the light turned green; it shook and shuddered, and then I'd feel first gear slap into place and hear it loud and clear: pop! Now second: pop! And here's third: pop! And here's another red light: shake and shudder and pop pop pop! I cursed the car like a stubborn mule; I pounded the dashboard and yelled, "Come on, you piece of shit, move!" Finally I got to David's house, and there was Irina's BMW parked behind his SUV in the driveway. The middle of a workday and David was home—oh yes, he knew, there was no doubt about it. I parked at the curb, and as I got out, I happened to look up and saw a small hawk with powder-blue and pinkish feathers perched above me on a telephone wire—a beautiful bird that almost seemed to know how beautiful it was and was sitting in its own spotlight so the world could admire it. It's so strange I happened to notice that. It slowed me for a second, and once again I thought, "What are you doing? You're just going to make things worse, showing up here. You ought to go home and wait for her to call." But I'd broken my phone, and I was sick to death of waiting. She was mine, she'd just told me so the other day, and it was too late anyway; I'd called the house, and I was standing right in front of it, and everything was so quiet I knew they must have heard me pull up. I walked up to that big Moroccan door and knocked and rang the bell. Nobody answered. There was a spade-shaped window with no curtain to cover it, so I stepped off the porch and looked through the window and saw part of the living room with the sunlight forming a pattern on the wall. Then a shadow passed over the pattern, and it sounded like somebody was whispering, but I couldn't tell if it was a man or a woman or what the whisper said. I went back to the door and really knocked now; I shouted Irina's name like Brando in *Streetcar*—"IRIINAAA! IRIIIINAAAAA!"—and I was thinking of breaking the door down when it suddenly opened, and there was David. He cracked the door maybe two feet wide and stood on the other side of it with a look of reptilian hatred in his eyes. It was a very cold look. His eyes never blinked, and his whole face was so tight, so perfectly pulled together, and he spoke in a soft voice that somehow caught me up short. He said, "She doesn't want to see you, Jason"—and it's hard to explain the effect that had. He seemed so serene, so sure of himself, and he looked right at me—no flinching, no blinking—when I'd been expecting something else entirely: shouts and shoves and threats. Plus he said my name, and there was knowledge in the way he said it, like he knew everything and something else besides: he knew she didn't want to see me, and nothing was going to change that—even if I hit him, I'd only be pushing her that much more to his side. I can see now it was all a trick, something he must have acquired as part of his upbringing, and even at the time I had a sense of that, yet I have to say it worked. I could barely find my voice. Then I did. I said, "Let her tell me that to my face." Yet my voice sounded so weak compared to the way I wanted it to sound, and he kept staring me down with eyes like a snake's and that serene tone designed to keep me off-balance. He said, "I just told you she doesn't want to see you. You're making an awfully big fuss out here, and she's afraid of you. Now get off my property, please, or I'm phoning the police. And don't try to contact Irina. She wants nothing more to do with you." Then he shut the door, and I heard him walk away, and for a second I stood there, stunned. She didn't want to see me. She wanted nothing more to do with me. But I hadn't heard those words from her own mouth, and I knew she was in there—I knew if she wanted to see me, she'd see me; she wouldn't have sent David—but I couldn't believe she could be that cowardly. But hadn't she *always* been that cowardly? She could never bring herself to tell him after months of saying she would, and now he knew, and she *still* wasn't going to leave him. And suddenly I felt my strength again; I pounded on the door and said, "Irina, come out here and talk to me! Don't send David to do your dirty work! If you've got something to say to me, come out here and say it yourself!"

She never answered. David did. From inside the house I heard him say, "All right, Jason, I warned you! I'm phoning the police now!" And at first I thought, "Go ahead and *call* the fucking police." But then I turned and saw an elderly couple in gym clothes paused on the street and gaping at me, and I pictured myself getting hauled off in cuffs with them still watching, and worse, Irina watching from inside the house. And I wasn't about to give her the satisfaction.

So I walked back to the street. I could sense the couple backing away as I got closer. Oh dear, what was *that* all about? The property values must really be sinking, *that* kind of thing going on. I got in my car and sped off, and for at least two hours I drove in circles. I don't remember where I went. All I know is I drove and drove, and it's a wonder I didn't wreck, but some part of me kept the car on the road while most of me was lost to dreaming. There she was, last December, saying she loved me. There she was, back from Prague, saying she loved me again. And all those nights and all those fights when she kept denying what I knew was true from the very beginning: she was never going to leave David. Why couldn't she have been honest? Why couldn't she have said this is it, and this is all it's ever going to be: a nice little affair, no strings attached? Was it *my* fault? Was I that unwilling to hear the truth? But I pushed her and pressed her as hard as I could, and all she ever said was the same old thing: be patient, calm down, it's all going to be fine, it's all going to be okay. And oh, sweetheart, I'm *so* sorry, it breaks my *heart* to see you this way. *What* fucking heart? Mine was the one that got broken. And I knew that was going to happen; I told her that the first time we broke up: I said, "One of us is going to get hurt, and I think I know which one it's going to be." Well, here I am! And it's so beautiful to see you cry, it makes me feel so close to you, and two days later she won't even see me to say it's over, she sends *him* to say it for her. What kind of person are you? But you're not a person, you're a cat. Cats don't just kill their prey, they play with it first; they tease it by releasing it again and again, and finally, when that game has run its course, they do what they were planning to do all along. Well, you're going to get yours one of these days. One day somebody's going to play you the same way you played me, and it's all going to come back to you, you fucking whore.

Yes, I can say it now—you want me to say it again? And David knows it too now, and he's never going to forget it, thanks to Astrid. Oh yes, Jim, you did me a favor after all. But you weren't doing it to help me. No, you wanted to get back at me for actually caring. And what did I tell you? I said I was going to kill you, didn't I? And I bet you think that's an idle threat. Well, I'm getting on the freeway right this second to come out there and kill you! You always said you wanted to die, right? Well, death is on the way! I'm like one of those right-wing beach kids, the kind that took you literally when you sang about breaking things. And the thing that's going to break, the thing that's going to fly apart as I beat you and beat you and beat you, is your motherfucking head!

...Four!

Brutal kids of this promised future
Cut the highways
With shards of truth
I call out to my young and black hearted
Do you believe in what I have seen?

...And You Will Know Us
by the Trail of Dead

There's no doubt in my mind that I'd now be a convicted felon if my transmission hadn't given out on the freeway halfway to Jim's place. Would I really have killed him, given the chance? Not deliberately. But I know I would've broken down his door to get my hands on him, and between that and the damage done to his person afterward, I would surely have logged some serious jail time. But it was five o'clock on a weekday afternoon—the worst hour of all for commuter traffic—and at one point, stuck in a multi-lane cluster-fuck, my car refused to budge; I ground down on the gas pedal and nothing happened. A long line of cars was stretched out behind me, and people honked their horns like they actually thought I was blocking them by choice, you fucking morons; and soon a Highway Patrol cruiser showed up, and the Nazis inside it pushed my car to the road shoulder. They called for a tow truck, and that finally came, and the middle-aged Mexican driver hooked me up and towed me to my regular mechanic in Echo Park. We talked as he drove, and I told him I'd come close to murder that day, and he laughed and said, "Well, shit, I do that *every* goddamn day"—and I have to say it helped a little, hearing that. It helped to remind me that other people have problems too. But for towing me all that distance, I had to pay him almost every cent I had on me, cleaning me out till my check had cleared; and I walked up the street to my place broke in every sense of the word, thinking, "What now? What am I going to do now?" I got home and slept for something like fifteen hours, and the next day I took a long walk in Elysian Park and decided I had to make some major changes. I decided I'd move back to New York and—do what exactly? I wasn't sure. But I knew I couldn't stay in L.A., not with Irina so close, and the only thing keeping me in L.A. was my so-called career, and that was certainly nothing to brag about. I called Avatar and told them I had to pull out of the kiddie flick, that I'd gotten a better-paying job, and they were great about it; they let me out of my contract. But I continued to work on *Landmine* in the hope that Horst would pay me enough to make a fresh start; and I'll never know how I managed to do it, since I was easily at my lowest ebb since the accident, but I finished within a week, and Horst was so pleased he was finally prepared to "tock about see munny." I called ICM and said, "Yes, I've got an offer on a screenplay and need somebody to help me negotiate," and they set me right up with an agent. Of course, I knew it could take a while before I had a deal, since agents love to haggle—that's all they really do—and I'd started the bidding at 200 grand, and I knew that was far too much for the likes of Horst. I was almost broke again when Trail of Dead came back through town late that July, and, looking for something to lift my spirits, I drove down to see them at a place called the Lab, and there in the parking lot was Buddy Lavrakis—just what I fucking needed!

But he was a different guy that night. He was weirdly sort of friendly. We talked about Jim for a long time before the show, and he said my instincts were completely right, that Jim despised himself for reasons Buddy had never been sure of, and if you made the mistake of being his friend, he'd despise you too. We also talked about Irina, and, for what it's worth, he said she'd come on pretty strong the night he'd taken her out to Jim's place, and afterward she acted like such a bitch, telling him to keep his hands to himself, he had for a fact driven off and left her behind on purpose. And for that I bought him a beer.

ACTUALLY, BY THEN I'D SPOKEN TO HER. She called one day, maybe a week after the debacle at David's house, and said she was sorry for leaving me stranded the way she had, but David wasn't ready to give up on the marriage, and he'd "made" her promise she wouldn't see or speak to me while they tried to work things out. Nor had she *wanted* to see or speak to me—not after I'd run my mouth to Astrid. I said, "It wasn't me, it was Jim! I never said a *word* to Astrid!"

"Well, you might as well have! I told you so many times not to talk about things, and *now* look!" Then we fought for a while as to whom was to blame for exactly what, till finally I said, 'Look, this is just pointless. You were going to stay with David no matter what. So stay with him, okay? And don't fucking call me anymore!"

But two weeks later she called again. It was over with David, she said. He'd gone through her computer and read the letters I'd sent her while she was shooting in Prague, and after a huge, horrible fight, they'd decided to part ways. Now she was putting her stuff in storage and heading home to Belgrade for the rest of the summer. She wanted to see me before she left, and I was tempted, I was; but I said, "Irina, you just don't get it, do you? What, do you think you can just call me up and I'll come running? I don't care if you're with David or not. There are some things you can't take back!"

So she went off to Belgrade, and I took up briefly with a woman named Celeste. I met her in the park one day. She was walking her dog, and I stopped to pet it, and from there we ended up swapping phone numbers. I told her from the get-go I was getting over somebody else, and she claimed she understood. Then one morning toward the end of August—the 21st, to be exact—I turned on my computer and found this waiting in my inbox:

Dear Jason,

I hope you are doing better. I'm doing much better since I came home. Now I have a chance to go to the University and I've decided I'm going to take it. I can't see any reason to come back to LA. It's over with us. David hates me. All of my friends there are talking about me. I know that I'll have to come back to finish things with David but I can do that next Spring when school is over. I'm going to study art and take some classes in graphic design. I have a friend who does very well with that and I think I need a "Plan B" if it doesn't work out with acting. I hope to do some acting here, too. The other day I almost booked a commercial. It was for coffee, can you believe that? I would have played a typical house wife [sic].

I'm sure that you don't care about this. But I wanted you to know that I've been thinking about you and some of the things that I did and I wish there was some way I could take it back. I'm so ashamed of myself. I never wanted to hurt you, I just didn't know what I was doing. I think I do now but it's not so easy to explain and you probably wouldn't believe me. And then sometimes I think that if this is the way things are then this the way they were meant to be and there is nothing any one could have done to change them. I would like to believe nothing happens without a reason. I just hope it's a good reason!! But maybe it's for us to make it that way.

There's much more I would like to say but I think I should keep this short. But please, if there's anything you would like to say to me I hope that you'll write me or you know you can always call. I just saw Bora, he's visiting also and he said he found these callings cards in LA where it's very cheap to call Europe. He said you can find them anywhere but maybe somebody there can give you better information. I have a new mobile which is 381 064 *** *** or you can call my home number which is 381 *** ***. Mornings and evenings are best. And if you don't write or call me I will understand and wish you all the best.

Love always,
Irina

PS
I still have your necklace. I'll send it back with Bora. I broke the chain a few weeks ago but I had it replaced. It's white gold, better than it was before.

CELESTE WAS FORTY, WITH AVERAGE LOOKS, but that seemed like just the ticket after being with Irina. It wasn't, but that was my fault, not hers: my every second sentence began with "I," followed by four more letters. It all came to a head the day I got that e-mail. I couldn't help but mention it, and she got upset and showed me the door. She liked me, and I liked some "teenager" from Eastern Europe. She cried about it too. I felt like a heel.

That night I got drunk and called Irina. There was more she wanted to say to me? Bring it on, bitch! There was more I wanted to say as well! I had a whole speech worked out—something to the effect of "Who's sorry now?"—but then she picked up right away, as I hadn't been expecting, and took me aback with her very first words: "Jason? Oh my God, I just had a dream you were going to call!" In her dream, she said, she was lying in bed when her phone rang, and, knowing it was me, she went to answer when "some woman" appeared and snatched the phone away. It was eerie: the woman she described sounded exactly like Celeste. I told her about Celeste, hoping it would hurt her, but she had something to tell me too. It seemed she'd recently bumped into an old acquaintance, somebody she used to have a crush on, and she'd slept with him once as a kind of "experiment." But the experiment failed, she said; all it did was make her miss me. I said, "Oh fuck, don't tell me that. You say the same thing every time!"

"Well, it's true. You don't believe me, do you? I don't think you *ever* believed I loved you. I think you think you have to be a big success first, and maybe *then* I could love you. And I know I did a lot of bad things, but I think I could've been perfect and it would have been just the same. You never believed we'd be together. That's why you had to talk about me: you wanted someone to *help* you believe it."

I had to admit she might be right. I didn't think so at first, but the more we talked, the more I realized I'd second-guessed her right from the start. How could she be with a loser like me? And, yes, I saw myself as a loser. I'd played in one of the best rock & roll bands of its time, and that's something I still believe, just as I believe *Sick to Death* is one of the better movies ever made about rock & roll, but it's not like the world ever backed me up. To the world those things didn't exist. So, after a while, you start doubting your own perceptions. You think, "Well, if nobody else cares, I guess it was never that good to begin with." And it went further back than that; it went all the way back to North Carolina. I'd excelled at sports and dressed like a preppie and dated the most popular girl at school, but everybody knew my family was struggling, and in various ways—some subtle, some not—I was forever being reminded I was second-best. And, come to think of it, I'd been the same way with Megan as I'd been with Irina: what was a girl like that—a girl who could've had anybody she wanted—doing with someone like *me*?

But Irina said I was too hard on myself, and that was partly why it hadn't worked out with us: if I didn't think something was possible, it wouldn't be. Not that she regarded herself as blameless. In fact, she said, she now realized that part of her had always tried to push me away. Maybe it was because of her father. She loved him so much, and then he died, so maybe she was afraid of being with someone who really touched her and potentially losing him as well. David never touched her, not really. He was safe. And like me, she'd grown up without much money, and David had taken care of her, and part of her was always afraid of giving that up.

"Well, come on!" I said. "I only told you that a hundred thousand times!"

"Yes, but I didn't know I felt that way! I didn't want to think it was true! But there's something else. This isn't so easy to talk about, but...remember what you used to tell me about leading guys on? Well, I've only been hearing it all my life! Even when I was very young, people said I was using my looks to get my way, or I was trying to steal their boyfriend, or they'd accuse me of wanting to sleep with somebody I had no *intention* of sleeping with. Every man I was ever with accused me of that. You were the same way. But David wasn't like that. His friends would tell him stories about me—'I saw Irina with another guy'—and he would *laugh* about it. Astrid wasn't the only one. *Everybody* told him that. He really trusted me, you know? And then, when he found out about you, he was so hurt, I felt like I had to stay with him just to prove I wasn't as bad as everybody always said I was. I know, it sounds crazy. I never realized I *cared* that much what other people think about me. But it wasn't just them, it was also *me*. I mean, when you hear something so many times, you start to think it's true. And it *was* true. I'm not a very good person, Jason. But I guess you know that."

"Oh, I don't know. You're finally being honest, that's a start. Besides, I'm not so good myself."

"Well, I think you're much better than *I* am. And I *want* to be a good person, and I know I *try* to be, but sometimes...I just can't help myself."

"Yeah, well. That makes two of us."

WE PROBABLY TALKED FOR TWO HOURS THAT NIGHT. We talked even longer a few days later. The bill for those calls later came to $700; but by then I'd found those calling cards her cousin had told her about, so we could speak as long as we wanted for a song and a dance. We decided we'd try again when she returned to the States the following spring. We had phone sex. We fought a couple of times. Nothing serious. Once she told me about a great-looking guy she'd recently met, and I said,

"Well, don't let *me* stand in your way! Go ahead and fuck him!" Then I realized it was *good* she was telling me that. She used to keep those things to herself, not wanting to make me jealous. And it would have. And it did. But in some ways Irina seemed like a different person. It was as if, realizing she'd kept certain truths from herself, she'd become a born-again truthteller. We discussed potential livelihoods when I moved to New York—*if* I moved to New York. My whole life hinged on my deal with Horst. He turned me down for 200 grand. Likewise 100. Then, shortly after Labor Day, he called me personally to say he'd give me seventy-five if I gave *him* sole credit for the screenplay. He said he'd been fooling around with it, making lots of changes, and it wasn't going to be my script by the time he was done with it. I haggled, asking him to throw in the ten percent I'd have to pay the agent at ICM. He agreed, and a few days later we signed the contracts. He was supposed to wire the full seventy-five straight into my bank account but said he was having cash-flow problems, and right now all he could give me was half. Still, that was close to forty grand, and the day I got it, I called Irina and said, "It's here! And you know what I want to do? I want to fly you over! Here, let me call the airline and book you a flight!"

But she said that wasn't possible: she'd just started classes, and it was too far to fly for a couple of days. Then I offered to fly to her, but she said no to that too. First, she said, I'd have to apply for a visa at the Yugoslav embassy in Budapest, and the regime was so suspicious of foreigners, Americans especially, so there was a very good chance I wouldn't get it. She thought the best idea was to wait a few weeks, during which she'd have her mother, who was a well-respected law professor, write a letter vouching for me, and from there she'd send the letter to the embassy, where her mother had a well-placed friend. But even then I might not get approved, so maybe we should make a plan for Christmas, when she could fly to L.A. or New York. I said, "But, Irina, that's three months away! And I'm climbing the fucking walls here, and I've finally got some money, and what good is it if I can't use it to see you?"

So this is what we eventually decided: she would personally bring her mother's letter to Budapest; and if I got the visa, I'd go with her to Belgrade, where I'd stay till the visa ran out; and if I didn't get the visa, we'd spend a few days together in Budapest, and that would have to be it. She couldn't stay longer on account of her classes, and I figured at least this way I'd get to see her, and afterward I could treat myself to some travel. There were so many places I'd never been: Athens and Istanbul, Moscow and Prague. (Scratch Prague!) Then, before I flew back, maybe we could see each other a second time in Budapest—if, that was, we got along the first time. Yes, everything seemed fine on the phone, but that was the phone. It might be very different in person.

So I called Delta and booked myself on the next flight to Budapest, and afterward I called Irina to give her my arrival time. Great, she said. She'd take a bus up from Belgrade and meet me at the airport.

THREE DAYS LATER, at nine in the morning on a mid-September Friday, my flight touched down in Budapest. The sky through my window was putty white, the runway darkened by a late-summer rain. I breezed through customs and walked out to see a number of men holding up signs that said BELGRADE. These were drivers, I later learned, who made their living escorting Serbs across the border. All around me I heard people speaking in overlapping tongues—English and German and Magyar and Serbian—and where the fuck was Irina? She'd stood me up! Terrence told me she would. I called him the day before I left, and he told me not to go, he told me I was out of my fucking mind, but I couldn't be made to listen. Then I felt a hand press softly against my back and turned to find her standing behind me. She'd cut off most of her hair—I'd been warned about that on the phone—and her eyes were red after riding the bus all night, but she was smiling just the sweetest smile, and the second I saw that, I knew everything was going to be okay, at least in terms of us. We got my bag and got a cab, and Irina gave the driver a slip of paper with the address of the Yugoslav embassy, and for at least forty-five minutes he pretended to be lost. Eventually, when I realized he was pumping up his fare, I told him to stop and let us hail another cab, at which point he magically regained his sense of direction and drove us straight to the embassy. It was right across the street from a park and plaza called Victory Square—a good omen, I thought. A sour-faced man answered the door, and his face soured further when we showed him my passport and the letter written by Irina's mother. He and Irina talked for a long time in Serbian, and I could tell by his bellicose body language alone that he was never going to grant me a visa. Still, I had no regrets about flying over, and I'd cross the border illegally if it came right down to it, you heartless bloodless loveless bureaucrat!

But then somebody else walked up behind him—a guy in his thirties, young for a diplomat—and he fairly beamed when he saw Irina, kissing her three times on the cheek. Obviously this must be her mother's friend. There might be hope after all. I wasn't so sure when he read the letter. Once again there was a long talk in Serbian, and the tone was deadly serious at first, but the longer the talk went on, the more the tone seemed to lighten. Then I realized what was happening: Irina was flirting with the guy, who was powerless to resist. He had that dreamy look in his eyes. He was charmed right off his feet. He turned to me and said in English, "So you are the lucky one." I said, "That's me." Then he walked through an official-looking door, leaving us alone; and Irina—I'd been gripping her hand the whole time, and now she squeezed mine really hard and said beneath her breath, "I think it's going to be okay."

"You think?" And she nodded cautiously like she didn't want to get my hopes up, or hers up either. Then her mother's friend reappeared and led us up some rickety stairs to an empty conference room on the second floor and told us to have a seat. He didn't say why. He just said to wait. And so we did for at least an hour; and the room was a grimy salmon color, and it smelled of stale smoke; and Irina whispered that it might be bugged, so we barely said a word; we just sat and held hands and waited. Then a different man opened the door and told me to go with him to fill out some forms and have my picture taken. That's when we knew I was getting the visa. We were so happy! We found a hotel a few blocks away (an Ibis hotel—there's a chain of them in Europe), and we spent the next two and a half days holed up there. I think we left just three times: twice to eat, and once to do some sightseeing. Aside from that, we stayed in our room, making up for the months we'd foolishly spent apart.

BELGRADE LITERALLY MEANS "WHITE CITY," and maybe it really was white once upon a time, but now it's full of dull brown buildings mostly dating from the Tito years. Much of the city was razed during World War II and the many wars before it; and all over town I saw the remains of the latest conflict, the twisted beams of shattered highrises framed by buildings perfectly intact and guarded by patrolling soldiers. Allegedly NATO had only bombed military targets, and, as such, they were still considered sensitive, so taking pictures wasn't allowed, as I learned one day the hard way. This was a police state, make no mistake about it, but there was an awful lot of crime—not street crime but mafia; and gangsters were media darlings who made the gossip rags side by side with homegrown pop stars. And there were many such pop stars—surprising for a country the size of Kentucky. Especially around the center of town I heard a kind of Turkish disco called Turbofolk wafting from kiosks selling bootleg records—Turkish because the Turks ruled Serbia for 500 years. You were never allowed to forget it. Practically every time I met a stranger, I was subjected to a history lesson, and the first thing I was usually told was: "The Turks ruled us for five hundred years. We almost beat them in Kosovo, but they came back at the last minute and we lost the battle." Even kids would tell me that. I found that fairly remarkable, since most Americans, regardless of age, don't know the first thing about their own history, except that Lincoln beat the British after Washington freed the slaves. But Serbs knew world history as well as their own; and often, as soon as somebody heard me speaking English with an American accent, he or she would pull up a chair and start yakking away. They loved our asses, and we'd just bombed them. And we'd bombed them before during World War II, when they were supposed to be our allies. But they held no grudges—they didn't like our leaders, but they sure liked us—and the boys wore jerseys for American teams (including baseball—a sport with no following in Europe); and the girls—well, they had a style uniquely their own, with skintight clothes on perfect bodies, and that mix of Slavic and Turkish features—fucking gorgeous! *Everybody* was gorgeous, at least to the age of thirty. My second night in town, Irina's brother Nebojša took us to a club called Bus, where stunning kids numbered in the hundreds writhed and spooned and sized each other up. It was a bit like that in the streets too: lovers kissing, guys on the prowl, packs of haughty girls. They were tough little bitches, but they had to be, given the lewdness of Serbian guys, and Nebojša was one of the worst there was. Not that, blessed with his sister's singular beauty, he lacked for avid partners. In fact, that night at Bus, we'd no sooner finished our first drinks than he bumped into one of his regulars, and, taking me aside, he said, "I go to fuck now! I be back one hour!" And, sure enough, he was back in an hour. He clearly wanted to cultivate our friendship. As an American, I was something of a status symbol.

Nebojša still lived with his mother, Nataša. That's par for the course in Belgrade. Most young people can't afford their own apartments, so they live with their parents till the day they get married and, sometimes, even afterward. Nebojša had recently lost his job, so, during the day, while Irina was at school, he'd drop by the place where I was staying to keep me company and get stoned with Dragan, the guy whose place it was. Dragan was an old friend of Irina's who produced commercials (that's how they knew each other), and since there wasn't much room at her mother's flat (Irina lived there as well), she'd asked Dragan to put me up. He had a large apartment in the center of town where, at night, I could look out my window and see party barges on the Sava River, strung with lights and blasting music. The rave scene was centered on the rivers (plural because the Sava met the Danube in Belgrade), and Nebojša was an aspiring DJ, so chances were, past ten o'clock you'd find him on one of the barges. Irina always said no when he invited us to join him. She'd go to clubs to check out bands, but she was never a fan of dance music—that night at Bus was one of the few times we ever went out dancing. She likewise never cared for drugs; but Nebojša *loved* drugs, and Dragan sold pot to supplement his income, not to mention smack. Belgrade was smack heaven, thanks to the Albanian mafia. We'd supposedly bombed Belgrade to save the poor, saintly Albanians from the mean old Serbs, but the Western media never mentioned the fine smack used to pay for Albanian anti-Serb terorism. Oh yes, it was fine smack indeed, and so cheap that even Nebojša could afford it, so that he and Dragan were constantly sniffing it, and a couple of times I took the straw, even though I'd promised Irina I wouldn't do drugs with her brother. She and Nataša were on a mission to straighten him out, and they knew about the pot, and they must have known he was doing ecstasy, but at the time neither was aware that his heart belonged to heroin. And, yes, I did fuck up a couple of times, but considering the many temptations on hand, I think I behaved rather well. Girls were constantly stopping by that place to service Nebojša, and again, as an American, I was a figure of intrigue, so let's just say I could easily have gotten some on the side. Nebojša wouldn't have cared. His whole life was sex, drugs and music, and one of his best friends was another dope dealer who pimped on the side and let his friends fuck his girls for nothing. This was Miloš, whose portrait, painted by Irina, used to hang on her bedroom wall in Los Angeles. I was offered one of Miloš's girls—his way of showing off—but, pretty as she was, she couldn't begin to compare with my one true love. And almost every morning my love would leave for class and rush back afterward to show me around, even though, past the first few days, there wasn't much to see. There was the center of town, which had somehow survived the many shellings and conquering armies over the centuries; and Kalamagden Park, with its Roman fortress still standing; and one Sunday we took a drive to a town called Novi Sad, and that was all very lovely, the rolling yellow fields like Kansas. And I toured an ancient church with ancient icons flaking on the walls; and I visited one of the world's finest military museums; and I hit a few clubs, including Bus, which were nice enough, but if you lived in New York at the time I did, they were nothing special. Belgrade *itself* was nothing special if all you were going by was looks alone.

But then we'd walk around at night and I'd see gypsies and gangsters and those gorgeous kids, as well as real-life *sponzoruše,* who reminded me of Brentwood trophy wives. And there were nightly protests across the street from the National Opera House—Opposition leaders speaking into megaphones, and crowds with banners calling for the removal of Slobodan Milošević—and posters plastered all over town with the raised fist of a radical student group called Otpor, which means "resistance." And later, at Dragan's place, making love or trying to sleep, I'd hear music from the party barges down on the river and see lights go floating by on black water at three in the morning. And long past dawn the late-night stragglers would stumble home, breaking bottles and singing folk songs out of tune, and with that we'd wake and go out to a bakery for yogurt and *burek,* a kind of pastry pie stuffed with meat or cheese or spinach or mushrooms. And if other customers heard me speaking English, they might stare at first, but eventually they'd walk up and ask who I was and where I came from and what I thought of Belgrade. *That* was the appeal: the people. They were so warm and so fucking alive! And Irina had always told me how "depressing" it was, and I could see what she meant—everybody was poor, and nobody could leave (at that moment, in fact, it was utterly impossible)—yet the less these people had, the more they seemed to live, just as they had less freedom than we supposedly have in America, but they were free *inside* themselves, which is where I think it counts. They'd been through these horrific wars, and so much of the world regarded them as monsters, but they at least struck me as *honest* monsters, unlike the ones in America, who'll steal you blind with a friendly smile. We're even monsters to ourselves: our whole lives are just work and more work; got to have this and got to have that; and hey, did you happen to catch that *Friends* rerun last night? There's no time for *real* friends. Besides, what would you do with them? Talk about *Friends*? Or maybe over the weekend you can see a movie made for twelve-year-olds, which by now is every movie, though nobody seems able to recognize it, and go back to work and talk about that. Or maybe you can do something with the kids; you can drive them back and forth to all kinds of activities, since they've got to be prepared; they've got to grow up and make lots of money, just like you want to do. And I really can't say I blame you. I know from firsthand experience it's a crime to be poor in America. And maybe that was my fault; maybe I risked and expected too much, but I always thought you had to think big to achieve the American dream. But the dream was over. I knew it was over for me. I had no desire to return to the States. I'd found what I was looking for, and it was all right here. And I thought Irina was going to be thrilled when I said as much, but in fact she was horrified. She said, "Jason, this place isn't for *you*! It's not for *anybody*! Everybody wants to get out! And most of the interesting people *have* gotten out."

"Well, your mother's interesting. Why is *she* here?"

But the first time I raised the subject, her mother was sitting across from us. She'd taken us out to dinner at a place called the Writers Club, and at first she seemed to side with Irina. Yugoslavia wasn't what it used to be. No, she said, when she made her first trips abroad, she was the envy of everyone she met. Of course that was in Hungary and Czechoslovakia—Yugoslavia was like paradise to them! Then Tito died and everything fell apart. It didn't happen right away—even during the eighties it was still a great place to live—but now when she read the papers, she was filled with shame. How could people keep voting for Milošević after all he'd done? He'd stolen their money and cut them off from the rest of the world while perpetuating these stupid wars, and why? For so-called Serbian nationalism? In fact, this restaurant was the birthplace of Serbian nationalism: the politicians used to come here to plot out the future. I said, "Well, the food's sure good. This is the best lamb I ever had."

"Yes, it *is* good, isn't it? That's why I still like it. And I have many good memories of this place. I used to come here with Aleksej."

Aleksej was Irina's father. I'd seen pictures of him, and he looked like an Italian movie star, like Renato Salvatori in *Rocco and His Brothers*. As for Nataša, she reminded me a bit of Jackie Kennedy, except she had some meat on her bones and her eyes weren't set so wide apart. She was one of the few Serbs I'd seen past a certain age who was holding on to her looks. What a fucking gene pool! And I asked Nataša why she didn't leave the country, and she said, "Well, I've thought about it. But my work is here and my son is here, and Nebojša is never going to leave. He's not so ambitious like Irina. And at my age it's not so easy to start again, and to tell you the truth, I'm sure I would miss it. Yes, things are bad at the moment, but I have to hope they're getting better. And we have a spirit here I've never seen anywhere else. Of course, I haven't been to that many places. I've never even been to America. But I don't think I would like it much. Irina was very unhappy there."

"That's not true," Irina said. "I *loved* New York. And that's where Jason is moving, and as soon as school is over, I'm moving there with him."

And that was the plan before I came to Belgrade. But that night, after Nataša had gone home, we walked around and talked about it, and Irina admitted that, in certain ways, her mother was right. There *was* a spirit here, and she'd missed that spirit the whole time she was living in America. And her family was here, and she had good friends, including girlfriends, which she'd always lacked and missed in America. Still, she couldn't see us living in Belgrade. It was fine for now, but knowing she was eventually going to leave was part of what made it bearable. I said, "But, angel, it's so cheap! We could live for years on the money I just made, and you know how expensive it is in New York. We'll go through all that money like nothing!" Plus, I said, it was obvious this place had a good effect on her. She was upbeat where she always used to be down. She was glowing like I'd never seen her before—and it was true, she was, even though I thought it was mostly the sex. Belgrade for me was an aphrodisiac, all that lust in the air. I felt like I was eighteen again. I was excited around the clock.

But Irina said she was mostly thinking of me. She said, "Sweetheart, I know you think you like it, but you've only been here *two weeks*. It's really *hard* to live here—especially for someone like you. There's no work; you don't speak the language; people would think you're a spy. There are people who think *I'm* a spy just because I moved back! And I know you think it's interesting, but, believe me, this is special. After a few months you'd be so bored you'd start to go crazy!"

And I remember exactly where we were when she gave me that speech. It was right outside Dom Omladine, where the hardcore kids put on shows, and as she spoke, a kid who looked exactly like Sid Vicious went strolling past. This kid had every detail right—the hair, the clothes, the chain and padlock around his neck—and I remember thinking it almost felt like a sign, him walking by just then, since my pseudonym on all those shitty movies was Simon Ritchie. Still, the true sign came a few days later, if you believe in such things. It was an event so overwhelming, there was no question I had to stay—even Irina was saying so. After that I went to Budapest to renew my visa and took a bus back to Belgrade. And this is where I've been ever since.

I OFFICIALLY MOVED TO BELGRADE a little over six years ago, as I write these words, and this book was begun shortly afterward. It was Irina's idea. She thought I was going to lose my mind without something to keep me occupied, and suggested I write a book. I said, "A *book*? What am I supposed to write a *book* about?"

"Write about Peewee. Write about us. You always tell such great stories. I think you need to start writing them down." And that December, when I went to L.A. to pack and ship my stuff, I thought about it and called her one night and said, "You know, I think I *am* going to write a book. But I've got to warn you: I'm going to be brutally honest about everybody concerned."

"You promise?" Yes, we'll see if she still feels that way when she reads it! I've shown her sections here and there, and she's really kept after me to keep going. There've been a lot of distractions. Not long after that Christmas, I met a kid named Nikola who was in a band called Funeral Pussy, and he asked if I could look at his lyrics, which he'd written in

English, to see if they sounded okay. Well, from there we ended up jamming, and next thing I knew I was in the band. It started off hardcore, but once I joined, we started branching out. We even cover Superego songs. I sing those. Nikola does the hardcore stuff. It's a bit like Scratch, a similar schism, and even though we treat it as a hobby, I'm amazed it's lasted as long as it has, what with our many sabbaticals. For example, I spent two months in L.A. in the summer of 2001 after Horst asked me to take another whack at the script. Plus Irina had to come anyway to settle things with David; and one night we all had dinner together, which is something I *never* thought would happen. I think he wanted a better idea of the man who broke up his marriage, and I decided he was basically a decent guy, if still a bit patronizing; and two years ago he married a Scottish girl and moved back to London, and every so often he writes or calls Irina, so, just as she always wanted, she was able to stay his friend. As for Astrid, I understand she's still single and living in Los Angeles, where she's doing extremely well as a costume designer. She was even nominated for an Academy Award. I won't mention the movie. She might decide to sue me. And that's why I've changed her name and most of the others and fudged certain details, though I'm sure all concerned will have no trouble identifying themselves.

At any rate, once Horst had paid me the money he still owed me, I took Irina to North Carolina so my family could meet the reason I'd moved to Siberia, as my dad insisted on calling it; and afterward she and I flew to New York for Terrence and Emily's wedding. (They're still together, but far from happy.) I was apprehensive about going to New York. I was afraid Irina was going to resurrect the idea of moving there, but in fact she wasn't that taken with it. She said something had changed, she wasn't sure what, and she could hardly wait to get back to Belgrade. She had prospects there. A friend of Dragan's was talking of producing a Balkan rip-off of *Sex in the City* called *Lasice*, which literally translates as "weasels," but in Serbian a *lasica* is slang for a hot, cool chick. There were three *lasice* on the show, and Dragan's friend wanted Irina to play one of them, and after the financing had fallen through a couple of times, he finally got it together. I later got involved myself, directing episodes and working with the writers, since Irina wasn't happy with the shitty story lines. Even so, the show was a hit, and Irina got written up in the tabloids with headlines like: VESNA'S BROTHER IS A JUNKIE.

(Vesna was the name of Irina's character.) And it was true: Nebojša had become a full-blown junkie. (He's since cleaned up.) I likewise showed up in the tabloids. In March 2003 I was almost deported for a supposed visa violation in the wake of a massive crackdown following the assassination of Prime Minister Đinđić. It was a very close call, and to make certain it never happened again, Irina said we should get married; and the day after St. Patrick's Day we did, and that got written up as: VESNA MARRIES AMERICAN LOVER. There were quotes from one of her exes, and they invented quotes from me, and while I personally thought the whole thing was funny, Irina was very disturbed by it. She started to realize that she was much too private to be a public figure, even on such a tiny scale. Plus she thought the show was idiotic, which it was, and she was insanely jealous of one of her costars, who was always flirting with me, and I was equally jealous of all those actors she was always having to kiss. So it was a big relief for both of us when the show stopped production a year and a half ago. (I'm writing this in 2007.) Still, I have no regrets about doing it, since we made great money by Belgrade standards; and when it was over, Irina said she was finished with acting; from now on she was concentrating strictly on her art. She resumed the classes she'd abandoned for the show, but I'm not sure what will come of that, since, last fall, we found out she was pregnant. It was the weirdest thing. Nebojša had knocked up a girl who insisted on having the baby, and seeing the way it clipped his wings, I was no longer certain I wanted kids. Neither was Irina, for reasons too personal to explain. Then her cat died after years of suffering, and Irina always treated that cat like a child, and almost the second it died, Irina got pregnant, though I know for a fact we were both taking every precaution. The baby's a boy, and he's due in late June, which means he could well arrive on Irina's birthday. We're going to call him Aleksej, which in English you'd spell "Alexi," and which, as I've said before, was the name of Irina's father. We also think it goes nicely with my last name.

Too good to be true? I know it will seem that way to those who don't trust happiness. Yes, I got "the girl." It all worked out in "the end." But this *isn't* the end. My life is a work in progress, as all lives are, and who knows what tomorrow will bring? Already much has changed since I moved to Belgrade—including Belgrade. There are a lot more tourists, for one thing, and a lot of Western companies have set up shop, and we now have Western-style laws, such as having to wear seatbelts, and eventually I expect there'll be no more smoking in public places and all the rest of that shit. It's also not as cheap as it used to be, though compared to the States the cost of living is nothing, and that's just perfect for a writer like me. I never thought of myself as a writer during my years of banging out screenplays, but this book has changed my mind, and now I think that if I'd grown up in a family that read, I probably would have come around to writing seriously a lot sooner. Peewee came from a family that read, and the last time I was in New York, I took Irina to meet his parents, and when I mentioned I was working on a memoir (which for legal reasons I'm calling a novel), Peewee's mom said, "You know, I always thought that's what Bernard was going to do. I think eventually he would've stopped with all that music nonsense and become a writer." Then his dad (who's sadly since died) said, "OH, HE WAS TOO SMART FOR THAT. HE KNEW PEOPLE DON'T GIVE A DAMN ABOUT WRITERS. ESPECIALLY NOW. ALL THEY WANT TO DO IS PLAY WITH THEIR COMPUTERS." Yes, even wasting away from leukemia, he still spoke at the top of his lungs, and his remark was right on the money, yet it also touched on one of my key motives for writing. Because every time I go back to the States, I see kids who look as bored as I used to be when I was their age and waiting for something—*anything*—to happen. And then something did. It wasn't just punk rock, it was learning I had a mind and how to use it. It was taking chances and learning how to live—same difference. And I was lucky, I had a great guide, and who do these kids have? The mainstream's full of Uncle Toms, and the Internet's full of crackpots. The underground? *What* underground? There's no pulse or resistance, and how can you miss what you've never known? And what difference can this book or any other make when so few people read?

Still, I have to hope. I have debts to pay—now more than ever. And what's scary is knowing that if one thing had gone just slightly differently, I wouldn't be where I am now. Suppose, for instance, I'd gone to that reading and prevented Jim from speaking to Astrid? Irina always says she would've told David anyway, and with time I've come to believe her, but I'm glad now she didn't. Otherwise she would never have fled to Belgrade. And I would never have followed.

BUT I DID. And by all rights I should never have gotten a visa, since at that time Milošević was running for reelection against the Opposition candidate, Koštunica, who was said by some to be funded by the U.S. Otpor was definitely being funded by the U.S., so an American like me was automatically suspect, and it was only because of Irina's charm and beauty that I wasn't turned away. The election took place a few days later, and Milošević claimed victory on state-run television, but everyone knew he'd rigged the vote, and the country was starved for change. The Opposition started staging those nightly protests in the center of Belgrade, and Otpor papered every public space in Yugoslavia with posters calling for a general strike to be spearheaded by a massive rally on the 5th of October. Milošević countered by placing more cops on the streets, but the nightly protests grew larger. Some said there was going to be a bloodbath, and Irina said I should leave the country, but then the borders were sealed to keep out arms and agitators, and at that point I couldn't have left even I'd wanted; I just had to wait till the strike was over, and hopefully, if the Opposition prevailed, I'd have my visa renewed. It didn't seem likely. Nobody *really* thought they could oust Milošević. In fact, we discussed the situation the night we had dinner at the Writers Club, and Nataša said, "It will be just like 1991. There was an outburst then, and one morning the streets were filled with tanks and no more outburst." Still, even if the protestors weren't deterred by a show of force this time, she thought Milošević would sooner level his own country than concede defeat—and I was talking about moving there!

On the morning of October 5th, I was at Dragan's place with Dragan and Irina and Irina's friend Milica. Dragan and Milica were going to the rally, and so were Nebojša and his pimp friend Miloš, who stopped by for a beer; and right before they all left, I said, "Wait. I'm going with you." Absolutely not, Irina said. We'd talked about going, but she was afraid that, being American, I might get singled out for arrest or worse, and it wasn't like I could turn to the American embassy for support. There *was* no American embassy. An angry mob had torn it down at the start of the NATO strikes.

But Nebojša took my side. I think he liked the idea that I cared as much about his country as he did; and it was true, I did, but I was also simply curious. Something big might happen—how could I miss it? Exactly, Nebojša said. He and Irina sparred in Serbian, and I never thought he'd change her mind, but then she turned to me and said, "Okay, you want to go? We'll go. But you have to stay with me the whole time, and once we walk out that door, I don't want you to say a word. I don't want the police to realize you're American."

It was slightly cloudy that day, and even blocks from the parliament building, where the rally was centered, the streets were packed. Some waved flags, and some blew whistles, and some were getting off buses from other cities; and Nebojša and Miloš led the way, pathfinders in this human forest. It was hard to move as we got closer to the parliament building, and a man in the distance was speaking on a megaphone, and suddenly the crowd erupted in boos. I later learned the election results had just been overturned by the Milošević-controlled Supreme Court, but at the time all I knew was that the mood had turned ugly, when a second before it had been almost festive. The crowd surged forward, on the attack, but then it surged back, and I saw a white cloud moving rapidly toward us and felt the effects before it arrived, as if the skin on my face had been sprayed with hot grease. People were jostling and scattering in all directions, and I grabbed Irina and took off running behind Nebojša, who was talking on his phone to a friend elsewhere in the crowd, trying to learn which streets were safe. Miloš was wearing a wire in one ear to get the play-by-play on radio, and his eyes looked like squashed red berries with the juice running out, and that goes for most of the eyes I saw that day, including Irina's. I almost wished we'd never come when I saw her face in so much pain, but too late now; we blindly trailed Miloš and Nebojša, at one point passing a special forces unit—the Red Berets—who were standing beside Humvees with gas masks and machine guns as if waiting for the command to open fire. But the command never came. The army had made a deal with the Opposition not to intervene, though nobody know it, and every second seemed like it might be our last. We turned down a street and saw a big cloud of tear gas coming our way, so we turned and ran in the opposite direction, but a cloud was coming that way as well. Then cops in riot gear came leaping through the cloud, and we thought they were coming for us, but they were themselves running away from packs of rabid kids. I saw one cop get pulled to the ground, beaten and kicked till he stopped moving. Guns were going off in the distance, and Irina said, "I think I hear tanks!" but no tanks appeared; and we kept dodging cops and tear gas, running and running, so that we probably covered ten or so miles in less than two hours. Protesters would pass us all beaten up, some wearing scarves as makeshift gas masks, and one removed his scarf and gave it to Irina—a gallant gesture, I thought. The air had the puke-banana smell of tear gas, but there was another smell too, and I saw that the sky was filled with swarming bees, and then I realized, no, it's smoke. Ashes fell around us like big black snowflakes, and Nebojša turned to me and said with a smile, "They burn the parliament building!" And he tried to lead us closer for a better look, but the fumes were too overpowering.

Still, he knew what was going to go next: RTS Television, the government's trusty mouthpiece. Then we all took off for that, and the second we got there, a bulldozer came flying around the corner and ripped a hole in the front of the building. Plumes of tear gas came rushing out and packs of kids stormed inside, and after what seemed like no time at all, a long line of cops emerged with their weapons removed and their faces rearranged. They walked right past us, obviously terrified that we and those around us were going to finish them off, but protestors started shaking their hands, and the cops responded in kind. I figured then it must be over. Nobody said so, but I noticed fewer people fleeing, and the looting had begun with no intervention. I watched a girl walk out of the TV station with her pockets stuffed with God-knows-what and her arms stacked with video tapes. I watched kids ransack a store owned by Marko Milošević, Slobo's hated son. We decided to head back to Dragan's place, and along the way we passed another unit of Red Berets, who, just like the cops, were shaking hands. Some protesters were crying, and not because of the gas or smoke; they were crying because they knew it was over. Yet nobody dared to say as much. We got to Dragan's, where he broke out a liter bottle of Johnny Walker, and that thing didn't last two minutes. The TV was going with a blank screen, and suddenly a man appeared and made an announcement, and the room exploded with cheers. Irina translated for me, even though it wasn't necessary. It seemed the station was—how shall we say?—under new management, and both the police and army were admitting that, gosh, it kind of looks like Slobo lost the election after all! Meantime, just in case the powers that be changed their minds, the man told everybody to return to the streets and stay there.

So we did as the man told us: we walked outside to a scene I'd never seen in all my days and know I'll probably never see again. Flatbed trucks carting giant amplifiers drove past blasting music, and people danced on rooftops and the tops of buses. They were dancing in the streets too, and strangers would come up and kiss us, and every time they spoke to me, I'd nod and say, *"Da,"* which at the time was one of the few Serbian words I knew. We walked behind the parliament building, where the fire had been extinguished and files of official papers were being tossed from the windows. Wheel-bottomed chairs were being tossed down as well, and kids were picking them up and racing them on the pavement. Then something small hit the top of my head, and I looked up and saw a guy emptying a box of red plastic cards, which Irina said were membership cards for the Communist Party. People scrambled to collect them as souvenirs, and we did too—we've still got them. Then Miloš and Nebojša left to meet some girls, and Dragan and Milica later broke off as well. Lust, as never before, was in the air.

But I stayed on the streets with Irina for the rest of that night, just strolling around that great big beautiful wonderland of chaos. It was hard to believe that one of the world's most despised governments had fallen that fast, and we'd helped, and by that I mean not just me and Irina but America too. And at that moment I was so proud to be American, yet I'd barely begun to consider the implications. Because this was the beginning of the end of a country I'd taken to heart, and whatever its crimes, it was holding out against so-called progress—the global village and convenience at any cost; safety and sense deprivation and rule by corporation—and one day there'd be nothing left but a ghost of its former self, and all the other lifeless Western states would praise themselves for bringing these savages in line. But wasn't it better this way? They'd suffered so much and caused suffering too, so maybe now there'd be peace and prosperity. And, speaking selfishly, I certainly stood to gain. I could stay now. And Irina wanted me to stay, and maybe now she'd want to stay herself. It felt like such a miracle, and part of that miracle was just being there in the first place, and I wanted to say thanks to every person who in some small way had helped to make it possible. Thank you, Gail, for a great fuck. Thank you, Mark, for spreading the word. And thanks to my parents for kicking me out of the house, and thanks to all those band members who turned me against music, and thanks to every Hollywood producer who refused to give me a break. And Terrence and Suzanne and Lucien? And Peewee? But I don't have to say a word to you, man; there's nothing you don't know. Oh yes, and there's someone else: the one I used to call my hero, the one who set me on this path before I even met him. And I haven't spoken to that guy since the day I thought he'd leveled my life, but, Jim, let me just tell you this now: somebody got the message. I'll always be grateful. And I pass the message on.

2000-2008
Los Angeles
Čanj
Beograd

Gratitude to the following for labor, support, feedback, inspiration, permission, and the occasional prod of memory:

Kenneth Gee, Karin Elsener, Jack Lanning, Danny Harmon, Bryan Price, Shawn Yanez, Jill Crenshaw, Michael Kellner, Michelle Nati, George Porcari, Jonathan Evison, Ryan Leone, Kate Bower, Jerry Neeley, Jane Gaffney, Burke Roberts, Miloš Brjnada, Vule Brjnada, the Brjnada family, Brin-Jonathan Friesen, Dan Starling, And/Or Press, Kristopher Young, Andy Seklir, Unwound, Maggie Vail, Kill Rock Stars, Jason Reece, …And You Will Know Us by the Trail of Dead, Interscope Records, Paul Draper, Ricky Williams (RIP), Michael Belfer, the Sleepers, David & Adriann Haney, Walter Haney & family, Sara & Robert Matthews, Jennifer Lynch, Sydney Lynch, Chris Kraus, Joseph Suglia, Scott Sterling, Goran Pacević, Sab (the great!) Grey, Matt Osborne, Jonathan Belli, Christopher Gee, George Tabb, Maximilian Hohlweg, Nik Coley, Ian MacKaye, Rude Buddha, Distortion Felix, Earlimart, Joe Keithley, Erin Broadley, Alexandra Kravetz, Wade Whittenberger, Bryce Martin, Pete Cechvala, Ely Morgan, Die Princess Die, Penelope Houston, the Avengers, Jim Ruland, Mark Ames, *The eXile*, Cornelia Lanford Goodwin, Mary Brill Kidd, Samuel Derek Parnell, Karen Hartman, Sarah Paradoski, *Search & Destroy*, *Flipside*, John Santana, Sabine Feuilloley, Dangerhouse, Teresa Patten, Patrick Gleason, Brian McEnroe, Jordan Hawley, the "Mash" family, Bernard Friedman, Lesley Hyatt, Bill Badgley, Ben Wildenhaus, Federation X, the 400 Blows, Chris Burnett, Paul Westmoreland, Vladimir Slavica, Nikola Ivanović, Ben Nuber, Penny Bloom, Ben Roberts, the Tribal Café, Humberto Terrones Esquivel, Suicide Girls Radio, Jared Forman, *A Beat of Their Own*, Tina-Louise Reid, Seamus Smith, J.T. Gurzi, Really Red, Joe & Heather D'Augustine, Sid Nicholson, Rachel James, Brian Cassels, Charlie Newmark, Monica Hayes, Mark Boone Junior, James Reid, Steven Blush, Marko Paljić, Brian Wohlgemuth, Chaz Zelus, Mark Hershey, Iron Cross, Negative Approach, Marcus Tingle, Justin Fairbanks Winchell, Flipper (I long since changed my mind), Srdjan Todorović, Srdjan Dragajović, Roger Cadillo, John Dentino, Jeff Spencer, Thom & Mickey & the Short Stop, Sonic Youth, Francis Schwartz (RIP), Rob Anderson, Bob Noxious, the Fuck-Ups, Chuck Dukowski, Paul Redmond, Target Video, J & N, Elliott Smith (RIP), Legs McNeil,

J. Spike Sasano, Radan Popović, Jason "Hawke" Hamilton, the Monorchid, Ken Segall, Rob Tepper, Corey Brandenstein, Austin Lovell, Jason "Gream" Gaona, Donnie Bockman, Mala Peikov, Tom Baer, Susanne Woche, Dana Allan Young, Dave Marley, Goran Bjelogrić, Dragan Bjelogrić, Mondo A-Go-Go Video, Dusty Paik, Mission of Burma, Robin McMahon, Kevin Cox, Steve Jones, Cockney Rejects, Subway Sect, Ivory Carlson, KXLU, TJ Nordaker, *Punk* magazine, Jim Jarmusch, Kahyeed Allahn, Colin de Andrade, Bahia Quire, Shiloe Swisher, Yuri Sivo, Brandon Perras, Jonathan Hall, Wire, Jason Lane, Laura R., Bedhead, Geoff Flint, Dylan Gordon, Shane Richardson, Jon Savage, Dave Dacron (RIP), Charlie Nichols, Michelle Munoz, Mary Roth, Betsy Roth, Mikael Paul, Bill Thompson, Clayton Savage, Mary Pleasant, Wire, John T. Woods, J.C. Rees, Vredrana Nanić, Dena Massenburg, Shotmaker, Jeremy Lowe, Rockets Redglare (RIP), Rhino 39, Nicole Turley, Kateri O'Neil, Paul Westerberg, the Replacements, Hedi el Kholti, DAVE COLE (all caps as demanded), Rocky Votolato, Jason Coover, Arlie John Carstens, Jenn Gardy, Anneke Rodina, Betsy Hall, Roro & Roxie, the Bizzurke Army, the Walkmen, Sonya Bekoff Molho, Richard Hell, Seung-Un Ha, Ryan McBride, Ian Vanek, Michael W. Dean, Milla Jovovich, the city of Belgrade, the people of Čanj, all of the fine medical staff who treated me on and the months following the worst day of my life, that kid with whom I got drunk at Czar Bar all those years ago (wish to God I knew your name), Kerry Kennedy (not a day goes by), Harry Bromley-Davenport (couldn't have pulled it off without you), and perhaps most of all Ghost Boy: may you grow to haunt the world as you will always haunt me. Semper fi.

D. R. Haney has actively participated in underground music, film, and literary circles for more than two decades. His writing has appeared in numerous journals, both in the United States and in Europe. *Banned for Life* is his first published novel.